Quintin Jardine gave up the life of a political spin doctor for the more morally acceptable world of murder and mayhem. Happily married, he hides from critics and creditors in secret locations in Scotland and Spain, but can be tracked down through his website: www.quintinjardine.com.

Praise for Quintin Jardine's novels:

'Well constructed, fast-paced, Jardine's narrative has many an ingenious twist and turn' *Observer*

'The perfect mix for a highly charged, fast-moving crime thriller' *Glasgow Herald*

'Engrossing, believable characters . . . captures Edinburgh beautifully . . . It all adds up to a very good read' *Edinburgh Evening News*

'[Quintin Jardine] sells more crime fiction in Scotland than John Grisham and people queue around the block to buy his latest book' *The Australian*

'There is a whole world here, the tense narratives all come to the boil at the same time in a spectacular climax' *Shots* magazine

'A complex story combined with robust characterisation; a murder/mystery novel of our time that will keep you hooked to the very last page' *The Scots Magazine*

By Quintin Jardine and available from Headline

Bob Skinner series:
Skinner's Rules
Skinner's Festival
Skinner's Trail
Skinner's Round
Skinner's Ordeal
Skinner's Mission
Skinner's Ghosts
Murmuring the Judges
Gallery Whispers
Thursday Legends
Autographs in the Rain
Head Shot
Fallen Gods
Stay of Execution
Lethal Intent
Dead and Buried
Death's Door
Aftershock
Fatal Last Words

Oz Blackstone series:
Blackstone's Pursuits
A Coffin for Two
Wearing Purple
Screen Savers
On Honeymoon with Death
Poisoned Cherries
Unnatural Justice
Alarm Call
For the Death of Me

Primavera Blackstone series:
Inhuman Remains

Quintin Jardine

SKINNER'S FESTIVAL

headline

First published in 1994 by
HEADLINE PUBLISHING GROUP

First published in paperback in 1994 by
HEADLINE PUBLISHING GROUP

First published in this paperback edition in 2009 by
HEADLINE PUBLISHING GROUP

Cataloguing in Publication Data is available from the British Library

ISBN 978 0 7553 5771 0 (B format)
ISBN 978 0 7472 4140 9 (A format)

Typeset in Electra by Avon DataSet Ltd,
Bidford-on-Avon, Warwickshire

Printed and bound by CPI Group (UK) Ltd, Croydon, CR0 4YY

Headline's policy is to use papers that are natural, renewable and recyclable products and made from wood grown in sustainable forests. The logging and manufacturing processes are expected to conform to the environmental regulations of the country of origin.

HEADLINE PUBLISHING GROUP
An Hachette UK Company
338 Euston Road
London NW1 3BH

www.headline.co.uk
www.hachette.co.uk

Dedicated to the memory of William Reid Jardine,

1908–1976

One

Panic was etched on the face of the clown on the unicyle. Even through the happy smile make-up, it registered as he struggled to regain his balance, rocking frantically backwards and forwards on his unsteady perch. His arms flailed, and for a second it seemed certain that he was gone, but with a violent last-ditch heave he pulled himself back to the vertical, straightening quickly in the saddle and resuming his compromise with gravity. The real-life smile returned behind the rictus.

He swerved suddenly towards Skinner and Sarah.

Under Bob's arm, Sarah's shoulders still shook with laughter from the sight of this silent struggle. She leaned against her husband as the clown drew closer. Fully in command of his steed once more, the unicyclist thrust out his right hand, offering them a leaflet. Sarah reached up and took it from him, waving him goodbye as he wobbled on towards his next target.

She studied the handbill. 'Le Cirque Mobile. Leith Links. Performances 7:30 and 10:00 nightly.'

'Hmm. Hope the rest are a bloody sight more "*mobile*" than him,' Skinner said, dryly.

'Let's find out some night. My treat.'

'Put like that, Doctor Sarah Grace Skinner, you're on.'

His wife hugged him tight with her left arm as they made

their way, slowly and haphazardly, through the crowds which thronged the open area at the foot of the Mound, around the grey-pillared Royal Scottish Academy, and its yellow stone neighbour, the National Gallery of Scotland. The classical formality of the buildings was in strange contrast to the garish make-up and dress of the Fringe performers who were milling around the pedestrian area, promoting the opening nights of their various shows.

Skinner's sweater was slung over his left shoulder, hanging from his thumb by its label. As the sun had climbed higher in the sky in the late August morning, its heat had caught him by surprise. He was a tall, strongly built man, grey maned but still looking younger than his forty-four years. He walked straight backed and broad chested, with a mass of curly hair filling the V of his open-necked shirt.

Sarah's lean and sinuous body seemed to fit perfectly against his, held by the tanned right arm which spanned her shoulders. Her auburn hair sparkled in the sun, and an easy smile played around the corners of her mouth as she relaxed against her chosen mate, enjoying the beauty of the morning.

Summer tends to by-pass Scotland in July, the month in which most of its families normally take their annual holidays. Those who can afford it make for the airports, *en route* for the Mediterranean, the Canary Islands or the Aegean. Those with no spending power, or no stomach for flying, either stay at home – adults in the pub, offspring watching satellite TV movies – or cling to wind-swept loch-sides in caravans, as the bleak season runs its course.

Then, in August, the penance is over. As the factories reopen and builders' buttocks peek out anew from jeans on construction sites across the country, the skies clear and the sun resumes its daily journey from Edinburgh to Glasgow.

This turn in the weather coincides with the opening of the Edinburgh International Festival. 'The Festival' is a misnomer in reality, for the season of the arts in Scotland's capital is a gathering of gatherings. From all over the world, performers and audiences come: for the 'official' plays and concerts in the grandest venues; for the connoisseurs' film event; for the conference of the mighty in television; for the jazz and blues concerts around the pubs and hotels; for the Military Tattoo in its steel arena on the sloping Esplanade of the great Castle; and, chaotically, for the Fringe – that magnet for hundreds of theatre groups ranging from the most professional to the rankest amateur.

As is the case with many who have migrated from west to east in Scotland, there was a part of Skinner which relished the time of the Festivals. They gave his adopted city an atmosphere which he could not imagine being matched anywhere in the world. For the best part of a month the capital buzzed with excitement; her streets filled with freak shows; her pubs, hotels and shops filled with visitors.

On the other hand, as Assistant Chief Constable Skinner, Head of Edinburgh's Criminal Investigation Department, there was an ambivalent tinge to his appreciation of this unique ambience. For the Festival month brought with it an invasion of pickpockets, conmen, shoplifters, and still the occasional drug-dealer, although the ranks of the pushers had been decimated by Skinner's own heavy hand and by the severity of the Scottish courts.

Still, despite that downside, this year's Festivals made Skinner even happier than the contented man he had become since his marriage. Already he and Sarah had spent days plotting their course through the hundreds of shows on offer to them and had worked out a rough running order. However, there were still some slots to be filled and, for those in doubt, midday window-shopping at the Mound had become yet another Fringe tradition.

Surrounded by the jangle of competing musicians, and the traffic noise from Princes Street, one hundred yards away, Sarah did not react at all to the sound of the explosion.

But Skinner tensed at once. First Sarah felt the bunching of the muscles of his arm. Then he took it from her shoulders, his hand reaching subconsciously towards his left side. He seemed to stretch, to stand to his full height. With eyebrows raised, he looked around, first to his left towards the west end of Princes Street, then right, towards Waverley Station and the Balmoral Hotel. He turned his back on the street, as his gaze swept up the jagged skyline as it rose to the Bank of Scotland Head Office, past the Assembly Rooms, and on towards the Castle on its rock.

Sarah tugged his arm. 'What is it, Bob? What's wrong?'

'Didn't you hear it?' The sharpness of his tone stung her, and she fired back.

'Hear what, for Christ's sake? All I can hear are guitars and fairground barkers. What am I supposed to have heard?'

'A bang. An explosion. A fucking bomb, that's what! But I can't figure out where it went off.'

'Are you sure, Bob? Couldn't it just have been some stunt here?'

When he looked down at her, his eyes were hard, but they softened at once at seeing the hurt on her face. 'I'm sorry, love. I didn't mean to snap at you. No, it wasn't as close as that. I reckon it was somewhere between two and four hundred yards away, but I can't pin down the exact location. It was a bomb though, for sure, I've spent too long on anti-terrorist training courses not to recognise that sound.'

He looked back towards Princes Street. The traffic was still flowing freely from west to east, but closer to them, on the street's south side, it seemed to have dwindled to a trickle. Only a public service bus and two cars could now be seen, slowing as the lights changed to red.

Skinner flicked open the button which secured the left breast pocket of his shirt, and took out a small mobile telephone. He switched it on, and keyed in a short-coded number. The headquarters switchboard answered within three seconds.

'This is ACC Skinner. Give me the duty inspector in communications control, fast.'

'Yes, sir.'

He heard the buzz as the call was re-routed. Once again it was picked up quickly.

'Central control, Inspector Good.'

Skinner knew the man, and was pleased to hear his voice; he had him marked down as experienced and unflappable. 'ACC Skinner here, Henry. Have you had anything through 999 from the Princes Street area within the last half-minute or so?'

'Princes Street, sir? Not that I've heard. Hold on a minute. Lads, anyone picked up—?'

Suddenly, Skinner heard an excited voice in the background. Then, louder, he heard Good issue orders to his officers. 'Get our nearest units there at once. Make sure all the other emergency services are on the way. Then get on to the Bomb Squad!'

Skinner heard the control room burst into activity as the inspector turned his attention back to him. 'That was something just then, sir. A shout from Waverley Market, from that big entertainment tent they stick on top of it for the Festival. A report of an explosion. It came in on 999. All services required. The caller said it looked as if there were casualties. Where are you just now, sir?'

'Dr Grace and I are only about two hundred and fifty yards away. We are on our way right now. You get hold of DCI Martin, and tell him to get there, pronto.' He pushed the '*end*' button, folded the telephone and replaced it in his pocket.

Sarah looked at him wide eyed, questioning, but calm. 'So?'

'See that big tent along there? The one with the flag in front? That's where it happened. You're needed as well, so let's leg it along there.'

Breaking into a trot, he set off out of the impromptu showground, its cacophony and its tumult still unaffected by the drama nearby. Sarah, gripping his hand, ran alongside him, keeping pace with his loping stride. Faced with a throng of pedestrians in Princes Street, Skinner pulled her behind him into its tree-lined Gardens. They ran across the grass, skirted the towering, grey neo-Gothic Scott Monument, and reached the exit which faced Waverley Market, the decked-over centre which provides the only shopping on the south side of Princes Street without compromising its famous skyline. They were confronted by a scene of panic and confusion around the big marquee. The entrance which faced them looked undamaged, but they could see that, towards the rear of the huge tent, a main support pillar had collapsed.

People stood around, some simply looking stunned, others in tears. Somewhere in the crowd a man was screaming hysterically. A few held handkerchiefs to head wounds. As Bob and Sarah took in the scene from across the street, a girl stumbled from the tent's wide entrance, above which the sponsor's name was emblazoned. Skinner guessed that she had been wearing a tartan uniform. Shreds of her skirt hung from her waist, and a piece of fabric still clung to her left arm as it dangled, broken, at her side. Her face was a mask of blood; her blond hair looked singed in places. If the girl was aware of being virtually naked, it concerned her not at all as she felt her way blindly forward with her uninjured right arm.

The crowd around them was growing thicker as people emerged from the shopping centre beneath the tent, shock replacing curiosity on their faces as they were gathered into the chaos.

Again Skinner took Sarah by the arm and pulled her after him, stopping the traffic with an upraised hand. They crossed the street together, jogged up the short slope back into Princes Street, and made their way towards the damaged marquee. Just as they arrived, a panda car drew up, and Skinner saw a traffic vehicle approaching also. He waited for its arrival, then called all of the four uniformed officers to him.

'What's your name?' Skinner asked the one sergeant among the four, feeling the inevitable pang of guilt which struck him every time he failed to recall the name of any police officer of promoted rank.

'Sergeant Holland, sir.'

'Right, Sergeant. Take charge outside here till a senior uniform arrives. Use your three constables to divert traffic: eastbound at the traffic lights past the Balmoral, westbound at Jenners corner, and southbound up in St Andrew Square.' He pointed for emphasis in each direction as he issued his orders. 'For now, you place yourself at the entrance to the tent and keep the public out. As more officers arrive, use them to clear the immediate area completely, to make room for the emergency services.'

Meantime, Sarah had gone to the assistance of the naked, blinded victim. She had taken off her own light cotton jacket and had draped it around the girl's shoulders, comforting her as best she could while quickly assessing her injuries.

Skinner called over to her as she worked. 'Love, I want you to round up the walking casulties and take them across the street into the Gardens; as far away as the Scott Monument, and behind it for safety. The sergeant here will route the ambulances to you as they arrive.'

Sarah nodded acknowledgement – but to the back of his head, for Skinner was already striding off towards the tent. She turned towards the crowd which had gathered in Princes Street. 'Hey! Are there any doctors or nurses here?' she shouted.

A middle-aged man and two young women raised their hands.

'Well, why the hell are you standing there gawping? Come over here and help me with these people.'

The two girls ran forward at once, but the man, though closest of the three, merely shook his head slowly, mouthing 'Sorry.'

Sarah stared at him, astonished. 'You're a doctor?'

'Yes.'

'So help here, for Christ's sake.'

The man shook his balding head again. 'I'm sorry, but I can't. I work in a hospital. My indemnity cover doesn't extend to situations like these.'

'In that case,' said Sergeant Holland, who had overheard the exchange, 'on your bike, or I'll do you for obstruction!'

The neon strip-lights were still working as Skinner stepped into the big marquee. It was sectioned off by a canvas divider which stretched almost its full width, with only a short gap on the right acting as a doorway. This partition was torn in two places, but that was the only damage apparent in that part of the tent. A small stage, fringed by a blue velvet pelmet and edged by potted greenery, had been set up against the perimeter canvas on the left. The paved deck of the Waverley Centre had been covered with green hessian flooring, and gold-painted, blue-upholstered seats were arranged on it, theatre-style, around the small stage. Two long rectangular tables stood against the tent wall opposite the stage. Each was covered by a white cloth, ruffled by the force of the blast but still held in place by boxes of wine-glasses, presumably there in readiness for the marquee's first Festival party.

Skinner did not notice the young man at first. It was a faint whimper that made him look across the rows of seats to catch sight of the figure sitting on the floor, his face buried in his hands, his shoulders shaking.

Skinner spoke softly, not wanting to startle the boy. 'Son, are you all right? Son.'

The youth turned his head slowly to look up him. His face was chalk-white, in awful contrast with the drying blood across his forehead. Then he stood up unsteadily, and Skinner saw the rest, of it smeared across the front of his blue and black striped Heart of Midlothian replica football shirt, spread also on his black denim jeans and matting in his hair.

'Go and see Danny, mister. Go and see him. Go and see Danny. Look at him. He's all over me.' He began to cry, softly at first, then louder. He slumped to his knees again and Skinner went closer, but he could think of nothing to do but put his hands on the boy's shoulders. For silent seconds he stood over the kneeling, sobbing young man in a strange attitude of blessing.

'We'll see to the lad, sir.' The voice came from behind him. He looked round to see an ambulance crew; a man and a woman in uniform. Nodding, but without a word, the big detective took a step back, then turned and walked towards the opening in the canvas wall.

As once it was clear to Skinner that the explosion had originated in the far right-hand corner of the tent's inner apartment. One of the structure's stout supporting pillars had been blown to fragments, and debris radiated outwards from that spot. Slowly, Skinner stepped towards the wreckage. But suddenly he paused, his eyes widening, as he caught sight of what was left of Danny, the boy he had been sent there to see.

All of his clothes had been blown off. The right arm and most of the right leg were missing. Forcing himself to look closer at the carnage, Skinner saw them lying a little way apart from the mangled torso. He tensed and stepped closer, keeping himself under control with an effort of will, as he took in the horror of it in stages. The corpse seemed to have been ripped open by shrapnel, for metal, glass and wood splinters were mixed in with the bloody mass. The top of the young man's head had been sliced off, and the bluey-grey brain matter spread out beyond it. Skinner then realised that some of this terrible cocktail had been splashed on the boy's friend next-door.

'Oh, Holy Mother of God.'

The voice came from behind Skinner – followed by the violent sounds of its owner vomiting. Skinner did not speak until the heaving had subsided. Then, still without turning, he said grimly: 'Didn't know you had got religion, Andy.'

There was no reply other than another bout of retching.

'You made it here fast.'

Detective Chief Inspector Andrew Martin, Head of Special Branch, and once Skinner's personal assistant, stepped up to stand alongside him. 'Not as fast as you, boss, but I wasn't that far away either. Sally and I were in John Lewis when I got the shout. She wasn't best pleased. As a matter of fact, she suggested it was a porky pie I had dreamed up to get out of shopping for her fucking curtains. To hell with her; I wish it had been a lie.'

'You should have brought her along to see for herself,' said Skinner. 'Christ, we get to clear up some right messes, but this one . . .' He shook his head, as his voice tailed away.

'Where were *you*, boss?'

'Along at the Gallery precinct, with Sarah.'

'You heard the bang?' Martin asked.

Skinner nodded in confirmation.

'What do you think it could have been? It looks as if they were installing beer kegs in here. Could it have been one of the gas cylinders?'

'No way, Andy. It was a bomb. You've been on the courses too. You know the different sound that explosives make. That was what I heard. Anyway, the beer and the gas bottles are all over there in that other corner.' He pointed a finger off to the left.

'This was no accident. Some bastard did this in deadly earnest. We'd best be very careful just in case he left us any other wee parcels. In fact, I think that for once we'll be sensible and get the fuck out of here until the Bomb Squad arrives and checks the whole place over. There's nothing we can do for poor Danny there, but we can empty the Waverley Centre, and the Balmoral next door.'

They walked quickly from the tent. Outside, more uniformed officers had arrived and were busy moving the crowds back. An ambulance was pulling out of the Princes Street Gardens gateway, with its blue light whirling. Two others stood by, waiting for passengers. Skinner caught sight of Sarah beside the Scott Monument, tending to Danny's friend, the boy from the tent. As he looked on, she wiped the blood from his forehead with a towel, then helped him, very gently, to take off his frightful shirt. For a moment, the youth held it away from him, at arm's length, then dropped it on the ground.

Four fire appliances had arrived. They were lined up on Waverley Bridge, at the spot where, normally, the tour buses took on their passengers. A senior fire officer, recognising Skinner, came across. 'What can we do here?' he asked.

'Nothing in the tent for now, but you could tell your people to evacuate the shopping station, and to close off the Station exit up the Waverley Steps.'

The officer nodded, his bulky helmet giving this gesture added emphasis. 'You've got it.' He turned and walked back towards the fire appliances, barking out orders to his men.

Skinner looked around for the highest-ranking policeman, and soon spotted a superintendent in uniform. He walked over and tapped the man on the shoulder. The officer spun round, impatient at first, until recognition brought him swiftly to attention.

'Afternoon, Archie,' said Skinner. 'Look, I want the Balmoral emptied. See to it, please. Then get on your radio and have someone tell the Transport Police, on my authority, that I want all trains stopped at Haymarket, and held up to the east. Until the bomb boys have cleared the site, I don't want any more people in that station than can be helped. If there's another bang, it could bring down the glass roof – if that one hasn't already!'

The man saluted and moved away to carry out his orders. Skinner retraced his steps and found Martin.

'Andy, you get down to your office. I want to know the minute someone claims responsibility for this mess. And even if no one does, I want the best analysis that your outfit can give me of the likely runners. I don't recall any recent intelligence in my other job to give me a hint of this, but I'll look again. You check your network for ideas.

'Maybe it's the Arabs getting even for us blowing out their plot last winter. Or perhaps it's the Paddies deciding to give Scotland a turn at last. Or possibly we've grown some new nutters of our own. I don't fancy any of those prospects, but the one I like least is the last one, the idea that we might have collected our own terrorist outfit. If that's so, I want to nail them quick and clean them out.'

Two

Martin had been gone for less than ten minutes when the Army Bomb Squad arrived from their base on the outskirts of the city. Major Gabriel 'Gammy' Legge, their commander, was well known to Skinner from countless call-outs to bomb hoaxes, and from their work together on security preparations for Royal and VIP visits to the city. The two stood beside the gold chairs, in the first area of the marquee.

'I suppose it was bound to happen one day, Bob,' said the slim soldier. His accent was that of an Ulsterman, but its harsher tones had been smoothed away by years of military service. 'All those false alarms, and then when the real thing comes we don't have a chance to defuse it.'

'You might have that chance yet, Gammy. There's all sorts of stuff lying in there needing to be checked out. There's something else in there, too. Maybe it'll make you and your lads think twice about being heroes. If it doesn't, at the least it'll sure as hell make you careful.'

The smile left the Major's face.

'Look out for yourselves, but, Gammy, I need the place checked out with all safe speed. I need to get the forensics people in, and I have to get the station reopened as soon as possible, before the effect of train hold-ups ripples all the way down to London.'

'Thank you, Robert, I'll take charge now.'

The voice breaking in on their conversation came from the entrance to the marquee. Surprised, and instantly annoyed, Skinner looked up to see the Deputy Chief Constable, in full uniform, bearing down on him.

DCC Edward McGuinness was in temporary command of the force, in the absence on holiday of the recently knighted Chief Constable, Sir James Proud. Skinner was aware that even at the best of times he was not the Deputy's favourite colleague. At the Chief Constable's regular management meetings, he and McGuinness were drawn almost invariably to taking opposite sides in any debate. Now Skinner guessed that to arrive at the disaster scene and find Bob in command, and matters well under control, was more than the other man could bear.

Mastering his irritation at McGuinness's rank-pulling, he mustered a smile.

'That's fine, Eddie. I'm glad you're here. Crowd control's for the uniform branch, anyway!'

The DCC reddened.

'I'd better fill you in, since you've only just got here.' Still smiling, Skinner seized him by the elbow and led him towards the entrance through the partition. 'The bang happened through there. Some form of explosive. We don't know for sure what, but from the pattern of destruction it could have been Semtex.'

He ushered McGuinness through into the second area. 'There have been some casualties, almost all of them superficial – apart from poor Danny there.'

The DCC had taken a few steps into the chamber, before he realised what lay on the floor. He started back in horror, but Skinner held tight to his elbow and drew him onwards.

McGuinness's ruddy face had gone grey.

'They can be hellish, these crime scenes, can't they, Eddie. I'm glad you're here to take charge of this one. I'll be in my other office if you need me.' He slapped the DCC on the back in friendly fashion, then turned and strode out of the marquee, his grim smile broadening with every step.

Three

Skinner's 'other office' was a small room in St Andrews House, the headquarters of government in Scotland.

Three months before, out of the blue, he had received a telephone call from Alan Ballantyne, then newly appointed as Secretary of State for Scotland. The surprising thing, he had thought as he answered that summons to a private meeting, was that Ballantyne had placed the call himself, rather than arranging an appointment through his Private Secretary. The unorthodoxy of this approach had soon been explained. A suave politician, Ballantyne was still a few years short of forty, and his rise to power had been meteoric. It had been helped along by a lack of alternative talent among his party's Scottish membership, but nonetheless, even with that dearth of competition, his appointment to the Cabinet had been greeted with some surprise on both sides of the Commons Chamber. Ballantyne was a stocky man, with quick darting eyes and a quiff of frizzy hair which, however expertly it was cut, invariably stood up from the rest in defiance of gravity, giving the appearance of a permanent overhanging question-mark.

At their first meeting in his office, the new Secretary of State had received the detective alone.

'Sorry about the mystery, Mr Skinner, but I'm finding that, as in your own job, there are one or two matters in mine which can't be delegated, or even discussed over the telephone. I find myself with a . . . shall we say a personnel problem. You will find many advisers to the Secretary of State listed in those office directories over there. But there is one who is not listed among the rest. I think you are aware of the job I'm talking about, and I believe that you're acquainted with the previous post-holder.'

He had paused then, palms laid flat on the polished mahogany surface of his desk, and had thrown Skinner a side-long glance which he still recalled vividly. Then he continued. 'Indeed, I believe that you may even have had something to do with the man's rapid departure from office.'

Skinner had said nothing, nor given anything away in his expression.

'If that's the case, Mr Skinner, you yourself have left me with something of a problem. So the way I see it, now it's up to you to solve it. Therefore, with the approval of your Chief Constable, I am inviting you to combine your present role within the police force with that of security adviser to the Secretary of State, in succession to Mr Hugh Fulton.'

At Ballantyne's suggestion, Skinner had called Jimmy Proud to discuss the offer there and then, and had found his chief enthusiastic.

'It's an honour, Bob, and it'll be the first time that job's been combined with active service in a police force. There's all sorts of ways it could help you here. Of course I think you should take it. Who do you think put your name up anyway? Mind you, combining the two jobs was my idea. There's no way I'd want to lose you from here, I'm not that bloody patriotic.'

And so Skinner had accepted – with one proviso. 'I don't want any more of this secrecy crap. It's well outdated. Hughie Fulton used it only to build up a wall of mystique around him – to suit his ego. So, if I take the job, I go into the directories, along with the doctors, the dentists, the social workers and all your other advisers.'

'If you say so,' the Secretary of State had conceded, 'but remember the confidentiality is most of all for your own protection.'

Skinner had laughed. 'Listen, Mr Ballantyne. I make enemies enough just by being head of Edinburgh CID. A few more won't bother me.'

And so he had accepted the appointment. In the ensuing weeks he had seen a lot of the Secretary of State, their meetings usually in private. Their relationship was informal and cordial, yet Skinner, despite his long experience of appraising people, still felt that he knew very little of the real man. This Secretary of State was an enigmatic, secretive character, and though Skinner had sought to pinpoint the special quality which had won Ballantyne his high office, it remained hidden to him.

Skinner had experienced no problems in coping with the extra workload of his part-time post. Most of it involved nothing more strenuous than writing reports to the Secretary of State on an assortment of questions relating to his personal security and that of his junior Ministers, or to the security of establishments which were the responsibility of government, directly or through its agencies. He had taken the precaution of following some of his own security advice, varying his daily routine rather more often than before, garaging his car when possible, and checking underneath it whenever it had been left in a public place for any length of time. But overall, his new job, which carried a modest additional salary, had made his life no more difficult than before.

However, it had given him, as a serving policeman, one very big advantage. As Hugh Fulton had been before him,

Skinner was now regarded as an active member of the UK Security Service. As such, he had access to the latest files on terrorism at national and international level, intelligence far more sensitive than any available to Andy Martin's Special Branch network. For example, Skinner was briefed fully on the Ulster Unionist plot, foiled earlier that summer, to assassinate President Clinton in New York, and on the secret elimination by the SAS, only a month before, of an underground organisation in Hong Kong which had been planning violent public opposition to the forthcoming Chinese take-over. He had been told of the rigorous international search for the ringleaders in each case, and of the harsh orders to be carried out should any of them be traced in Britain. He knew the true operational strength of the various Northern Irish para-military groups, and was aware of the routes which were used to smuggle weapons and explosives to the British mainland. He had heard rumours, too, of the summary justice meted out to those terrorists who, by chance, fell into the hands of the SAS rather than the police.

But he knew of nothing at all, on either the MI5 or the Special Branch networks, which offered the faintest clue to the identity of the perpetrators of the Waverley Centre explosion.

Four

Much of the information held by MI5 is stored on computer. Skinner had access to it through a modem and a dedicated 'secure' telephone line. Seated before his terminal in his St Andrews House office, he gained entry to the network by keying in his personal code, a five-letter password known only to him, which was made up of his parents' initials.

The colour screen lit up, to be filled rapidly by a directory. One by one, Skinner selected all of the most recent intelligence files, then others which had any bearing on UK security or UK nationals, or which attempted to predict future trends in terrorism. He found a forecast of renewed Irish activity on the mainland in late September through early October, with a flash that a 'major event' was planned for the week of the Conservative Party Conference. There was a warning of possible trouble within the Chinese community in the wake of the recent Hong Kong incident. Another file reported that a senior government Minister had become a major security risk because of an active homosexual relationship with a military attacheé from a North African embassy. There was a warning posted of the possibility of further Basque nationalist activity against British tourists arriving on flights into Malaga and Alicante airports. But there was nothing – nothing at all – to suggest the likelihood of terrorist attacks in Scotland.

After closing the last file, Skinner stared for a few seconds at the blank screen, then, with a shake of his head, signed out of the network. He picked up his secure telephone and called Andy Martin's direct-line number, which was also scrambled.

'How're you getting on? I've turned up nothing here.'

'Me neither. One thing I have done, though, is track down the managing director of the firm that sponsored that marquee – some big knitwear outfit or other – to check whether they've got any serious business rivals, or if there are any former employees with a grievance. He's thinking over the second possibility, but said there's no chance of the first. He claims he knows all his rivals personally. They're all in the same golf club. He reckons that alone would rule out any nasties.'

Skinner chuckled. 'Course it would! You can't play golf with a man, then bomb his business. Just isn't done! Got any other theories, m' boy?'

Martin exhaled noisily at his end of the line. 'None that are worth a stuff, boss. I've checked out the Nats and some of the wilder boys in the home-rule wing of the Labour Party, but there's absolutely nothing on any of the characters we've got on file to suggest that they'd be capable of this. And just suppose there is a Home Ruler out there of a mind to do something stupid, why the hell would he do it in some bloody tent? He'd choose a high-profile target, wouldn't he? No, my best guess is that it's linked in some way to the sponsors of that marquee. And that's all I've got.'

Skinner grunted. 'And as far as I'm concerned, you haven't even got that. OK, Andy. I'm on my way down to Fettes. We'll need to work out a statement on this, and get it out before the media start a public panic through lack of solid information. See you shortly.'

Skinner was turning the key of the five-lever Chubb lock to

close his office door when his mobile telephone started its trembling call sound. He dug it out of the breast pocket of his shirt and pushed the '*receive*' button. 'Skinner.'

'Bob, it's Alan Ballantyne here. I'm at Number 6. Can you get here right away, please.'

Skinner recognised concern, almost alarm in the Secretary of State's voice, but made an effort to keep his own tone relaxed. 'Sure, Alan. I'm at the House just now. I'll be with you in five minutes.'

'That's good. But use the back door, will you. I don't want anyone to know you're here!'

Five

Skinner's new BMW was parked in his reserved space in the St Andrews House courtyard, where he and Sarah had left it earlier that day.

As he pulled out of the exit gates held open for him by a security guard, he saw the traffic tailed back from the closed section of Princes Street, so he nipped across the flow and headed eastwards, turning into Regent Terrace. Just three minutes later he pulled off St Colme Street and up the rising driveway which led into the car park at the rear of Number 6 Charlotte Square. After parking, he called Andy Martin to warn him that he had been delayed, but without telling him exactly where he was. Then he climbed out of the BMW, locked it securely, headed over to the anonymous blue-painted back door, and rang its brass bell.

The official residence of the Secretary of State for Scotland had been gifted to the nation by an aristocratic family, to be used for that special purpose. It is a noble Georgian building in the centre of the terrace extending along the north side of Charlotte Square, Edinburgh's finest. Unlike Downing Street, there is no ministerial office in Number 6. Its only business function is to serve as a venue for government receptions and official dinner parties. However, its private apartments are occupied frequently by Scottish Office ministers, particularly those with rural constituencies. Alan Ballantyne was Member of Parliament for a sprawling seat in the north-east of Scotland. Skinner knew, too, that he had a shaky marriage, and that he used his Edinburgh residence on occasion as a bolt-hole.

The back door was opened by a beautiful woman. She looked to be around thirty, and was dressed in a silk blouse and a perfectly cut beige skirt. About Sarah's age, Skinner thought, and he doesn't have any sisters. Dressed with money, too. *Careful, Alan, careful.*

The blonde's accent sounded even more expensive than her clothes. 'Mr Skinner?' He nodded. 'Come away in, you're expected. I'm Carlie, by the way. A sort of friend of the family.' She led him up a flight of stairs which ascended to an austere hallway at street level. At the top she turned to him. 'Alan's waiting for you in the drawing-room. Do you know the way from here?'

Skinner smiled. 'Yes, I've been here a few times. Usually get to use the front door, though.'

Carlie returned his grin, and disappeared through a door at the back of the hall. Skinner continued up a second flight of stone stairs. One of the double doors to the drawing-room lay open. He entered and closed it behind him.

The magnificent room extended across the full width of the house. Its original fixtures had all been preserved, and the antique furniture and fittings were in tune with the period of the building itself.

The Secretary of State for Scotland stood leaning with his left forearm on the mantelpiece of the big empty fireplace. His right hand held a heavy crystal glass, in which a peaty liquid swirled. Skinner was astonished by this, as he knew the man rarely drank alcohol in any form.

Ballantyne turned at the sound of the closing of the door. 'Bob, am I glad to see you. Want a drink?'

Skinner shook his head. 'Too early for me, Alan.'

'Me too, as a rule, but when you hear what I have to tell you, you'll understand why. First things first, tell me about this explosion. Everything you know or suspect. Don't worry about anyone walking in on us. There's no staff here today, and I've told Carlie not to disturb us.'

Ballantyne led the way over to two finely carved, tightly upholstered armchairs at the far end of the room. They sat down, facing each other. Skinner leaned forward, his forearms on his knees, and looked the Secretary of State in the eye.

'Well, first of all, there was no warning, no tip-off, no chance to clear the place. Whoever planted that bomb meant for it to go off, and didn't care a bit about casualties. Mind you, I don't think that it was meant particularly to cause injury. It was placed in a corner of the tent, and the lad who was killed – a poor wee bugger called Danny Baker – was just unlucky. He was standing right next to the thing when it went off. It blew him to bits, and hurt quite a few other people, but none of the survivors seems to have been critically injured. The boy's body probably shielded the rest of them. We don't know for sure, but the army people think it was some Semtex device. So it wouldn't have been very big, and could have been stashed in anything: a biscuit tin, or any container like that. Something took the top of the boy Baker's head off; it could have been the lid.'

As Ballantyne winced at the thought, Skinner went on. 'So, despite the recklessness, I think that this was meant as some sort of demonstration. The objective could have been just to bring down the tent and attract public attention. But it's the *why* that beats me. As for *who* our somebody might be, I've looked at all the obvious candidates, and I don't fancy any of them. There've been no hints from the intelligence networks of anything cooking, so it looks like either a random nutter or a completely new set-up. It's the Semtex that worries me most of all. You don't steal that stuff from construction sites. Anybody who can get his hands on Semtex is either tied into an international terror group, or has serious cash at his disposal. I wish to God I knew which it is.

'The thing that surprises me, Alan, is that we haven't had a call yet. I'd have expected whoever did this to have been in touch by now, identifying himself, telling us what it's all about, and making some specific demands. But so far, there's been nothing at all.'

Ballantyne leaned back in his chair. 'That's where you're wrong, Bob,' he said softly.

Skinner's eyebrows rose. The Secretary of State, normally laid-back and self-assured, seemed as tense as the mainspring of an over-wound watch.

Ballantyne jumped up and strode across the room to a fine Georgian writing table. He picked up a brown A4 manila envelope and walked back towards Skinner, thrusting it before him.

'There you are. Take a look at this. It was handed in at St Andrews House by a motorcyclist half an hour ago. The security staff checked that I was here, then sent it along to me. Read it, man.'

Skinner took the envelope from Ballantyne, noticing that the man's hand was trembling. A white address label was stuck precisely in the centre.

The words on it were neatly typed:

Alan Ballantyne, MP
St Andrew's House
Edinburgh
To be opened by Addressee only.

In contrast to the neatness of the label, the envelope itself had been ripped open crudely. Skinner prised its sides apart with two fingers, and saw inside a single sheet of white paper. Taking it by one corner he withdrew it carefully and laid it on the open palm of his left hand. He looked at it for a moment then began to read.

To the so-called Secretary of State for Scotland.
From the Fighters for an Independent Scotland.

By now you will have learned of the demonstration staged earlier today by the true representatives of the people of Scotland, for the benefit and enlightenment of you and your colleagues in the government of the occupying power. Be in no doubt that this was only a small token of the resources which are available to us, and it is no more than a first warning.

Our demands are simple and clear. Your Westminster Parliament will agree at once to take steps to annul the fraudulent Treaty of Union, and to restore full power and authority to the Estates of Scotland, through its properly elected Parliament. We have been compelled to take this stern action by the intransigence of your government, and by the collaboration of the so-called opposition parties, in denying Scotland its birthright.

Today's operation should be interpreted as a declaration of intent. At the moment of writing this communiqueé, we cannot know whether it will be completed without casualties. But if people have been killed or injured, they should be seen as martyrs to the Scottish cause. The same will be true of those others who will be called upon to sacrifice themselves if you do not yield to our demands.

The Edinburgh International Festival has been chosen as the stage for our drama. We hope that this will be a play in one act only, but unless Scotland's independence is restored at once, there will be further scenes, escalating in their violence until you, the oppressors, are forced to submit. Scotland deserves that the whole world should see her regain her freedom. With this in mind the contents of this letter are being released simultaneously to the media. Future communiqueés from us, should they be necessary, will use the code word *Arbroath* to demonstrate their authenticity.'

Skinner pursed his lips and whistled softly. He glanced up at Ballantyne. 'Wordy bastard this one, is he not. Lovely turn of phrase. Poor Danny'd be chuffed to know he's joined the great honour roll of martyrdom.' He paused and looked at the note again. 'What have you done about the bit on the end?'

Ballantyne looked puzzled. 'What do you mean?'

'Come on, Alan. Get a grip. What have you done about the press?'

'Nothing so far. Do you take this thing seriously?'

Skinner pointed to his right foot. 'See that stain on my shoe? That's blood. Too effing right I take it seriously.' He took out his mobile telephone and punched in a number. 'Andy? It's Bob. Listen, I need you to act fast. The Secretary of State's had a letter claiming responsibility for our bomb. They say they've put it out to the press, too, but they don't say how. Chances are they'll issue it by hand or by telephone. I don't think they'd be daft enough to use a fax. Get hold of Alan

Royston, our Press Officer, whatever golf course he's on, and tell him to get his arse into the office. While he's doing that, you put out a holding statement on the explosion via our Mercury distribution network. Don't say much, just that the cause is being investigated. Then tell Royston to field all incoming calls. And while you're at it, tell DCC McGuinness that's the SB party line and that he's to stick to it. Better still, he's to say nothing at all.'

'Will he take that from me?'

'He'll take it from me. Use my name. Once that statement has gone out, I want you to stop all other coverage. Use your duty staff, and get them calling round all the media. If anyone hasn't received the letter yet, then tell them about it. Whatever the case, say that we hope it's a crank, but that we need a complete news blackout on it while we study the contents, run forensic tests, and so on. They can say that they're calling on my behalf, with the full authority of the Security Service, and that D-notice procedures apply. If any editor refuses to co-operate, arrest him, and let me know.'

Skinner heard Martin gasp at the other end of the line.

'That's a bit beyond D-notice procedure, boss. We can't just lift an editor because he won't do what we ask. We don't have the—'

Skinner cut him off short. 'Andy, I don't think you'll need to go that far, but if you do, you'll find that the Secretary of State has just given me the authority I need. That covers it. Now don't waste any time. Get on with it. As soon as that's under way, here are a few other things that'll need doing. First locate all the Scottish Office ministers, plus the Lord Advocate and the Solicitor General, and give them all Special Branch armed close protection. Then get round all the police forces in Scotland and advise them that all public buildings, police stations, the lot, should upgrade their alert status to one level short of the maximum.'

He cut the line and turned to Ballantyne. 'Did you hear that, Secretary of State? I need you to sign a piece of paper.'

'Don't I need Downing Street approval?'

'You've got more power than you realise, Alan. You should read the new Act. The Home Secretary in England and you here in Scotland have the right to take certain actions on the advice of the Security Service, and to tell Downing Street afterwards. Well, thanks to you, I'm the Security Service, and I'm giving you that advice now. There's no such thing as an anti-terrorist branch in Scotland. But if we have grown our own provos after all these years, you're going to have to put one together quickly. The faster we move, the better the chance of killing the beast at birth, and it'll be easier if we can control the flow of information.'

Skinner looked Ballantyne straight in the eye, and the Secretary of State returned his gaze. He looked full of doubt, but slowly nodded his head.

'OK, Bob. You're on. If you take the letter that seriously, I'll back you that far. Set up your anti-terrorist squad. You're in command. You can have your emergency power to control the media. All I ask is that, before you use it, you remember that I'd like to be re-elected in a couple of years time! What else do you need? Tanks?'

Skinner grinned. 'Naw. Air cover'll be enough! I'll pick my own team. Mostly they'll be people I know and trust. I'd like to bring in someone with Irish experience. I'll expect full co-operation from other forces where necessary, but I've got no worries on that score. Have your Private Office call every chief constable to a briefing in St Andrews House tomorrow morning, and I'll tell them what's going on. I have a local problem in that McGuinness is standing in for Jimmy Proud. I'd appreciate it if you would call him yourself and tell him politely to keep out of my hair. I don't want any nonsense from that quarter.'

His composure completely restored, Ballantyne nodded his head vigorously. 'You'll have all that. I'll call my PPS now, and I'll have the Solicitor's Office draw up that paper and get it here for signature today. That way, if you do have to jail the Controller of BBC Scotland, at least you'll be doing it legally! You *are* certain that this wasn't just a gas explosion, aren't you?'

Skinner shook his head. 'Alan, if that was a gas explosion, then I'll never use my cooker again.' Then quite suddenly, his expression changed. His grey eyes had lost their warmth. 'Look, I'd love to be wrong, but I'm not. Like it or not, you've got some big decisions to make, my friend. For what it's worth, here's how I see them.

'Do you, could you, close down the Festival? No way! It's too big and it's too late. Everyone's here, tickets are sold, and the shows start tonight. Do you warn the public? I'd say not at this stage. It'd be too easy to start a panic; and we would for sure frighten off thousands of visitors. It could just be that all our friends are aiming to do is to disrupt the Festival, for now at least. If we let them do it that easily, then we're in real long-term trouble. That letter gives us nothing solid to go on. All we can do is hunt these people as best we can, and hope we get lucky. But, chances are, the next move is theirs. We, all of us, have got to live with that probability.'

He paused, looking hard at Ballantyne. Then he said, 'That's policeman's advice, Secretary of State, and for a reason I'll tell you shortly, it's the most honest you're ever likely to receive. It's not a political judgement; that's your arena. But these are decisions that need to be taken now.'

Ballantyne returned his gaze. He had respected Bob Skinner from the beginning of their relationship, but now he began to understand the very strange thing that Sir James Proud, imposing and unimpeachable as ever in full uniform, had said as they had discussed Skinner's appointment. '*Bob is the son I never had. He's clever and intuitive as a detective. He's strict but fair as a commander. He's charming and generous as a man. Yet inside all that, there lives also the most fearsome human being I know. I hope you never have to encounter that side of him.*'

Looking into Skinner's eyes, Ballantyne felt, for the very first time, the faint chill of something else in the man, something very hard and formidable, and perceived at last an inkling of what Proud had meant. He had never sought to learn in detail the circumstances which had led up to Hugh Fulton's resignation, although he knew that something had caused bad blood between him and Skinner. Now he realised with certainly that Fulton had been mortally afraid of his successor. Suddenly and irrationally, Ballantyne was glad that he did not know why.

He forced himself to consider the choice he had to make, the choice which Skinner had set out for him. There could be only one decision.

'The show goes on. Warn the Directors of the various Festivals if you consider it necessary, but no one else. Keep this thing under wraps for as long as you can. Issue a further statement through your press office, saying that you are still looking into the causes of the explosion, but at the moment it looks like a gas leak of some sort. Pick your team and use whatever time the news blackout buys you as best you can. Maybe we'll get lucky.'

Skinner nodded. 'Very good, Minister,' he said, formal for

the first time. 'That's how it will be. Now I'll tell you just how objective my advice was. If this lot are going to start blowing up the Festival, as they threaten, then that makes my daughter a target. She's performing in a play on the Fringe. It could have been her lying in that tent today, and when I find these characters, I'll go just as hard as if it had been her. Meanwhile, I'm on the spot. Do I tell Alex to pull out, without telling her why, or do I follow your orders to the letter, and keep my mouth shut, letting her run the same risk as the rest?'

'For God's sake, Bob. Of course you must get her out of it!'

'Thanks, Alan, but that has to be my choice to make. It won't be an easy one. There are so many *what ifs*. The best answer is just to catch these bastards before this thing gets any bigger. I'm off to do that now.'

He picked up the letter and its envelope and made for the door, but stopped just before he reached it.

'Oh, Alan, here's a piece of non-police advice. You could find photographers hanging around here today. If Carlie might be a problem in some newspaper picture, best not let that happen, eh.'

'Thanks, Bob. Point taken.'

Six

Skinner was deep in thought as he slid the BMW into St Colme Street. On impulse he indicated to the left and drove up the cobbled slope of Glenfinlas Street, turning left at the top into Charlotte Square.

As usual, all of the parking bays in the Square were occupied. Scores of cars, and not a few camper vans, bearing German, French and Belgian registration plates, were nosed in on the angle, facing the gardens in the centre, their tails pointing back towards the one-way traffic as it circulated clockwise. The space on the outer side of the wide street, normally kept clear by yellow lines, was mostly full, the vigilance of Edinburgh's redoubtable traffic wardens being relaxed on Saturday afternoons. However, there was a vacant slot only a few yards from Glenfinlas Street, just outside the head office of one of Scotland's largest public companies. Skinner reversed the BMW in, switched off the engine and sat looking thoughtfully at the pavement across the street from the Secretary of State's front door.

With its fund managers, its surveyors and its few remaining lawyers on the golf course rather than at work in their offices, Charlotte Square was usually one of the quietest spots in central Edinburgh on Saturday afternoons. Occasionally, special weekend events were held in its gardens; on the grass among the trees, around the oxidised bronze equestrian statuary on its marble plinth. Two years before, an age ago to Skinner, this green space had been covered with marquees serving as the venue of the biennial Edinburgh Book Festival. But, for this year at least, the Festival was being staged in different surroundings, in the City's newly opened international conference centre. Now, as Skinner looked across the expanse of grass, he saw only a few recumbent sunbathers enjoying the warmth of the August day.

He scanned the pavement opposite Number 6. Its surface was raised above the level of roadway by four cobbled steps, and so he could observe the pedestrians clearly. He saw two elderly grey-haired ladies, wearing shapeless hats and coats even in flaming August, their backs to him, walking slowly in step, with the same rolling gait. 'Afternoon tea in the Roxburghe, I'll bet,' he murmured to himself, smiling at this enduring tradition among the aged well-to-do of Edinburgh. As Skinner watched them, the two old ladies drew alongside and passed a bulky, bearded figure who was leaning against the railings, idly adjusting the camera which hung on a strap round his neck.

'Denis,' he said aloud, recognising one of the city's best-known news photographers.

He was on the point of climbing out of his car to talk to the man, when suddenly his eye was caught by a motorcyclist astride his vehicle in one of the parking bays on the corner: a tall figure, in black leathers, with a metallic blue crash helmet. He wore the livery of one of Edinburgh's many motorcycle delivery companies. That's odd, thought Skinner. Why the hell was a bike courier at work on a Saturday? And if he was supposed to be working, why the hell was he sitting on his arse in Charlotte Square, doing bugger all?

Deciding to postpone his chat with Denis the

photographer, he settled back into the driver's seat of the BMW, keeping as inconspicuous as any good detective should be. The leather gear made it difficult to judge the man's age, but Skinner knew that most of Edinburgh's delivery riders were in their early twenties, and his build and bearing seemed to bear this out. The courier held a folded newspaper in his left hand and gave the appearance of studying it intently. But Skinner noticed that, every so often, he would glance along the street – looking in the same direction as Denis the photographer – towards the Secretary of State's front door.

What the Devil is he up to? Skinner thought. Was he a tip-off man for the *Sunday Mail*, maybe, looking for action around Number 6?

As he gazed at the man, intrigued, his view was obscured for a moment by a black Rover Sterling with a familiar figure in the back seat. The car drew to a halt outside Number 6, and Lord Peters, Minister of State for Scotland and, as such, Ballantyne's deputy, heaved his girth on to the pavement. He tapped the car on the bonnet in dismissal and made towards the big brown door, tugging a key from his pocket as he walked.

Skinner looked across towards Denis, who was snapping off frame after frame of the Minister's arrival, then glanced across at the motorcyclist. The man had dropped his newspaper and now was holding a mobile telephone. There was a brief scene of pantomime as he put the earpiece up to his crash-helmet, then set the instrument down on the saddle of the bike and began to fiddle with his chinstrap.

'Let's check this boy out,' Skinner muttered to himself. He jumped from the car and began to trot across the street. 'Hey, just a minute!' he shouted as he ran.

The rider gave up his battle with the chinstrap, and reached inside his jacket with his ungloved right hand.

Later, it would strike Skinner as remarkable that he had not registered surprise when he saw the gun. But, at that moment, all that concerned him was reaching the nearest cover.

It was a small weapon, possibly a Beretta. The man swung towards him, his left hand coming up to join the other in a marksman's grip. By that time Skinner's trot had accelerated into a sprint. He reached the other side of the street, which was mercifully free of traffic, and threw himself full-length between a couple of parked cars. He was still in mid-dive when he heard the two shots, and the zinging sound of the ricochets as the bullets flew off the tarmac behind him.

Lying face-down, aware of the pounding of his heart, he tried to work out his next move. But in the very moment that he realised that he did not have one, he heard the motorcycle roar into life. Skinner pulled himself into a crouch behind the car which was his shield. Tyres squealed as the rider swung out of his parking bay against the traffic flow, barely missing a red Peugeot which was cornering at speed. Skinner stood up in time to see the silver-grey bike racing off down Glenfinlas Street, but a second too late to read its registration number.

'Bob!' The shout came from behind him. Skinner turned and saw Denis the photographer lumbering towards him. 'What the hell happened there? Were those gun-shots? Are you all right?' The big man was out of breath by the time he reached Skinner.

'No panic, Denis. It's okay. There's no harm done. What did you see anyway?'

'Nothing much. I just sort of heard the noise and caught a flash of you ducking between those two motors. Only I didn't realise it was you till you stood up. Who was the guy on the bike? I'll be looking twice at Apache Couriers next time they turn up on one of my jobs, I'll tell you.'

Skinner thought fast. 'Courier, my arse. That was a boy we've had under surveillance as a suspected drug-dealer.' He put a hand on Denis's shoulder and said, conspiratorially, 'But listen, old mate. You saw nothing – understand? All that you heard was the bike backfiring. The fact is, my imagination got the better of me, and I got the wrong idea and jumped for it. Now, for God's sake, not a cheep about that in your bloody rag or I'll be the laughing-stock of Edinburgh.'

Denis looked sceptical, but nodded. 'Well, if you say so, Bob. If you say so. But it's a bloody queer backfire that can put a hole through a window thirty yards away!'

He pointed across the street to Number 8. Skinner's eye followed his finger. In the top right-hand pane of one of its ground-floor windows there was a neat round hole, cracks fanning out from it like rays from a tiny, dark sun.

'Honest to Christ, Denis. See vandals these days. Nothing's sacred any more.' A guileless look crept across his face. 'What brings you here today anyway?'

Denis looked embarrassed. 'You shouldn't ask me that, Bob. Secrets of the trade and all that. The truth is, as usual, I don't know. Us photographers, in our army we're just the bloody infantry. I'm told to get along here and get some pics of Ballantyne and of anyone else that arrives here, so that's what I'm doing. But I'm not told why. Same old bloody story. Every other photographer's at bloody Tynecastle covering the football, and I'm stuck here watching a fucking door!'

Skinner sighed out loud, in mock sympathy, silencing the rising tirade. 'Ah, well, big fella, sometimes there's no justice at all. Sounds like a right boring afternoon, but good luck to you. Me, I'm doing something really exciting. I'm off to take the wife to Asda.' He raised a hand in farewell and strolled across the road towards his car.

'That'll be bloody right!' muttered Denis, towards his disappearing back.

Seven

As was usual at weekends, a heavy gate barred entry to the sloping driveway which rises up to the main entrance to Edinburgh's police headquarters building.

Denied access to his parking space, Skinner drove on out of Fettes Avenue, and used the side entrance in Carrington Road. The civilian security guard manning the entrance barriers recognised him, but nonetheless inspected his photographic warrant card carefully, knowing that the ACC would have roasted him had he done any less.

Skinner entered the building at basement level, in the rear, and made his way up four flights of stairs to Andy Martin's office – on the same level as his own in the Command Suite, but in the main four-storey section. The Detective Chief Inspector's room opened off the main area of the Special Branch office. In the outer room, Skinner recognised Detective Constables Neil McIlhenney, a Special Branch regular, and Barry Macgregor – borrowed, he guessed, from week-end duty with the Crime Squad to help with the call-round of the media.

'Afternoon, gentlemen. Had a busy time?'

'Not as busy as you, by the looks of it, sir,' said the normally phlegmatic McIlhenney, pointing towards Skinner's lower half. 'Been playing football wi' the lads?'

Skinner looked down and noticed for the first time the split across the right leg of his denims, just above the knee. 'Hah. Not quite football, Neil, but a bit of fancy diving all the same.

'Mr Martin in?'

'Sir.' McIlhenney nodded in confirmation, and Skinner walked on up to Martin's door, rapped on it, and pushed it open without waiting for a response.

The Special Branch commander was seated behind his desk, his shoulders hunched and the telephone pressed to his right ear. He glanced up at Skinner, his eyes taking in the torn jeans and registering surprise. He pointed awkwardly and unnecessarily towards the phone with his left hand, then towards a filter coffee-maker on a table beneath the room's only window.

'Sorry, sir, but my boss just came in, and I missed that.' He paused, listening to the voice on the line. 'I appreciate your point, but you have to understand our situation too. Our information is that today's explosion was quite possibly accidental. If this hoax letter appears anywhere, it could cause quite unnecessary public alarm, not to mention its effect on such a popular international event. Every other news organisation in the UK has already agreed to a black-out of that letter. You'll lose nothing by co-operating.'

Skinner was listening intently now. 'Who is this?' he mouthed silently to Martin.

'Hold on one second please, sir,' the Chief Inspector said to the telephone. 'I have to speak to my chief.' He pressed the privacy button. 'It's an American guy, sir. He's chief editor, or some such title, of Television News International, that satellite channel that we always hear about on other people's news bulletins. I called his bureau chief in London about the black-out. He told me he had to refer upwards, and this is the result. The bloke's mouthing on about global responsibility. Sounds like he's after a world scoop, and since his channel's on in every newsroom in this country, if he runs the letter we've got trouble – emergency powers or not. Everyone else is playing ball, but if this arsehole publishes it, they all will.'

Skinner's eyes glinted. A dangerous smile hung around the corners of his mouth. He held out his right hand towards Martin. 'Gimme. What's his name?'

'Albert Neidermeyer.'

Skinner took the receiver from Martin, earpiece first.

'Mr Neidermeyer? My name is Bob Skinner. I am in charge of this investigation, and the request made by Mr Martin comes directly from me. As you've just been told, we don't want to start a major public fuss over a letter which could well have been sent in by a crank. Every other news outlet in the country has agreed not to publish that letter for the time being so I'd be grateful if you would instruct your man in London to go along with—'

Neidermeyer cut in. 'Listen, mister. I'm in charge of the world's biggest news organisation. We didn't get that way by dropping our pants every time some guy like you comes by. We have viewers everywhere, and we don't keep news from them on the say-so of just any copper. What did you say your name was?'

'Skinner. Assistant Chief Constable Skinner. Edinburgh CID.'

'Skinner.' Across the Atlantic, there was a pause. 'Say, weren't you the guy who—'

This time Skinner cut in. 'Yes, I probably was. Look me up. If your information library is any good, I'll be there. While you're doing that, let me tell you what I'll be doing at this end. I'll be making one telephone call. About two minutes later, you'll find that every one of your satellite transponders has been shut down for repair. The more fuss you make, the longer that repair will take. I'm not just talking about Europe. I'm talking home base too. I'm talking everywhere.'

'Bull Shit!'

'Try me. You want to find out what's possible, then force me to make that phone call. I don't care how big a fish you are in your own pond. If you want still to be swimming there tomorrow, you'll do what we request. If the situation changes, we'll let you know. For now, please be sensible and co-operate with us.'

For a few seconds there was silence. Then Neidermeyer gave a loud sigh. 'OK, Skinner. Experience tells me that if anybody makes a threat that heavy, then he can probably make it good. So I'll do what you ask. But, pal, you'd better be right every step of the way. Otherwise you'll have the full resources of the world's biggest news organisation after your ass!'

Skinner gave a strange cold smile. 'Thank you, Mr Neidermeyer, for showing such good sense. I'll bear your promise in mind, but just be sure that you don't forget mine!' He put the telephone back in its cradle. 'There, Andy. Like my old mother used to say, a problem shared is a problem halved. And in this case, solved.'

Martin looked at him curiously. 'I suppose you could have done that thing with the transponders.'

Skinner grinned back at him affably. 'Well, maybe it wouldn't have been just as easy as that. I might have had to make two phone calls.'

He took several steps across to the window table and poured coffee into two mugs. He added a little milk to his own and handed the other, plain black, to Martin. Then he took the folded envelope enclosing the letter from the back pocket of his jeans, and tossed it down on the desk.

'That's what the fuss is about. What d'you think?'

Martin extracted the letter and scanned it quickly. 'Where was this handed in?'

'St Andrews House. By motorbike courier. About half an hour after the bang.'

'Well, I suppose this could be from some idiot who saw the fuss over the explosion in the centre of town and decided to take the piss out of the polis. But he'd need to have moved very fast. From the look of this, too, he'd also have needed access to a computer and a bubble-jet printer. Mind you, that doesn't mean much these days, given the size of some of the kit around.

'What about the courier?'

'I haven't checked that yet. But I think that when we ask the security men at St Andrew's House, we'll find he was wearing an Apache Couriers vest. And when we check Apache Couriers – and we will – we'll find that they had no one working today, but also that either one of their new recruits has gone missing or one of their vests has been nicked.'

'What makes you think all that then, boss?' Martin asked warily.

Quickly, Skinner described the incident in Charlotte Square. 'Ripped my new Levis too. I'll take it out of the bastard's hide when I catch him, see if I don't. Not, of course, that there's a cat's chance that we will catch him. Nonetheless, we'll put a call out for a tall guy with a metallic blue brain-bucket, riding a silver grey bike. You never know. Anyway, that wee encounter removed my last doubt that this letter could be just kidology. Our man was on look-out duty, reporting all arrivals at Number 6 to someone else, our anonymous correspondent no doubt. We've got to assume that they were watching the back door as well, and they'll have seen me come and go. They probably wanted to see how Ballantyne would react to the letter. By now, since they've heard nothing on the radio, they'll be finding that out. I wonder what their next move will be.' He winced. 'Painful for someone, I have no doubt.'

He pulled up a chair and sat down, facing Martin across the desk. 'What we've got to do now is put a unit in place to deal with these characters. Ballantyne's given me all the power and authority I need . . . for now at any rate.'

Martin raised his eyebrows. 'You worried about him?'

'He's a politician, Andy. I always worry about them. Their judgement gets clouded by the ballot box – then, depending on what sort they are, they either shit themselves or overreact. And our Secretary of State's just one man on the ladder. There are others with more clout than him. But, in any event, the ball's in our court, so let's run with it and set up our anti-terrorist unit. I want a team briefing in this office at 3:45. Then I want to meet all of the Festival directors in a hotel somewhere in the city centre. You set that up, will you. Make it for five o'clock.'

'That's short notice, boss.'

'The fuckers who planted that bomb didn't give us any notice at all!' said Skinner, tersely.

He sat silent in thought for a few seconds, then went on. 'Our team has to be tight. I want people I know and can trust – not too many of them, but enough. They've all got to be able to take sector responsibility, if they need to, for running a part of what will be, in total, a very big security operation. Naturally, Andy, you're my second-in-command. As my personal assistant, Brian Mackie has to be in, too. And I'll have Maggie Rose and Mario McGuire. They've been over the course with us already. They're both tough and we know for sure they don't get rattled.'

'I thought you wanted them kept apart, because they're going together off-duty.'

'I've had second thoughts on that, but you'll figure out why in a minute. I'll call their divisional commanders and put them on temporary secondment. Then there's those two outside, Neil and Barry. They're in the know already, and they're good guys, so we'll have them too. You tell Jimmy Hodgson, the Crime Squad gaffer, that I'd like to borrow the boy Macgregor until further notice. Do it nicely, mind you. He's his own boss in this place. I need someone through in the West, too. Although these lunatics say that it's the Festival that's under threat, you never know when this could turn into a cross-border affair.'

'Who'll you want over there?' asked Martin.

'Willie Haggerty. Who else?'

'Haggerty? What about McKinstery? He's Special Branch in Strathclyde.'

'Not any more he isn't. He's out, and Haggerty's in.'

Martin's eyebrows shot up. Skinner smiled at the surprise written on his face. 'You Special Branch guys aren't allowed to get together as a group – in case you form your own secret police force – so there's some excuse for you not to have noticed the changes that have been made lately.'

'What d'you mean?'

'I mean that *you* are now the only surviving Special Branch head who was in post during Hughie Fulton's time. Since I took over, the commander in every other force has been posted elsewhere. It's happened in stages, but it's happened. McKinstery was the last to be moved.'

'You've done all that?' Martin's voice rose in surprise.

'Let's say that I've persuaded all their Chief Constables that it was a good idea.'

'But why?'

'Remember when we had that carry-on last winter, and big Fulton seemed to know everything that we did?'

Martin nodded.

'At the time, you and I pinned some of the blame for that on Roy Thornton, up at the Court. As it happens we were right, but only up to a point, for there was a hell of a lot he didn't know that Fulton still found out. I wondered at the time who the big bastard's touts were, and it didn't take me long to find out, once I took over his job. All your opposite numbers in Special Branch were feeding him stuff that even their own bosses – my equivalents – didn't know. In short, they were all in his pocket. Alec Smith, your predecessor, was at it as well. When Sarah and I started seeing each other, he reported it to Fulton, and big Hughie had her vetted.'

'How did you find that out?'

'The stupid bastard kept a file on me. As soon as he quit, the locks on his office door were changed, and so he didn't get the chance to destroy the file before he left. He's in Ibiza now, retired. Be just as well for him if he stays there.'

'Why didn't he approach me when I took over?'

'Take that as a compliment. He must have decided that you were incorruptible, as far as I was concerned. I guess that Alec Smith told him that. Actually, Alec did make one brief attempt to talk me into giving his job to someone else, but he changed horses when he saw my mind was made up, and he backed you instead.'

'Who was the someone else?'

'If I told you, it might prejudice your view of a perfectly good copper – who is, incidentally, in the uniformed branch now.' Skinner paused reflectively. 'Anyway, all Fulton's boys are gone now. They're either back in uniform, on promotion, or they're retired.'

Martin shook his head. 'But I liked Davie MacKinstery. Alec, too for that matter.'

'No need to stop loving them, Andy. The fact that they were Fulton's touts didn't make them bad people. He set the rules and got away with it, thanks to his reputation and his power. I don't condemn anyone for not crossing him. Still, when I took over, I decided that I could never trust anybody who had previously reported to Fulton on that basis. Hence the complete and total clear-out.' Skinner's tone grew heavy. 'One thing stays the same: all the new guys talk to *me* regularly. The big difference is that none of them keeps secrets from or spies on his bosses in his home force. It's an open system now – as far as it *can* be in our game.'

Martin stared at the surface of his desk, his brow furrowed. 'Christ, boss. I knew you had clout, but to clear the whole of Special Branch . . .'

'Forget it, Andy. It's history, and only the Chief Constables know that it's happened. So, for this emergency, it'll be Haggerty in the West, Bill Finlay in Aberdeen, and Peter Buxton in Dundee – as and when we need them.'

He stood up and walked over to the window. 'There are two other people I'm going to include on our team. One's a counter-terrorist specialist from the SAS: I guy I met when I was away at that seminar in Yorkshire last month. His name is Arrow, Captain Adam Arrow, and he's got years in Ireland and other places under his belt.'

He paused. Martin looked up at him.

'Not another one of *those* guys, Bob, please?'

Skinner smiled softly. 'No, son. There'll never be another of them – anywhere. Not while I'm around, at least. Arrow's a good guy. His speciality is counter-terrorism: IRA, UVF, it doesn't matter to him. He loathes them all. He's put a few active service men into early retirement, one way or another. Just recently, he was involved in sorting out something particularly nasty that the Loyalists were planning. Arrow knows something of what happened last winter – but not everything.'

Andy Martin looked at Skinner, and held his eyes. An awkward silence hung in the room, until Martin broke it.

'Bob, I'm your closest colleague, and you've never told even me the whole story of that night. You've changed since then, you know. I tell you this as a friend, that I've noticed a side to you that wasn't there before. Just now and again, it's as if you're somewhere else, in a very scary place. Maybe only people who really know you can see it.'

Skinner had his back to Martin as he replied. It was perhaps as well that the younger man could not see the expression in his grey eyes. 'Andy, I try not to let any of my thoughts show on the outside, but *that* was something of a night.' Then, suddenly Skinner laughed out loud. 'And I've got a fucking great bullet hole in my leg to remind me!'

The tension broken, Skinner quickly changed the subject. 'Now, the last member of the team. I want to include Sarah. What d'you think? Can I have my own wife on my team?'

Martin looked thoughtful for a second, then looked up and nodded. 'Yes, boss, I'm all for it. She knows how you think, and she's got her Masters in criminal psychology, too. If she can help you, she's helping us all. And since she's still a part-time police surgeon, technically she's an insider as well.'

'Right, Andy,' said Skinner emphatically. 'That's our team picked. Now let's get it on the park. The game's started and the other side's a goal up already!'

Eight

From the privacy of his own office in the command suite, Skinner made six quick-fire telephone calls. The first two were to the divisional detective superintendents at the Torphichen Street and St Leonards police stations, who were, respectively, the line officers Maggie Rose and Mario McGuire. He told them that each would be losing his best sergeant for an indefinite period. He expected no questions or protests, and received none. The third call went to a private number.

The phone was answered on the second ring, and a familiar deep voice sounded on the line. 'McGuire.'

'Hi, Mario. ACC here. Are you alone, or is anyone I know there with you?'

'Well as it happens, sir, DS Rose is watching a video in the living room. Me? I'm in the kitchen as usual.'

'In that case, Sergeant, I've got good news for you, and bad news for Maggie. You heard about this morning's bang in Princes Street?'

McGuire grunted assent.

'Well, I'm setting up a unit to co-ordinate the search for the cowboys who did it. I want my best on it, so you two are in. Get yourselves down to Fettes right away, and meet me in the SB suite.'

Next he dialled the mobile number of Detective Inspector

Brian Mackie, his personal assistant. As Mackie answered, Skinner could hear the din of a crowd.

'Where are you, Brian?'

'Tynecastle, sir. Kicked off five minutes ago. The Jam Tarts are one down already.'

'So am I. Give the rest a miss and get into the office.'

For his fifth call, Skinner switched to a green scrambled telephone on his desk. Seconds later he was connected to an MI5 duty officer. He identified himself, and asked the woman to call him back in confirmation. When she did so, he asked her to do everything necessary to have Captain Adam Arrow report to him personally at police headquarters in Edinburgh by 10:00 am the next morning.

Finally, he called his own home number in Edinburgh. Sarah and he had just moved into a bungalow off Queensferry Street, even closer to Fettes Avenue than the flat in Stockbridge from which they had recently moved. He assumed that Sarah herself would answer his call, but he was wrong.

'This is 957 0825. Alex Skinner speaking.'

He smiled at the unexpected sound of his daughter's voice.

'Hi, kid. I thought you were rehearsing up to the last minute.'

'No, Pops. Our director decided that we could only get worse, so he gave us the afternoon off, to rest up. Curtain goes up at 8:00 sharp. Will you be able to get to it, with all this bomb stuff and everything? Sarah told me about it. In fact will you get home at all this evening, Pops? There's someone here I'd like you to meet. My new leading man, you might say.'

'Don't think so. Better postpone the introduction. But unless something else happens, I will make it tonight. So you be good, and if you can't be good, just be sensational. Now put your stepmother on, okay.'

'I think she's in the shower. No, I lie. Just a sec. Sarah! It's your old man!'

Moments later, he heard Sarah's soft New York drawl. 'Hello, honey, where are you?'

'At HQ. Did you get everything cleaned up at your end?'

'Eventually. No other serious casualties. That poor girl looked in worse shape than actually she was. A bad scalp cut; lots of blood – most of it ended up on me. God, was I a mess. I've just done washing it off. Next I'll have to wash the shower-curtain. It looks like that scene from *Psycho*. When will you be home?'

'Not for a bit yet. But, that's not why I've called. Look, I want you up here now. I'm putting a team together and I want you on it. I need somebody with your sort of expertise, so why not you?'

'Well . . .' she tried, but failed, to sound matter-of-fact. 'See you in twenty minutes.'

Nine

Detective Inspector Brian Mackie had found that getting out of a football ground just after kick-off can be more difficult than gaining entry. Having been forced earlier to park his car a mile from Tynecastle Stadium, he found himself the last to join the team in the Special Branch suite. As he arrived, apologetically, the clock on the wall was just approaching 4:00 pm.

Nevertheless, Skinner greeted him with a smile. 'Hello, Brian. We were beginning to think you'd hung on there for the pies and the Bovril. Hearts were 3 – 1 up at half-time, in case you hadn't heard.'

'I always had faith in them, boss.'

'God knows why. OK, grab a seat and let's get on with it.'

Skinner walked over to a pinboard fixed to the wall. 'Most of you will know each other, I think. But, Maggie, Mario, have you met Barry Macgregor here?' The two sergeants nodded towards the detective constable who, at twenty-four, was the youngest of the group by several years. Maggie Rose gave him a friendly smile.

'Mind you, even if you hadn't met him, you'd have marked him out, nae bother, as Crime Squad just by the hairdo.' Macgregor's mousy-blond hair was shoulder-length. It was pulled back into a pony-tail, and some of it was braided and ringed with white beads. The young man grinned, shaking his head vigorously from side to side to make the beads rattle.

'All of you know Dr Sarah Grace, from various crime scenes and elsewhere. Be in no doubt that, although she's my wife, Sarah's here now as Dr Grace, police surgeon, criminal psychologist and fully fledged member of the team. If she slips up, she'll get bollocked just like any of the rest of you. For me,' he said with a sudden broad grin, 'the downside is that if I slip up myself, she'll let me know – in her own special way.'

Then the smile left Skinner's face. 'That's the last laugh you'll get from me for a while. We've been brought together here – and it's a reunion for all of us but you, Barry – by a very nasty incident which took place this morning. For those of you who've only heard the news reports, I'll tell you now what we're dealing with – as far as we know. An explosion took place in a hospitality marquee on top of Waverley Market at around midday today. It could be that it was meant to go off at 12:00 noon exactly. There was one fatality, an unfortunate lad named Danny Baker, who was too close to the seat of the blast to have stood a chance. His next-of-kin have been told. Apart from the boy Baker, there were no serious casualties, although around twenty people wound up in the Royal with shock or minor injuries. I've just told the Press Office to issue a statement that we are investigating the possibility that the explosion was caused by a faulty gas bottle.'

He paused for a moment. 'This may shock you good people, but that is an out-and-out lie. "Gammy" Legge, the bomb expert, has just confirmed that it was caused by approximately one pound of Semtex. He believes that the explosive was hidden in a metal tool-box, on account of some bits of scorched shrapnel dug out of the poor lad Baker and three other casualties. That fact makes it very clear that we must take very seriously the contents of this letter which was delivered to the Secretary of State at St Andrews House shortly after the explosion.'

He went from person to person, handing each a photocopied sheet. 'Read it, note the details, then each of you make sure you shred your copy before you leave this room. No copies other than mine must be taken out of this building. The original is currently at the forensics lab. Although the lads there will take until this time tomorrow to prove it, I am quite certain that it, and the envelope in which it was delivered, will yield no fingerprints other than those of a couple of security guards, the Secretary of State, DCI Martin and me. They will also tell us that it was originated on a word-processor using a common software package – WordPerfect or some such – and printed on a laser or bubble-jet job with no distinguishing features. In other words, the sort of kit that thousands of punters buy across the counter at Dixons every year.

'However, I could be wrong. You never know, the scientists might find a set of dabs that'll let us wrap this business up by tomorrow night. If that happens, I will personally treat you all to a fine steak dinner – but don't set your taste buds going in anticipation! Mr Martin has made sure that neither the existence nor the content of that letter will be mentioned in the press, radio or television, for the meantime at least. That will piss off our friends no end, but I don't expect any further action from them within the next twenty-four hours.'

Mackie raised a hand. 'You said "our friends", sir. Couldn't it be just one bloke? Couldn't this letter be a con?'

'It could be – but it isn't. First, it'd be a very resourceful individual who could lay hands on a pound of Semtex unaided. Second, at least one person, and maybe two, had the Secretary of State's residence under observation after that letter was delivered, reporting on arrivals and departures to someone on the other end of a mobile telephone. This is clearly a terrorist group and, to my mind, a very determined one.'

Martin, at the back of the group, opened his mouth as if to speak, then closed it tight as Skinner froze him with a warning look. Only Sarah noticed this silent exchange.

Skinner continued with barely a pause. 'Because of that, I want every one of you – except Dr Grace, of course – to be armed at all times during this investigation. You'll have SB arms and ammo, issued under Mr Martin's authority. You won't need to hand them in at the end of each shift. Each of you draw them from Brian Mackie at the end of this briefing.'

Martin had already taken his own gun, under Skinner's authorising signature. He carried it slung in a shoulder-holster inside his baggy leather jacket. Skinner had not drawn a weapon, for reasons which he had kept to himself.

'I hardly need to say that this is only a precautionary measure. I don't want any Cowboys and Indians out on our streets. But in the unlikely event, and all that, I want you able to respond in any way you need to. Whether they meant it this time or not, these characters have shown that they're prepared to kill. That means you have to be ready to drop them, if it comes to it. Anyone got a problem with that?'

He glanced in the direction of Barry Macgregor. The young man understood the reason. Unsmiling this time, he shook his head so slightly that his beads made not a sound.

'OK. We may not expect further immediate action, but we have things to do now. We've had a direct threat to the whole Festival, and we have to privately warn all the personnel involved. There's no way that we can cover all the venues. Mr Martin's been pulling some figures together. They should give you an idea of the scale of our task. Andy?'

The detective chief inspector, powerfully built and blond haired, took Skinner's place at the front of the room. His green eyes were made even more vivid by his tinted contact lenses as he fixed a piercing gaze on each member of the team in turn.

'Those of you who ain't culture vultures – and I have to admit I'm not myself – will probably be surprised by just how big this Festival is. I should really say "Festivals", because this year there are six different ones all running at the same time. The Festival proper – that's the Official job, the one the City backs – it's relatively small. Over the next three weeks, starting tonight, it will put on about one hundred and fifty events, concerts, opera, poof's football – sorry, ballet – and plays, in more than a dozen different venues. On the other hand, the Festival Fringe, despite its name, is the biggest event of the lot. This year it'll put on several thousand individual performances of all shapes and sizes, in over a hundred venues. They range from church halls to circus tents, and they're all over Edinburgh. Two of them are even staged out of town, in Musselburgh.

'Then we've got the Film Festival. Very prestigious. Not Cannes, or anything like it, but it still attracts some high-quality film premieres, and some big names. That what's-her-name, the one with the big voice-box – *you* know who I mean, Neil – she's due in for it next week, and she'll have to be looked after. Put your hand down, Macgregor, Sergeant Rose will draw that job. The Film Festival takes place mostly in the Filmhouse, and in that other cinema up Tollcross. This year there are about a hundred screenings, and five will involve personal appearances by directors and stars. The best thing about the Film Festival is that it only lasts for a couple of weeks, not the full three.

'The Jazz Festival has an even shorter run: nine days, to be exact. It's been scaled down a bit over the last couple of years, but it still puts on eighty shows – or is that "gigs"? – in nine halls. The Jazz Festival, so a friend tells me, tends to attract fewer tourists than the rest. It's for real aficionados, and it's the big week of the year for all the local jazzers. There is also a strong correlation between the Jazz Festival and the consumption of strong ales and lagers, which won't make our security job any easier.

'The Book Festival is different entirely. It only happens every other year, and it's an exhibition as much as anything. This year, they've stuck it in the new Conference Centre in Lothian Road. That makes it easy for us, 'cause there's all sorts of security built in there.

'As well as all that lot, we also have a Television Festival. That only lasts for a few days, and it's more of a talking shop really, but it still pulls in some very high rollers. Scottish Television puts a lot of money and effort into it, and all the big UK names – from the BBC, the Commercial network and now from satellite – turn up. There's an international contingent, too. Guess who's coming this year, boss? Your mate Al Neidermeyer of Television News International.'

The rest of the team looked puzzled. Skinner laughed.

'If we should happen to meet, Andy, I'm sure the pleasure'll be all his!'

Martin grinned and continued. 'When I'd tallied that lot up, I thought that all we needed to make up the set was an international gathering of arms dealers. Then I realised that, in a sense, we have. Because on top of it all, although it isn't part of any Festival, there's the biggest event of them all, the Military Tattoo. Three weeks of night-time performances on the Castle Esplanade, six thousand seats for every performance, and every one of them sold in advance.

'Taking it all together, the Festival involves thousands of live performances at a couple of hundred different venues. No one knows for sure how many people will be taking part, but it'll be in the tens of thousands for sure. As for spectators, working it out on a bums-on-seats basis, it's reckoned to be around a million.'

Barry Macgregor let out a soft whistle.

'Remember,' Martin went on, 'these are the performance events. I haven't mentioned the various sorts of art exhibition that'll be running. There are about a dozen regular galleries in Edinburgh, and quite a few other places are pressed into service. So that's what's happening in our city over the next three weeks. And we've just had a threat to it of a lethal nature.

'The idea of calling it all off is a non-starter. The Government can't be seen to give in to terrorism, and neither, for that matter can the police service. And, anyway, it's too late. So our job is to protect it, the whole event, as best we can, and the best way to do that is to catch the people behind the threat. On that front, as the boss has said, there are no leads so far. On the security side, I have only two bits of good news. The first is that we can forget the exhibitions, during the day at least, and also the Book Festival. All of those have high-calibre private guards as a condition of their insurance cover. There's a very big exhibition in the National Gallery – Rembrandt's greatest hits or something. We'll give that special attention at night. The second bonus is that we can forget the Tattoo. It's a military event, and the military will look after it. But the rest is up to us. Boss?'

'Thanks, Andy.' Skinner took the floor again. 'Right. First, I'll state the obvious: that which you're all thinking. We don't have anything like enough polismen and women to give proper protection to all those venues. And, in any event, the game plan is to keep this whole business from becoming public knowledge for the moment at least. But, within these four secure walls, I'll tell you frankly that I don't think we've a snowball's chance of doing that for too long. If this lot are as determined and resourceful as I think they are, they'll soon find a way to force us to go public on their threatening letter. In the meantime heavy police presence at *all* the Festival events, even if it were possible, would be counter productive, as it could only alarm and annoy the public.

'No, what we must do is plan on the assumption that any future incidents will involve high-profile targets. Therefore, we're going to concentrate on the biggest venues. The news blackout on that letter will buy us maybe a day or two, so let's put that time to good use. In an hour from now, Mr Martin and I are meeting all of the Festival directors, save one, in the George Hotel. We're going to tell them what's happening and what we're doing about it. Then we're going to swear them to secrecy for as long as we say so. I am operating – and, therefore, so are you lot on my team – with the benefit of certain extra powers afforded me by the Secretary of State. If anybody plays silly buggers with us, we can, as a very last resort, bang them inside. We've only had one problem so far – with the guy Neidermeyer from TNI, that Mr Martin just mentioned. All our own people are toeing the line, and so will the Festival directors. The reason I'm going to brief them is because you'll need their co-operation. I want you lot, starting this evening, to recce all the major venues, and then check in here tomorrow morning with reports on how each one can be protected effectively with the minimum visible strength. I'm not using uniforms, if I can help it. If this crowd do start taking pot shots at Festival events, then our boys and girls would be sitting targets in their blue suits and funny hats.

'Brian, I want you to give everyone here a list of the venues.

Cover all the Official Festival venues: that's the Usher Hall, Lyceum, King's, Empire and Playhouse, at least. Cover Filmhouse, and the telly Festival venue, too. Cover all multiple centres, where they've got more than one theatre; that's places like the Assembly Rooms and the Pleasance. Oh, and cover the Traverse. Remember, that's part of Saltire Court, and our friends may decide that a building named after our Scottish national flag would make a prime target. I want your reports to include details of all entrances and exits at each place. By that I mean public, performers' and vehicle entrances. Produce for each hall and theatre a security plan. If you think we need to shut a few entrances and slow the normal flow in and out, don't be afraid to make that recommendation. As long as we can empty a place in a hurry, if we need to, it doesn't matter to me how long it takes to fill it. Bear in mind too that, by Tuesday at the latest, all performers and stagehands will have passes, and will need to show them on their way into the building.'

Sarah spoke for the first time. Skinner sensed her striving to appear as formal with him as she could, to stake out no special position within the team. 'Won't that involve thousands of people? And will the photo-booth machines be able to cope?'

He nodded. 'Sure, we'll have to issue thousands of passes. But I'm going to second the Scottish Office Information staff to do the processing. And the passes won't be photographic. They'll be credit-card style with a signature on the back. We'll make every applicant sign their pass in the presence of the issuing officer, and then we'll make them sign in and out of their venue every day. But come on, doctor, tell me. What's the real reason for the passes?'

Sarah felt as if everyone in the room was watching her. A frown-line appeared suddenly above her nose, emphasising her concentration on his question. Then, just as suddenly, her face lit up.

'It's all about the application forms. You want every performer or stagehand to fill in an application form.'

Skinner was pleased at her perception, but kept it to himself. 'Right, They fill in the application form. Then Mr Plod feeds the details into his great big computer, and if his great big computer is any bloody good at all, out pop all the nasty secrets. Unless we turn up a very nasty secret indeed, something like a convicted paedophile giving a one-man show for kids in the back of a Transit, we do nothing precipitate, but we keep a very close watch on all the odd-bods, to see where we get led.'

Skinner switched his gaze to Macgregor. 'What else do we do, Barry?'

The young detective beamed with pleasure. 'Hotels, sir. Everyone checking into a hotel is asked to fill up a registration form. We just expand them a bit, if necessary. Then, every day, we collect copies of all the completed forms and stick them through the computer as well.'

'That's the game, son. And what do we get out of all that? Probably sweet FA, but we do it anyway. And, just like with all the other routine precautions we're taking, we hope that God's luck's on our side.'

He paused to look around the room, fixing his eyes on each member of the team in turn. When he spoke again, it was in a gentler tone.

'OK, my good people. Go out there and do your very best – and, as usual, that'll be good enough for me. But, as you do it, keep this thought in your minds. I saw that poor boy today. I know in my heart that this one will get even nastier than today before it gets better. We've got other people's lives in our hands here. Let's not let them slip. While you're at it, look out for yourselves, too. I love you all, as friends as well as colleagues, and I don't want any mishaps. Go to it. This is a no-leave job, so I'll see you all tomorrow morning.'

Ten

'Andy,' said Skinner, and nodded for Martin to follow as he headed for the door.

They left the room, Sarah following on their heels and waving goodbye to the rest of the team as she closed the door behind her.

Bob paused in the corridor and turned towards her. 'Sorry, love, Andy and I have a few things to do. No need for you to hang around here any longer. What you could do for me when you get home, though, is look at your copy of their letter – which I see you did not shred before you left the room.'

'Uh-oh, my first blooper.' Sarah turned a shade of pink.

'And hopefully, your last. Still, let's put it to advantage. Read it carefully, study the language, the style, anything in particular that strikes you, and see if you can come up with some sort of a psychological profile of the author.'

'Yes, boss!'

'And, once you've done that, burn it!'

She nodded. 'Yes, sir, will do. See you later. We will get to Alex's play, won't we?'

'No problem. I'll rest easier if I've taken a bloody good look at that venue myself, anyway. I'll be home for 7:30, latest. We can eat after the show, so book us a table somewhere, eh?'

He started off towards Martin, who stood waiting at the end

of the corridor, but she held him back with a gentle tug at his sleeve.

'Bob. In there, earlier on, I had the impression that Andy was going to say something important, but you shut him up. Was it something that you didn't want the whole team to hear – or just me?'

He looked at her wide eyed. 'Don't know what you're on about, love. When did I ever chop Andy off in public – and before you lower ranks, too?'

The unmasked doubt in her expression countered the wide-eyed innocence in his. 'Skinner, you are being evasive. We *will* discuss this later.' Her tone left no room for doubt.

'Nothing to discuss. But I'll see you.' He strode off to join Martin.

As soon as they were out of sight, the big ACC cuffed the Head of Special Branch lightly around the ear. 'Dropped me in it there, mate, haven't you. Don't tell me you weren't on the point of chipping into my briefing with a homily about gun-toting motorcycle messengers in Charlotte Square. Christ, if I hadn't been looking at you at the time! There are things you need to break to the wife in private – if you choose to break them at all. Now I've got no choice!'

Martin wore a guilty look that was rarely seen. 'Sorry, boss. I just didn't think.'

Skinner considered his point made. 'It's OK, son. I chose to bring Sarah into the team, so it's half my fault for putting you in the situation, anyway. There's another side to it, though, and a good reason not to tell the team about my wee bit of excitation. These Apache Couriers are all over town. I'd hate to think of what might happen if next week one of them even looked sideways at one of our team while reaching into his jacket. Bang, bang. Dead courier. "Oh, you were only getting a hankie out were you. Sorry about that. Just a wee mistake." No, thank you very much! Not even Proud Jimmy would see the funny side of that one.'

They had reached Skinner's office in the Command Suite. 'Come on in, Andy, and I'll let you halfway in on a state secret. I told you I've already accessed available files on the MI5 computer from my other office, and come up blank?'

Martin nodded.

'Well, not all the stuff's on computer. With all these hackers and folk like that, and viruses and so on, the plain fact is that information technology doesn't have the security you need at the very top level – or at the bottom level, depending on how you see these things. There are files still kept on paper, in London, behind a very thick door with a very long combination and a very loud alarm. I'm going to use my secure phone to brief the MI5 analysts to look at them all, and prepare me a list of people to be considered. It probably won't be a long list, but I'll bet they'll have some entries for us. This will all be stuff I probably haven't seen myself. I'll have picked up bits of it now and then, just wee scraps of information, but the total picture is gathered together by section teams in Head Office.'

He sat down in a chair at the side of his desk and pulled his scrambled telephone to him.

'While I do this, Andy, could you access your SB stuff through my terminal, and run another list for me. Journalists – anyone you've got on file, either here or in branches in the rest of the country. Look at their special interests and their known associates. I fancy we'll want to talk to one or two of them, too, when the moment comes.'

'That not a bit of a risk, leaning on journalists?' asked Martin.

'Who said anything about leaning on them? We'll just say

we're consulting them; it'll make them feel important. The hack is not yet born who is so hairy backed and anti-establishment that he doesn't want the polis owing him a favour. You do that, while I make this call. Then we'll get off to the George to scare the shit out of the Festival directors.'

Eleven

The George is not the most imposing of Edinburgh's first-division hotels, but it is one of the best. It is situated on the street from which it takes its name, and its narrow entrance affords clients a greater degree of privacy than its massive rivals at either end of Princes Street. It is possible to slip virtually unobserved into the George, while entry through the wide doors of the Caledonian or the Balmoral, past their liveried and effusive keepers, is always something of a performance.

Skinner and Martin arrived at the hotel in the BMW just after 5:00 pm, finding a parking place with unusual ease, as the Saturday shopping crush had eased off. Martin, who enjoyed special relationships with every hotel manager in the city centre, had asked for a private room for their meeting. He carried a briefcase as they walked into the hotel. Six of the seven Festival directors were waiting for them. Only Trevor Golley of the Book Festival had been unavailable. None of the six had been told in advance that the others would be present. As the two policemen entered the room, the low buzz of conversation stopped, and half a dozen faces turned towards them.

Skinner broke the ice. 'Good afternoon, ladies and gentlemen. I must thank you for coming along here at such short notice, and in response to such a mysterious invitation.

We appreciate how busy you must be just now, so we won't keep you long.'

Three large Thermos jugs lay on three occasional tables in the centre of the room.

'Everyone all right for coffee, before we begin?' An assortment of grunts and nods came from around the room. 'Right, if you'll each find a seat, I'll explain what all this is about.'

The long room had no windows. It was furnished with three deep and comfortable two-seater sofas and two armchairs. The policemen each took a chair, leaving the sofas for their guests. As the directors sat down, Skinner saw that they seemed to sort themselves unconsciously into natural pairings.

Harriet Nelson, in her second year as director for the 'Official' Festival, sat on the left-hand sofa, alongside Colonel Archie McPhee, organiser of the Military Tattoo. Even seated, Harriet Nelson was an imposing woman: tall, heavy featured and with flaming red hair. She had won her spurs in the arts in her late twenties, as one of the very few leading female orchestral conductors, and had wielded her baton in concert halls around the world for almost two decades. Her appointment as director of the Edinburgh International Festival had been announced by the governing committee as a major coup, which indeed it was.

Colonel McPhee, the Military Tattoo director, was in his own way as imposing as his neighbour on the sofa. Before his retirement from active service, five years earlier, he had been a battalion commander in the Parachute Regiment, and had seen bloody combat in the Falklands. He was in his early fifties, with close-cropped, receding hair, a sharp nose and piercing, perceptive eyes. He was dressed in light slacks and a short-sleeved green shirt, an outfit which emphasised an impression of total physical fitness.

The director of the Film Festival, Julia Shahor, sat directly facing Skinner and Martin, next to the one person of the six whom Skinner had not met before, whom he knew therefore to be Ray Starkey, head of the television event. Julia Shahor's shock of very black hair exploded in a natural Afro, framing a small, pale but unforgettably attractive face. She wore a voluminous white robe which covered her from neck to ankles. She was a small woman, the youngest of the six directors by at least seven or eight years, Skinner guessed. She had come to the Film Festival ten months earlier, on a one-year contract, and like Harriet Nelson she had been regarded as a catch for Edinburgh. She was still in her twenties, but already she had built a brilliant career as a screenwriter. It was said that her ambition was to emulate one of her predecessors by using the Festival as the springboard for a career as a movie director in America.

Ray Starkey wore large, yellow-framed spectacles, with lenses which made his eyes seem huge. He was very fat, and dressed incongruously in a pale blue Armani suit, with a grey shirt, yellow braces, and a tie which seemed to have been hand painted, badly, that same afternoon. Skinner knew that Starkey had come to run the television event after having been a casualty of the 1991 commercial television licence auctions. He had been programme controller with one of the losing franchise-holders and had waited in vain for a year for one of the winners to offer him a contract, before being invited to take up the Festival post.

Finally, seated together on the sofa to the right of the two policemen, were David Leroy, the director of the Fringe, and Jay Hands, his counterpart at the Jazz Festival.

The Edinburgh Festival Fringe enjoys a reputation as one of the great showcases for new-wave theatre and new performing talent. Many artists now world-famous had made their first impressions upon public consciousness at Edinburgh Fringe productions. David Leroy's appearance was completely at odds with the avant-garde style of his Festival. While many of his performers found kaftans and sandals *de rigueur*, the Fringe director could have been taken for a successful big-firm chartered accountant. Even on an August Saturday he wore a blue Austin Reed suit, black Loake shoes, a white shirt with a thin blue stripe, and an Edinburgh Academy Old Boys' tie.

However, Jay Hands, the longest-serving of all the directors, was much more in tune with the image of the grizzled jazzman. Even seated, he seemed round shouldered. He was in his late fifties, tall and lean, with a sallow complexion and lank grey hair which looked two months overdue for a trim. He had the tired eyes of a man who played with a jazz band several nights a week, then stayed on after the show.

The six directors now sat in waiting, some looking curious, some – Nelson and Hands in particular – showing an edge of annoyance. Skinner smiled his warmest smile. 'For those of you who haven't met us, I'm Bob Skinner, Assistant Chief Constable and head of CID in Edinburgh. It's a matter of public knowledge that I also act as security adviser to the Secretary of State. My colleague here is Detective Chief Inspector Andrew Martin, head of Special Branch in Edinburgh. Some of you may have guessed why we've asked you to meet us.'

Only two reacted in any way. Archie McPhee smiled tightly and nodded. Jay Hands looked puzzled.

'For those of you who don't already know, we have had what we describe in police-speak as "a serious incident", specifically an explosion. It happened at midday today at a Festival hospitality venue in Princes Street. In fact, we now know that it was a bomb attack on the Festival itself.'

He paused. Opposite him, Julia Shahor's eyes seemed to grow impossibly wide.

'Jesus Christ!' whispered Jay Hands.

Skinner went on. 'Shortly after the bang, we received this. Would you all read it, please.'

He handed his copy of the letter to Harriet Nelson. She scanned it slowly, then, white faced, handed it to Archie McPhee. By the time Jay Hands had finished studying the letter, and handed it back to Skinner, all six directors looked considerably shaken.

'Before any of you ask me, I'll tell you that we are taking this letter at face value. We believe that the people behind this atrocity are serious. We don't know the first thing about them yet, but we do know that anyone who can lay hands on a pound or two of Semtex is unlikely to be a one-hit wonder. Therefore, ladies and gentlemen, we have to believe that the Festival events for which you are responsible are now all under threat. More than that, while I don't want to alarm you unnecessarily, we have to assume, for safety's sake, that each of you could be a target.'

He studied each face in turn. The expressions ranged from the incredulity of Ray Starkey to the serenity of Julia Shahor. As Skinner had expected, the first to speak was Archie McPhee.

The colonel's eyes seemed to gleam with memories of conflict as he asked softly: 'What would you like us to do about it, Bob?'

'I'd like all six of you to co-operate with us, but, Archie, I'd like you to do a wee bit more than that. The Tattoo isn't run by the army, but it is military in nature, and it does take place at what is in fact an army base – the Castle. I'd like you yourself to take on responsibility for extra security. Pull in soldiers from Craigiehall if you have to. You won't have any difficulty getting them. I can promise you that. At the moment I'm considering whether I need help from other quarters for the wider task. Is that okay with you?'

'Certainly!' said McPhee emphatically.

'Thanks. Now, everyone else, the first thing to say is that we do not believe that we should, nor do we even believe that we could call off any or all of your Festivals in response to this threat. And that isn't just a police view. It's a decision of the Secretary of State. So Mr Martin and I have two tasks. First, we have to take steps to protect all the Festival events, organisers, performers, and audiences, as best we can. Then, having done that, we must make it all unnecessary by catching these terrorists and putting them away. I have already set up a team to tackle both those jobs.'

He described the instructions which he had issued earlier to his own team.

'When my officers make their security checks, they'll do so discreetly. I don't want to cause any more public concern than is necessary. At the moment, that lettter's between you, us, and some very co-operative newspaper editors. We've secured a news blackout on it, otherwise you'd have heard about it before now. I would ask you to assist my people in every way, as they assess each of our priority venues. If they need specific help or information, please let them have it without question. If any curious managers ask you what that was all about, the party line is that it is routine procedure. Please stick to that.'

Skinner look around and smiled. 'OK so far? Good. That's what we're doing about the buildings. Now for the people – and this is where you're asked to give us the greatest help.

As part of the security operation we need to ensure that each participant can be identified, and also that we know when they're on site. That means a pass system for everyone who is performing at every Festival event, front or back stage, primadonna or call-boy.'

There was a collective cry of protest from five of the six directors. Only Archie McPhee stayed relaxed, sprawled comfortably back on his sofa. The Military Tattoo had operated its own pass system since its inception.

'You can't mean *everyone*!' said Harriet Nelson.

'That's impossible!' said David Leroy.

'I do, Ms Nelson – and it isn't, Mr Leroy.' He looked across at Martin. 'Andy, explain how we'll go about it.'

Martin waited until he was sure that he had the full attention of every one of the six. He flashed a wide smile at Julia Shahor, who responded with a small one of her own.

'As Mr Skinner has said, it's important that we are able to check people's identity and that we know precisely when they're in their venues. God forbid, but we could have another incident like today's, or an arson attack, or even just a warning that we take seriously enough to act upon – and if this threat becomes public knowledge we could have every drunk and nutter under the sun calling in hoaxes. If anything like that were to happen, we'd have to clear the place in question totally, and account for everyone supposedly there. Ticket stubs would tell us how many people are in the audience, but we need a pass system for the performers. Agreed?'

His last word was a statement rather than a question. Martin sat forward on his chair, accidentally swinging his holstered pistol into full sight. His vivid green eyes were intense as they scanned the three sofas. Five heads nodded. Even Colonel McPhee sat up straight.

'Good. Now let me tell you how we'll do it. These passes needn't be photographic. They'll be credit-card style, and they'll be signed on the back by the holder, in the presence of the issuing officer, when they're allocated. We'll use experienced Scottish Office personnel to process the applications and issue passes on the spot. They'll be based in your various offices. So what we'd like you to do, as soon as you all get back to your offices, is to organise a circular to every performing company that's here so far. It should advise them that the fire safety officer has demanded that, in the light of new regulations, all performers and crew will have to carry passes and show them whenever they enter their venues. Here's a draft for you to work on.'

He delved into his briefcase, produced a handful of copy letters, and handed them round.

'This asks everyone involved to report to whichever Festival Office is appropriate, between four and seven o'clock tomorrow evening, and to take with them some form of personal identification.'

Jay Hands broke in. 'What if they don't possess any?'

'We won't actually turn anyone down on those grounds, but I think you'll find that nowadays everybody carries something with their signature on it. We'll put experienced people into your offices to do the job. It'll be painless, I promise you – no worse than the queue at the building society on the last Friday of the month.'

He grinned at the six directors. Julia Shahor smiled back; the rest reacted with an assortment of grunts and snorts.

'Of course, you and all of your staff will require passes, too. Even you, Colonel McPhee, in case you need to go backstage at any *other* event.'

The colonel acknowledged with the faintest nod of his head.

Harriet Nelson voiced again her earlier concern. 'No exceptions at all?'

Martin shook his head. 'Ms Nelson, if the Royal Ballet had the ghosts of Fonteyn and Nureyev appearing in *Swan Lake*, I'd want them to have passes. There are no exemptions when it comes to security. Even the Prime Minister has to carry a pass for the House of Commons.' He looked around the room once more. 'Your circulars should make it clear that, as from Monday, anyone without a pass just doesn't get in. So that this daily signing-in routine isn't a burden with the larger companies, we'll put our own plain-clothes people in to look after it. The smaller groups should be able to handle that end themselves.'

Martin picked up his briefcase again, and lifted the lid. 'As Mr Skinner said earlier, we have to consider every foreseeable threat, however remote it might seem. For example, these terrorists may decide that it's easier to target individuals than venues. You're all prominent people, and we have to keep you safe. If any of you want round-the-clock police protection, just ask and you'll have it. In my view, that's not necessary, but just say the word. Anyone?'

The room hung with tension, but no one spoke.

'OK, but my offer stays open. For what it's worth, I think a constant police presence would be a greater irritant for you than the risk justifies. But there are some simple precautions which you should take all the same.'

He reached into his case and produced two bundles of small volumes, one bound in blue, the other in russet brown. He handed a copy of both to each of the directors.

'These two wee books contain advice on security procedures. The blue one relates to office security, tells you how to look out for suspect parcels in the mail – stuff like that.

The brown one deals with personal security, tells you the bad habits to cut out – like going to work every day at the same time, by the same route. It tells you how to search your car, and what to do if you think you're being watched. That last bit's quite important. If any of you do believe that you're being followed, don't just try to scare the suspect off by shouting "Murder! Polis!" Only do that if you feel you're in imminent danger. What you should do is stay in a crowd, if you can, and try to find some unobtrusive way to let us know about your situation. Do you all have mobile telephones? Yes? Well you'll find a telephone number written in the brown book. Short-code that into your phones. In a real emergency, all you'll need to do is punch in that one number and you'll be straight through to my office. Remember, we don't just want to frighten these people off. We want to catch them, and keep them – for a hell of a long time.'

He closed his briefcase, snapped the locks shut, and spun the combination wheels. 'That's all I have to say. Sir?'

Skinner took his cue. 'So that's the situation, ladies and gentlemen. I'm sorry you've been handed this extra worry, but, hate it as we may, we're all involved in this crisis. If anybody has any questions, we'll deal with them now. And if anybody wants to ask us, or tell us, anything privately, we'll deal with it here too.'

Julia Shahor's slim hand crept up tentatively, like a child at school. 'Could I have a word with Mr Martin in private?'

'Sure. Would the two of you like to step out into the corridor?'

The policeman held open the door for the Film Festival director, then closed it behind them. Outside she turned to face him, her cheeks slightly flushed.

'What can I do for you, Miss Shahor?'

'Julia, please.'

'OK. What can I do for you, Julia?' He looked into her eyes and had to stop himself from adding, '*. . . and if I can, I will.*' She really had very attractive dark brown eyes. And, even under the Jesus dress, all the rest looked in fair working order, too.

'Well, Mr Martin . . .'

'Andy, please.'

'Well, Andy, I heard what you said in there about no exceptions. But, you see, we've got this mega star coming. You know—'

'Yeah, sure, what's-her-name.'

'That's right, her. Well, I'm just afraid that if we ask her to apply for a pass, that . . . well, you know her reputation – that she'll just tell us to take a flying you-know-what. That's what she's said to be like.'

Martin almost laughed out loud, but restricted himself to what he hoped was a reassuring smile. He gazed deep into the brown eyes. 'I hear you, Julia, but I just can't make any exceptions. I'll tell you what I can do, though. Since she's so high-profile, I can bend the rules a bit. How would it be if you and I went to her hotel, and processed her there ourselves? And you have a back entrance, she can sign in there on the night.'

'Andy, that'd be great. The only thing is, whenever she makes an appearance like this, she wants to pose out front. She'll never agree to sign in at the back door.'

'She will if the alternative could be a high-velocity round between the eyes. Tell you what, why don't I come up and check out the venue myself?'

'Would you really? That'd be great. Can you come up tonight, maybe? We're screening the European premiere of the new Costner movie as our launch event. You could look things over, then stay on for the film – as my guest, or course.'

'I'd like that. And I'll even leave this thing behind in the office.' He tapped the gun under his left arm.

She laughed. 'Terrific. Just ask for me at the door. Better come about 7:30. The film starts at 8:15.'

She waved over her shoulder as she walked away. Martin stood gazing after her, until the door opened and the other five Festival directors emerged, followed by Skinner.

Martin was still smiling as he and his chief went back into the room together. He poured them both coffee from one of the Thermos jugs.

'What's the grin for?' said Skinner, accepting a cup. 'Christ, you haven't bloody scored with Crystal Tipps there, have you, Andy? See you, boy, you'd shag Desert Orchid if you could catch it. If I ever find out that you talk in your sleep, I'll have to think again about you as head of Special Branch.'

Martin's grin was suddenly a little forced. 'You can say that, Bob, but since you put me in this job, I haven't been able to keep a girlfriend for more than two months at a stretch. They say it's because they never know where I am.'

Skinner laughed out loud. 'Bollocks! It's because they *do* know where you are. You're usually with some other female! Come on, let's get moving. I've got to get ready for Alex's show. And you've got to fix up these Scottish Office people for tomorrow, then get home and take your ginseng and Vitamin E. You wouldn't want to go limp on wee Julia.'

Twelve

Dropped off by Skinner at Fettes Avenue, Martin entered the building by the back door and trotted up the stairs from the basement level to his office.

He was pleased to see that, save for Barry Macgregor, who was manning the telephones, the Special Branch suite was empty. It was 6:20 pm, and it was Saturday, but he knew this meant, not that everyone had finished for the night, but that the inspection of the chosen venues was already well under way. Sitting down behind his desk, he read the ex-directory telephone number which Skinner had written down for him on the back of a business card, then picked up his secure telephone and punched it in.

A clipped, slightly cautious voice answered. 'Hello, Michael Licorish.'

Andy Martin had met the Head of the Scottish Office Information Directorate on a few occasions, and had seen him in action in one or two high-pressure situations. Licorish had impressed Martin each time as an unflappable, no-nonsense performer, who could keep his media people under control, out of respect as well as his authority, and at times when others would be running for the nearest exit. He had been deputy director in those days, waiting patiently for his crusty old military predecessor to complete his last few months.

'Michael, hi. Andy Martin here. Special Branch. Remember me?'

The responding voice lost its cautious edge. 'Hah. I should forget? What can I do for you, Andy?'

'I take it that you'll have heard by now, the real story of our so-called gas explosion in Princes Street today.'

'Mm. I know all about it. Secretary of State briefed me this afternoon. Told me about the warning letter, too. And about Bob Skinner's anti-terrorist unit. Seems a strong reaction for this S of S, between you and me.'

'Needed though, as it's turned out.' Martin described Skinner's encounter with the motorcyclist.

'Jesus, Andy. S of S didn't tell me that.'

'He doesn't know. It happened after Bob had left him. Now you appreciate how serious this is, I hope you won't quibble over what I'm going to ask you for.'

Martin explained the plan for a pass system, and all of the reasons for it.

'We're going to have to process a hell of a lot of people very quickly, so the sooner we can get started, the happier I'll be. My outfit is having the registration forms printed overnight, and the passes too. What I'd like you to do is to provide us with suitable staff to handle the accreditation at the Festival office venues, from tomorrow evening onwards. I could put police personnel in to do it, but your people are properly experienced in this sort of thing. They'll handle it faster, and the performers won't get prickly the way some people do when they have to deal with us.

'What d'you say?'

'I say *yes*, if you'll pick up any overtime tab.'

'Done.'

'Right. How many will you need?'

'Tomorrow, six good people. Two each at the Festival and Fringe offices, and one at each of the Jazz, and Film festivals. The television thing doesn't start for another week. After that, their job will be continuous at least up to the third weekend, with completely new companies and solo performers coming in all the time. But we'll draw up a rota of registration times at all the offices. That'll let you run it with two people at the most – maybe only one.'

'That sounds fair. I'll line my people up. I'll use my tour escorts; they're smooth talkers. And my publicity section people; they do this sort of thing on royal visits. Where will you want them, and when?'

'Ask them all to report to Fettes at 2:30 tomorrow, and to ask for DI Brian Mackie. We'll brief them then, and allocate them around the offices.'

'You've got it.' There was a pause. 'Here, does this mean that we get to meet that glamour girl, her with the . . . If it does, I might come along myself!'

'Nice one, Michael, but I've put myself down for that painful task.'

'That sounds like corruption to me, Andy! See you.' The line clicked dead.

Martin grinned. Suddenly he thought again of Julia Shahor, her black hair, her pale, heart-stopping face and her dark brown eyes. He snorted. 'Crystal Tipps, indeed! Shag Desert Orchid, indeed! Ginseng and Vitamin E, indeed! Giving away your own secrets, Bob?'

Thirteen

Skinner raised a hand in farewell to Martin, as he dropped him at the Carrington Road entrance to police headquarters.

He pulled the BMW away from the kerb, its steel sunroof fully open. The day was beginning to cool, but the August evening sun still blazed from the west in a cloudless sky. Looking down as he reached for the on-button of the radio/cassette, his eye was caught by the rip in the knee of his denims, and in the same instant his mind swept back to Charlotte Square, replaying the incident with the motorcyclist.

Analysing the incident as he drove the short distance home, several things struck Skinner in succession. The first was the sheer speed of his own reaction to the threat. He had known instinctively that the man was pulling a gun, even before he had seen its barrel. The second was that he had felt no fear. Twice in his life, now, he had been exposed to direct gunfire, and on neither occasion had he been afraid. Was it simply that there had been no time for the luxury of terror, or was the answer somewhere deeper inside him, more complex and more sinister? Was he a man who actually courted and enjoyed danger? Was there even in him a touch of the psychopath?

He cast his mind back through his career, recalling the many criminal psychopaths who had crossed his path over the years. One in particular stood out from the crowd: a merciless killer whose most striking feature – apart from his total lack of concern for his victims, or his own safety – had been his absolute coolness. Catching him had been the toughest job of Skinner's career. Yet, as he thought of his own peril, and of the danger he had faced on another occasion, Skinner recognised something of that killer in the way he himself had reacted to each situation. Cool, unflappable and, if he was totally honest, ready – if it came to it – to kill another human being without a scrap of remorse. That was the reason why, when the firearms had been issued earlier, he had declined to take one himself. For Skinner did know fear, deep in his heart: fear of the easy confidence and skill with which he handled a lethal weapon, and of his readiness to use it.

The final thing to strike him in this self-analysis was that it was now far too late to dream up a good story for Sarah to explain away the rip in his jeans. He would have to handle it as best he could. That thought snapped him back to the present, just as he turned the BMW into the narrow driveway of his home. He pressed a remote signalling device and the door of the double garage swung up. Running the car inside, he parked alongside Sarah's Frontera Sport, then entered the bungalow by the back door, closing the garage doors with his signaller as he did so. That was one of the small, routine security precautions which had become a fact of his life.

The kitchen was empty, neat as usual save for five crumpled Safeway bags lying on one of the work-tops. Skinner checked the fridge and found that it had been re-stocked. He took out an opened carton of orange juice and took a swig, leaning his head back and pouring it into his open mouth, Spanish-style. As he replaced the carton and closed the door, two brown arms wound round his waist and a chin dug itself into the centre of his back. From its position he could tell that Sarah was barefoot. And from the warmth flowing through to him he guessed that nakedness was her overall condition.

'Hi.' Her voice was muffled slightly by his shirt.

As she spoke, he felt her right hand at work. In a few seconds, she had loosened the buckle of his belt and unzipped his denims. At the same time, with her other hand she unfastened, quickly and skilfully, the buttons of his shirt. When she had finished, he turned into her embrace, facing her, shrugging off his shirt in the same movement. She threw her left arm round his neck, pulling his mouth down to hers. As they kissed, her right hand moved lower down, quickly finding and releasing the object of its search. He gripped the top of her thighs and lifted her clear of the floor, feeling both her strength and her softness as she wrapped her legs around him, not really needing her guiding hand as she lowered herself, to draw him deep into her. He found her mouth as she gyrated against him, tasting slight saltiness. Gradually her movement grew faster, her body bucking and heaving, her legs gripping him tighter than he would have believed possible.

She cried out aloud, once, twice, three times, and then suddenly, so did he, as he felt himself erupt inside her – coming and coming until he thought he would never stop. But at last Sarah's movements began to slow, until he settled gently against him, and he became aware for the first time of her weight, on his hands, arms and shoulders.

He whispered in her ear. 'See, if the window cleaner came now . . .'

Bob felt her laughter well up, from inside her. She hugged him, gripping him tight once more with her thighs.

He walked them, still locked together, through to their bedroom and laid her on the bed. He settled on top of her but she rolled him over and sat up, keeping him still hard and inside her, as she reached down to strip off the rest of his clothes. Then, slowly, she began to move again, her eyes misty and her body glowing with a light sheen of sweat. Her fingers ploughed their way into the hair on his chest until he drew her down close to him again and rolled her over, thrusting deeper and hearing her gasp with what he thought for a moment was pain, until it stretched into a long sigh of pleasure. She arched her back and swung her legs up, gripping him yet again, and pushing with her thighs in perfect time with his thrusts. Her head was flung back, her chin upturned, her neck as if offered to the wolf. Strands of her auburn hair clung to her damp face. She began to climax again, throwing back her arms, using only her legs to pull her centre tight to him, and once more they came together, gasping and crying, and finally laughing at the skill and energy of their love-making, and glorying in the sheer pleasure of being one together.

Eventually he rolled away, to lie on his side, propped up on his left elbow. With his right index finger he traced the line of her nose, while smoothing back her damp hair, where it had stuck to her forehead and to the sides of her face.

'Love you, doctor.'

'Yeah. And I you, copper.' She reached up and rubbed his cheek. 'You're on the edge of needing a shave.'

Since their engagement on New Year's Day – and their subsequent April marriage – theirs had become the deepest, closest and most powerfully physical relationship that either had ever known. In their intimacy Sarah had been cautious at first, holding herself back, still with the memory of her earlier, failed engagement in New York. But as a wife, she had developed a sexual frankness and an appetite for congress which often astonished her and always delighted Bob. With his daughter Alex now independent of them, living in her Glasgow flat during university term-time and for most of the summer, they had full freedom to enjoy each other, and eagerly they took advantage of it.

Bob, despite being in his mid-forties, had evolved sexually, too. He often thought of himself in the fifteen years between Myra's death and Sarah's arrival in his life: a quiet, private, thoughtful man, a loner; good qualities for a high-achieving detective but barriers on the road to happiness. For all of those years he had been wounded inwardly, like Sarah, but more severely. His few brief sexual encounters with available women – never at his home, and always when Alex was away with her grandparents or at school camps – had been deeply unsatisfying and had left him grieving afresh for his daughter's dead mother. So when he had first met Sarah, in the line of duty, and had felt immediately drawn to her, it had been in spite of himself, and his nature, that he had followed his instincts. And now he was, he knew, a far better man for it. He had still only a very few close friends, Andy Martin and James Proud top of the list, but he had become more approachable, more ready to laugh with others, and to share his thoughts with them. He perceived, too, that he was now more active in his support of those in trouble, where before he might have offered no more than sympathy. At first he had worried whether the new Skinner might be too soft as a commander, but he had realised quickly that the qualities which he had felt himself developing were strengths rather than weaknesses.

He had now lapsed into a reverie, from which Sarah

recalled him abruptly, by propping herself up on an elbow and tweaking his nose.

'Hey! I'm still here, you know.' She glanced down towards his right leg. 'Going to tell me about that now?'

Bob glanced down to see the red raw scrape on his knee. He looked at Sarah and grinned.

'All right. I'm in Charlotte Square, and I'm watching this motorcyclist outside Alan Ballantyne's place, you know Number 6. I think he looks a bit iffy, so I decide to check him out. I'm on my way over to talk to him when he reaches inside his jacket. That bomb must have got to me more than I thought, because I decide he's going for a gun, and I dive for cover. In fact, what's he got in his hand is nothing but a mobile phone. Did I feel like a prat? Yes I did. Worst of all, big Denis from the *Scotsman* saw it all. Ask him.'

He said it all with a smile, thinking: *That last part was a clever touch. Hope it does the trick.*

Sarah's eyes narrowed as she weighed up the plausibility of his story. 'What did the biker do?'

'He got the fright of his life. Imagine. He hears what he must have thought was a nutter shouting and running at him, then sees him diving about in the street. He revved up his bike and bombed off. What else would you expect?' Bob kept smiling, his fingers mentally crossed, as she looked at him for a few long seconds.

'Well, if that's all. Lie there and I'll clean up that knee.' She swung herself off the bed and walked on tip-toes into their shower-room. A few seconds later she reappeared, leaning on the doorjamb with an uncapped bottle of Dettol and a wad of cottonwool in her hand.

As always, the sudden sight of his wife naked gave Bob a rush of pleasure, even although he had seen her thus only a few seconds before. He smiled as his eyes took in her long legs, her smooth belly with the dark heart of mystery at its base, her high, proud, full breasts.

In her turn she looked at him, stretched out on the bed with the special relaxation that only follows great sex: grey maned but still vibrant with the spirit of youth, long, lean and muscular. He smiled at her again, but she kept her face straight.

'Think it's funny, huh. Spread 'em, boy, and take your medicine.'

He did as he was told, rolling on to his back, his legs forming a V. She knelt alongside him and padded the scrape on his knee with the cotton wool, now well soaked in the antiseptic. She held the bottle of Dettol upright in her left hand as she worked.

He winced as the antiseptic stung, smiling a stage smile through clenched teeth.

'That's a brave soldier,' she cooed.

Then, suddenly, she straddled him again, sitting on his legs, immobilising him. She switched the Dettol bottle to her right hand, holding it, not upright this time, but almost horizontally with her thumb over the top. It hovered menacingly above his lower mid-section.

'This stuff stings. Don't it just?' she said.

Bob laughed involuntarily, taken by surprise. He looked at the bottle, unsure of what would happen next.

'Was that really how you scraped your leg, big boy?' she said, mock menace in her tone.

The grin stayed on his face. 'Well, no. The truth is, I was at the zoo, and I got too close to the alligator. Naw, that's not it, I was crossing Princes Street, and I was run over by a bus. Or maybe it was when I tried to jump the food queue in Marks and Spencer.'

'Ok, ok, ok! I give up already.' She jumped to her feet and put the bottle on the bedside table.

'Now, for God's sake, get a move on. It's almost seven and we have to be at the theatre for eight.'

His grin grew wider. 'Exactly. So what's the rush.'

He reached up and drew her to him.

Fourteen

They arrived at the Pleasance theatre complex with only three minutes to spare.

For eleven months of the year, the Pleasance is used by Edinburgh University and its graduates as a leisure and recreational facility, and thus makes little or no impact on the life of the city. But during August it is transformed into a cosmopolitan centre for the performing arts, throbbing with activity eighteen hours a day. Bars, cafeterias and two theatres are set around a central courtyard filled with benches, chairs, and tables. Around one corner of the cobbled yard, rows of canvas seats are set out, making the area into a third and impromptu theatre, used by the ragbag of idealists and solo performers who, unable to find or fund a venue, flock to the Fringe regardless, ready to make use of even the crudest stage to further their dreams of glory.

Bob and Sarah saw Alex before she spotted them. Wearing her stage make-up, she stood at the top of the stairway which led into Pleasance Theatre 2. Her eyes scanned the crowd; her arms were folded tight across her chest and her brow was knitted with impatience – and gathering disappointment. Even caught off guard, the girl still looked stunning: tall and slim, with big, round blue eyes and a jumble of long dark hair, shining with natural highlights, which fell around her wide shoulders like a shawl.

As they approached, Bob and Sarah saw her rise on her toes, stretching up to peer as far into the crowd as she could. Then, with a shrug of frustration, she dropped back on to her heels and made as if to turn away.

'Alex!'

At Sarah's cry, she turned and caught sight of them at last, as they reached the end of a snaking queue of around forty people leading towards and then up the stairway entrance.

'Where have you two been?' she called down to them. 'I was beginning to feel like I'd been stood up. Listen, when you get in, do me a favour and sit well to the back. I don't want to be able to see either of you, or catch your eye during the show, in case it makes me freeze. Wish me luck!'

Bob smiled up at her. 'Break a leg, kid, or whatever!' he shouted. Sarah blew her a kiss. Alex waved to them and disappeared into the theatre.

There were only a few of the steeply tiered seats left when they entered, but they found two in the third row from the back, close to a spotlight. None of the cast would look in that direction for fear of being blinded.

Alexis Skinner was five weeks short of her twenty-first birthday. She was the only child of Bob's youthful first marriage, which had been cut tragically short by the death of his wife in a simple car accident when Alex was only three years old. She had no clear memory of her mother, and Bob had brought her up virtually alone – with the occasional help of his parents – in the cottage in Gullane, the East Lothian golfing village, where he and Sarah now shared their off-duty time. Myra, Alex's dead mother, had left a sizable endowment policy to provide for her education at one of the Merchant Company schools in Edinburgh. However, the young Alex had demanded that she be allowed to stay with her friends in East

Lothian, stamping her tiny foot to emphasise the point. Eventually, Bob had let her have her way. Gullane Primary and North Berwick High it had been, and both schools had done well by her. University had been a different matter, as she had chosen to read Law at Glasgow. Now, three years on, she was about to enter her Honours year, on track for a First, with a string of commendations and prizes to her name. She intended eventually to pursue a career at the Scottish Bar. To her father's private delight, recently she had been awarded a Faculty of Advocates' Scholarship, to help her through her period of pupillage and over the first months of her career in advocacy, where traditionally a newcomer had little or no earning capacity.

When Alex was five, Bob had invested her school endowment fund in a Ivory & Sime capital growth trust, switching to an income fund when she was ready to leave school. Her 'private means' – as sometimes, with mock grandeur, she described her mother's legacy – allowed her to live a frugal but comfortable student existence. Freed from the need to find a part-time job, she had been able to pursue her interest in the theatre, which had been developing since the start of her university career, gathering pace as she gained more confidence in the progress of her studies. After a year in the University drama club, she had joined a rather more ambitious theatre society founded by, but no longer restricted to, Glasgow's wealthy and influential Jewish community. Bob and Sarah had seen her perform in two productions, each a musical, and had been surprised by the way her naturally powerful singing voice had developed under coaching. It was now good enough to have attracted interest outside the theatre group. As Sarah knew – daughter and stepmother having decided to keep it a secret from Bob until the release of the album – she had been used as a backing singer by a Glasgow rock-group which was already internationally successful, and still seemed to be moving on an upward career path.

This Fringe show was far different from anything she had attempted before. In fact, Alex had said, it was the most difficult thing their group had ever tackled: a stage version of Tom Wolfe's book *The Right Stuff*, telling the story of the pioneering American Mercury astronauts. No music, just straight drama. And for the first time Alex played the female lead. She was cast as 'Glamorous Glennis' Yeager, the wife of the first man to break the sound barrier. When not involved in dialogue, she narrated in spotlight from side stage, as the story developed. She had enlisted Sarah as American accent coach and, throughout July, the Skinner household had rung to the sound of Transatlantic conversation. On occasion even Bob had found himself joining in.

Bob and Sarah settled into their seats, as the last light dimmed to blackness. Then suddenly in a brilliant stage illumination there were Alex and the male lead, miming a chase in which Alex was steadily overtaken and thrown to the ground, in what the skilful stage-lighting effect made believable as desert. The Yeagers' strange courtship ritual began a play which unfolded its gripping story over two and a half hours. Before the show, Bob had held private reservations about a play which attempted to tell the whole story of early space exploration in a makeshift theatre. However, when it was over, he conceded to himself that it had worked, thanks to the intensity of the fellow players and, of course, to Alex's exceptional performance.

The final curtain was received with thunderous applause and a standing ovation, a rarity on the Fringe. Eventually, after three encores, the applause quietened and the audience began to file out. Bob and Sarah made their way down to the front. Less than a minute later, Alex appeared through a side door. She was followed, a few paces behind, by a muscular blond man, an inch or so under six feet in height, dressed in jeans and a T-shirt.

'Well, what did you think?' she bubbled, still on a high from the warmth of the applause. 'Was it ok?'

'Ok?' said Bob. 'It was brilliant. You could take that anywhere. Well done, baby. Always knew you were a star.'

'Yes, terrific, kid.' Sarah hugged her.

Alex kissed them both. 'Thanks, Pops. Thanks, Sarah. You really mean it?'

They smiled their replies, as Alex turned and beckoned to the man waiting behind her.

'There's someone I'd like you to meet. This is Ingemar Svart, known as Ingo – our lighting genius. We imported him from Sweden specially for the show.

'Ingo, meet Bob and Sarah Skinner, my Dad and Mum.'

Inwardly Sarah was enormously pleased by Alex's introduction, but she held up a hand. 'Please, Alex! That's step-mum. I'm only nine years older than you, remember. Hi, Ingo, it's nice to meet you. I thought your lighting was great.'

'Thank you. I am also pleased to meet both of you.'

As he returned the Swede's firm handshake, Bob was struck by the clarity of his ice-blue eyes, and by the easy confidence with which the man, whom he judged to be around thirty, returned his appraising gaze. He tried, but failed, to read his thoughts through his calm expression. Behind the smile, Ingo Svart was impassive.

Alex reclaimed his attention. 'Pops, d' you mind if we pass on supper? There's a first-night cast party, and we've really got to go to it. You two could come with us, if you like.'

As his daughter spoke, Skinner caught sight, over her shoulder, of a tall, balding figure framed in the door at the side of the hall.

'No, babe. Thanks, but we won't. I want to have a look round here. Then we've got our table booked at the Waterfront. Can't let it go to waste. You go on, though. Enjoy yourselves. You've both earned it. Now, I must say hello to Brian over there.'

He walked with Alex and Ingo back across to the side door. Detective Inspector Mackie smiled, and nodded a greeting to Alex. Then he stepped aside and held the door for her and her companion, before turning back to Skinner.

'Evening, boss. Good show?'

'I'm biased, I know, but it was one of the best things I've seen in a long time. A Fringe award-winner for sure. How're you doing?'

'Fine. I've just been scouting round this place – and the other theatre. No problems with either from a security viewpoint, but the bars and that open courtyard scare the hell out of me. It looks virtually impossible to make them secure, as things are just now. Mind you, there are only two ways into this complex. How would you feel about blocking the back way, and then searching everyone as they come through the arch?'

Skinner shrugged his shoulder. 'I'd feel uneasy about it, but maybe we don't have a choice. Think through the pros and cons and give me a recommendation in the morning. While we're here, why don't you walk me through it. After that, we're off to eat. Want to join us?'

'Thanks, boss, but I won't if you don't mind. I'm rubber-ducked. So I'm bound for an early night, Saturday or not!'

Fifteen

As Skinner and Sarah chose their late supper from the blackboard menu in their crowded dockside restaurant, a mile or two away Andy Martin's evening was moving towards a satisfactory conclusion.

Earlier he had inspected Filmhouse, the base of the Film Festival, from its attic to its cellars. There seemed to be no wasted space at all in the building, and it seemed to pose no problems. Its two purpose-built cinemas had numbered seating, and everyone entering had to pass through a single wide foyer before reaching either of them – or the restaurant and bar. Julia Shahor had quickly agreed to his suggestion that she should install two video cameras in the foyer, but placed where they could be seen clearly, their value being deterrence rather than detection.

They had sat side-by-side in front row seats during the film, an intense drama set in revolutionary France. Before the dimming of the lights for the screening, Julia, a designer outfit replacing the white robe she had worn earlier in the day, had launched her film Festival with a short, assured and politically clever speech about the economic importance of the British movie industry, ending with an appeal to the financial leaders who made up a sizable chunk of the invited audience to recognise the earning potential of a successful film by providing risk capital for worthwhile projects. When she had finished, and had taken her seat by his side, Andy had realised that his earlier assessment of the woman as naive or gauche had been well wide of the mark. So he had warmed to her even more.

After the film, they had eaten in the Filmhouse restaurant, at her suggestion. They had discussed the film itself, and others which were to be the highlights of the ensuing Festival. They had made small-talk, learning more about each other as their conversation developed, sparring gently with words, each establishing in the process that the other had no serious entanglements. And then, just as Andy had been deciding what might happen next, and how he should play it, she had beaten him to it.

'I don't suppose you'd feel like giving a working girl a lift home, do you?'

In the same moment as Bob Skinner's baked red mullet was placed before him by the Waterfront's young waiter, Andy closed the passenger door of his red sports hatch and Julia settled into her seat. The moon was bright and clear as they drove through the New Town. As Andy changed gear, turning into Northumberland Street, Julia reached out and stroked the back of his hand. Her touch was featherlight, and he felt a tingle run up his arm.

'I bet all the girls say this, but you're quite different from my idea of a policeman. Although you're not just any old policeman, are you? You're one of the Special kind.'

He laughed. 'Not that Special, honest. And what all the girls say, after a while at least, is more like "Typical bloody copper!" – followed, as a rule, by a slamming door.

'Along here, did you say?'

'Yes, just around the corner. But it gets narrow. If you park there, we can walk the rest.'

Julia's home was a two-storey mews house in the lane which linked Dublin Street and Northumberland Street. A tiny flowerpot garden, surprising in the heart of the city, was divided off from the roadway by an iron fence with a narrow gate. She put a hand on its latch, then suddenly stood on tiptoe and kissed him. Her face shone in the moonlight which flooded the lane. Andy was reminded of the taste of honey and the scent of fresh lemons.

'I'm really just a nice Jewish girl, you know. Come in and I'll prove it.'

Andy knew that if he tried to speak, it would come out as a husky croak. So he said nothing, but followed her into the cottage, closing the gate quietly behind him.

The house had no hall, and the front door opened straight into the living room. It was in darkness, and so the woman's voice, when it sounded from the far corner, took him completely by surprise.

'Julia?' The accent was guttural, unspecified middle European.

'Yes, auntie, it's me.' She flicked on the light. Andy saw, sitting in the corner, a small grey-haired woman. She turned her face towards them, with a smile which the policeman thought had something strange about it. 'I've brought a new friend home. His name's Andy Martin. He's a policeman. Andy, this is my Aunt Dorrie – Mrs Rosenberg.'

Andy smiled towards her and knew with certainty, as he did so, that Mrs Rosenberg was completely blind. Julia tugged at his sleeve, pulling him towards an open door which led into the kitchen. At the same time she spoke across the room to her aunt. 'I'm going to make coffee. Would you like some?'

'No, thank you, dear. I'm off to bed. My radio programme finished some time ago. Very pleased to meet you, Mr Martin.'

She stood up from her chair and began to tap her way expertly, with a white stick, towards a door on the far side of the room.

Andy was still recovering from the surprise. 'Very pleased to meet you too, Mrs Rosenberg,' he said belatedly. 'Goodnight.'

As the old woman left the room, he followed Julia into the kitchen.

'There. I told you I was a nice Jewish girl. And all nice Jewish girls have to have little old Jewish mothers – and, if not, aunties.'

'How long . . .?'

'Three years now, but her sight was failing for five years before that. It's a very rare condition. Seventeen cases currently on the record in the UK. The vision starts to go in the centre, and the blind spot just widens out until it's all gone. Quite incurable. Uncle Percy took her everywhere, looking for a different opinion, but all the diagnoses were the same – and all the prognoses. She can't see a thing now, not even the faintest hint of light. Hardly any point in her coming to a film festival, is there? But she said she'd just like to be here in the city while it was on. She can hear, though. Can she hear! A mouse hiccup at fifty paces, she says.'

Julia drew Andy's head down towards her and kissed him. 'So we'll just have to be very quiet. Won't we?' she murmured.

Quieter than mice, and being careful not to hiccup, they tiptoed upstairs. Much of Julia's bedroom was filled by a king-size brass-framed bed, positioned opposite a narrow white-curtained window. The drapes were tied back to allow in as much light as possible. Andy felt inside the doorway for a light switch, but she placed a soft hand on his arm to stop him.

She led him gently towards the bed and, without speaking, began to unfasten his shirt, kissing his chest as each button came undone. Her hunger for him was frank, honest, and somehow touching in its fragility. For his part, where he would normally have been confident and dominant, now he felt as awkward and clumsy as an inexperienced teenager. He was amazed to find that his fingers were trembling as he fumbled with the catch of her dress, but eventually the zipper came free and unfastened in one long movement.

She stepped out of the expensive garment and laid it on a chair near the bed. And when she reached out her arms to him, and moved towards him, her pale skin shining in the silver light like fine china, he embraced her with a catch in his throat, and with the knowledge that he had come to a pivotal moment in his life, after which nothing would ever be as it had been before.

Julia was generous and tender and enormously affectionate in her love-making. He responded to her touches, as she did to his, with shivers and gasps, allowing her to express herself as she chose, as she introduced herself to his body. He took pleasure in her tenderness, finding himself excited as never before by her patience and by the relaxed fashion in which she unfolded herself to him. He drank deeply from the well of her passion, matching her pace where he would once have rushed, holding back to sustain her as she climaxed, letting go only when he could control himself no longer. As he did, he scaled a peak of pleasure which he had never reached before, realising as he stretched himself on its summit, that he was experiencing for the first time all the sensations of a genuine union between two bodies and souls.

When they had reached the other side of the mountain, they lay side by side on the fluffy cover, naked, smiling at each other in the moonlight. Martin felt enriched, and it came to him with the greatest clarity that the essential ingredient, intimacy, had been missing from the string of hollow, purely physical relationships in which he had been involved over the previous few years.

'I don't do this ever, you know,' she whispered to him, very softly. 'On the first date, I mean. Not very nice Jewish behaviour at all.'

He blew gently into her ear, and smiled as her back arched and her nipples hardened in a second. Then he turned her face to his and said very softly: 'Would you believe me if I told you that was the first time I've ever made love?'

Her eyes widened and she opened her mouth to speak, but he stopped her with a kiss.

'It's true. Until now, what I've known has been no more than screwing.' He paused. 'Suddenly, I'm scared. This is new territory for me. We met what, eight hours ago? – and yet . . . Well, it's incredible. I'm a logical man, I'm pushing thirty-five, and here I am, gone, shot, stoned . . . in love, I think. Do you think I'm crazy?'

She laid two small fingers across his mouth. 'If you are, my darling, it's contagious.' She took his hand and placed it between her breasts. 'Feel here. I'm shaking.'

It was true. Under his touch, Andy could feel a faint trembling mixed in with the steady pounding of her heart. He moved his hand round and drew her, gently, close against him. He nodded his head towards the window. 'Maybe it's just that full moon. Maybe tomorrow . . .'

She smiled. 'Maybe. But it doesn't feel that way to me. In the meantime . . .'

She pulled his head towards her and began to chew his earlobe, gently. A shaft of pleasure ran down his body, all the way to his toes.

'Julia!' Mrs Rosenberg's voice came in an insistent whisper from the open doorway.

In her surprise, Julia bit down sharply on Andy's ear. He managed to stifle a yelp. Taken completely unawares by the silence of the woman's approach, and forgetting that she was blind, he reached out automatically for his clothes.

The whisper came again. 'There's someone downstairs. Someone trying to get in.'

'Are you sure, auntie?' Julia whispered in return.

'Of course I'm sure. At the front door. As well we have a policeman here.' In the moonlight, he saw her smile faintly into the room.

Martin was into his slacks and shirt before she had finished speaking. Barefoot, he moved silently through the doorway and crept downstairs. He and Julia had left the living-room door ajar when they had gone up. He stood behind it and listened. At first there was nothing, only a heavy silence, until he heard a scratchy, creaking noise, which he recognised as a jemmy on the door-frame.

Keeping out of the moonlight and close to the wall, he slid into the room and up to the front door. Grabbing the oval handle of the Yale lock, he twisted it and pulled, hard. The door swung open, only to be stopped after a few inches by a brass security chain, fixed peculiarly a few inches above floor level.

'Shit!'

Martin closed the door again and freed the chain, then pulled it wide but, in those few seconds, the intruder had bolted. The garden gate swung creaking on its hinges. He had just time to see what he was certain was a male figure disappearing around the corner. As he ran from the lane into the sloping Dublin Street, he saw his quarry at the foot of the hill, racing into Drummond Place. Martin gave up the chase. Seconds later he heard a motorcycle bark into life, then roar away. He jogged back to the house, where he found Julia standing in the doorway, once again wearing her white robe.

'Sorry, love. He got away. I'd have had him, but I didn't notice the chain.'

'You were in the kitchen when I fixed it. I do that every night without even thinking. A previous occupant installed it down there. He must have been a midget. Oh, but, Andy, thank God you were here. So much for my precious alarm system!'

Martin looked up at the big red box above the door. 'Don't blame that too much. The guy's pumped some quick-dry stuff into it. A pound to a pinch of pig-shit, this was the container.' He knelt and picked up a long cylinder, with a pistol grip at one end, and a nozzle at the other. 'Yes. Sure enough. Quick-dry mastic: a sort of rubber solution. Your alarm probably still thinks it's working. It won't realise it's been choked to death. I don't suppose it's linked to the Gayfield police station?'

Julia shook her head.

Together they went back indoors, Martin carrying the mastic tube.

'Where's your aunt?'

'I made her go back to bed.'

'Well, go and tell her everything's ok, but first show me where the phone is. I'm going to call this in.'

'It's in the kitchen. Will that mean police here tonight?'

He chuckled. 'Apart from me, you mean? No, I'll tell them I'm handling things here. But for the next half-hour or so I want anyone going through this city on a motorcycle pulled over and questioned. On you go, now. Put your aunt's mind at rest.'

She started towards the stairs, then looked back at him from the doorway. 'Andy,' she said quietly. 'Will you stay till morning?'

He smiled his widest smile. 'And the morning after, and the morning after that; as many mornings as you want. Try and stop me. You, lady, now have the highest-ranking personal bodyguard in Edinburgh.'

She was waiting for him under the duvet – after he had made his call and issued his orders to the Gayfield night-shift. Her white robe lay on the floor, the curtains were drawn, and a lamp on the bedside table was lit. He undressed and slipped into bed beside her.

As she hugged him, he felt her shiver very slightly.

'Andy, you don't suppose there could have been any connection between that burglar and the things you told us about this afternoon.'

He shook his head vigorously. 'Not at all. That was just a Saturday-night chancer. The sort of thing that happens every weekend in life, in any city.'

As she smiled and pulled him towards her he hoped that he would never have to lie to her again.

Sixteen

'I know it's a big *if*, boss, but she is connected with the Festival.'

'Yes, but hold on, Andy. You said yourself that the curtains were open at the front of the house: downstairs and upstairs. And your car was parked round the corner. The guy probably just guessed, wrongly, that the place was empty. How was he to know that you just like having it off with the curtains open?'

'Aye, very funny, Bob. Look, damn few opportunists come equipped with a cylinder of mastic to fuck up any alarm system they might happen to come across.'

'OK, maybe he was a professional Saturday-nighter.'

Skinner saw Martin's frown deepen, his expression made even darker by the stubble on his chin. He put a friendly hand on his shoulder.

'Look, Andy, I know you're worried about this girl. Nothing's impossible, and the chances are we'll never know whether there was a connection. But one thing's for sure: after having a close shave like that, there's no way the bastard will come back.'

'Maybe so, boss, but I'm still having that house watched, and Julia escorted to and from work. And once the alarm's fixed, it's being linked to Gayfield.'

Skinner whistled at Martin's vehemence. 'Here, this sounds serious. How long have you known this lass? One day? Is this the Andy Martin that I know, and that dozens of women have come to love in vain? Your thinking must be affected, right enough. Otherwise, last night you'd have let that boy get all the way in the door! Then you could have stiffened him and we'd have got all the answers that we're just guessing at now. That's what I'd have done if I'd been there – and been thinking straight, that is!'

Skinner and Martin were alone in the private office of the Special Branch suite. It was 8:50 am on Sunday morning, and the headquarters building was weekend quiet. But suddenly, they heard the outer door open.

'Someone's keen,' said Skinner. 'We told them nine o'clock.'

There was a soft knock on Martin's door. 'Come!' he shouted.

The door opened and a little round man, no more than five feet four inches tall, seemed to roll into the room. At first Martin was reminded of a football, then, noting the way in which the little man appeared to taper inward and down from the shoulders, decided that he looked more like a spinning top.

The newcomer had a friendly, inquisitive smile, and receding gingery, close-cropped hair. He wore a Harris tweed jacket, unusually heavy for August, a check shirt, and grey trousers. His black shoes were polished to a high shine.

'Hello, Bob, 's good to see you again.' There was a twinkle in his eyes as he stretched a hand upwards towards Skinner. The accent was unmistakably North of England, Lancashire or thereabouts, Martin guessed.

Skinner shook the outstretched hand and returned the smile. 'Adam, good to see you, too. Glad you're here, although I didn't expect you to make it so fast.'

'You kiddin'? I was in fookin' Belfast. You get a chance to get clear of that place, you don't hang about. Natives are fookin' restless over there just now. Whatever you've got here, it'll be a fookin' holiday by comparison.'

Skinner smiled grimly. 'Hope that's the way it turns out, mate.'

He turned to Martin. 'Andy, this is Captain Adam Arrow, Military Intelligence, Special Air Services, counter-terrorist adviser. You name it, he's the lot. He and I met at that security seminar I went to last month. Adam. Meet Andy Martin, DCI Special Branch. He might only look like a lad, but he's been there, done that.'

'That's enough for me,' said Arrow.

The two shook hands, and Martin was suddenly aware that the little man was immensely strong.

Arrow turned back towards Skinner. 'OK, Bob, so why have I been pulled out of t' fookin' frying-pan? All that the Five woman said was that you'd asked for me as a specialist.'

Skinner waved him over to a chair. 'Sit yourself down, and I'll tell you.'

Quickly but comprehensively, he briefed Arrow on the crisis, describing the Waverley Market bomb, Ballantyne's letter, his own encounter with the motorcycle gunman, and finally even Martin's late-night tussle.

'Like as not, Andy's incident had nothing to do with all this, but he's not so sure.'

Martin cut in: 'Let's just say I'm taking no chances.'

Arrow nodded his round head vigorously. 'Quite right. As Bob says, it's a long shot, but it's best to keep an eye on the lass. If it were connected, they might just have another go. Unless you identified y'self. Didn't shout "Stop in t' name of the law", or owt like that, did you?'

Martin grinned. 'No. I did shout something when that chain stopped the door, but it wasn't anything like that.'

Arrow nodded. Then he looked up at Skinner. 'Tell you one thing already, Bob. Nowt to do wi' Ireland, this lot.'

'Why so sure?' Skinner asked.

'Loads of reasons. Your average Paddy, whatever side he's on, wouldn't write it all down, then nail it to Secretary of State's fookin' door. It'd be telephone warning every time. Then there's t' tone of yon letter. It's ponderous. Pretentious almost. This bastard is a new hand at the game. He's feeling very important – or at least he's trying to make us think he is. Then there's your biker. Irish wouldn't do anything so fookin' stupid as to shoot at a civilian. And you didn't shout "Police", either. Most of all, our intelligence is pretty good when it comes to things like this. We're good at monitoring their contacts wi' other organisations. I reckon if they'd been in touch with anyone over here, there's a fair chance our guys'd have stumbled on it. No – no Irish link 'ere. This is a new lot, and that's a big problem.'

'Why so big?' said Martin, quizzically.

''Cos it means we know fook-all about 'em, that's why. No established behaviour pattern. In Ireland we know how the fookers think. Gives us whatever edge we have. Lets us guess what they're likely to do. We don't always guess right. But when we do, and we're in the right place, then they can get out the black gloves, beret, tricolour – or the Union Jack; we don't play favourites – and the hearse.' Arrow's small bright eyes hardened, and his voice dropped to not much above a whisper. ''Cos they'll fookin' need 'em.'

He looked sharply across at Martin. 'This lot's starting from scratch. That'll make it harder for us. What have you done so far on the security side, Bob?'

'As much as I could in, what . . .' Skinner looked at his slim gold wristwatch. '. . . less than twenty-four hours.'

He described the steps which had been taken, the security checks, the pass system.

'All that's in place. My people are coming in this morning to finish writing up security reports on each of the higher-risk venues. We've designated about two dozen of them. Once I've looked through them, I'll be able to judge how I'm off for manpower.' His glance at Arrow held a question in it. 'If I decide I'm a bit light, and need some extra cover for special places, how are your lot placed just now?'

The little man paused, as if he was deciding how frankly he could answer such a direct question. Then, with an imperceptible nod, he said: 'I think we could give you some help. We've got quite a few over in Ireland at the moment. Then there's others up to no fookin' good in the Middle East. There's a few bastards out there we're going to get even with, and one in particular. We lost some guys in the Gulf War, and we haven't forgotten them.'

Suddenly the eyes lost all their jollity, as his mind turned over a bitter memory. 'We never forget things like that. We've nailed a few of the guys responsible already, but there's more to get yet. That lot think it's Mossad.' He chuckled – a quiet sound which chilled Martin to the bone. 'But it ain't. Fookin' pussies, Mossad are, compared wi' our lot when someone upsets us.'

He looked up at Skinner, and the genial smile returned. 'Still an' all, I reckon the CO could sort out a dozen or so good lads for you. You'd have to ask through the politicians, mind you.'

Skinner nodded. 'I know – and I probably will. Meantime there are some things we can do in-house. Andy's pulled a list of odd-ball journalists from the SB files, the sort of guys whose names pop up in criminal investigations, or who are known to make heavy use of criminal sources. There's about a dozen of them, and they've all still to be interviewed. As well as that, I'm expecting a report that I asked Five to do for me last night. It's on its way up now, by courier.'

Arrow raised his eyebrows. 'Too hot for fax or telex, then.'

'Mm.' Skinner nodded. 'Tell you what, Adam. Are you checked in anywhere yet?'

'No. I'm stoppin' at Redford, wherever that is.'

'I'll get someone to show you. In fact, we'll give you the grand tour, while we're at it. Let's see, who was the early-shift guy out there again?'

He pressed a buzzer on Martin's desk. A few seconds later his question was answered, as Mario McGuire appeared in the doorway.

'Sir?'

'Morning, Mario.' Skinner introduced Arrow to the big dark-haired detective. 'Captain Arrow's new in town, Sergeant. It's your first time here, Adam, isn't it?'

The little man nodded.

'Mario,' said Skinner, 'I'd like you to give Captain Arrow a run-around. Take him out to Redford Barracks first, to drop off his kit. Then show him Festival Edinburgh. Let him get a feel of the place, show him some of the venues: the Usher Hall, Lyceum, Assembly Hall, places like that. Take a look at the Pleasance. Grab some lunch there, maybe, and I'll see you both back here around two. Is that okay with you, Adam?'

'First-rate. There a bar at this Pleasance place, then? I'll be fookin' gaspin' by then, I reckon. Looks like I'm out of the fryin'-pan in Belfast and into the fookin' fire here, right enough.'

The two men, one large, one little, left the room, looking incongruous side-by-side. Yet, as they left, Martin found himself thinking that, of the two, big, hard and powerful as McGuire was, if forced to make the choice he would rather tackle three Mario McGuires, than a single Adam Arrow.

As the door closed behind them, Skinner turned back to Martin. 'OK, Andy. Let's have a look at that list of journos.'

From a secure cabinet which he opened with a key, Martin produced a yellow folder. Coming to stand beside Skinner, he laid it on the desk and opened it to show a list of names in alphabetical order.

'They're all here: fourteen in all. Five in and around Glasgow, six in Edinburgh, one in Haddington, one in Stirling, and one in Dundee. Only five of them are employed full-time on the staff of newspapers. The rest are a mixture of freelances, mostly writers and researchers, but two describe themselves as television producers.'

Skinner pointed to a name in the lower half of the list. 'Aye, and that one's our number-one target.'

Martin followed his finger. 'Mr Frazer Pagett. Yes, I agree. Christ, he'd take the huff if we didn't feel his collar. He'd take it as a slur on his reputation as an investigative journalist if he didn't get a visit from us.'

Skinner shook his head. 'No,' he said vehemently. 'That's just what he's not going to get. I want him watched. I want his phone tapped. In fact, I want taps on everyone on that list.'

'Don't we need Ballantyne's signature to do that, boss?'

'We've got it already. That piece of paper he signed yesterday gives me authority to do as I think fit. And I think fit now to start telephone surveillance on all the people mentioned here. The half of them probably believe they're being tapped all the time, anyway. As far as Mr Pagett's concerned, we're going to let him sit on it for a few days. Listen to him, look at him, and just see if he says or does anything funny. He's the only guy on your list that I take seriously. The others are just unscrupulous reporters, or nutters. We'll give all of them the courtesy of a visit right away. Word of that'll get back to Mr Pagett, and it'll make him nervous. When we finally do go to see him, I want him as jumpy as possible.'

Martin closed the yellow folder. 'I'll need your written authority for Telecom to set up the phone taps.'

'No, we're not going to use them. There's a guy in the Scottish Office: Mel Christian, Director of Telecommunications. Here's his home number.' Skinner scribbled on a memo pad, tore off the page, and handed it to Martin. 'Call him right away. Use my name. Tell him it's a Beta operation. That'll get his attention. Tell him what you need and he'll make it ha—'

He was cut short by the trembling tone of his mobile phone. He took it from his pocket and pressed the *'receive'* button. 'Hello.'

'Bob. It's Alan B. Can you come to St Andrew's House, right away. I've had another.'

Seventeen

The three flags hanging limp on their poles seemed to emphasise the Sunday morning quiet, making the massive grey stone building look for all the world like an abandoned fortress.

Skinner pulled the BMW into a parking space opposite the tall brass-bound double entrance doors, one of which was slightly ajar. Across Regent Road, the morning sun, as it rose skywards, shone brightly on the foliage of Calton Hill, but the foyer of St Andrew's House – which was north-facing – was in shade.

His eyes took a second or two to adjust to the gloom as he stepped into the big entrance hall, which was made even darker than usual by the closed outer doors. He waved his pass at the security guard on duty in his booth.

'Morning, John.'

'Morning, Mr Skinner.'

As he crossed the hall he noted that the alert board had been changed from the low-grade of the previous day to the yellow state which he had ordered. He stepped into the waiting lift and pressed the button marked 5.

Arnold Shields, Ballantyne's Private Secretary, was working at his desk in the Secretary of State's outer office. Another man sat in a chair in the corner, reading avidly the sports section of *Scotland on Sunday*. Skinner had taken three paces into the room before the man looked up. Recognition flooded his face.

In the same instant, he dropped the newspaper and sat bolt upright.

For a second, Skinner fixed the man with a glare. Then he turned to Shields. The Private Secretary was tall, thin and dapper. He was also sharp, perceptive and destined for high office, as were all those who were appointed to his important post. Sunday morning or not, he was dressed in a dark single-breasted suit, striped shirt, collar and tie. He was a reserved man, with an unfailing formality of manner which added to his overall air of aloofness. He did not mix socially with colleagues, and none knew anything of his private life. Although he was respected universally, he was regarded, just as universally, as stand-offish, and was disliked by his colleagues as a result.

Skinner knew more about Shields than any of the man's office peers. He and Martin had handled the meticulous vetting to which Shields had been subjected before being offered the Private Secretary post. They had discovered without difficulty that he was a practising homosexual, and had a stable, twelve-year-old relationship with a partner in the Glasgow office of an international accountancy practice. After considering their course of action for some days, Skinner and Martin had taken the unusual step of talking over the situation with Shields and his friend. They had been persuaded by the discussion that, although the relationship was private, it was not secret, and that it could not possibly lay either man open to blackmail. Skinner had approved the appointment, keeping the information he had uncovered entirely under wraps.

Shields rose from his chair and extended his hand, as Skinner approached his desk.

'Mr Skinner. Good morning. The Secretary of State is expecting you. Go right in.'

Ballantyne was working his way through a pile of

correspondence as Skinner entered. 'Sit down over there, Bob. I won't be a moment. Read that in the meantime.' He pushed a brown envelope across the desk. 'It was handed to the doorman at the Caledonian Hotel at nine o'clock. Motorcyclist again, but no courier's livery this time. This one just wore denims and a crash-helmet. The manager of the Caley sent the letter straight along here.'

There was a faint catch in the Secretary of State's voice. Skinner studied him closely, as he worked. The tension of the previous day showed in his face once more, as he scrawled his signature across a letter. He cast it, in its folder, on to the pile in his out-tray, then picked up another, barely reading it before signing. Skinner thought that the man looked strung-out and nervous. Was that all down to this the terror threat, or could some of it be due to that designer blonde, Carlie, he mused.

He looked down at the envelope which Ballantyne had handed to him. It was the twin of the previous day's, addressed in the same way, with a white label. He drew out the letter and read.

To the so-called Secretary of State for Scotland.
From the Fighters for an Independent Scotland.
Code word Arbroath.

The failure of the media to report yesterday's demonstration, or to publish our letter leads us to conclude that you and your colleagues in the Government of the occupying power have secured their silence by coercion.

Clearly we cannot allow this situation to continue. If your censorship is not lifted by 1:00 pm today, and if, by that time, yesterday's statement of our demands has not been broadcast on radio and television, we will take further stern action to force you to accede. No warning of that action will be given, and full responsibility for its consequences will rest entirely with you.

Skinner sank into a chair by the window and read the letter through once again. As he was finishing, Ballantyne put the last of the green folders, its letter signed, in his out-tray. He rose from behind the desk and crossed the room, to sit in a facing chair.

'What d'you think, Bob? What'll they do?'

'I don't know, Alan. If I did, I'd stop them from doing it, and that would be that.'

'Well, what can *I* do?' There was a note of frustration in the Secretary of State's voice.

'Maybe we should do what they ask. We've bought some time, and used it as best we could. Our plans are made, and even now they're being put into action. We can't keep this genie in the bottle for ever, so we might as well thank the media for their co-operation and tell them they're free to run the letter.'

'Absolutely not!' Ballantyne's tone was suddenly strident. Skinner was alarmed to detect hysteria lurking not far below the surface.

'We can't do that. I won't do that! It would be a surrender to terrorism. And the Prime Minister would never countenance it. I spoke to him last night. He's quite resolute.'

Skinner shook his head. 'That's inspiring news. Look, Alan, there's no surrender about it. You were gung-ho yesterday, and that was right, but it doesn't do to be tough just for the sake of it. Sometimes you've got to use this.' As he spoke he tapped the side of his head. 'You can't believe, surely, that we can keep the truth from the public for ever. What's the point, anyway? As I said, we've bought our time and used it wisely, by putting in extra security everywhere. That'll start to show soon. Give it a day or two, three at the most, and the public will begin to figure out that yesterday's bang wasn't any gas explosion. And, listen, these bastards are right about one thing. We have coerced the bloody media! We did it for a purpose, and now we've achieved it, we should thank them for their co-operation and let them go ahead.'

Ballantyne jumped from his seat. 'No!' he shouted. 'It's a matter of principle.'

Skinner stood too. He glared down at the man, and when he answered, his voice was raised also. 'I've had a taste of politicians' principles in my time, Secretary of State, and I've noticed that they have a nasty tendency to get innocent people killed. Do you think this outfit are kidding? "Stern action to force you to accede." Whatever that means, it's a direct threat.'

'You seem to forget they've threatened more action, come what may – unless we hand them the keys to the kingdom, that is.'

Skinner slapped the walnut-panelled wall in frustration. 'I don't forget that at all, but there's no sense in pushing them into more violence, when we've nothing immediate to gain.'

Although still shaking, Ballantyne had recovered at least some of his composure. 'I'm sorry, Bob. I am adamant. The Government must stand its ground. We take the decisions; your job is to protect. That's what I expect you, and your people, to do.'

Skinner glowered at him, making no effort to hide the flame of his anger. 'I hope you realise you could be signing some poor sod's death warrant. Not your own, though; you're safe enough. As for our job, we're already doing it. But since you're making it difficult for us, you can come up with some extra resources. I want some SAS people up here. You can quote the Prime Minister's resolve, to get the OK from MOD. A dozen will do me. I'm told they're available.'

Ballantyne retreated across the room to the citadel of the ministerial desk. 'Yes, I'll do that for you. Bob, I'm sure it'll be all right.' His tone had changed; now it was almost placatory.

Skinner too had cooled down. 'I hope it is, Alan. It's your shout. If you're wrong, it'll be as if our disagreement never happened. I won't ever cast it up to you, but you'll have some job forgiving yourself.'

Ballantyne said nothing. He stood behind his desk, head bowed.

Skinner looked at him coolly for a few seconds, then changed the subject. 'What time are the Chief Constables coming in?'

'Twelve noon. I thought we'd see them in the third-floor conference room. I'll welcome them, and you can give them the low-down. I spoke to McGuinness personally, as you requested, and explained that you were working directly to me on this thing. I told him that if you need to ask for his co-operation in anything, he's to give it without question. I'll tell the Chiefs that too.'

Skinner looked at his watch. It was five minutes before ten. 'OK. Thanks. Look, I'm going back down to Fettes. I've got one or two things to do there. I'll be back for ten to twelve.'

'Fine. See you then.'

As he left the room, Skinner knew that something had gone for ever from his relationship with the Secretary of State. He had previously thought more highly of Ballantyne's judgement, yet there was more to it than that. He was deeply disappointed in the man. Skinner's creed was built on unswerving loyalty: to family, to friends, to colleagues, to country. The Secretary of State's implacable refusal even to consider his view had left him feeling personally betrayed, and he knew in his heart that he would never be able to look at Ballantyne in quite the same way again.

He closed the door quietly behind him. If Shields and the other man had heard the raised voices, neither gave the slightest sign.

Skinner smiled at the Private Secretary. 'I'll be back for that other meeting in a couple of hours, Arnold.'

Shields simply nodded in acknowledgement.

Skinner beckoned the other man to follow him into the corridor. When they were alone, he turned on him. 'Detective Constable Howells, just what the hell do you think you're here for? You are an armed Special Branch officer assigned to close protection of the Secretary of State. I walk into that room and you're in there reading the fucking funny papers. If I had been a bad guy, you'd have been dead in one second, then Mr Shields, then the Secretary of State. Your job is out here, not in there. You have to assume that *everyone* who comes on to this floor unannounced is a bad guy, and be ready to act until you find out different. Do you know what happens to detective officers if they screw up badly enough around me? Night-shift in uniform on the beat in fucking Eyemouth, that's what. You've just walked perilously close to having a permanent smell of fish in your wide nostrils. So don't do it again. Clear?'

The detective, who was two inches taller than Skinner, nodded vigorously. 'Clear, sir. Sorry, sir.'

'OK, incident closed. But be on guard in the corridor from now on.'

He started towards the lift, then looked over his shoulder.

'I'll be back. You'd better be the first person I see on this floor.'

Eighteen

The courier was a woman. She was seated in a corner of the main Special Branch office, sipping coffee and reading a magazine. When Skinner entered the room, she stood up at once, recognising him from the photograph which she had been shown early that morning in London.

Forestalling Brian Mackie's attempt to introduce her, she came towards him, hand outstretched. 'Good morning, sir. My name's Mary. I'm from Five. I have some papers for you from London, which I believe you're expecting.'

Skinner shook the woman's hand. 'Yes, that's right. Thank you for coming all this way.'

Mary was carrying a brown leather satchel. She fished a key from the pocket of her blue woollen jacket and unfastened the heavy brass lock, releasing the catch with a flick of her thumb. She withdrew a long white envelope and handed it over.

'Mission accomplished, sir. Now may I call for a cab back to the airport?'

Skinner held the envelope unopened in his hand. 'Thank you, Mary. No need for a taxi. Even on a Sunday I think we can find you a driver.' He looked across to Mackie. 'See to it please, Brian.'

'Sir!'

'DCI in?'

'Yes, boss.'

He thanked the messenger once more, and excused himself.

Martin was speaking softly into the telephone. He was seated in his swivel chair with his back to the door. When Skinner entered the room he swung round, making a wind-up motion with his left hand. 'Got to go now. I'll pick you up at around one o'clock.' He paused for a second, as he listened to the voice on the line.

'If you're sure your aunt will be all right at home, we'll go to my place. I need to shave, badly. See you then.' He was still smiling as he replaced the receiver in its cradle.

Skinner shook his head and laughed. 'I don't believe what I'm seeing here. A thirty-something schoolboy. Everyone's cracking up today. First Ballantyne turns into General fucking Patton, now you turn into fucking Romeo.'

Martin looked at him curiously. 'What's up with Ballantyne?'

Skinner's good humour disappeared as he described his altercation with the Secretary of State. 'I hate these boys when they decide to get brave, Andy. It's always some other bastard that winds up bleeding.'

'Let's hope not this time.'

'Yeah. Anyway, forget that for the moment and let's look at what's in here. It's my report from Five.'

He drew up a chair and sat down, facing Martin across the desk. Slitting open the white envelope, he drew out its contents, three sheets of A4 folded top to bottom. He scanned the first sheet, and glanced across at Martin.

'This says they've been through all of the most sensitive running files on politicians, and found only one that fits the bill.'

He put the covering letter to one side and studied the two-page report.

'We know about this guy all right. Grant Forrest Macdairmid. Labour MP for Glasgow Marymount. He used to be a right wee hoodlum when he was a youngster. Ran a gang and did time in Barlinnie Young Offenders, till he got into politics and started doing people over legally. He's on the ultra-nationalist wing of the People's Party. Advocates direct action to secure Home Rule. But there's a twist to him: he's a monarchist. Wants to set up a Scottish Parliament with a head of state on Scandinavian lines – you know, what they call a minimalist monarch. A king with a day job. He's even got a candidate picked out: a descendant of the Stuarts. Our potential king is an Italian who barely speaks English, but that's nae bother to our Mr Macdairmid. The general view of him is that he's just a nutter, but worth watching nonetheless. He's got the sort of humourless zeal in his eye that alarms the likes of you and me.'

'Mm. I know what you mean,' said Martin. 'I've seen him on telly. Have we been paying him any special attention?'

'Up here? The Glasgow Special Branch keeps a tap on his phone. It's never picked up anything more sinister than an order for a carry-out Chinese. That probably means that he expects to be tapped. He makes a load of noise in public, but in private – well the transcripts read like he's a real A-1 bore. That's what he's like up here.' Skinner tapped the report on the desk. 'According to this, though, he comes out of the closet when he's in London. Five were giving him a sort of general look-over a few weeks back. They tailed him to an Irish club in Camden Town. It seems they walked into a sort of terrorist jamboree. All shapes and sizes: Irish, Basques, neo-Nazis,

Libyans, all jabbering away, pissing it up, and our man Macdairmid right in the midst of it all.'

'So what did the Five guys do?'

'Hung around long enough to commit as many faces to memory as they could, then beat a retreat. Apparently, so says this report, they had a problem; one of the Five guys was a gal. This was a real hairy-arsed place and they felt too obvious, so they split. When they got back to the shop, they dug out the picture gallery, spotted four or five faces, and realised what they had been into. They sent the heavies round right away, but the party had broken up. They've been tailing Macdairmid ever since. No more contacts, but three weeks ago, as soon as Parliament broke up, he went on holiday.'

'Where to?'

'Ready for this? Tripoli. One of the world's prime sources of Semtex and other choice ordnance. He got back to Glasgow last Thursday.'

'Fucking hell!'

'Couldn't have put it more eloquently myself. They searched his luggage at the airport. He had a big hold-all thing as hand baggage, and when he caught the shuttle, they X-rayed it, but they couldn't search it without making him suspicious. He could have had anything in there.'

Skinner folded the report, replaced it in the envelope, and handed it to Martin. 'Here, lock this in your safe. So Mr Grant Forrest Macdairmid MP has been installed as bookies' favourite. We need a round-the-clock job on him.'

'Want me on it?'

'No. Your wee friend Julia and I both need you here. Anyway, it's a Glasgow job: one for Super-Haggerty. Dig out his home phone number for me. You've got it here, haven't you?'

Martin nodded. He flicked through his Filofax until he

found the Glasgow number, dialled it and handed the receiver to Skinner.

Two rings later a gruff voice answered. 'Hello.'

'Willie? It's Bob Skinner.'

'Mornin', sir. Sunday mornin', too. What's up? Ye got a crisis in Edinburgh? Is it rainin' or something?'

'It's about to rain on your weekend, fella. I need you through here. I'm seeing your Chief and others in about ninety minutes in St Andrew's House. I want you there to hear what I've got to tell them. It'll save me having to repeat myself. Are you fit to drive? I know what your weekends can be like.'

'Aw, come on, sir. You ken very well I'm teetotal.'

Skinner laughed ironically, and replaced the receiver.

'Scotland can sleep easy in her bed, Andy. Haggerty's on the job. Speaking of which, take a few hours off and see your new girlfriend. There isn't a lot you can do here till the troops finish their reports from last night. Me, I'm going along to kill some paperwork till it's time for my briefing.'

Martin smiled his new contented smile. 'Yeah, okay, boss. I think I'll do that. Before I go, though, one thing occurs to me about Macdairmid. If he's such a nutter, why doesn't the Labour Party get shot of him as one of their MPs?'

'They can't,' said Skinner. 'You see he's really a Nat. Apparently an extreme nationalist splinter group, like that old Seed of the Gael thing from ten years back, infiltrated the Marymount constituency Labour Party, took control, deselected the last MP, and installed the boy Macdairmid. He's untouchable by Head Office. They'd love to find a good excuse to bump him, but they haven't come up with one yet. Labour are desperate to keep the whole thing hushed up. None of the other parties know, not even the official

Nationalists. If they found out, they'd crucify them, and so would the voters. Funny game politics, eh.'

Martin grunted. 'Not when you start playing it with Semtex, it isn't.'

Nineteen

'Macdairmid? That bampot? Surely he's all wind and piss, sir.'

'That was my impression too, Willie, till Five told me different.'

The last of the Chief Constables had driven or been driven away from St Andrew's House, and the Secretary of State had departed for Charlotte Square. Skinner and Detective Superintendent Willie Haggerty, the new head of Special Branch in Glasgow, were sitting alone in the big conference room, which still reeked of the smoke from Sir John Govan's pipe. The Glasgow Chief, two months from retirement, had smiled cheerfully through the coughs and splutters of his colleagues.

The big table was still littered with the debris of the buffet lunch which the Secretary of State had provided. Haggerty munched on the last of the sandwiches as he considered Skinner's story.

'Christ, that's amazin'. We listen in tae the guy's phone and he never as much as breaks wind. Down in the Smoke and he's off tae a Murder Incorporated smoker! And tae Libya fur his holidays! Looks like he could be our man, right enough.'

'Not our man, Willie. One of them, perhaps, but not the only one. He was home in Glasgow when the bomb went off, and when the first letter was delivered, and when that biker took a shot at me.'

'How d'you know that?'

'Because I've read the transcripts. The tap picked up three calls during that time. One at 11:20 to his wife – they're separated. One at 11:30, to his girlfriend. One right on the stroke of midday, to the Chief Reporter of the *Sunday Mail*. It's the third one that interests me. Twelve noon on the dot, the same moment that the bomb goes off, and he phones a mate on a newspaper.'

'What did they talk about?'

'That's the strange thing. He calls the bloke up to ask what time the Rangers game kicks off. Says he thought it could have been one o'clock rather than three, but that his *Daily Record* hasn't been delivered that morning, so he can't check. Says he realises the newspaper guy isn't a football fan, but could he find out and call him back on his home number. What does that say to you?'

'That he could have been trying tae fix himself up with an alibi for twelve noon?'

'Most juries I've known would call that a reasonable conclusion. Especially if you tell them that Rangers weren't playing at all yesterday. Their game's today.'

Haggerty washed down the last of his sandwich with lukewarm coffee. 'So what d'you want me tae do, Mr S?'

'I want you to be like sticking plaster to him, Willie. Everywhere he goes, everything he does, everyone he talks to, I want to know. I'll detail a couple of guys to work with you. If he goes for a shit, I want to know how many sheets of paper he uses. If he goes to Confession, I want to know how many Hail Marys he gets as his penance.'

Haggerty's eyebrows rose. 'If he's a Rangers supporter, he's hardly going tae Confession!'

Skinner laughed. 'That's the other funny thing about the

phone call. Grant Macdairmid's a Catholic. Not too many Tims at the Rangers end!'

'No' for long, at any rate!' said Haggerty with a snort. 'Right, sir. Leave it tae Haggerty's heroes. Every contact he makes will be reported back to you daily. What about other checks? Can you get us the authority to look into his bank accounts?'

'You've got it. Anybody gives you problems, call me. Use this number.'

He picked up a paper napkin and a rollerball pen, and wrote down the number of his mobile. As he did so, as if on cue, the phone itself, which was lying on the table, sang into life. He picked it up and pressed the '*receive*' button.

'Hello.'

'Boss, it's Andy.' At once, Skinner sensed the tension in Martin's voice. 'I need to see you at the Sheraton – now. Suite 207.'

'What's the problem?'

'Ballantyne's bravery. Someone's bled for it – to the death.'

Twenty

In fact there was very little blood. Yet Skinner recognised the odours of death as soon as he opened the bedroom door in the Sheraton suite.

The woman lay curled on her left side on the floor, in the centre of the room. Her right arm was thrown out in front of her, the hand palm downward. Her short, greying hair was wet, and plastered to her head. The left side of her face was pressed to the carpet. Her right eye seemed to stare at Skinner's feet as he stood in the doorway. Her expression, even in death, was one of pure aggression, accentuated by the fact that her top lip was curled back in a snarl from her prominent teeth. Her pale pink towelling robe had fallen open. Beneath her heavy left breast a single puncture wound was visible, dark red and vivid against the postmortem pallor of her skin. From it, a thin trail of blood ran down to form a small scarlet blot on the robe, which was marked also by a second stain, yellow-hued, beneath her hips.

Martin stood over the body. Sarah was by his side.

'Who is she?' Skinner asked.

Martin opened his mouth to answer, but it was Sarah who replied, in a strange soft voice.

'Hilary Guillaum. *From Buffalo, New York*. The world's greatest mezzo-soprano. I first heard her sing there, in a summer concert, when I was twelve years old. She'd come back to Buffalo to do a charity recital in an open-air theatre. My dad took me, and I thought she was wonderful. The second time was thirteen years later, at the Met. She sang *Norma*, and she was just glorious. She was due to sing at the Usher Hall tonight. I tried to get tickets for us, but they were sold out.'

She shook her head and looked at the floor, biting her lip as she fought to regain her professional detachment.

Skinner stared at the body. He too had heard Hilary Guillaum sing, on the records and CDs of her repertoire which made up a large part of Sarah's collection. He pictured in his mind the photographs – on the record sleeves and boxes – of a beautiful, confident statuesque woman with hair piled high and an extravagant cleavage, as he now looked more closely at the fleshy lump lying on the floor. He saw not the slightest similarity between the two.

'Death doesn't compromise with dignity, does it.' Skinner spoke his thought aloud into the quiet room.

'Tell me what happened, Doc.'

Sarah banished all memories of the Metropolitian Opera House from her mind, and went to work. 'You see it there, Skinner. Single knife wound, lower chest area, left of centre. Made by a very sharp, double-edged weapon with a long blade, thrust in and upwards into the heart. Death ensued certainly within ten seconds. It would have been caused by shock, not haemorrhage. That's why there's very little external bleeding.'

'So show me how it was done,' he said. 'Andy, you be the victim. She couldn't have been far short of your height.'

'That's right,' said Sarah, with an appraising glance at Martin. 'And there's no sign of any struggle.

'OK, let's see. Andy, over here, please.' She led him towards the door to the ensuite bathroom. 'This is where it begins.

She's just had a shower, OK. She's been across at the Usher Hall doing sound checks. She dries off and plasters her hair back, then goes into the bedroom.'

'Does she hear something that makes her go back in?' Skinner asked, knowing the answer but looking for confirmation.

'No. She didn't tie her bathrobe. But whoever killed her was in the room, waiting. Either behind the door, or else it was someone she was expecting, someone whose appearance there was quite normal and didn't cause her any alarm. Because she still didn't tie the bathrobe.'

'Do we know if she was here alone?'

Martin answered. 'Her husband travels with her occasionally, but not this time. There's always a voice coach, male, and a secretary, female. They were both still at the Usher Hall from the time she left there at 1:00 o'clock until the secretary came back across here and found her at 2:15.'

'So,' said Skinner, 'she was either taken completely by surprise, and overcome quickly and easily by someone very fast and very strong, or she was taken completely off-guard by someone she knew or didn't regard as a threat. If we look at the second of those options, it brings us back to the fact that she didn't tie the robe. That means that she either had a boyfriend – or girlfriend – in town that we don't know about, or—'

Sarah broke in. 'Or the person in the room was another woman.'

'Would a woman have had the strength to do that?'

'If she took her by surprise, yes, no question. Looking at the wound, the weapon must have been so sharp that a child could have killed with it. It happened one of two ways. Either like this . . .'

She took a pair of long scissors from her bag, and held them as one would grasp a knife. She beckoned to Martin, and positioned him with his back to the bathroom door, close to where the body lay. Then she stepped up to him, quickly, spun him round with her left hand on his right shoulder, and imitated the upward thrust of the knife, pulling him down by the shoulder and towards her as she did so. Instinctively Martin's right hand came up and caught Sarah's shoulder.

'. . . or like this.'

She stood Martin with his back to the dead Hilary Guillaum. She held the scissors inverted and point-upwards against the inside of her forearm, concealed from his sight.

'Let's assume that the killer was in the room, and that Hilary had just come in from her shower,' she said. 'He or she could have made as if to go into the bathroom. Then . . .'

Again she stepped in close, grasping Martin by the shoulder, letting the scissors fall into her hand and stabbing upwards. Again, instinctively, the detective pushed against her with his right hand, but she was able to hold herself close to him.

'Right, I buy that so far,' said Skinner. 'Now, how did the victim react?'

'You saw how Andy grasped my shoulder? I'd say she did the same. See how the fingers of her right hand are still partly closed. Rather than break that grip, the killer just let go of the knife and took her weight as she fell to the floor. If it had been pulled out at this point, blood would probably have spurted, but she must have been dead within a second or two of hitting the ground. When it was removed that's all the bleeding there was, apart from a drop or two from the blade. Look, there's one here on the sleeve of the robe.'

Skinner stepped up to the body and bent over it. He examined it closely, comparing its posture in his mind against Sarah's description. Suddenly, as he looked at the victim's right hand, his brows tightened and he bent closer.

'Andy, look here.' He spoke without looking up.

Martin crossed the room to his side.

'Look at this.'

Very gently Skinner lifted the right hand. Stiffness had not yet set in. Indeed the body was still warm, as well as supple. He turned the hand so that Martin could see the fingers.

The nail on the third finger was split. A small piece of lemon-coloured cloth was lodged in the tear.

'At least that'll give the technicians something to do,' said Skinner. 'The place looks clean as a whistle otherwise.'

Martin was still examining the fragment. 'Boss, I know that's only a wee bit of cloth, but it looks to me like the same colour as the uniform the hotel's domestic staff wear.'

'What, the chambermaids, you mean?'

'Yeah.'

'Right, I want the whole place searched, top to bottom. When are we getting some manpower here? I saw young Macgregor at the door when I came in, but no one else around. How come you're here, Andy, but not the divisional CID?'

'Dunsmuir, the general manager, knows me. When the victim's secretary found the body, she managed to control herself, and called him straight up to the suite. He all but shit himself, and then called me – or at least he phoned Fettes and asked for me. Young Barry out there called me on my mobile. By that time, I was dropping Julia back at Filmhouse, just next-door. I rang Sarah first, then you. I thought you'd want to decide how we handle this one.'

'Fair enough. Before I do that, call down to your pal Dunsmuir. Ask him to line up his chambermaids, count them, and see if they're all present and correct.'

Martin picked up the telephone at the side of the bed, and carried out this order.

As he finished, Skinner said, 'That florid remark of yours earlier, about Ballantyne's bravery – were you just assuming that poor Hilary over there relates to the other thing?'

'No, sir. Come next door and I'll show you why I said it.'

He led the way to the suite's sitting room. A small coffee table was placed amidst a semicircle of four armchairs, arranged to face a picture window which offered a panoramic view across Festival Square to the Usher Hall, then, above and beyond its copper roof, to the western ramparts of Edinburgh Castle, rising from the vertical face of the great rock in which their foundations were set.

An envelope lay on the low rectangular table. Even before he picked it up and read the white label, Skinner knew what it was. It was addressed in the same way as its predecessors. Skinner opened it carefully and drew out the letter inside. He then read it aloud to Martin and Sarah.

To the so-called Secretary of State for Scotland.
From the Fighters for an Independent Scotland.
Code word Arbroath.

The fact that you are reading this letter means that you have chosen to ignore our ultimatum, and that an innocent person has suffered the consequences of your folly.

After this demonstration, you will not be able to keep from the world our just demand that you and your

> cohorts quit our beloved country and restore to us the democratic rights which were stolen from us almost three hundred years ago.
>
> This lady, and international celebrity, has died so that world attention will be focused on our struggle, and so that international pressure will be brought to bear upon you, to force you to withdraw from our land.
>
> Accede now, and no more blood will be spilled. Force us to continue, and you will find us resolved to take whatever action we believe to be necessary during this global Festival, and thereafter, to drive England and its institutions from our beloved Scotland.

As he finished reading, Skinner looked up at Sarah. 'Same author as the one you read yesterday, d'you think?'

'Certain.'

'Single author or more than one?'

'Probably just one. Give me some time and I'll try to work up a profile. There's something odd about the language, though.'

'What d' you mean?'

'I don't know exactly. It's very formal. These people are on a jihad, yet there's something dispassionate about their language.'

'Well think on it some more, and see what guesses you can make about the kind of person our writer is. Andy, we keep this one in-house for a while. No flashing blue lights, please. Get the technicians in now, and bring in Divisional CID to help interview everyone we can find who was in the hotel from midday to 2:30. What have you done with the voice coach and the secretary?'

'They're in their own rooms. Neil and Maggie are with them.'

'Good. Keep them on ice for now. I'm going across to tell the Usher Hall manager that he's got no show tonight. Then I'm off to tackle Ballantyne. We can't put a blackout on this one.'

Twenty-one

Skinner was halfway across Festival Square, the plaza which lies between the Sheraton and Lothian Road, when his phone sounded again. He stopped and sat down on a bench to answer it. The wooden seat was hot to the touch, such was the force of the sun.

'Boss, it's Brian here. I've had a guy on from the States, going absolutely apeshit. Said his name was Albert Neidermeyer from TNI, or something. He claims to have had a call at his London office, tipping him off that some American opera singer's been killed in Edinburgh. And, boss, he says the caller used the proper code-word. Now he wants you to confirm if it's true. He says if it is he's going to blow it and – his words, sir – fuck all you Scots bastards and your threats. Seems he doesn't like you at all, chief.'

'I'm chilled with terror,' said Skinner, icily.

'He left a number. Wants you to call him back personally.'

'Bugger that for a game of soldiers. Soldiers! There's an idea. Is Adam Arrow with you?'

'Yes, boss. He and Mario got back here twenty minutes ago.'

'Right. Adam's an English bastard, not Scots, but he'll do. Ask him if he'll do us a turn and call Neidermeyer back. He's to stall him, bullshit him, tell him we don't know what he's talking about, but we're looking into it. Ask Adam to spin him out for as long as he can. That should be quite some time. Neidermeyer won't understand a fookin' word Adam says.'

Skinner pressed the '*end*' button, and carried on across Festival Square.

Twenty-two

Again, it was Carlie who opened the rear door of Number 6 Charlotte Square. She had on the same skirt she had worn at their first meeting, but with a different top; silk once again but fastened at the shoulder, Chinese style.

'Hello again, Mr Skinner. What's the crisis this time?'

He can't have told her any of this, thought Skinner as he tried, but failed, to return her easy smile. She read the concern written on his face and turned serious herself. 'Alan's waiting for you upstairs. He's working on some papers in the dining room.'

Skinner made no move towards the stairway. Instead he stood his ground, gazing coolly at the woman, and saying nothing for several seconds. His expression was one of undisguised appraisal.

She was unflustered by his scrutiny, and when at last he opened his mouth to speak, she beat him to it.

'I know who you are, Mr Skinner, and what it is you do for Alan. And I can guess that you're wondering where I fit in. What sort of a family friend I am, how close, and to whom. If I won't tell, does it get to the point where you take me down to the cells and beat me with rubber hoses?'

In spite of himself, Skinner smiled at her frankness, and her jest. 'No. I have other people who do that sort of thing.'

She grinned in her turn. 'Stop, I give in.' She spoke in a

light, cultured Scots accent; rural and north of the Tay, Skinner guessed.

In a flash she was serious again. 'Look, you'll be aware, surely, of the stories about Alan's marriage being on the rocks.'

Skinner nodded.

'Well, they're true. Of course I know that most women in my position would claim this, but I'm not the cause of it. I'm the consequence. Honor Ballantyne opted out of Alan's life five years ago. She lives in London full-time now. She has her own career, and she's having an affair with a Liberal peer. Just so you know everything about me, I live in Alan's constituency. I'm a partner in a firm of solicitors in Aberdeen, called Goldstone and Ferris. Look me up: Charlotte Mays, spelled M-A-Y-S. Tenth on the list of partners out of fourteen. I specialise in Maritime Law. I've passed my Rights of Audience exams, and appear occasionally in the Court of Session.

'I've paid my subs to the Tory Party since I was twenty-three, but I didn't do anything for them until last year. Then a girlfriend got me involved in organising the constituency Christmas dance. I met Alan there, for the first time. I thought nothing of it. I was too busy selling tombola tickets. The next thing to happen was that my friend persuaded me to go on a branch committee. That was how I really met Alan. We went canvassing together in the spring, and it just took off from there. This is the first time I've been sort of "in residence" here. Alan thinks we should come out into society in easy stages. Everybody in the Constituency Association knows about us already, and they all seem to approve. They haven't had an MP's wife there for God knows how long, and they feel deprived. So, far from being a shameless hussy, I'm almost the flavour of the month.'

'What about the other political parties?' Skinner asked. 'Won't someone run to the media?'

'Not in politics, Mr Skinner. In our constituency, the SNP are the opposition. Their standard-bearer is screwing his secretary, so he won't say anything. The Liberals don't play the game that way, as a matter of principle, and as for the Labour candidate, he's one of my partners at Goldstones. No, the real problem is Honor Ballantyne. Alan's asked her for a quiet divorce, but she's looking for a horrendous amount of money to agree. They have two daughters, you know. One's ten, the other fourteen. So it's stalemate on that front, for the moment. Alan's even thinking about counter-suing, claiming adultery with the Liberal peer.'

'Silly bugger if he does.'

'As a lawyer, I agree with you. As one of the points in the triangle, I'm selfish. I just wish it could be sorted out.' For the first time, traces of pain and frustration showed through the outer shell of her self-assurance.

Skinner's smile was sympathetic. 'I understand that.

'Look, I'm sorry to have pressed the question, Miss Mays—'

'Carlie, please.'

'OK, Carlie. But since you know what my job is, you'll understand why. I'm responsible not just for advising Alan on security policy, but for his personal security as well. I have to know everything about him, and to know about everything that could affect him, and the Government.'

'Yes. I understand all that. So what do you think? Do we worry you?'

Skinner decided to tell her the truth. 'Yes, the way things are, you do. Your relationship, as long as it remains secret, could lay Alan open to all sorts of external pressure. My duty is to the office of Secretary of State, not to a man, or to an MP, and my advice can't take your interests into account. But you might like it nonetheless. On the basis that he's serious about you, I would advise that you go public, and take what political flak there is. But that's business for later. Right now we have a crisis to handle.'

Together, Skinner and Carlie Mays climbed the stairs. She ushered him into the dining room and closed the door behind him.

Ballantyne was seated with his back to the door, at the end of a long mahogany dining table strewn with paper. A bulky document case, bound in red leather, lay open at his feet. He looked over his shoulder as Skinner entered the room, and, laying his thick Mont Blanc fountain pen down on the table, went over to greet him.

'Bob, hello. You sounded very serious when you phoned. What's happened?'

Quickly, Skinner informed the Secretary of State of the murder of Hilary Guillaum, then he handed him the third letter. As he read it, Ballantyne slumped into one of the dining chairs. When he had finished he laid the single sheet of paper on the table and leaned back in his chair, with his right hand trembling over his eyes.

'Oh, sweet Jesus Christ. We're responsible, Bob. If we only hadn't stood on principle.'

At first, Skinner thought that Ballantyne's use of the plural included him, too, until he remembered his earlier claim to have consulted the Prime Minister. He said nothing as the Secretary of State sat lost for a while in his panicking thoughts, but watched the man gradually compose himself again. Eventually Ballantyne stood up from the table and walked over to the Adam fireplace, its hearth lit by imitation coals. He leaned against the mantelpiece, as he had done in the drawing room twenty-four hours before, and looked back across the room towards Skinner, who was still standing near the door.

'Well, Bob? Did we sign her death warrant?'

The tall policeman stared back at him, dispassionately. As he did so, all of his gnawing doubts about Ballantyne surged up to the surface. There was a clear trace of panic in the man's eyes, and the faintest trembling still in his movements. Skinner doubted that Ballantyne had ever dreamed of his prestigious office throwing him into the midst of such a crisis. Now his expression begged for absolution; and relief washed across his face when Skinner gave it to him.

'No, Alan. I don't think you did. Not this one, at any rate. The way this murder was done, it was planned well in advance. I had a call on my way down here. We've made two solid discoveries at the Sheraton. The first was a chambermaid's uniform stuffed in a servicing cart on the same floor as Hilary Guillaum's suite. The second was its original wearer, in a cleaner's cupboard. She was in her bra and knickers, trussed up like she was ready for the oven, and blindfolded and gagged with tape. The girl's still hysterical, but when she's calm enough to talk, she'll confirm for us, I've no doubt, that she was grabbed from behind by more than one person, bundled into the cupboard and stripped of her uniform. They'll have gagged her at once so that she couldn't scream, then blindfolded her so that she couldn't see any of them. If we had published that letter, Hilary Guillaum might well be alive now, but I'm pretty certain she'd still be dead tomorrow. Remember, they've promised more incidents, and we've been assuming they'll look for high-profile targets. What the third letter tells us is that they'll be looking for international targets as well. Hilary Guillaum's murder was well planned. They didn't just knock her off to force you to go public. They'd have done it anyway.'

'What do we do now? Give in to them?'

Suddenly Skinner's disappointment in Ballantyne swelled to overflowing. 'Christ, man, where is it about giving in? Look, you're the politician. You take the decisions. I'd have thought it was pretty fucking obvious what you do, but I'm just a poor simple copper. Dig up the Prime Minister wherever he is. Tell him you're going to call a press conference today to lay out the whole scene. You're going to say that Scotland is under terrorist attack, and that the Government is determined to see the threat off. While you're at it, you should call on all the opposition parties to make public declarations of support for your position. You tell the public that all possible steps are being taken to protect Festival venues, and that you're counting on them to show their contempt for the terrorists by making it business as usual.'

'What if the PM disagrees?'

'You're not asking him, you're telling him. Neither of you has any option any more. Hilary Guillaum's been murdered, remember. That's major international news, and the enemy's already called a satellite news channel with the story. Of course, they used the code-word. On the way down here, I told my guys that they could confirm the information, and give the details. It'll be on air in the States by now, and here too for those who tune in to that station. Everyone else will follow it up. The genie's out of the bottle, Alan.'

Ballantyne spun round to face Skinner. '*You* said they could confirm it,' he shouted, suddenly red faced. 'On whose authority?'

'On mine!' Skinner roared back. 'This is a murder. It's my city, and I'm in charge of the investigation – not you. My call. End of story – or you can find yourself a new security adviser.'

The Secretary of State looked at him with a mixture of amazement and apprehension, realising that he was seeing just a flash of the danger in the man: the frightening Skinner of whom Sir James Proud had spoken. Quickly he backed down.

'Bob, you are quite right. Please forgive my outburst. This affair is preying on me. I will do as you recommend. And I'd like you to be with me when I confront the press. I have a number to contact the PM, so let's raise him now. Then we'll have Licorish call the press conference. Let's see. It's nearly four now. Shall we invite everyone here for, say, 5:30?'

Skinner's anger was, as usual with him, quick to dissipate. 'Sounds fine, Alan. Sorry I blew my cool, too.

'Where is the Prime Minister anyway?'

'He's at EuroDisney with his family – and with a small press contingent. He's given all of us orders to be nice to the French, though God knows why. This seems to be his way of setting an example.'

'OK, then, so you dig him out of the Magic Kingdom and update him on the real world. Meanwhile, I'll get Licorish moving.'

Skinner hurried from the residence, and, from his car, he called the Director of Information and instructed him to set up a meeting with the press for the time that he and Ballantyne had agreed. Then he called Martin.

'Andy. A check for me please.

'Miss Charlotte Mays. Solicitor. Age thirty-something. Partner in a firm called Goldstone and Ferris, Aberdeen. Everything there is to know, please. I'm on my way back.'

Twenty-three

'There must be fifty people in there.'

The Secretary of State was staring nervously at a monitor screen set up by the police audio-visual unit in the Special Branch Office suite. On the advice of Michael Licorish, the press briefing had been transferred to the main hall at Fettes Avenue, both because of the potential turn-out and because of the difficulty of providing full security cover at St Andrew's House at such short notice.

'I can't ever recall such a turn-out for a press conference in Scotland. Can you, Bob?'

'One or two. But they had to do either with murder or football. You see, you only deal with politics as a rule, so when you have a press conference up here, or even at Westminster, you see the same half-dozen or so faces, again and again. Whereas if we have a briefing here that's to do with a really sensational murder case, we'll have a turn-out not far short of this one. Best of all, though, is if it's anything to do with football, say crowd misbehaviour, or stadium regulations. Then they're breaking down the doors trying to get in. The press are governed by the laws of supply and demand, just like any other business, and the sad fact is, Secretary of State, our stuff sells more papers than your stuff!'

Andy Martin, who had vivid memories of earlier occasions, looked at Skinner thoughtfully, but said nothing.

Ballantyne grunted. 'Sad fact indeed, Bob. Violence and soccer. The twin opiates of the masses. Come on, Michael,' he said to Licorish, with forced humour, 'lead on and let's face the scribbling classes.'

There were six television crews crammed together on a hastily erected platform at the back of the hall, behind theatre-style seating which held around forty newspaper and broadcast journalists. Most were home-based Scots, but the numbers had been swelled by writers and broadcasters from England and beyond, currently in Edinburgh on assignment to cover the Festival, but pitched suddenly into the midst of the fastest breaking story of the day.

The three participants, with Licorish in front and Skinner bringing up the rear, entered from a door to the right of the table at which they were to sit. It was placed in front of a simple blue backdrop, kept for media occasions, which had been assembled quickly that afternoon by Alan Royston, the police press officer. The noisy air-extractors in the high-ceilinged hall had been switched off. The day outside was still blazing hot, and already many of the audience were perspiring freely.

Ballantyne took the seat in the centre of the table, with Skinner on his right. The two were introduced formally to their inquisitors by Michael Licorish. Ballantyne opened a blue folder, which he had carried with him into the hall, and produced a prepared statement which he began to read to the hushed assembly.

He recounted the events of the previous thirty hours, from the Waverley Centre explosion to the murder of Hilary Guillaum. He thanked the media for their restraint in withholding publication of the first threatening letter, saying that it had allowed full security measures to be put in place at each of the major Festival venues, without alarming the public unduly in the process. But he made no mention of the second letter.

As he reached his conclusion he said: 'As most of you will know, Assistant Chief Constable Skinner also acts as my adviser on security matters. I am very pleased to say that at my request he has formed, within the past twenty-four hours, an elite anti-terrorist squad to deal with this new and unexpected threat. I have assured him that he will have all the facilities he needs to enable him to catch this group and shut it down. He bears a heavy responsibility, but I have every confidence that he will succeed. At the same time, the public can have confidence that the security precautions which have been taken under his direction will prove effective, and that the horrifying actions perpetrated by this ruthless group will not be repeated.

'The people of Scotland, whose Festival this is, have been targeted by this group of desperate men. They have given the lie to their bluster about freedom by their willingness to use violence against those same people whose imaginary cause they purport to champion. I ask all Scots, and those who are among us as our guests, to show their support for the actions I have taken by declaring business as usual at the Edinburgh Festival. I pledge that these bandits will be hunted down and punished to the full extent of the law. We can all feel safe under the protection of Mr Skinner and his team, while these terrorists should know that they will have no refuge while they remain among us. Scotland will not give in to them. The Government will never accede to their demands.' Ballantyne paused, and stared across at the rows of seats, then beyond them at the television cameras. 'I give them warning that their days are numbered. Thank you all.'

Skinner's face was visibly grim as Ballantyne finished. He

had been staggered by the Secretary of State's assumption of copyright over the creation of the anti-terrorist squad. And he had been shocked by the way that he had been set up. He knew that Ballantyne's promise of total safety at the Festival was a sham. Equally he knew who had been placed squarely in the firing line should things go badly wrong. All of his burgeoning doubts about the Secretary of State's valour in a crisis crystallised finally into a certainty that the man was innately treacherous.

A question broke into his thoughts.

'Mr Ballantyne. Dave Bassett, TNI Bureau Chief, London. I'd like to ask about the reference to an ultimatum in the second communiqué. I have information that this relates to a warning given to you this morning that – and I quote my source – "stern action" would be taken unless you lifted the news blackout by midday.'

'Who told you that?' Ballantyne snapped back.

'That doesn't matter. If it is true, what was the point in holding out?'

The Secretary of State stared at Bassett. As Ballantyne replied, Skinner felt him shaking beside him.

'Yes it is true that we received such a communication. Mr Skinner was involved in our decision. Perhaps he can best explain our thinking.'

There was a faint smile of acknowledgement on Skinner's face as he glanced towards Ballantyne, but his eyes, locking on the other man's for a fraction of a second, said something completely different.

'Thank you, Secretary of State. Mr Bassett, all I can say to you is that we took a view at the time. I don't believe that our decision led to this unfortunate lady's murder. I am quite certain that it was planned all along, and it's quite clear that she was chosen as a victim who would attract the maximum international attention. You'll agree with that, I think.'

Bassett nodded.

'These are ruthless, evil people,' Skinner went on. 'We've had only a little over twenty-four hours to weigh them up, but it seems clear to me already that they are not operating on any spur-of-the-moment basis, and that they are well resourced both in terms of equipment and manpower. Yesterday's atrocity and today's were both well planned. The bomb used a sophisticated and fairly rare type of explosive, one that hasn't been encountered before in the UK. We believe that two or three people were involved in Miss Guillaum's murder, and that one of them may have been a woman. We have to assume that what has happened so far is part of a longer-term strategy. My officers and I have to try to anticipate each move as far as we can, and aim, at the same time, to make the city as safe as we can.'

John Hunter, a veteran Edinburgh reporter, and an old friend of Skinner's, raised a hand. 'Bob, can you tell us something about the precautions you're taking?'

'Some of them are obvious. For example, we're sealing up litter bins and welding down underground access covers. All traffic cones will be taken off the streets so that no one can leave anything nasty under them. On-street parking by private motorists, other than residents displaying valid permits, will be banned in the city centre. We're setting up temporary car parks and running shuttle bus services free of charge. Our press officer will issue details of locations as you leave, and they'll be published in tomorrow's *Scotsman* and *Evening News*. We're putting other things in place as well, but I'm not going to talk about them.'

Bassett broke in again. 'Mr Skinner, can the public really

have faith in your guarantee of safety, as just expressed by Mr Ballantyne? It didn't do Hilary Guillaum much good, did it?'

Skinner glared at the fat man, as he sat sweating in his short-sleeved shirt. It was a look which said: 'Don't challenge me, friend. Don't push, it could be dangerous.' Even in the superheated hall, he felt an alien coldness spread over him. He was under fire again. This time there were words, not bullets, but the intent was as hostile, nonetheless.

Bassett picked up the warning in the eyes, and when he spoke again, his tone was noticeably more circumspect. 'I mean aren't these people fanatics, and can you protect one hundred per cent against types like that?'

Skinner stared at him for a few seconds more, then slowly shook his head. 'No. No, I don't think they are fanatics. A fanatic is a person suffering from an excess of zeal. Look it up in your *Consise Oxford*. I don't see that here. Nothing these "Fighters for an Independent Scotland" –' his voice was tinged with scorn '– have said leads me to believe that they are willing to fight to the death, at least not their own. They make bold statements about sacrifice, but only sacrifice by others. You won't find any of them charging into a hail of gunfire. People like that can be dealt with. The other sort, the true fanatics, are always likely to do damage simply because they don't expect to walk away.'

He looked away from Bassett and directly towards the bank of television cameras. 'I cannot say to the public that there is no risk. Of course there is. The plain fact is that this city and all of its people are now under terrorist attack. But I can say three things. First, these people will not succeed. Second, each of us can help knock them on the head by looking out for, and reporting to the police, anything that looks at all suspicious. Third, it isn't a matter of just making them go away. These are murderous louts who have killed two people, and who are going to pay for it. That's my promise, to you and to them.'

Like Ballantyne before him, but instinctively, he too paused and looked directly at the cameras.

'We're all in this together, and the world is watching us. So let's stand up to these terrorists, let's smoke them out, and let's have justice for Danny Baker, for Hilary Guillam, and for us all.'

He held his gaze on the cameras for several seconds. And then something happened; something quite unexpected and quite unique. John Hunter first, then a second, then three more journalists began to applaud, all of them Scots, and all of them long in the media tooth.

Taken aback and embarrassed, Skinner rose from the table, motioned Ballantyne and Licorish to their feet, and led them from the hall.

'Good on you, Bob,' Hunter called out just before the swing-door closed behind them.

Skinner led Ballantyne up a short flight of stairs. Licorish remained behind in the corridor to cope with the media as they left, and to answer any remaining questions.

At the top of the stairs, Skinner opened the door to the command corridor with his pass key, and held it open for Ballantyne. It had no sooner closed behind them than the Secretary of State turned on him.

'Nice speech, Bob.' His voice was laden with sarcasm. 'I didn't realise you were a politician too!'

The other man was there inside him again, so swiftly that Skinner could not keep him bottled up. It was as if someone else, not he, grabbed Ballantyne by the throat and slammed him against the wall. And for his part, Ballantyne, raised to his tiptoes and beginning to purple, saw the menace in Skinner's unfamiliar expression and heard the threat in his cold, hard, quiet voice.

'You set me up in there, mister. You put your miserable politician's hide first, and everything else second, you chicken-hearted little bastard. "It's all down to Skinner." That's what you were saying to those people. "If it goes wrong, it's his fault. Hilary Guillaum? Don't look at me. I'd have done as they asked and gone public. Ask Skinner about it. Anything else goes wrong, blame him." I'd thought more of you than that, but now I know better. You're the sort who would lay down the life of his best friend to save his own, aren't you, Alan. Without a second fucking thought. When the shit hits the fan, we know where to find you: hiding under the table, keeping your nice suit clean. When this is over, pal, you can get yourself a new security adviser. Until then do not, repeat *do not*, fuck me about again!'

Twenty-four

'Come on, Bob. Snap out of it. The girls'll be back in a minute.'

'Eh, what? Oh, sorry, Andy. I was somewhere else.'

'You still mad at Ballantyne?'

'What makes you think I ever was?'

'Come off it. I was watching you when he put you on the spot back there.'

'Nah. That was no problem. Here they are. Let's go.'

He stood up and led the way out of the Filmhouse bar, to meet his wife and Julia Shahor as they emerged from the ladies' room. The evening's performance, a Louis Malle feature, was scheduled to begin in only a few minutes. They had almost reached the auditorium when Julia was called to the telephone.

'Go on in, you two,' said Andy. 'I'll wait for Julia.'

She was gone for only a few minutes. As soon as she reappeared at the foot of the staircase he could see that something was wrong. She looked close to tears.

'What is it, love?'

'Oh Andy! She's cancelled!'

For a few seconds a frown of puzzlement creased his forehead. Then his eyebrows rose. 'What, you mean . . . what's-her-name?'

'Yes. That was her agent. She's heard about Hilary

Guillaum, and she's said that no way is she coming. The bitch! How could she! What a coward.'

'And that's what other people will think, sweetheart. It's not surprising, though. I've a feeling she could be the first of many. Damn shame, though. I was looking forward to processing her in person!'

'That's all right,' said Julia, squeezing his arm and brightening up in an instant. 'You can process me instead!'

Twenty-five

Bob and Sarah had been home for only ten minutes when Alex turned up with the supper guest she had invited earlier in the day.

'Hello, Ingo. Good to meet you again.' Bob stretched out a hand to the Swede, as he stood in the doorway of the sitting room. Smiling, he looked the younger man square in the eye. Ingo shook his hand powerfully, holding his gaze unblinking, with a faint but confident grin. 'Come on through. Sarah's working one of her microwave miracles.' Bob led the way through to the conservatory, where an oval table was set for four.

Supper was a spicy lemon chicken dish, which Sarah had prepared earlier in the day. Bob helped her to serve it, spooning out portions of light, fluffy rice. Since Ingo would have to drive later, Bob decreed that they would all drink Gleneagles spring water which, he assured their guest, had more life to it than most white wines, and certainly more than any from north of the Mediterranean or south of the Equator.

Alex was still on a high from her evening's performance. She spoke so fast she was almost breathless, as she rushed to tell Bob and Sarah of the group's first review, which was scheduled to appear in the next morning's *Scotsman*, and which would be 'absolutely rave', or so their director had been assured by the arts editor. He had said that it would make special reference to the quality of the lighting, and of its importance to the flow of the play.

'Isn't Ingo brilliant, folks? And it's only his hobby!'

'You're not a professional electrician?' Bob's question spoke volumes. His inflection was such that it was as if he had said straight out, 'Tell me all there is to know about you, young man.'

Suddenly silenced, Alex looked at him curiously.

'No, sir. Not in that sense,' said the Swede. 'I have a degree in mining engineering, and now I do what you would call post-grad research at university in Sweden. The theatre work I do for fun, as something different. And it helps me pass this summer.'

'But it's unpaid?'

'Yes, my amateur status remains intact!' He laughed, self-assured.

'They must look after you well in Sweden. Here, damn few postgraduates can afford to be amateur at anything.'

'In Sweden is no different. But I have a scholarship.'

'A good one, obviously.'

'Big enough for me anyway. It comes from a foundation set up by a South African mining company. The story goes that they were anxious to atone for their racial policy, and so they decided to set up scholarships at universities around the world, mostly for black students of mining. But what they found was that only Sweden would take their money. Of course there are very few black students in Sweden, and none at all in mining engineering! Still, the scholarship is very generous and so, for someone who is no more than a researcher, I am, as you say here, rolling in it.'

Only Alex did not join in the laughter.

'So what brought you to Edinburgh?'

'I have heard much of your Festival. I had hoped to come with a Swedish group, but they could not raise the cash. It was suggested that I write to the Festival people and offer my services. To tell truth, I was coming anyway, but the Glasgow people had an emergency, they call me, and here I am, in this very fine play, in your lovely city.'

'What sort of emergency?'

Alex broke in. 'I thought I'd told you. Our regular lighting technician went on holiday to Gran Canaria last month. On the way back, the Spanish airport police searched his rucksack, and found lots of white powder in a big talcum tin. Only it wasn't talc. The story goes that it was a kilo of heroin. He's in jail now, waiting to be tried. He swears he's innocent, that it was planted on him.'

Skinner laughed out loud and shook his head. 'Sorry, love. The smack smuggler isn't born yet who won't say that when he gets nicked. Doesn't matter whether it's Las Palmas or Las Pilton, the story's always the same. "Who? Me, officer? Never saw it before in my life." We had this lady once, off a holiday flight at Edinburgh. The stuff was tied up in a French letter, hidden, shall we say about her person. Know what she said? That her boyfriend has asked her to take it through, but that he had told her they were the diamonds for her engagement ring, packed in icing sugar. Romantic, eh. The only trouble was she was travelling alone. She claimed her boyfriend had missed the flight.'

'Hold on, darling,' said Sarah, breaking in. 'I could almost swallow that.'

Bob raised his eyebrow in an exaggerated gesture. 'You could what?'

Her mouth fell open and she flushed bright pink.

'Be that as it may,' he went on, '*we* didn't. Turned out the boyfriend was her husband, a Spanish brigand with a ton of form. They missed him in Malaga. They said they reckoned he was hiding out in La Gomera, till he could get across to Africa. We keep waiting for him to turn up on visiting day at Cornton Vale. No joy yet, though. Not one visit in five years. Some husband, eh.' He shook his head. 'No, sorry, Alex. Your lighting man got greedy, and got caught. You might see him again in around fifteen years.'

He smiled back across the table at the Swede. 'So the lights man's ill wind blew you some good, Ingo.'

'Yes, sir. So it seems.'

'Enough of the "sir", the name's Bob, remember.' He twisted the top off the Gleneagles bottle and topped up his guest's glass. 'Is mining a family thing, Ingo? Is that what your father does?'

The Swede laughed. 'No, no. Nothing like that. The opposite, I should say. He was an airline pilot with SAS.'

'There's a coincidence,' Skinner muttered.

'Pardon?'

'Sorry, a private joke. Rude of me. I have one of his colleagues working with me just now, in a manner of speaking. SAS: Scandinavian Airlines. How about your mother?'

'Ah. Like Alex, my mother died when I was very young.'

'Ahh. That's too bad. Anyway, enough of that. Dig into those strawberries.'

By the time the meal was over, Skinner had learned a great deal about Ingemar Svart. But he had been concentrating so hard on his gentle cross-examination that he had failed to notice the frown as it gathered and deepened on his daughter's face. Alex had hardly closed the door from saying her goodnight to the Swede, when she squared up to him.

'Pops, just what is it with you?'

'What do you mean?'

'You interrogated Ingo like a suspect.'

Bob laughed, but he was taken aback by an edge in her voice which he had never heard before. 'Your artistic imagination's running away with you.'

'Like hell it is. You gave the guy the third degree. You were rude and inquisitive. Are you coming the heavy father or something?'

'Hey, calm down, girl. A man comes into our house with my daughter; it's natural to want to know something about him.'

'Not his collar size and inside-leg measurement, for Christ's sake. What is this? Since when did you bring the office home with you.'

For the first time that he could remember, Bob Skinner raised his voice in anger to his daughter. 'Since when? Since innocent people started to get killed in Edinburgh, for no reason other than being useful propaganda fodder, or for just being expendable. Did you see the TV news this evening? Recognise anyone – such as me? Get used to it, honey. Till this thing's over, no one in this town's going to be a stranger to me. Did you collect your pass tonight?'

Alex looked puzzled. 'Yes. So what?'

'You filled in a form?'

'Yes.'

'Right. Even now, as we stand here shouting at each other, the information on that form, and on every other form we collected tonight, is being run through a computer. That's called security. It's called taking precautions. It's all we can do against these people. God knows, it's not much, and it's probably useless, but at least it's something. Our best protection is all the information we can get about all the people in this city. That includes your friend Ingo.'

'And me?'

'Yes. Crazy as it may seem: *and* you. Just in case, through in Glasgow, you've fallen in with the sort of people who do the sort of things Sarah and I have seen close up in the last couple of days. And just in case, as your father, I'm too close to read the signs.'

'Then thank you, Father, for your love and trust.' The living-room door rattled on its hinges as she slammed it behind her.

Bob turned to Sarah. Amazement, tinged with hurt, showed on his face. 'What the bloody hell was all that about?'

'Hey, big man. Cool down.' She wound her arms around his neck and kissed him slowly, ruffling his hair. 'Read the signs, Dad. She thought you were attacking her man, so she defended him.'

'What d' you mean, her man?'

'I mean that our Alex has got it bad, and it shows – to everyone but you, that is.'

'But she's only a—'

'Slip of a girl, you were going to say? Oh no she isn't, my darling. Oh no, she isn't.'

Twenty-six

SCOTLAND DEFIANT AGAINST TERROR.

The banner headline of Monday Morning's *Scotsman* blared up at Skinner from the table as he joined Sarah for breakfast in the conservatory. He picked it up and saw himself on the front page, seated beside a subdued Ballantyne at the press conference, and looking hard at Dave Bassett as he faced him down.

He scanned the accompanying stories, which took up the entire front page, then turned to the leader column. He snorted quietly as he read the editorial, which praised the Secretary of State for displaying a firm and resolute face to the terrorists, and for his good sense in handing over complete responsibility to his security adviser.

'Mr Skinner and his newly formed squad bear a heavy responsibility,' it read. 'We are confident that they are up to the challenge. Yet it must be noted that however distinguished they may be as police officers, they are inexperienced in facing the type of threat which now confronts them. While no blame can be attached to any individual for failing to prevent the two deaths which took place at the weekend, security precautions are now in place and the public have a right to expect them to be effective.'

He threw the paper on to a chair and glanced at Sarah. 'Did you see the leader?'

She nodded, unsmiling. 'Odd, isn't it. It seems to say that Ballantyne's done all he possibly can, and that from now on it's all down to you if anything else happens.'

Bob shrugged his shoulders. 'Joe Compton, the editor – he's an old chum of Ballantyne, and it bloody well shows there. That's politics for you.'

'What are the chances of some other calamity happening?'

'Depends what they want to do. It'll be dangerous for them to target *individuals* from now on, but unless they've run out of Semtex we can look for some more bangs. There's bugger-all we can do about someone leaving a Marks & Spencer bag in the middle of Marks & Spencer, for example. That's what I expect, anyway. My reading of these characters says that they won't expose themselves to direct danger – not the ringleaders at any rate. What d' you think? Got any sort of a profile for me yet?'

'No chance. I've only got three short letters to go on, and frankly there just isn't enough in them to tell me anything about the man who wrote them.'

'Man? Is that an assumption?'

'No it is not. That's one thing I am fairly sure of: it wasn't a woman who wrote them. There's something about – how do I say? – the posture of the language that is decidedly male. Very assertive. Confident. In fact *certain*. Let me put it this way. If the writer of those letters isn't a man, then we're looking for someone as forceful as Germaine Greer – or, and it's just a thought, for more than one person.'

Twenty-seven

When Skinner reached his office he found ample evidence that the security operation was in full swing. His in-tray was piled high with folders, each one listing a different Festival location.

He picked one off the top of the heap. Its subject venue and its contents were noted on the front. He murmured quietly to himself as his eye scanned down the page.

'Signet Library.
'Description of venue.
'Potential hazards.
'Risk assessment.
'Recommendations.
'Inspecting officer's signature: Margaret Rose, Detective Sergeant.'

He opened the folder and read the report. As he expected of a Maggie Rose job, it was thorough, concise, and its recommendations were sound. The Signet Library, she had concluded, was an unlikely target. It would be the location of only four events, each of them part of the 'Official' Festival.

The spectacularly beautiful, pillared room, with its valuable collection of volumes arranged on two levels, was well alarmed. All of the potential access points, other than the main door, were bolted shut, and there was permanent building security all year round. Maggie Rose recommended that the security firm be deployed on a round-the-clock basis, with regular and ostentatious visits by uniformed police officers. Finally she proposed that, during performances, an armed officer, in uniform, should be posted at the main entrance. Her report closed with the suggestion, couched in properly respectful terms, that her senior officers might consider whether widespread deployment of high-profile armed police, in uniform, at all major venues might offer the double benefit of deterring would-be terrorists, while boosting public morale.

Skinner closed the folder and smiled to himself. 'Nice one, Maggie. You'll make inspector before that man of yours, I reckon.' He picked up the telephone and told Martin of her suggestion.

'She's right, boss. We might have enough people to do it, but they'll all have to be qualified marksmen. That could give us a problem.'

'No problem at all. Adam Arrow's SAS guys arrive this evening. Ask him if he minds us sticking them into police uniforms and using them as armed sentries.'

'Will do. Adam's right here.'

Skinner read through the rest of the reports. Each one was marked '*Actioned*', with Andy Martin's initials alongside. When the last of the reports had been consigned to the out-tray, he came upon a ribbon of computer printout sheets, still in fan-fold. A glance told him that they were the results of at least the first checks on the application forms completed by Festival performers. Subjects were listed by name, nationality, and home city. Almost all were marked '*Nothing Known*'. Occasionally there would be a note of some past encounter with the law, mostly motoring offences, with a few drug-use or theft convictions scattered among them. He flicked through the sheets, scanning the names, which were listed as they had been fed into the computer. Near the end, he found the entry for which he had been looking.

'Svart, Ingemar. Age 29, currently residing at 43 Close Avenue, Stockbridge. Student. Swedish national. Interpol check run. Nothing known.'

'Hm. Just as well for you, pal.'

He was about to toss the sheaf of paper into his out-tray when a name at the foot of the page caught his eye. For an instant it made his stomach drop, but a quick look reassured him.

'Skinner, Alexis. Age 20, currently residing at 20 Fairyhouse Avenue, Ediburgh.

Student. Nothing known.'

The sight of Alex's name listed there with the herd, and vetted with the rest, touched his heart. He laughed, but it was forced.

'Just as well for you too, my girl.'

He spent the next half-hour trying to restore a semblance of normality to his working life. In spite of Jimmy Proud's assurance, at the time of his promotion, that the attainment of Chief Officer rank would not affect his operational status as a working detective, inevitably Skinner had become caught up in the bureaucracy that all high command brings with it. He read through the pile of reports, circulars and standing orders which had been left in his pending tray by Ruth, the secretary he shared with the other two Assistant Chief Constables.

Fortunately, most were circulation copies of documents which had been dealt with by Harry Gass, the ACC responsible for Management Services. He absorbed their essence as quickly as possible, committing them to memory as best he could. The few which called for his executive action he placed to the side, to be dealt with when his concentration was less affected by the immediate crisis.

Eventually he gave up. He picked up his jacket and headed along the corridor to the Special Branch suite. The outer door had been labelled 'Anti-terrorist Squad'.

Adam Arrow was seated behind a desk, reading the *Sun* and looking bored.

'Come on, Adam. You've had the Mario McGuire tour of Edinburgh. Now I'll give you the Bob Skinner version.'

They left the building and climbed into the BMW, which was parked in one of half-a-dozen reserved spaces in front of the main entrance.

Skinner's tour of Edinburgh followed none of the usual routes. Arrow noticed the absence of open-topped, green Guide Friday tourist buses in the parts of the city through which he was driven.

'All this, Adam.' Skinner said as he drove, 'all this is ours. This is where my people and I work most of the time. There's little or no corporate crime in Edinburgh, or anywhere else in Scotland, you know. My Fraud Squad, and the Regional Crime guys, occasionally get to deal with a bent lawyer diverting clients' funds, or with some idiots who think they can get away with mortgage swindles, but dishonesty up here mostly involves poor skint bastards turning over the DSS for a few extra quid. Normally, the city centre's as clean as a whistle. Edinburgh, at the top end of the social scale, is a city of Holy Willies. Not like Glasgow. You'll find far more spivs and hooligans through there. But down here – in the bits of Edinburgh that the visitors don't get told about – is where my CID does its real hard slogging. I've seen detective officers in tears of sheer frustration at the work they have to face here. I've lost a couple of them through emotional breakdowns. Ten years ago this place was Smack City; we had one of the worst drug problems in Europe. Every week we found at least one kid dead up a close with a needle hanging out of his arm.

'We had families living in hell, respectable people but with a drug-dealer next door, who'd be turning the stuff out through his kitchen window like ice-cream. And these poor folk would be terrified that, if we turned the place over, the guy's pals would assume they'd grassed, and they'd get a kicking, or worse. And that happened too. I remember once when some of my lads busted a dealer. One of them knew the bloke next door slightly. He nodded to him, just briefly, as they took the villain away. Two nights later, the same neighbour staggered into his house with his throat cut, and bled to death on the living-room carpet in front of his wife and kids.'

Arrow hissed, grim-faced, sucking breath between his teeth. 'Is it still like that?'

'Not so bad now. It took us years, but we broke most of the big drug-dealers. None of them was hard to find. Christ, they used to fit steel doors to their council houses, so it would take longer for us to bash them in. The trick for us was to catch them dirty. We just kept battering away at them, though. We used every legitimate trick in the book: bogus DSS investigations, officers dressed up as meter readers, council workmen, you name it. One by one, we nicked them, and when we did, our judges did the business. As a policeman I've got a lot of time for the old boys in the High Court, in their red robes. "Dealing in Horse, my man? That'll be fifteen years of your time, thank you very much. Next case please." They didn't piss about when we needed them.

'All the big dealers are gone now. There's still a fair bit of drugs about, but it's well underground now. There seems to be a different distribution network. The estates aren't blighted and terrorised the way they used to be, but they're still hard, violent places. These blocks of flats might not look so bad, at least not the ones that have had a lick of paint, but a lot of them are still castles of misery, lived in by poor, frightened people, bullied by the DSS, the tally-men, even at times, I have to admit, by the police.'

He negotiated a roundabout, glowering across at Arrow. 'But do you know what hacks me off, Adam? Back in the Eighties, there we were tackling and beating one of the worst drug problems in Europe, and few if any people outside Edinburgh knew or cared about it. They didn't know, because it wasn't hot news. It was like murders in Ireland, everyday occurrences, so it only got a wee bit of coverage, short lived and mainly local. Didn't matter that it was a tragedy. It had no news value. Yet look at Edinburgh now. Some arseholes set off a firework and murder a primadonna, and we've got every news organisation in the world demanding to know what we're going to do about it. The world's unjust, Adam. A rich and famous person becomes a victim, and we have a media shit-storm. OK, well and good, and so we should have. But where were they all eight years ago when that poor wee man died in his front room, with his blood spraying all over his three-year-old daughter? Just two newspapers carried that story. *Two:* that's all.'

As Skinner spoke, they wound their way through the area which had been the battleground in the fight against the dealers. Wester Hailes, the windows of its high-rise blocks glinting in the sun. Niddrie, beginning to look scruffy again a few years on from its last cosmetic repainting. Pilton, much of it still grey and terrible, its poverty proclaimed by the boarded windows, the steel shutters guarding its shops even as they did business, and the burnt-out cars in its school grounds.

Skinner swung the car down towards Newhaven and the east. 'Enough, Adam, enough. Now at least you know that all human misery isn't concentrated in Belfast. Come on and I'll show you the other side of my patch. I need to clear my mind.'

They drove through Leith and Seafield, by-passed Portobello, and headed out of the city on the A1. As they passed the Craigpark retail centre, he glanced across at his passenger.

'You a golfer, Adam?'

'Not so's you'd fookin' notice, but I play.'

'Good lad. It's too nice a day to waste.'

Twenty minutes later they were in Gullane, in Bob and Sarah's 'other house', as they had come to call it. As Adam admired the garden in full bloom, Bob delved into a cavernous cupboard, emerging eventually with his golf kit, Sarah's ladies' clubs, and a pair of her studded shoes which proved an ideal fit for the stocky little soldier.

Gullane number-one course was mostly clear. There were no party bookings, and as Bob looked down the first two fairways and up to the third tee, high on the hill, he could see only one match, nearing the long second green in its peculiar ravine. He recognised the players: two of the club's many retired bankers.

Waved on to the tee by the bespectacled starter, he showed his guest the line to the first green with a low straight shot, hit with a two iron. The ball seemed to run for ever on the hard, brown fairway.

Arrow selected Sarah's metal three wood, teed low, and

boomed off a drive which headed straight for the far side of the roadway, and for the garden of one of the big white houses which ran parallel to the fairway on the right. But just as Skinner's hand crept up to cover his eyes, the ball drew back in towards the fairway, cleared the waiting sand-trap, bounced, and ran on to finish only twenty yards or so short of the green.

'"Not so's you'd fookin' notice," indeed!' Skinner mimicked.

They each took four, then halved the next three holes, before Arrow's aggression lost him a ball on the difficult, rising dog-leg fifth. Skinner was still one up when they climbed on to the seventh tee, the highest point on Gullane Hill. Like all first-time visitors to the famous old course, Arrow was stunned by the finest view in golf. The wide estuary of the River Forth sparkled in the sun, its waters flat calm at ebb tide. The watermark was so low that the grounded wreck of the Great War submarine in Aberlady Bay could be seen clearly.

Bob recited the names of each of the six golf courses which were in view from the hill-top, then pointed his way along the Fife coast opposite, past Kirkcaldy and the Methil rig yard, on to the East Neuk villages, Largo, Earlsferry, Elie, St Monans, Pittenweem, Anstruther and, in the far distance, Crail.

'By Christ, Bob. Why bother to play fookin' golf? Why not just come straight up here and enjoy it?'

Skinner laughed. 'Many's the time I've wished I had done just that, mate. And it tends to be all downhill from here, in more ways than one.'

Their match continued as tight as it had begun. Each was fiercely competitive, and Sarah's clubs seemed to suit Arrow perfectly. However, Skinner's straighter game gave him the edge, until they shook hands on the green of the short sixteenth, after the little soldier had missed a ten-foot putt for a match-saving half. Both to celebrate and to demonstrate, on the seventeenth tee Bob took out his boron-shafted driver for the first time, and sent a huge shot soaring over the downward-sloping fairway. His body English seemed to give the shot extra yardage as it squeezed over the cross bunkers guarding the approach to the green.

Arrow came very close to following him, but his ball found the sand.

As they walked down the steep slope, the little soldier looked up at his partner. 'Cool bugger most of the time, ain't yer, Bob. It's as well you don't give people the same treatment you gave that fookin' ball there. Tell me something. You've told me one thing that makes you angry, but is there anything that makes you really mad, really blow your stack?'

As he continued down the hill, Bob looked deep into himself, as if searching for the other Skinner, the one whose appearance he dreaded, as if analysing him, working out what brought him to the surface. Eventually, on the ridge above the bunker, he stopped, and leaned on his clubs.

'That's a better question than you know, Adam, and it's a tough one to answer honestly. But I'll try. You say I'm a cool bugger, but you're wrong. I might be controlled, but that's a different thing. There are, I think, just two things that would make me lose self-control. Christ, I hope there are only two. One is any direct threat to my nearest and dearest: to my wife Sarah or my daughter Alex. Most people would say the same. The other one is betrayal. An act of serious betrayal. That gets me. And if that betrayal is bad enough, then – well let's just say I'm not so nice to know.'

Arrow looked at him shrewdly. 'Betrayal. You mean like what that prick of a Secretary of State of yours did to you at your press conference?'

Skinner's eyes narrowed as he took out his putter. 'Who called the prick a Secretary of State, Adam, that's what I'd like to know,' he said softly, with a cold smile, rolling the ball into the hole.

Twenty-eight

The world was still turning on its axis as normal when Skinner and Arrow returned to Edinburgh from Gullane.

It looked like any other Festival Monday afternoon as they drove along Princes Street. The hospitality marquee above the Waverley Centre had been repaired. Banners bearing the sponsor's corporate logo fluttered from poles set on its supporting pillars. A few guests stood in the entrance, drinks in hand, enjoying the summer day.

Skinner rolled down the windows of the BMW. The sunroof had been open all through the journey from Gullane. As they drove along, they took in the sounds of the street. Competing bagpipers, some live, some no more than taped Muzak floating from the open-fronted shops, competed for attention above the noise of the traffic, vehicular and human. The open-air Fringe sideshow at the Mound was in full swing. Edinburgh was alive: full of bustle. The capital was wearing its bright Festival face, as if there was no threat, as if no crisis existed.

Back at Fettes, Arrow headed for the car which had been assigned to him, and drove straight off to Redford Barracks to await the check-in of his SAS unit. His men were travelling north on various afternoon flights from Heathrow, in groups of two or three.

Skinner settled back into his swivel chair, behind his

desk, at precisely two minutes before 4:00 pm, just in time for his regular Monday meeting with his deputy and the six Divisional heads of CID. As Commander he needed to know everything that was going on throughout the force's sprawling territory. At the same time these weekly meetings as a group encouraged a healthy exchange of information among colleagues.

Once Ruth had brought in coffee and the obligatory chocolate digestives, he gave his fellow detectives a comprehensive run-through of the threat and the security operation. The summary briefing took only ten minutes.

'So that's what we've done,' Skinner said finally, 'and that's who's in the anti-terrorist squad. Any questions, gentlemen?'

'One, sir.'

Skinner looked across at Douglas Armstrong, a big, bluff man from Dalkeith. Armstrong was his nominated deputy and, as a Detective Chief Superintendent, a rank above the Divisional heads. 'Whose side are the politicians on?'

'If you mean our own Board, they're solidly behind us, as always. If you mean ministers, they're backing us too, for the moment at least. We've got a job to do. Let's just do it as well as we can, and earn any thanks we get at the end of the day. And when I say we've got a job to do, I mean you too, whatever your Division, aye, even you down in the Borders, Ron. These people must have a home base. For all the high-flown language, and all that crap, this is just another bloody gang. We don't know how big it is, but there has to be a gang-hut somewhere, a place where the boss is, a place where orders are given – a place where these letters are typed. Even if they're so well organised that they never meet as a complete group, there is still movement and contact between them. They communicate through letters, not over the phone, and they use pretend couriers. There's a contact point, when the courier picks up his envelope – unless of course, he's the author, but that's unlikely.

'So we're not just looking for people, we're looking for that place as well. I want you, in your Divisions, to put all your people on the alert, uniform as well as CID, to keep an eye out for any possibility, however slight. The only forensic knowledge which we have is that the notes were produced by a computer or word processor using a fairly obscure typeface called Venice, and that they were printed on Conqueror paper by a Hewlett Packard Desk-jet.'

He handed each man a manufacturer's brochure showing the ugly but functional square-shaped printer, and a sample sheet of Conqueror paper with its clear watermark.

'If any of your people find anywhere where they see those two items together, they should report it back and let us follow it up. I don't care who the owner is, whether it's your wife's brother or the parish priest, each case is to be reported back. We're checking out all printer stockists and paper suppliers. Both these items are sold over the counter, but we already think we know where the printer was bought: a shop in Queensferry Street, last Tuesday. Buyer paid cash and left a phoney address for product registration. All the assistant could describe was tallish male, may have been dark haired, but he wore a hooded tank-top and shades, so she couldn't be certain. She didn't remember his accent. The shop doesn't sell Conqueror paper, but there's a stockist in William Street, and we're checking it out now.'

'Any prints on either letter?' asked Armstrong.

'No, Douglas, not a smear. Gloves all down the chain. So, gentlemen, unless any one of you has anything else on your patch that's about to go pear shaped, and you need to tell me about in private, that's it for today. See you all here next week, on a group basis again, I think, unless you hear different. Go to it, and good luck.'

Twenty-nine

Heading for home, Skinner was in the act of closing the door of his office behind him when another thought occurred. He went back to his desk and picked up his scrambled telephone, keying in one of forty pre-programmed numbers.

The call was answered brusquely on the first ring. 'Hello.'

'Willie. Skinner here. How are you lot getting on with our pal?'

'No' bad, sir.'

'How are my guys doing?'

'First class. That's a hard big bastard, that McIlhenney. And the boy Macgregor, he's so sharp he'll cut himself.'

'Well just you keep an eye on him and see that he doesn't. Now, what about Macdairmid?'

'He's spent most of the day at the Constituency Labour Party offices. Ah had a tap put on them too. Is that OK wi' you?'

'Yes, for now, but just make sure you remember to take it off as soon as Macdairmid's eliminated as a suspect.'

'Shame! But yes, sir. That's understood. No' that it's produced anything yet that would interest you, other than the guy haranguin' lassies in the Housin' Department, threatenin' them that their jobs 'll no be safe if they don't do as he says.'

'He's not saying he'll use his political clout to have them sacked, is he?'

'Not straight out. Naw. Well it isn't enough for a charge, if that's what ye're thinking; it's nothing that the Crown Office needs to tae hear. Mind you,' Haggerty mused, 'if someone dropped a copy of the transcript tae the *Sun*, it might finish him as an MP.'

'Don't bother yourself, Willie. Nice thought as it is, it would cause too many problems. Anyway, we've got enough on the guy now to make sure that he's quietly de-selected, and we'll do that at the right time. For now just keep tabs on him and see if he leads us anywhere.'

Haggerty grunted. 'Understood. There is one thing, sir. The boy does have a funny habit. Twice, he left the offices and went fur a pint in a pub on Greenlands Road. McIlhenney and Macgregor took turns tailing him. Apparently, each time, he only had a half-pint, and hardly touched that. But each time, he used the pub pay-phone. 'S'that no interesting?'

'It's funny, for sure. It could be anything, though, that he didn't want heard in the office. Calling the girlfriend for example. Still, we'll take a punt on it. As soon as you see him heading for the CLP offices again, put a tap on that pub phone, and let's see what we get.'

Thirty

The rest of the day passed peacefully. Bob and Sarah took in a one-man show, based on the life of Houdini, in a converted church hall in Newington. The star – 'A game guy,' as Bob declared later – performed several of Houdini's easier illusions as part of the show, prevailing upon members of the audience to verify that he was securely chained, or straightjacketed, or boxed in, whatever each trick demanded. Sarah's enjoyment of the show was dampened slightly by a constant niggling fear that Bob's mobile telephone would ring, but it never did.

They returned to their bungalow in Fairyhouse Avenue at around 10:30 pm. Half an hour later, Andy Martin and Julia Shahor arrived for a late supper after the evening's film performance. It was partly a social visit, and partly an opportunity for the two detectives to touch base on the day's events.

While, in the conservatory, Skinner told Martin of Grant Macdairmid's peculiar visits to the pub in Greenlands Road, Sarah and Julia chatted in the kitchen.

'How's your aunt reacting to all the excitement?' Sarah asked.

'She's taken herself off,' said Julia, a note of disappointment creeping into her voice, giving it sudden depth where normally it was flat and devoid of accent. 'She said that I had enough on my hands without having her around, and so she insisted on going back home to Uncle Percy in Brighton. I put her on the Gatwick flight this morning, and he was going to pick her up at the other end. I'm sorry in a way. She likes to be around when it's busy, to help me as best she can. She still does little things about the house. I said I didn't want her to leave, but she had made her mind up.'

'So you're there on your own now?'

Julia smiled. 'Well, not exactly. Andy says that since his work has become involved with mine, and since he insists on looking after me, after my scare the other night, it makes sense for me to move in with him for a week or two. That is nice of him, is it not.'

Sarah laughed. 'Nice! It's amazing. For as long as I've known Andy Martin, he's been adamant that he'd never let a girlfriend hang her clothes in his wardrobe. This sounds serious. He's not the head-over-heels type; and that's not the way you strike me either.'

'I didn't think I was. But when I saw him on Saturday, something just went into melt-down. Earlier tonight he asked me to marry him.'

Sarah's mouth dropped open in amazement. 'He did what! What did you say?'

'I said that he should ask me again in a month. If he does, and if I still feel this same way, then I *will* marry him, and just as fast as I can.'

'Good for you, lady. Bob and I didn't hang about either. We took a little more time over it than you and Andy but, still, we only met last year. He had to be a bit more cautious though, having the other love of his life to consider.'

'What, do you mean his job?'

Sarah smiled again, and shook her head. 'Apart from that! No, I meant Alex, his daughter. If she and I had hated each other, it'd have been difficult for him – and for me too, come to that. It was fine, though. I love Alex. She's like my kid sister, only she's no kid. It's funny, but your moving in with Andy – it's come just at the right time, in a way. It might help Bob understand something he doesn't fathom yet.'

'What's that?'

'Alex and Bob had their first real row last night. I mean their first ever. She brought her new man home for supper, and Bob gave him the third degree. After he'd gone, Alex just blew her stack. So did Bob. This afternoon she came back from her theatre while he was out – she's acting in a play – and picked up some of her clothes and things. She's moved in with Ingo, the boyfriend. I promised I'd break the news to Bob.'

She saw a look of apprehension cloud Julia's face, and was quick to dispel it. 'Don't worry. I won't let it spoil our evening. I'll wait till afterwards, to tell him.'

'What will he do?'

'Well, he might just go and find Ingo and give him a quiet going over.' She paused, and Julia's mouth dropped open, a frown creasing her forehead. Sarah grinned. 'But I think I should be able to stop him doing that. Especially now that I can remind him that you and Andy are in the same situation. He'll sulk for a while, but he'll be OK. Alex wouldn't do anything just for the sake of hurting Bob, and he knows that.'

'Would it help if I asked Andy to talk to him?' said Julia, tentatively.

'God no! Andy treats her like a sister, too. He's known her since she was a little girl. He'd probably have Ingo deported! No, don't say anything to him. We'll let Bob sort himself out first, then he can sort out Andy!'

At the insistence of Sarah and Julia, no shop was talked during supper. Instead Bob replayed, shot by shot, his round of golf with Adam Arrow. The walk in the sun had added a pink touch to his tan and a bleached hint to his hair. His account rose in its superlatives until it climaxed in his description of his eagle two at the seventeenth, passed off casually at the time, for Arrow's benefit, but in fact, a life-time first.

'And what happened at the eighteenth?' asked Andy.

'Trust you, boy. I was going to gloss over that, but OK. Gave it the long handle again, didn't I. Stuffed my drive in that chest-high rough up the right. Bunkered my second ball. Took eight. Anyway, by that time I was thinking about work again.'

In a sense that was true. In fact, as he stood on the tee, he had been considering still, in depth, the subject of betrayal.

Thirty-one

He seemed the usual Skinner on arriving at his office next morning, but Ruth, ever the perceptive secretary, caught a preoccupied, slightly sharp edge to his 'Good morning'.

'Where's Alex?' he had asked, as the door had closed on Andy and Julia seven hours earlier. Then Sarah had told him. He had taken the news better than she had thought he might, but his reaction had opened a new shaft of concern for Alex in Sarah herself.

'Sarah, love, in all of her life since her mother died, the girl's never known disappointment. Some of that I've seen to, but most of the credit's hers. She's never failed an exam in her life. And as far as I can remember, or at least know about, she's never made a serious error of judgement. But I suspect that she's made one this time.'

'What do you mean?'

'I mean that guy Ingo isn't right – not for her at any rate. There's something about him that I don't like. I can't say what it is. All I can tell you that in my time I've interviewed a lot of people in the course of police investigations. I've reached the stage when I can usually smell the wrong ones. And believe me, that fellow smells wrong. He's a self-centred bastard, and he doesn't give a damn about Alex. He's just taking a loan of her.'

'Come on, Bob, you're hardly being objective.'

'I'm hardly objective about criminals either, but I'm usually right.'

Sarah reached out a hand and touched his cheek, whispering as she did,

> ' "Fair seed-time had my soul, and I grew up,
> fostered alike by beauty and by fear." '

'What's that?'

'Wordsworth. It just came into my head, thinking about you and Alex. Your relationship is beautiful, Bob, but there's fear there too. Your fear, every father's fear, of what might happen to his little girl.'

He shook his head. 'I wish it was so simple, or so poetic, lover, but the hair on the back of my neck prickled the first time I ever met the guy, when Alex introduced him just as one of the squad, without even saying there was something between them. And the day I stop trusting the hair on the back of my neck – that day I'll be finished as a detective.'

'Well if you really believe that, what are you going to do?'

'What can I do? I can't talk her round. It's gone too far for that. I could put the fear of God into him, but to do that properly I have a feeling that I might have to break at least one of his legs! And what would that do for me and Alex? It'd never be the same again.

'No, I – what do I mean *I* – *we* just have to accept it for now, but watch the situation and be around to pick up the pieces when he dumps her and buggers off back to Sweden.'

They sat up until 2:00 am discussing Alex's decampment.

Back in his office, faced once again with the tyranny of his pending tray, Bob could feel the loss of those few hours' sleep, but he persevered until, by mid-morning, he had worked his way through most of the heap of files and folders.

Just after 11:00 am he was interrupted by a call on his private line. He picked up the receiver and heard a familiar voice echoing through a bad international connection.

'Bob, Jimmy here. I've just seen a copy of yesterday's *Telegraph*. What the hell's going on there?'

Sir James Proud's celebration of his recently conferred knighthood was taking the form of a four-week break with Lady Proud in Lanzarote. 'Twenty-eight days of doing absolutely sod all,' he had announced before his departure. His holiday still had almost twenty-one of those days to run.

Skinner was not in the least surprised by his call. 'Hello, Chief. I thought you'd be on the phone as soon as the news caught up with you. If you've seen the *Telegraph*, you probably know it all. Since the murder of the Guillaum woman, we've had no more incidents, or any further contact from the terrorists. That's nearly forty-eight hours now. We've put as much security in place as we can, including some of the boys in black from Hereford. Maybe we've scared them off, but I have my doubts.'

'How's Ballantyne taking it?'

'I don't want to talk about that.'

For a few seconds there was only a whistling sound on the otherwise silent line, as Proud considered the implications of Skinner's reticence. When he spoke again, there was a warning in his tone.

'You watch our friend, Robert. Like most politicians, he's not to be trusted. Look, I'll try to get a plane out of here. I should be back home there.'

'No you shouldn't. What could you do that I haven't done? Besides if you've read the Torygraph, you'll know that this isn't a force matter anyway. Officially, it's in the hands of an anti-terrorist squad, and I'm in command, courtesy of our friend Ballantyne. So you just lie in the sun with Lady Chrissie, and try to enjoy doing all that bugger-all that you were looking forward to.'

'But, man, I'll feel terrible, worrying about you lot.'

'Why should you? Do you think all crime stops in Edinburgh just because you've gone on bloody holiday? Think of it as just another investigation.'

Proud grunted. 'I suppose you're right. I have to admit that Chrissie did give me the start of a very black look when I mentioned going back home. How's McGuinness getting on?'

'Not bothering me.'

'And Sarah? How's Sarah?'

'Terrific. She's taking years off me.'

'And Alex?'

'Playing house with some Swede at the moment. Much to my displeasure, I have to say.'

'Take some advice from an expert, Bob. Let her get on with it. When you're her age, no one else knows anything about life.'

'That's more or less what Sarah says too.'

Warning pips sounded on the line. 'OK, boss, thanks for the call. Now go on. Get back to your sunbed.'

Proud laughed. 'All right. If you're certain. It's true what they say, by the way. I have to get up at 7:30 to book our places. So long.' The line went dead.

The rest of the day passed peacefully, apart from the distraction of a mid-afternoon bank robbery at the Bank of Scotland in Picardy Place – a crime which was almost refreshing in its normality after the tumult of the weekend.

The bearded senior manager's terse and vivid description of the raiders struck a chord with the investigating Detective Chief Inspector, and a replay of the bank video confirmed his suspicions. Within three hours of the crime, arrests were made and the stolen £33,000 recovered.

Thirty-two

Bob and Sarah decided to give the performing arts a miss that evening. Instead they visited a private view of a major exhibition of Inca treasures in the Royal Scottish Museum. After their guided tour, they mingled with the rich and famous of Edinburgh and various members of the visiting glitterati, at a drinks reception in the Museum's main hall, under its magnificent high-arched glass ceiling.

They had just spent some time in confusing conversation with one of Scotland's leading young jazz saxophonists and his identical twin brother, and were circulating towards the next group, when they were confronted by a stocky, bull-like, crew-cut figure sweating in his pink shirt and white cotton jacket, even in the controlled climate of the Museum.

'Skinner?' The man seemed to bark rather than speak.

Skinner nodded, hackles rising instantly.

'Al Neidermeyer. We spoke on the transatlantic horn on Saturday. Remember?'

'Oh yes, I remember.' Skinner's voice was suddenly soft. He felt Sarah's hand tighten on his arm, as if she was holding him back.

A vein throbbed on the side of the shorter man's bullet-like head. 'I want you to know that I'm watching you, Skinner. You fucked me around. I don't forget that. You slip up just once on this case, and I'll make you international bad news. I'll screw you so hard your eyes'll pop. You get me? Now tell me what the fuck you're doing to catch these people.'

A slow, cold smile spread across Skinner's face. Beside him Sarah was trembling in fury. She made to speak, but Bob, still smiling, silenced her with a slight movement of his hand. The chattering of the groups of guests around them had stilled, and a circle had opened up around them. The closest bystanders stared selfconsciously into their wine glasses. 'Mr Neidermeyer – or can I call you Al? You're new in town. You're probably jet-lagged. And, like my wife, here, you're an American. All that cuts you one piece of slack. You've just used it up.' The smile left his lips. 'So now you listen to me, and listen well. Here you get the same rights and privileges on this story as any other member of the foreign press. In your special case, that means you're at the back of the queue. You want to ask any questions about this investigation, you contact my information office. You don't waylay me in a public place. Understood?'

Suddenly his voice was different, still quiet but hard now, and very, very cold. 'And one more thing. You ever talk to me like that again, or block my way, or use language like that in front of my wife, and you'll either be on liquids for a week, or locked up, or both.

'Come on, love. Time we were going.' He slipped an arm around Sarah's waist and led her from the Museum.

Thirty-three

An hour later Sarah was still seething. She sat on the edge of the bed in her matching pink bra and panties, pulling a brush through her hair. Bob lay naked between the sheets.

'That little jerk. Who the hell does he think he is? Guys like him give all us Americans a bad name. What an asshole! If I ever see him again . . .'

Bob laughed and shook his head. 'Calm down, Doc. You're getting as red in the face as he was. I'll tell you what, why don't you phone Don the Consul and report him?'

She frowned at him. 'How can you be so calm about it? He threatened you in front of all those people.'

'Yeah, and I threatened him back. I don't think he'll do it again. If he does, I'll just have to call my pal Joe. To hell, maybe I'll do that anyway.'

'Who's your pal Joe?'

'The FBI guy in your Embassy in London. I wonder if old Al would fancy a full-scale IRS tax audit.'

Sarah looked at him. Even now, he was still capable of surprising her. 'Could you fix that?'

'Damn right I could. Now forget that bastard, and come here. There's a fella wants to talk to you.'

In an instant, she slipped out of her bra and panties and into bed, reaching for him. Just as he drew her close to him, the telephone rang.

Sarah swore softly, rolled over and picked it up. 'Hello?'

'Sarah? It's Maggie Rose here.' At once, Sarah was aware of the tension in the detective sergeant's voice. The woman was struggling hard to stay in control. 'I'm sorry, but I need to speak to the boss.'

Frowning, Sarah handed over the receiver.

Bob took it from her. 'Yes, Sergeant. What is it?'

'It's a bomb, sir. In the Assembly Rooms. In the Music Hall. They've done it again. Oh, my God, but it's awful. Get here, please, sir! Just get here, please!'

Thirty-four

George Street was closed off along its entire length, from Charlotte Square to St Andrew's Square. A uniformed officer, stationed at the junction of Queen Street and Frederick Street, recognised Skinner and Sarah instantly, and waved them through.

They parked in front of the double-windows of Phillips, the fine art auctioneers. Clad in the jeans and sweatshirts which they had pulled on after tumbling out of bed, they raced across the street, past the police cars lined along the central reservation, and past the rank of ambulances which stood like blue-beaconed taxis at the arched and pillared entrance to the Assembly Rooms.

At once, Skinner spotted Deputy Chief Constable McGuinness standing in the doorway, looking out into the street. The portly policeman was in evening dress, as if he had been summoned from the opera. His normally ruddy face had a yellowish tinge, and his eyes gave a clear hint of what lay inside.

Skinner greeted him sympathetically. 'Hello, Eddie. What's happened?' Even as he spoke two paramedics hurried past, bearing a keening victim on a stretcher towards one of the ambulances. He looked down at their burden, and in spite of himself, he felt his stomach knot, and his testicles tighten. It was a girl, young and blonde. Her left ear and part of the left side of her face had been sliced off. Through the mess, Skinner could see white bone. A long shard of wood protruded from her belly. Her hands, all bloody, were grasping it as if she were holding on to her pain and, through that, to life itself.

McGuinness's lips moved as if he was speaking, but no sound came out. Instead his eyes filled with tears as he followed the girl on her stretcher. For the first time in his life, Skinner found that he felt sorry for the Deputy. He knew that most of McGuinness's career had been spent in administration, and yet here he was visiting his second charnel-house in only four days.

'Go and sit in one of the cars, Eddie. You don't have to look at this. You can't help these people.'

But the Deputy Chief Constable shook his head, blinking the glaze from his eyes. Then, as Skinner looked at him, he straightened his back and clenched his jaw. 'No, Bob. I realise that things like this come with the job.'

Skinner patted him on the shoulder with a new-found sense of camaraderie. 'Good man, Eddie,' he murmured softly. 'Jimmy would be pleased with you.'

As he led Sarah into the foyer of the Assembly Rooms, they were met by a babel of sound. The shouts of the emergency teams mingled with cries of pain from victims. Somewhere not too far away a man was screaming.

Carrying her bulky first-aid bag, Sarah looked around until she saw a nurse in uniform. 'I'm a doctor,' she called out to the man. 'Where's the medical centre?'

'Up those stairs, in the big room to the left.'

She turned to Skinner. 'Bob, I'm . . .'

'Yes, of course. I'll send for you if I need you.

'Maggie Rose said it was in the Music Hall,' he said to no one in particular. Then he caught sight of Andy Martin standing at the foot of the wide staircase to the right, waving to him.

'Boss,' he called. 'This way.'

Skinner followed Martin up the staircase. At the top he made to step into the big Music Hall which he knew so well, but Martin caught his arm.

'No, boss. Come up to the gallery. You'll get a better idea there. And listen, prepare yourself. It's not a pretty sight.'

Martin led him through the access door to the balcony, and up a second flight of stairs, much narrower than the first. As he stepped into the auditorium, Skinner's eyes screwed up involuntarily, taking in the horror. Glass was strewn across the full width of the upper seating area. White stuffing, much of it stained crimson with blood, protruded from torn tip-up seats. A line of pockmarks ran irregularly along the painted back wall of the gallery. The whole upper area of the hall looked as if it had been strafed with machine-gun fire.

As soon as Skinner looked down into the body of the hall, he realised why. The framework of the huge, ornate chandelier, which had been the main feature of the room, now hung twisted and tangled, suspended from the ceiling by only a few wires. Its heavy crystal fittings were virtually all gone. Skinner saw at once that the blast had torn them off and sent them whistling like heavy-calibre bullets into the balcony seats.

He walked down the few steps from the doorway, and looked into the body of the theatre. From the way the wreckage was spread out, he could see that the explosion had taken place mid-stage. The lower part of the auditorium was filled with temporary tiered-stall seating. The rows of seats nearest the front, and thus closest to the explosion, were below stage level, and seemed to have been shielded from the worst of the blast. He could see that those in the middle and towards the rear had been riddled with a savage assortment of wooden, glass and metal shrapnel. Skinner remembered the girl on the stretcher, and guessed that it was the debris of the stage furniture.

Suddenly he was overwhelmed by the horror of it all. 'Jesus Christ, Andy. What a mess.'

Martin had been working at the scene for some time, but he too was still ashen faced. 'Hellish. We've got at least twelve dead, and who knows how many injured. A few of them won't make it. There was a girl there . . .'

'I know. I saw her, I think. Sarah came with me. She's gone next door to do what she can.'

'That's good, boss. Maggie Rose is there too. She was in the building – down in the foyer, and thank Christ not in the Hall – when it happened.'

'She holding up OK?'

'Maggie? Are you kidding?'

'That's good. Now tell me what you've worked out so far.'

'Well, as you can see, the bomb seems to have exploded right on the stage itself. The show was an Australian musical called *Waltzing Matilda* or some such. The cast was bang – oh Christ!' He paused, aghast at his choice of words – 'in the middle of one of their big production numbers when it happened. We can account for three bodies on stage, but there's another one missing. We reckon she's probably just been blown all over the fucking place. You can see what the blast did to the big chandelier. The folk upstairs caught the worst of it. One or two of the poor sods were just cut to pieces. The audience downstairs didn't do too well either. The people at the front and at the back got off lightest; mostly shock, some deafened, a few scrapes. The folk in the middle caught the stage debris. They were lucky the frame of that big chandelier didn't come down on them as well.'

Martin paused, to bring his rising voice under control. Skinner looked over into the mid-section of the big hall, which was flooded by the temporary lights which had been set up. Many of the seats were torn and, as in the upper area, some were stained scarlet. More blood trails led up the aisle towards the exit door.

'By the time I got here,' Martin continued, 'they'd taken eight people out dead from the audience. Five more are touch-and-go. One woman had her hand sliced off. Her boyfriend had to put a tourniquet on her.' He paused, gulping in breath. 'The worst casualties are on their way to hospital. Most of them are being treated here.'

Skinner caught sight of 'Gammy' Legge kneeling in the centre of the scorched blackened stage. 'Do we know anything about the type of bomb yet? Was it the same as Saturday?'

'There's an old guy reckons he can describe it for us. He's a weird old boy; he's either tremendously excited or a bit hysterical or both. He can't stop talking. I've sent him downstairs with a PC. Do you want to talk to him?'

'Too right. Let's get to him before he starts to embroider it.'

Martin led the way out of the Music Hall and down the wide carpeted staircase, back to the foyer. The Fringe café-bar in the rear ground-level hall had been turned into an emergency canteen. A number of survivors, more shocked than injured, were sitting around on stacking chairs, drinking mugs of hot sweet tea.

Skinner could hear the old man's shrill, hoarse voice rising above the hubbub even before Martin pointed him out. He was standing on his tip toe, clutching a white mug, with his chin stuck out, bellowing and gesticulating with his free hand to the young officer detailed to look after him. His small stature was accentuated by the wizening and shrinkage which the advancing years had brought with them.

Skinner could see at once why Martin had thought him weird. More than anything else, he looked like a large monkey in fancy dress. He had a broad flat face, and a high forehead, from which his long, thinning hair swept back. Skinner noted with surprise a sprinkling of black still showing among the grey. A small gold ring looked garish in his left ear, but somehow it was in accord with his crew-necked blue-and-white hooped sweater, and comfort-cut black jeans. He wore open-toed sandals, without socks. He might have been, Skinner estimated, anywhere between sixty-five and eighty.

Martin introduced them. 'Boss, this is Mr Charles Forsyth. Mr Forsyth, ACC Skinner.'

The little man turned and looked slowly up at the figure towering above him. 'So you're the great Bob Skinner! I've met you once before. Must be nearly twenty years ago. You were just a raw-arsed sergeant then!'

The man's voice was still raised and hoarse, and Skinner guessed this was his normal tone. He looked at Forsyth afresh, trying to place him in his memory, but failed.

'Well I'm pleased to meet you again, Mr Forsyth, although I'd rather it hadn't been here, and in these circumstances. So you were in the Music Hall when the explosion happened. Tell me, were you there alone?'

'Call me Charlie. Aye I was alone, thank Christ. Mary – that's my girlfriend – she was feeling a bit off-colour, and anyway, she didnae really fancy the idea of Aussies pretending tae be song-and-dance men. Don't know what brought me, truth be told. It's out of my usual line, all that prancin' poofter stuff. I'm a writer, y'know,' he added inconsequentially.

Skinner was not surprised by the revelation, but decided instinctively not to pursue that line of conversation.

'Where were you sat, Charlie?'

'Downstairs, three rows from the back. If I'd been three rows further down . . . The guy in the sixth row, straight in front of me, caught a big lump of flying timber or something, right in the throat. It took the poor bastard's head half off. And that could have been me. Mind you, I've always been lucky. I remember once in Burma . . .' His voice trailed off, as if he had suddenly discovered that this detail of his war-time memories was no longer there.

'Andy says you can describe the explosion, Charlie,' Skinner prodded, gently.

The little man's eyes lit up at once, and he seemed almost to straighten from his stoop. 'Aye, too fuckin' right I can! It was the radiogram.'

'What?'

'Well this nonsense – I won't dignify it with the name of a play – was set in the early Sixties and the stage was dressed with props from that time. Gate-leg table, chintzy chairs, that sort of stuff – and one of those huge standard electric radiograms they had back in those days. You'll be too young to remember them, maybe. Great big bastards they were. They weighed a ton. That's what blew up! I was lookin' straight at it at the time. It just seemed to disintegrate, and puff outwards in smoke, and everything else on stage along with it. Funny, looking back it's as if it happened in slow motion.'

'Are you certain?'

'Certain? Of course I'm fucking certain. I was there, wasn't I? There was a lassie standing right alongside it. Lamentable Christ, what a sight! I remember once I saw this big Nigerian soldier take a direct hit from Japanese artillery. The only thing left was his boots. Great big boots they were, with his great big fucking feet still in them. I'd ordered him tae stay under cover. Christ, ye couldnae tell those boys anything at all. Hearts of lions, brains of fieldmice.' His voice tailed off, the awful memory of the evening reviving another horror of the past, taking him back to the jungles of fifty years before.

Skinner calmed the old man's excitement. 'Thanks, Charlie. Thanks very much. You're a good man. You've given us the first eye-witness account we've had since all this business started.' He turned to the young PC. 'Constable, organise a car. Have Mr Forsyth taken home.' The man set off obediently.

'Ta,' said Forsyth. 'Ye know, Skinner. All this, it makes me glad I'm not long away from the wooden waistcoat. I grieve for Scotland when this can happen. Good luck to you, son. Catch these fuckers.'

As he left the little man in the canteen, Skinner wondered about his reaction. What kind of man could witness such appalling carnage and still describe it so matter-of-factly? Then he realised quite simply that, perhaps an eighty-year-old could do so: someone knowing that his lease on the planet was running out, taking every day as a bonus, caring only about that day and the next, and hopefully the day beyond. The horror of that evening might be blocked out easily by a man like that, and a strange satisfaction drawn from the privileged position of being an important witness, from the unexpected burst of warmth at being the centre of attention once again, rather than being just another lonely old man shouting his bizarre reminiscences to gather himself an audience.

Thirty-five

In the foyer, DCC McGuinness now seemed in full control both of himself and of the situation. The stream of casualties out to the ambulances had subsided.

Skinner went to check on Sarah in the first-aid room, which was still crowded with bleeding, shocked victims, waiting mainly in silence for attention. He realised that the decision to treat the less seriously injured at the scene had been a wise one. Edinburgh's main hospital casualty departments would have been swamped by the numbers.

Sarah estimated that she had another thirty minutes of stitching and patching to do. 'Look, you'll want to start work on this. Why don't you just leave me the car key and go off with Andy?'

'Yes, I'll do that,' he agreed. Handing her the big BMW key, he kissed her on the forehead and went downstairs. In the lower hall he was intercepted by Alan Royston, the police Media Relations Manager, who had set up a makeshift press office in a room to the left of the foyer. He led Skinner to where a dozen reporters stood waiting. There he explained to them what had happened in the Music Hall, describing the scale of the destruction. He answered the questions of the group as best he could, and agreed finally to Royston's suggestion that the journalists and photographers should be taken together into the hall to see for themselves. As he was making his way towards the exit, Al Neidermeyer arrived. There was a television cameraman puffing at his heels, a city freelance whom Skinner knew by sight.

'Well, copper,' snarled Neidermeyer. 'So much for your security. How many more people did you let die here tonight?'

Once more, Skinner felt his self-control valve begin to strain. He glanced quickly at the camera to make certain that the red action light was unlit. The cameraman was looking away, embarrassed. Then his right hand swept upwards in one short, swift motion. As it passed close to Neidermeyer's face, he flicked the second finger with his thumb, lightning-fast. The broad fingernail caught the American, very hard, square on the tip of the nose. Neidermeyer howled, and instantly his eyes flooded with tears.

'I warned you about pushing your luck, Al,' Skinner whispered. 'Too bad you didn't listen.' He swept the man from his path and left the building.

Thirty-six

Andy Martin was waiting for him outside. He saw the anger in Skinner's eyes, but an inner caution stopped him from asking what was wrong. Instead he suggested that they go and talk things out at his flat near Haymarket, rather than return to the headquarters building.

They found Julia Shahor there when they arrived, home from the Film Festival. She greeted Martin, obvious anxiety turning quickly to relief. Radio Forth RFM was playing, and the television was on, with Teletext On 3 on screen, carrying the latest news on the explosion. A Royal Infirmary spokeswoman had confirmed the current death toll at fourteen; the condition of two other victims was said to be critical.

For a time, they stared grim faced and speechless at the news bulletin on the screen. Then Martin handed Skinner and Julia a Beck's each from the fridge, taking a tin of Tennent's LA for himself. He joined Julia on the sofa, facing the television, while Skinner settled on the floor, his back against the wall.

It was Skinner who broke the silence – broke the spell cast by the horror of the Assembly Rooms. 'Andy, my brother, we've been kidding ourselves to think that we could prevent something like tonight. And we've been underestimating these people. They're good: very well planned. We've got to catch them before it goes any further. But I do not, for the life of me, know how we're going to do it.'

For once, Martin had no word of encouragement to offer in reply.

Skinner finished his Beck's in one swallow, straight from the bottle. He got up to fetch himself another, then resumed his seat on the floor. With a wry smile, he said, 'But that's me seeing the glass half-empty. The positive side is that at least we've got some straightforward police work to do, thanks to good old Charlie Forsyth.'

'What do you mean?' asked Julia.

'Well, first we have to check every member of every other company that's been using that venue. Then there's the stage props. That exploding radiogram. No fucking way – oh, sorry, Julia – did they bring that all the way from Oz. They must have sourced it locally.'

'Maybe I can help you there,' she offered. 'I know of only three companies in Scotland which supply stage props. I looked into it earlier this year, when I needed things for a display I put on at Filmhouse. One's in Glasgow, one's down towards the Borders somewhere, but the biggest by far is here in Edinburgh. Let me see. What was it called? Proscenium Props – that was it. It was based in a big warehouse out to the west of the city, near Sighthill.'

'Good, Julia. Thanks for that. Well, Andy, that's a priority task for first thing tomorrow – I mean this morning. Find out where those props came from. Then we'll find out all there is to know about everybody on the supplier's payroll – like whether any of them has been handling Semtex over the last few days.'

He drained his second Beck's then pushed himself up from his hard seat on the floor. 'Right, that's it for me. I'm off home.'

'Want me to phone for a patrol car to pick you up?' asked Martin.

'No, no. Don't do that. The boys are too busy for taxi runs tonight. I'll walk. It's not that hellish far from here.' He paused. 'It's a nice night, and it'll let me pull some things together in my head. So long, Julia.'

Martin walked him to the front door of the second-floor flat. He looked quizzically after his chief as he disappeared down the brightly lit, curving stairway. Eventually he closed the door and rejoined Julia in the living room.

She caught the faraway look in his eyes. 'What is it?' she asked.

'It's the boss. He's got one of his niggles, I can tell.'

'What do you mean?'

'How do I explain it? Every so often, on a really difficult job, when we're pursuing a particular line of enquiry, Bob'll decide that maybe it's not quite right: that all the bits don't fit that jigsaw. But he'll keep it to himself, just niggling and worrying away at the thought, like a dog at a bone, until either he's satisfied himself that, yes, we are on the right track after all, or until he comes up with a completely new approach.' He broke off. 'But enough of that. Heard from your aunt?'

'Yes, she's fine.'

'Which side of the family is she from? Mother or father?'

'Actually . . .' said Julia hesitantly, as if looking for the right words, 'neither. She's a sort of courtesy aunt, really. She was at school with my mother. They were very close.'

'In Israel? Funny, I wouldn't have thought that. Her accent sounds more European.'

'No, not in Israel. Somewhere else. The thing is – well, the thing is, my parents broke up when I was a girl, and I went to live with relatives in Israel. I got in touch with Auntie again when I came to the Sorbonne.' Suddenly she looked troubled.

'But, Andy, I really don't like to talk about all that. It was a bad time for me, and it is best left in the past.'

'Sure, love,' he said, soothingly. And in a second it was forgotten. 'He's some machine, old Bob, when he gets one of his niggles going. Wonder what it is this time? One thing's for sure though: sooner or later, we'll find out!'

Thirty-seven

The first rumblings of discontent appeared in the hastily written leaders of the following morning's *Scotsman* and *Herald*, while in the tabloids the rumbling was a full-scale earthquake. One late-edition banner blared, 'PLOD FIASCO: BOMBS HIT OZ'. This articulate headline filled two thirds of the front page, and led a story filled with hastily assembled 'bystander' condemnation of the security operation in general, and of its commander in person. Resisting the urge to crumple it up and throw it across the room, Skinner read it through to the end. He noted grimly that the only critic identified in the story was Al Neidermeyer.

While the more serious Scottish dailies were more circumspect, notes of concern rang in them all. The sombre leader in the *Scotsman* went so far as to praise Skinner as an outstanding detective, but developed its theme of two days before, wondering whether counter-terrorism was suited to his skills, and whether the crisis might be better placed under someone else's command.

'Like who, for instance?' he muttered to the empty room.

Michael Licorish and Alan Royston had scheduled a media conference, to be taken by Ballantyne and Skinner, at 10:00 am in the main hall at Fettes Avenue. In preparation for the inevitable grilling, the ACC read all of the reports which lay on his desk, including one from the Royal Infirmary which put the final death toll at eighteen, including the girl he had seen on the stretcher. Her name had been Alice Carroll, and she had been seventeen years old. Also listed at the end of the report was Alice's elderly grandmother, untouched by the shrapnel, but who had died of a heart attack shortly after the explosion.

Skinner had just finished his perusal when Ruth buzzed through on the intercom to tell him that Licorish was waiting outside. 'OK,' he said, 'send him in.'

The Information Director came in a few seconds later. Skinner could see an embarrassed look in his eyes, and knew that he had some uncomfortable news to break. He took a guess.

'Where's the Secretary of State, Mike? I thought he'd be here by now.'

'That's just it, Bob. He can't make it. He asked me to apologise to you, and to ask you to take the chair in his place. He said I was to tell you he still has every confidence in you.'

'That's fucking big of him. What's his story?'

'It's to do with a family friend having just died. Between you and me, it's actually a friend of Mrs Ballantyne. You know how it is with them?'

Skinner nodded. But he wondered if Licorish knew how it was with Ballantyne and Carlie.

The Scottish Office man continued, almost sotto voce. 'She's been having an affair with a Liberal peer, Lord Broadgate. But it seems she was too much for him. He had a stroke during the night. She phoned S of S in a bit of a panic, and he caught the first shuttle down to London.'

'Mmm,' Skinner muttered. 'Nice of him.'

As he looked at Licorish, he sensed something else. Before he could ask, the civil servant produced a brown envelope which he had been holding behind his back. 'This arrived just after he left.' He pushed it across the desk.

The latest letter was brief and to the point.

> Ballantyne, you and your lackeys must believe us now. We have shown you what we can do, and we will not stop until you give us back what is ours. Now we have the attention of the international community, and we have its support. Withdraw from Scotland before its people rise up and join us in throwing you out.

Skinner threw it down on the desk.

'What the hell is that? It's just fucking rhetoric. They kill an American. They kill Australians. They kill their own Scots folk. These people have to be crazy, or playing for very big stakes. Is Scotland that important?' He rose from behind his desk and led the way to his meeting with the media.

In the briefing room, the media corps – even Al Neidermeyer, his nose noticeably swollen – were unusually subdued as Skinner described the scene in the Music Hall, then listed the dead. Finally, he put down his notes and looked at his audience.

'There's little I can say to you that I haven't said before. This is a well-organised, well-resourced and completely ruthless group of people. What happened last night was beyond words – beyond mine, and I think beyond even yours, eloquent as you all may be. The thing that I find most incredible is that Scots people could treat other Scots in this way, whatever justifiable cause they think they have. Last night, I talked to an eighty-year-old man who told me that he grieved for Scotland. I share his grief.

'Having said that, I can tell you that there is now some sign of outside involvement in these atrocities. The explosive used in both attacks is a new type of Semtex. So far it's been unknown here. It hasn't even turned up in Ireland. Until now, no one has been aware that there was an illicit market in this material. The country of manufacture is pretty jealous of its reputation, and its government felt sure that all batches were accounted for. It seems they were wrong. We now know that there was a break-in at a French military arsenal two months ago, when a quantity of the stuff was stolen. We're pretty certain that's the explosive used here. Before all this started, we never had an inkling of any embryonic Scottish terrorist organisation. It's asking a lot – of me, at least – to believe that such a group has existed all along, with a plan so detailed that it involved stealing high explosives from an arsenal in France.'

Skinner's old friend, John Hunter, interrupted him. 'Bob, are you suggesting that all this might have been contrived outside Scotland, or that there might be some foreign involvement?'

'I can't say that for certain, John, but whatever this group is, it's tied into some sort of network.'

'Irish?'

'I don't know. I know someone who definitely doesn't think so, but sooner or later I'll find out for sure! Thank you, gentlemen. From now on, in the light of these events, I'm prepared to take briefings on a daily basis, at 10:00 every morning, here, but that's all for this morning.'

Skinner rose to his feet. There was a stampede for the door as the media corps rushed off *en masse* to file their French connection copy.

Thirty-eight

A message, written in Ruth's neat hand, lay on Skinner's desk when he returned to his office. *'Call DC McIlhenney, Glasgow. Urgent.'* She had noted down the telephone number.

Using his secure telephone, he keyed it in. 'Neil? ACC here. What've you got for me?'

'Morning, sir. Our man Macdairmid's an early bird. He pitched up at his Party offices at 9:00 this morning, but he was only there for twenty minutes, then off down to that pub of his. It's got an early-opening licence for night-shift workers at the factory up the road.

'Barry beat him there. He was waiting when he arrived. Sure as God made wee green apples, he ordered a half-pint of Gillespie's then used the pay-phone. The Glasgow technical boys had their tap in place, and got the whole thing.'

'Interesting?'

'As Mr Haggerty would say, "Too bliddy right it is, sir." But you can judge for yourself. There's a motorcycle polisman heading along the M8 right now with a copy for you. He should get it to you in half an hour. I'll tell you one thing, sir. That Macdairmid – for an MP he's bollock-deep in something that's definitely non-Parliamentary. That's bliddy certain!'

Thirty-nine

Bridie Lindwall, writer of the new musical revue *Waltzing Matilda*, and director of the Brisbane Youth Theatre Company, was still in a state of shock when Andy Martin and Brian Mackie were finally allowed into the private room in the Murrayfield Hospital in which she had been installed, thanks to the provision of generous private health insurance by her show's Australian sponsor.

Ms Lindwall had been given a heavy sedative by the junior doctor who had treated her at the Royal Infirmary immediately after the explosion, and so it was midday before Martin and Mackie were allowed to interview her. Even then, Martin had needed to use his Special Branch clout to overrule the senior house officer in charge. At first, Martin thought that talking to her was like interviewing mist. The two detectives were unable to hold the woman's attention for more than a few seconds before a distant, glazed look washed across her face, as her fuzzy memory took her back to the night before, fitting together jagged fragments of recollection to form a jigsaw picture of confusion and terror.

'Ms Lindwall,' Martin said finally, as gently as he could but with an edge of steel to hold the woman's concentration, 'we have to know where you sourced your props for the production. The explosion happened in centre stage. We believe that the bomb was hidden in a piece of prop furniture.'

The woman was sitting up in bed, propped against a mound of pillows. She turned her freckled face towards him.

'Explosion? Oh yes, the explosion. How is everyone? It all happened so fast. Little Kelly, how about her? Is she all right?'

Martin sat down on the side of her bed, and took the woman's hand. 'Don't worry about the others. Just concentrate on yourself. You've had quite a shock. Now we need very badly to know about those props. Where did you get them? Was it Proscenium?'

The woman frowned as she tried to clear a path through the flotsam of her memory. 'Proscenium? No. We went there first, but they couldn't give us everything we wanted. Eventually we found someone who could, in a little place with a funny name, south of Edinburgh.'

'What about the radiogram? You remember, the big thing in centre stage. Did you get that there, too?'

She shuddered. 'The radiogram.' Her voice rose. 'Yes. I remember the radiogram. I was standing in the wings. There was a flash, and I was being pushed backwards by a great big hand. Yes, it was as if the radiogram reached out and pushed me.'

She shot bolt upright in the bed, starring wide eyed at Martin.

'OK, now. It's all right.' He put his hands on her shoulders, and eased her very gently back on to the pillows. 'We think that's where the bomb was hidden, Ms Lindwall – in the radiogram. Now, can you remember where you got it?'

She nodded her head vigorously. Suddenly she seemed more in focus. 'Yes, that was one of the items that they couldn't give us at Proscenium. We had to go to the place with the funny name to find that.'

'That's good, Ms Lindwall. Now one other thing. When you

weren't actually using the theatre – when the other companies were using it – what did you do with your props?'

'We have a storeroom allocated to us in the basement. All our stuff's locked up there between shows.'

'Who keeps the keys?'

'I do. Both of them. The theatre management doesn't want the responsibility of looking after anyone's kit.'

'Have you ever given a key to anyone else?'

'No. No one at all.'

'You don't recall seeing any sign that anyone else might have been in that store?'

'Nothing at all. Everything always looked normal.'

'Ok, Ms Lindwall. That's been very helpful. Now you get yourself some more rest.'

She grabbed his arm as he stood up. 'Aren't you going to tell me about the rest of them. How is everyone? How is little Kelly?'

Martin decided that economy with the truth would be in everyone's interests. 'Look, Bridie, obviously with a bang like that there were a few other scrapes, as well as your own. We don't have the full details yet, but I'll arrange for someone to come by and talk to you as soon as possible. Now, you just relax. And thanks again.'

Mackie closed the door of the private room gently behind them.

'Nice one, Andy. I wouldn't have fancied telling her that one of her guys is dead because wee Kelly's arm was blown right through his chest!'

Forty

McIlhenney's motorcycle officer arrived with the promised tape cassette, five minutes ahead of schedule. Meanwhile Skinner had called Adam Arrow to his room to await its delivery. When Ruth brought the package in, she found the two seated in armchairs beside the low coffee table. Skinner accepted the clear plastic cassette and dropped it straight into a tape-recorder placed in the centre of the table. Once his secretary had closed the heavy door behind her, he pressed the '*play*' button.

For a few seconds there was only the hiss of the tape. Then they heard seven coins drop, one by one, followed by the musical beeps of a thirteen-digit telephone number being keyed in on a modern instrument. Seconds later a ringing began in monotone. The call was answered on the sixth ring, in a tongue that sounded like Arabic. The voice was guttural, the accent heavy. Neither listener was able to identify the language.

Grant Macdairmid's response in English was strangely hushed, far removed from the bellowing rant for which he was locally famous. 'Hello, Glasgow here. How are our arrangements coming along?'

'Everything is progressing very well. We will be able to move on to the next stage on Saturday. The second delivery will be made then.'

'From the same French source?'

'Yes.'

'That's good. My people have things well in hand, too. The police don't have a bloody clue. And they're stretched so tight just now, they're starting to come apart.'

'Yes, I see that your compatriots are keeping them very busy. That worries me a little. Their approach is so high-profile and you are, shall we say, so well known, might it not mean that your security people will soon turn their attention to you?'

Macdairmid laughed softly. 'Look, we went over all that at the start. I'm a public figure, an MP. Yes, the SB plods keep an occasional eye on me; it's sort of like a ritual dance. I can always slip their gaze, like now. And they wouldn't really expect me to be involved in something like this. Grant Macdairmid, MP, windbag, demagogue and general nuisance, that's my reputation. But the real view of our friends in the cheap suits is Grant Macdairmid, MP, all fart, no shit.'

This time the other man laughed. 'Ah, my friend, if they only knew you as I do. Why, you're *full* of shit!'

There was a moment's silence as Macdairmid tried to work out whether he had been insulted. Then, deciding to make allowances for the other man's poor grasp of colloquial English, he ignored the remark and went on. 'So it's Saturday. Where do we take delivery?'

'I suggest that we do it in Edinburgh. The police there are fully occupied.'

'Yeah. Why not?'

'So where do we meet?'

There was another silence. Then Macdairmid laughed softly. 'There's a bookseller's in George Street called James Thin. On the first floor there's a coffee shop. Most of the time it's full of old people and young mums and kids, but during the Festival there's all sorts in there. I'll have my person there by 11:30 am. Are you using the same courier as before?'

'Yes.'

'Fine. So identification will be no problem, then. It's all gone well so far, but they've seen nothing yet. Once I get my hands on your next consignment, we'll really make Scotland go off with a bang!'

There was a click as the receiver went down.

Skinner switched off the player. He and Arrow stared at each other in silence across the table.

'Fookin' hell!' said the little soldier, eventually.

'Yup, that just about sums it up,' said Skinner. 'He's right, you know, Adam. We do think of him as just a loud-mouthed wanker, capable of causing bother up to a point, but no further. I mean, I know the Five computer spat out his name, but I didn't think for a minute that he'd have the stones to be into this sort of thing. From the sound of it, I was wrong.'

'So what do we do, Bob? Pick him up?'

'On what grounds? One meeting in a pub in London, which he'd claim was a co-incidence? One funny telephone call? Even anti-terrorist squads need evidence, if they're going to go around arresting MPs.'

'I'm not a copper, Bob.' Arrow spoke slowly, as if weighing his words. Skinner noted that his accent had disappeared. 'Let me go underground for a couple of days, and you'd never hear of the man again.'

Skinner looked at him steadily and seriously. 'Adam, I know what can happen in Ireland, but it's not going to happen here. I'm a policeman, not a judge. Listen, chum, I knew a man once for whom that was the only way. You may have gone to the same school, but you're not like he was – so far. Be careful you never get that way, because if you do, sooner or later you'll come up against someone like me, who'll have to stop you.'

Arrow smiled at him, and when he spoke, the accent was back. 'Rather not come up against you, Bob. Don't worry, mate. That's not my choice. But these people are fookin' butchers, so I had to make the offer.'

'Ok. Enough said. Anyway, taking Macdairmid for a trip wouldn't necessarily stop anything. He may be mixed up in it, he may even be a leader, but no way is he doing the heavy stuff himself. No, we'll watch him like a hawk till Saturday, then we'll pick up his messenger, and the other one. Now, that's a job you can handle. My face is too well known.'

'Be glad to. Will you give me someone to work with?'

'Sure. It'll be McGuire and Rose. McIlhenney and Macgregor are already watching Macdairmid, so it could be they'd know the messenger by sight, and he in turn might clock them. So you'd better have a different team. And if it comes to a bundle, McGuire's your man!'

'I can hardly wait.'

'Right, I'll brief them. Now what about the other voice on that tape. Any ideas?'

'Not a voice I know, put it that way. It sounded like a fookin' Libyan, though.'

'Could have been, but I'm hardly an expert in Middle Eastern languages. I'll have copies of the tape made and get someone on a plane down to London. We'll let Five have a listen, and Six for that matter. Let's see if it strikes a chord with anyone down there.'

Forty-one

Stow – the place with the funny name – was a drab little village.

'It's pronounced as in "cow" not as in "blow",' Mackie, a Borderer himself, explained to Martin.

They reached Stow just on 4:00 pm, after a forty-five-minute drive down the A7, the road from Edinburgh to Galashiels and the Borders heartland of rugby football. The place clearly offered no attractions to delay the northward flood of tourist traffic on the scenic route into Scotland.

The business base of 'Frank Adams, Theatrical Props', as the *Yellow Pages* listing read, was difficult to locate, even in such a pocket-sized community. Eventually, with the help of the sub-postmistress, they found their quarry in a cluster of buildings which, Mackie guessed, had once been part of a small farm.

Before leaving Edinburgh they had checked out 'Frank Adams, Theatrical Props' as far as they could, using the Department of Social Security and the Inland Revenue as their starting points. The business had only two staff; Francis Snowdon Adams, listed by the tax office as self-employed, and Hugh Minto Dickson. Both were in their forties, with Adams three years the elder at forty-seven.

From a friendly bank manager, contacted through the DSS, they had learned that Mr Adams made acceptable annual profits from business contacts all around the UK. These were steady throughout the year, and peaked during August, and also over the Christmas season when the British pantomime craze was at its height. The company operated on a cash-and-carry basis. Mr Adams owned the premises, and his overheads were restricted to the two salaries, rates, heat and light, motor expenses, hotel costs arising from his buying and selling trips around the UK, stationery, including a modest catalogue, stock purchases and insurance. To the bank manager's certain knowledge, the last category included a substantial indemnity premium to cover death or injury to any customers arising from defective stock.

'Wise man, Mr Adams,' Martin had commented.

Although Adams lived in Lauder, a few miles away from Stow, the bank manager knew him well not only as a customer, but also as a neighbour. He had described him as a forthright man, with abiding interests in rugby football, golf and cricket, but little else. He was also an avowed Conservative, who regarded nationalism and its exponents as 'just plain stupid'.

Hugh Dickson was employed as stock controller, dispatch clerk and book-keeper. He was exceptionally well paid, possibly – the bank manager surmised – due to the fact that he was Mr Adams' brother-in-law.

Neither man was personally extravagant, although Mr Dickson, who was single and lived in Stow rent-free in a cottage alongside the company's storage barns, was known to have a close relationship with the village pub. However, he was known most of all for his reluctance ever to leave Stow. It was said that his last journey of more than one-and-a-half miles had been to Galashiels by bus, eighteen months before, to buy clothes and Christmas presents for his sister, her husband (his employer), and two nephews. Mr Adams and Mr Dickson enjoyed a cordial, proper relationship, but, said the bank manager, they could not be described as bosom companions.

Martin related all this account to Mackie as the Detective Inspector drove them southwards down the A7.

'From the sound of it,' said Skinner's personal assistant, 'we'll get nothing from these guys.'

'On the face of it, that's right, but maybe there's someone else in the chain that we don't know about, someone who fits in between them and the Aussies.'

Both men were taking a coffee break in the company's small office, when Martin and Mackie arrived unannounced. Neither Adams nor Dickson seemed in any way surprised by their visit.

Frank Adams stood up to greet them, shaking each by the hand, and making steady eye contact. He was a big man – not exceptionally tall, but big – with a hand that swallowed even Brian Mackie's oversized paw. As Martin looked at him, remembering his own rugby days, he guessed that once he might have been a member of the closed brotherhood of front-row forwards.

'We've been expecting you guys, after that thing last night,' said Adams. 'We supplied that company – but you'll know that already, I suppose.'

Dickson remained seated. Even in his chair he seemed dwarfed by his brother-in-law, yet he had that air of aggressive self-assurance that small men often adopt to compensate for their lack of size.

'Never under-estimate a wee man,' Skinner had said of Adam Arrow. 'That one there'll kill you just as dead as anyone.' The words returned unbidden to Martin, as he returned Dickson's confident gaze. He switched his attention back to Adams.

'What exactly have you heard or read?'

'Only that the explosion happened on the stage itself, in mid-performance. Nobody would leave a bomb just lying about, so it must have been planted somewhere.'

'You guessed right. Tell me about the radiogram you hired out to the Australians.'

'That big bugger? Was that it? Christ, you could hide a depth charge in there. Look, it was nothing to do wi' us. I'll tell you that right now.'

Martin laughed lightly. 'Mr Adams, if I thought it was, we'd have come in here with guns and flak jackets. You'd have to be very stupid indeed to hide a bomb in your own gear and then sit here waiting for us to turn up. You're not that stupid, are you? Or you, Mr Dickson?'

Adams grinned; possibly in relief, Martin guessed. Dickson looked mortally offended.

'No, what we do need to know is whether anyone else had access to that radiogram while it was still here. When was it hired out last? Could it have been passed on directly from one renter to another?'

Adams rubbed his chin, thoughtfully. 'Hughie can check the stock sheet, but I'm certain it hadn't been out for two years. And we always have kit brought back here first, just so we can check it's OK. We make our customers pay for the insurance of all our stock, under our own policy. Delivery back here is one of the conditions. And we take a twenty per cent value deposit.'

'So who else had access to it here, other than you and Mr Dickson?'

'Nobody!'

Martin was surprised by his vehemence. 'You haven't seen any sign of a break-in?'

'No, nor heard any. All our storage buildings are alarmed like bank vaults. You try and get insurance without that, these days.'

'And you've had no visitors?'

'No, we haven't.'

'It's your busy season. You haven't taken on any casual labour?'

'No.'

'Look, we're not the DSS. If you have, you can tell us. It goes no further.'

'No, I tell you!' Adams' tone was insistent.

'OK, OK.' He glanced at Mackie. 'That's as far as we can take it, Brian. Thanks, Mr Adams, Mr Dickson. We won't take up any more of your time now. I'll dictate a statement back at the office and have a uniformed officer drop it in for you to approve and sign.'

They had almost left of the building when they heard Hugh Dickson call out. 'Frankie!'

The detectives stopped and looked back. The little man had stood up. He was looking not at them but at Adams, a strange pleading expression on his face.

'Look, Frankie, this is nae use. Sister or no', I won't say a word tae Shona, I promise, but ye've got tae tell them about the lassie.'

If looks could kill, thought Martin, as Adams glared at his brother-in-law, we'd have a murder on our hands here. But then the big man's eyes dropped, and his shoulders sagged.

'Aye, Hughie. You're right enough. I've got to, haven't I. But mind, if you do say a bloody word to Shona . . .'

Martin broke in. 'Listen, Mr Adams. If you don't tell us whatever it is right now, I'll arrest you and do you for wasting our time. Then Shona'll find out for sure! Now, cough it up!'

Adams led them back into the office. This time he offered them seats. Mackie produced a notebook and pen.

'About three weeks ago,' Adams began, 'this girl showed up, looking for work. She was American. She said her name was Mary McCall. Said she was working her way round Britain, that she was skint, and needed a job. Most of all, she told me, she needed a roof over her head. I said I didn't need any help – that Hughie and I could manage fine. Hughie, by the way, he was down the village getting coffee and stuff when all this happened. Then she says if I give her a job and a place to kip, she'll make it worth my while. I ask her what the hell she means, and you know what she does?'

Before Martin and Mackie could hazard a guess he went on. 'She comes straight over and unzips me. Then she gives me the most memorable . . .' Adams closed his eyes and shuddered. 'Christ, man, I thought she was gonnae . . .' He stopped, and glanced at Martin, in a strange, conspiratorial, man-to-man way. 'Anyway, that was how Mary persuaded me to give her a job. Not that she did much work . . . standing up, at any rate.

'There's a wee flat above the garage across the yard. I let her stay there. I was giving her one every night. Once or twice I didn't go home, but Shona thought nothing of that. Sometimes I kip over there, if Hughie and I have had a few bevvies after work. I didn't mean it to go on for more than a few days, but, man, she was something else. She fucked like a jackrabbit! Hughie here caught on quick enough . . . He wasn't best pleased at first, but he laughed about it eventually. He called it the old ram's last stand.' He glanced across at his brother-in-law with a sheepish grin. The smaller man looked at the floor.

'How did it end?' asked Martin. 'I take it that it did end.'

'Oh, yes,' said Adams, 'it ended. I came here last Saturday night, after golf. Shagged me stupid she did, just like always. I came back across on Sunday, about midday, and she was gone. She didn't have much in the way of baggage, but what she had was away. She left not a trace behind her. No goodbye note, no "Thanks for a great time", no nothing.'

'Did she have access to your stores while she was here?'

'Sure. She helped Hughie check out some orders.'

'Including the Australian stuff?'

'Aye, I think so.'

'That's right,' Dickson confirmed.

'When was that?'

'Last Thursday,' said Adams. 'They wanted it delivered by Friday for their rehearsals.'

'And she disappeared on Sunday morning?'

'Right.'

'Did she take anything?'

'Steal anything, you mean? No. Nothing. The petty cash tin was there, too, wi' two-hundred-odd quid in it, but it was untouched.'

'You didn't see her leave, Mr Dickson?' asked Martin.

The man shook his head. 'No. I had nothing tae do wi' her. Ah'd rather have a good pint tae a blonde any day. Ah stayed out of her way as far as ah could.'

Martin looked back to Adams. 'How good a description can you give us?'

'Try this. Five feet nine or ten. Shoulder-length hair, blonde but dyed. Tanned, all but her bum. Legs right up to her arse. Very narrow waist, explosive hips, firm bum, wide shoulders, good-sized firm tits with wee pink nipples. Two moles low on her back. Appendix scar. Blue eyes, wide mouth, good teeth, long eyelashes. Oh, yes, and very strong.'

'Eh?'

'Aye. She's got exceptional strength on her for a woman. She challenged me to arm-wrestle once. I had a hell of a job getting her arm over, and I'm no pussy.' He rolled up his shirt sleeve to display a massive forearm.

'Did she ever talk about herself?'

'Not much. She said she came from Iowa, that she'd run away from home when she was sixteen, seven years ago. Said she'd been abused by her stepfather, but that she didn't want to talk about it.'

'Did you ever see her passport?'

'No.'

'Right. We'll need to get a technical team down here, to go over the flat where she stayed. Will you show us now, please.'

Adams led them out of the office and across the yard, past Mackie's Mondeo and past a silver Audi which the detectives assumed belonged to Adams.

A flight of narrow steps led up to the little flat, which had only two rooms. One was the main living area and the other, which opened from it, contained a single bed and a small wardrobe. A shower room and toilet opened off the top of the stairs.

'If this is our girl,' said Mackie, 'chances are she's wiped the place clean.'

Martin looked into the shower-room. The toilet seat was up. He turned to Adams. 'Do you always leave it like that?'

The man grinned. 'Aye. Bad habit of mine. The wife's always getting on to me.'

'Not so bad this time. I'll bet you we get a print off that, if nowhere else.'

Forty-two

Six called just after four. Copies of the Macdairmid tape had been rushed down on the 1:00 pm shuttle, carried by a Special Branch typist. She had handed them over to a motorcyclist waiting at Heathrow, and they had reached their destinations by 2:45 pm.

'Sorry to take so long to respond.'

Skinner thought for a moment that the Deputy DG was joking, but remembered that she had no sense of humour. The woman was rarely flippant, and most certainly never on a scrambled telephone.

'It took us a little while, because we believed we were listening to an Arab. But we were wrong. The reason he sounds that way is because he learned his English in Libya. Actually, the subject is a Peruvian. Our friend Macdairmid has got himself into some seriously bad company. The man on the telephone is Jesus Giminez.'

She paused.

Skinner knew the name at once. He had been shown the file on Giminez, a legendary figure among the world's security services. The man was an international terror consultant, wanted in many countries around the globe, but most of all by the Israelis. He was known to be responsible, either as hitman or as planner, for a string of political assassinations over around thirty years. His name had run like a scarlet thread around the world's trouble spots until 1991, not long after the death of Robert Maxwell, when he had vanished abruptly from the distant surveillance which the international intelligence community had managed to maintain, tenuously, for a quarter of a century. Some believed that he was dead, but the most commonly held opinion was that at the age of fifty-five he had decided to retire, like any businessman might. One of the most impressive things about Giminez had always been his anonymity. Other terrorists had become household names, but, to the international media and to the world at large, Giminez had remained unknown.

'Of course, we had no idea he was active again,' the Deputy DG continued. 'God knows what he's up to, but an operation like the one you've got on just now is right up his street. And if he was involved, he'd run it through someone just like Macdairmid, a radical front-man with an axe to grind. One thing about Giminez, his only principle is money. He works for cash only. Big cash. So if he's a player, someone's paying him: not less than seven figures sterling. Can you think of anyone in Scotland with access to that sort of cash?'

'It's possible, but what about contact? The man's a shadow. So how do you set about hiring him?'

'He has an agent, believe it or not – or rather a string of them. They're contactable through officials of a certain Middle Eastern government with a very dark name for that sort of thing.'

'But if *I* wasn't aware of that, how could someone like Macdairmid be in the know?'

'Well, he is an MP, after all. He *does* mooch around Whitehall. You can get anything there if you really want it. Of course, maybe *they* approached Macdairmid.'

'Meaning?'

'Meaning if your thing up there wasn't hatched in Scotland at all. Not everybody loves us Brits. You should know that more than most. Suppose someone wanted to do us a really bad turn. We've already got Ireland on our hands as an endemic problem. Stir up Scotland, then the Welsh, then a bit of ethnic warfare – in Bradford or Manchester, say. Mix all together, and Britain would become ungovernable. Our economy, our whole society would collapse. You know, Bob, I really do think you should catch these people.'

Forty-three

Andy Martin's guess had fallen just short of the mark: his technicians found not one but *two* sources of fingerprints. From the toilet seat, the scene-of-crime team had lifted perfect prints of the thumb and first three fingers of what they suspected, by taking and eliminating the prints of Adams and Dickson, to have been Mary McCall's right hand. And they had excelled themselves by taking from the toilet-roll holder the thumb and first finger of her left hand.

Everything else in the tiny garage apartment had been wiped clean, meticulously – and, as was clear to the technicians, by someone who had known exactly what she was doing.

Martin and Mackie had arrived back at Fettes Avenue with the prints at 9:10 pm, and had found Skinner still in his office.

'You say she split on Sunday morning? You think she's our woman, then, Andy?'

'Yes, boss, I do indeed. I think that our Mary deliberately gets herself tucked in beside randy old Frank Adams, and has time to take her pick of the stuff he's got going out to Festival companies – she had a choice of seventeen customers. She picks the Aussies, and plants her bomb in the radiogram with a timer set for mid-show – Adams told us that she had a Fringe programme in the flat – and stays under cover in Stow till last weekend. She gives old Frank one to remember her by, then nips up to Edinburgh on Sunday morning, either by bus or hitching, and teams up with the rest of her team to kill poor Hilary Guillaum. She's a big strong girl, says Frank. Well able to handle the knife work.'

'Yes,' said Skinner, his eyes bright with interest. 'It fits, all right. Brian, get out to the lab now, if not sooner and compare those prints with everything we lifted from Hilary Guillaum's suite at the Sheraton, and from that chambermaid's trolley. While you're at it, dig up a technician and get me blow-ups of those prints – top quality they can manage. Get back here as soon as you can. I'll be waiting. We'll see if the States can help us.'

Forty-four

Adam Arrow and 'Gammy' Legge arrived together. The two soldiers had met before in Ireland, and were resurrecting old stories as they walked into Skinner's office, just after 9:30 pm.

'So, put yourself in my place, Gammy. There you are, you search the fookin' house when the fella's out and you find, hidden in his fookin' bedroom, a bomb wi' the timer set to go off in thirty-six hours. I ask you, what would you do?'

'I suppose I'd send for me. What did you do?'

'Ah, but you weren't about. No, I just moved the timer forward thirty hours and fooked off. Six hours later, and so did 'e – sound asleep in his bed. Smashin' dream, he must have 'ad.'

Skinner put his hands over his ears. 'For God's sake, Adam, keep those stories to yourself. I'll assume you made that one up.'

The little man laughed. 'Course I did.' His eyes twinkled.

Skinner decided not to pry further. Instead he gave each man a beer from the small fridge standing in a corner of his office, and briefed them, as they drank, about the day's discovery at Stow.

'Does our assumption about the bomb sound right to you, Gammy? Could the timer have been set as accurately as that?'

'Yes. That's how she'd have done it, all right. They've got some really pricey timers these days, although if she really knew what she was about, she could have done it with the programming chip from a video. So in theory we could have sleeper Semtex bombs lying around all over Edinburgh.'

'Christ, that's all we need!'

'Ah, but in practice it's a different matter.'

'How come?'

'Thanks to some technical spec the manufacturers sent me, I've been able to work out how much of this super-Semtex stuff was used in each of our two explosions. The good news is that the total matches exactly the quantity nicked from that French arsenal. Add the fact that all of the rest of the world supply is accounted for, and in safe hands, and we reach the conclusion that as far as this super-Semtex is concerned, the bastards are out of ammo.'

'That's a relief; but what if they have conventional explosive? Maybe there are still sleeper bombs lying around.'

'If there are,' said Legge, 'then our dogs'll be able to smell them, or we'll be able to pick them out with some other little tricks that we have. We've already given every Festival venue a really thorough sniffing, and we'll keep on doing so on a regular basis.'

Skinner looked across at Arrow. 'All that makes our friend's meeting on Saturday even more interesting.'

The little soldier nodded. But Major Legge looked puzzled, until Skinner described the surveillance of Macdairmid, without actually naming him.

Arrow cut in. 'Did you find out who the other fooker was on the line?'

Skinner nodded, but said nothing. Instead he slapped a thick folder which lay on his desk. It was labelled '*Most Secret*', and had arrived by courier from MI6 only two hours earlier. It contained the career history of Jesus Giminez.

Arrow raised his eyebrows, but asked no more questions.

'Well,' said Legge. 'Good luck to you cloak-and-dagger Johnnies. Tell you one thing, though. If your geezer is expecting another consignment of those special fireworks, then he's likely to be disappointed, unless there's a second factory that no one knows about, because no one else is keen to be caught with their drawers down like the French were.'

'Hah,' Skinner snorted. 'Brave words, Gammy, but from what we've seen so far of this outfit, someone's arse is going to be exposed to the four winds!'

Forty-five

The two soldiers had been gone for only ten minutes when Brian Mackie returned with blow-ups of the six Mary McCall fingerprints. He brought too the opinion of the technicians that a fragment of a print taken from the chambermaid's trolley in the Sheraton Hotel could have come from her right hand.

'That's a start,' said Skinner. 'Now let's see how far our luck will run.' He led the way along the corridor to the Special Branch suite, past the duty officer in the outer area, and into Martin's empty office. A fax machine with a scrambled line sat on a table in the corner. Skinner picked up its telephone handset and dialled in a London number.

'FBI.'

Skinner was always struck by the frankness of the Americans. They knew and valued the respect in which the Bureau was held around the world, and were never shy of announcing its presence, even in foreign countries.

Joe Doherty was the FBI's senior man in Europe, based at the Embassy in Grosvenor Square. He had looked Skinner up on a tour of Special Branch heads when first posted to the UK in 1989, and they had been in touch ever since.

'You dragged yourself in, then,' said Skinner.

'Yup; I said I would. But this better be worth it.'

'Let's hope so. Joe, I'm going to fax you down six fingerprints. I'd like you to scan them into your magic machine, the one that connects back to the States, and see what it tells you – if it tells you anything at all, that is. I'll wait here. You'll get me on Andy Martin's direct line.' He gave him the number.

'OK, Bob,' said Doherty. 'Go for it.'

Skinner loaded the fax, selected half-tone quality, and keyed in the FBI's London number. The six pages took just over five minutes to transmit. He settled down to wait.

'Brian, this could take a while. You can go home if you want.'

'No way, boss. I want to see what he turns up.'

On Martin's office television, they watched the remainder of 'News at Ten', then midweek football. Rangers were two down in a League Cup tie to Motherwell, Skinner's team, when the telephone rang.

'Bugger it,' he swore, but switched off the television set as he picked up the receiver.

'Bob!' Doherty's excitement rang down the line, taking Skinner by surprise. 'Know who you've got there? Typhoid friggin' Mary, that's all.'

'And who the hell is she?'

'Typhoid Mary Little Horse. One of the most celebrated members of the American underclass. Hit-woman, bank-robber, political activist, terrorist, highly skilled with firearms, knives and explosives. You name it, that's Typhoid Mary. Deadly is her middle name. She styles herself a native American freedom fighter, but she's just a plain killer. We lost sight of her when she broke out of jail in Kansas last year. So what's she into over here?'

As quickly as he could, Skinner explained the detail of the Music Hall bomb, and summarised Adams' story. When he had finished, Doherty whistled loudly down the line. 'That's

Mary, both times. She's great with explosives, and she likes to kill people. But I'll tell you this, Bob. If she has Scotch blood, then you're a friggin' Sioux Indian.' Doherty paused, then went on. 'Couple of things for your Mr Adams. First the moderately good news. Not everything she told him was a lie. She was indeed raped by her step-daddy when she was sweet sixteen, and she did indeed run away from home. The detail that she left out was that, before she ran away, she cut his heart out . . . and I mean that literally, my friend.'

'Sounds like our friend Frank might have been lucky.'

'Well, no, Bob. You can't exactly say that. For now comes the really bad news for the Adams family. Mary can kill you in a whole lot of ways, but in one that's the most certain of all. She can kill you with her snatch, without you even being there – like she's probably killed Mrs Adams by now, through her poor sap of a husband. Her nickname's an understatement. We've got Mary's prison medical records. Bob, she's HIV positive. Look, I'll fax you up her picture. Better find her, man, before she screws the whole of Scotland to death!'

Forty-six

'So that's the story so far, Alan. A Scots MP mixed up with an international terrorist, and a crazy squaw killing people all over Edinburgh.'

The Secretary of State looked stunned. He leaned back in his chair and stared for several seconds up at the ceiling, affording Skinner a clear view of a large bruise, perhaps the size of a thumbprint, on the right side of his throat. Eventually he looked back across the desk. Their Sunday confrontation had not been mentioned, but a coldness hung between them, one which each man knew would never dissipate completely.

'This MI5 woman's theory, what do you make of it?'

'Mary Little Horse showing up makes it the best one we've got. You can count on the fingers of two hands the people in Scotland who could afford to fund this thing, and still have three fingers left over. I know; I have counted. Then you can rule out all of them as being too old, too straight, too boring, too law-abiding. None of the radical groups have the dough either. Yes, Alan, it all fits.'

'So what do you do now?'

'Well, I'm holding my morning briefing in an hour. I've got Crown Office permission to issue photographs of Mary Little Horse, and to put out a "Do not approach" warning.' As he spoke, Skinner opened the folder on his lap and handed across the desk a copy of the computer-generated print which Joe

Doherty had faxed to him. Ballantyne looked at it and saw an attractive blonde girl, expressionless in the standard prison mug-shot.

'I'll leave out the HIV bit,' Skinner went on. 'Stow's only a wee place, and I'm sure the story of Adams and the Yankee dolly-bird will be all over town already. The press coverage will produce a ton of calls, all of them rubbish no doubt, but if the heat makes her run for it, it'll have served its purpose. If I can't catch her here, I'd rather she was somewhere else.'

He paused and looked Ballantyne in the eye. 'But even if we do get rid of this girl, that doesn't solve our problem. She's a mercenary, and someone's brought her here to do a job. There may well be others, and we have got to expect other attacks. With that Semtex stuff used up, I'm less worried about more bomb attacks, but there are other things they can get up to. Like picking out more big-name assassination targets, for example. There are two events that really worry me. One is Fringe Sunday, and the other's the Fireworks Concert in Princes Street Gardens on the last Thursday of the Festival. One's held in a park, the other takes place after dark, and they're both too big for us to give them total protection. So I want to cancel them both.'

Ballantyne sat bolt upright in his chair. 'Absolutely not! I've made my position, and the Government's position, quite clear on that. We will do nothing that concedes an inch to these people. They cannot be allowed to claim a single victory through the threat of more violence. These events will go on as scheduled, and it's the job of your team and of your force to police them. Better still, it's your own job to catch these perpetrators. You've shown me some progress, but now I expect more concrete successes. Protection and detection, that's what I want to hear from you, Bob – not retreat and vacillation.'

It was Skinner's turn to jerk upright in his chair. An angry retort formed on his lips, but was stilled as he realised that something else was troubling Ballantyne. By now he knew the man well enough to read like a book the ups and downs of his personality, and he sensed clearly a second layer of concern, beyond the Festival crisis.

'Alan, is there anything else that you want to tell me?' he probed.

The Secretary of State sighed, and slammed his right fist into his left palm.

'Oh damn it! Yes, Bob. Look, I'm sorry I was so sharp there. You're right, I have another problem. You heard about my trip to London yesterday?'

Skinner nodded in silence.

'My wife has been absolutely devastated by the death of her, shall we say, friend. She regards it as some sort of punishment upon her. The upshot is she announced to me last night that she intends to resume our marriage. To make a fresh start.'

'Mm,' said Skinner, 'I can see that might be a problem. I had a talk with Carlie, Alan – for security purposes, you understand. I know the situation.'

'Yes, but you don't know about this.'

He produced a brown manila envelope from his desk drawer and pushed it across to Skinner, who picked it up and shook out a letter.

The salutation was the same as the earlier communications, but the message was different. Skinner read it quickly.

Attached is a photograph of the lady with whom you have been carrying on a liaison. We have others of you both which are more explicit, and in which the press will be interested. Accede to our demands, Ballantyne, or the people of Scotland will learn what a dishonourable man you are.

Clipped to the letter was a photograph of Carlie leaving Number 6 Charlotte Square by the back door.

'What do they mean, *other* pictures, Alan?'

'Haven't a clue, Bob. Why would they do that, anyway?'

'Keeping up the pressure, Alan. On you, on me, on us all. They know we're unlikely to ask for media help on this one. I'm afraid you're just going to have to take it on the chin when they show us what they've got.'

'Is there nothing I can do?'

'Yes. You have a choice. Announce that your marriage is over and that Carlie is the next Mrs Ballantyne, or – get her out of the country!'

Forty-seven

The Mary Little Horse story caused a sensation at the Thursday morning briefing, even without the intimate details of her relationship with Frank Adams. Skinner's carefully worded statement, warning the public to be on the look-out for the woman, together with her photograph, caught the media corps off guard.

'So where does that put your investigation?' With some of his belligerence recovered, Al Neidermeyer put the first question.

'It puts a new slant on it, that's for sure. Inevitably you have to be a bit sceptical about the real nature of a so-called patriotic organisation that gets itself involved with a foreign criminal like Typhoid Mary.'

Skinner saw the eyes of the *Sun* reporter, seated in the front row, light up at his use of her nickname.

'I regard this as significant progress. For legal reasons, I can't go into much detail, but we need to talk with this woman urgently in connection with the death of Hilary Guillaum and the *Waltzing Matilda* bombing. She's a striking girl: the sort who stands out in a crowd. She is also very, very dangerous, I am assured by the FBI. So any member of the public who thinks they've spotted her should give us a call at once, but otherwise leave her well alone.'

Forty-eight

Reported sightings of Typhoid Mary began to flood the Fettes switchboard, from the moment the first reports were broadcast. Indeed the earliest claims were made even before the first edition of the *Evening News* had hit the streets, giving her photograph page-one prominence.

As Skinner had surmised, all the calls were fruitless. Members of the public from as far afield as Barra and Lerwick called in to declare that they had seen the native American fugitive, but although these sightings were all followed up, none was even close to the mark. The only action that the police saw was when a young lady with a pronounced Sloane Ranger accent was detained in Shetland, before being identified as the daughter of a minor peer, on a back-packing tour of the Scottish Islands.

As Thursday stretched into Friday with no sign of further action by the Fighters, Skinner was able to report an incident-free twenty-four hours at the next morning's briefing.

Forty-nine

When Skinner returned from the Friday press conference, he found Alex waiting in his office. As he entered the room, she jumped up and rushed across to him.

'Hi, Pops.'

He took her into his arms and hugged her.

'Pops, I'm sorry. You're under all this pressure and I behave like a selfish, love-sick cow. I am really, really sorry.

'Am I forgiven?'

His face lit up as he smiled at her. Suddenly the world was a better place. 'Yeah, just this once I'll let you off with a caution. How are you and the boy getting on?'

'Fine. Ingo's great. He's so bright, and I just love him to bits. Don't worry, though. I'm not going to do anything daft like rushing off to Sweden with him. I've got a degree to finish first, and a diploma to get after that. He's got his course to finish, too. Once he's done that, he says he'll find a job in Britain, in the theatre if nothing else, and we can be together for good.'

In spite of his misgivings about the Swede, Bob grinned. 'Sounds like you've got his life thoroughly organised for him, just like you organised mine for twenty years.'

'Exactly. But you've got someone else to do that for you now. Even Andy, I hear from Sarah, may have found the love of his life. I have to have someone to look after.'

'Well, babe, all I ask is that you look after yourself as well. In fact put yourself first for a while.' He decided it was time to change the subject. 'How's your play then? We must pay it another visit.'

'We're doing great. It won't be announced in the *Scotsman* till tomorrow, but we've won a Fringe Award. Why don't you come to the Sunday show. It's being presented then.'

Sunday? Bob referred to his memory for a second. 'Sorry, can't do that. Sarah's got tickets for Le Cirque Mobile, or something, down on Leith Links. Tonight we're doing a movie with Andy and Julia, his new girlfriend, and tomorrow . . .' He paused for a second. 'Tomorrow I might be busy. So we'll come some time next week.'

Alex did not notice his momentary preoccupation. 'Le Cirque? I've heard of them. They're all bikers or something like that, aren't they. They're supposed to be terrific.'

'We'll see,' he said, although his tone implied doubt. 'All that carbon monoxide inside a tent doesn't sound too great to me. I'd rather be at your show, darling, believe me, but Sarah's dead keen on it.'

Alex laughed. 'It'll be all right. Sarah can pick 'em, you know.

'Well, look, Pops. If I don't see you at the theatre, I'll look out for you at Fringe Sunday.'

'No!'

His sudden vehemence stopped her in her tracks.

'Look, babe. Do just one thing for your old man. Steer well clear of Fringe Sunday.'

'But why? All the gang are going.'

'Just for me, give it a miss.'

She looked hard at him. 'You think something bad might happen? Do you know something?'

'Let's just say I'll feel happier if I know I don't have to look out for you there.'

'Well, my old Dad, if it makes you feel happier, I'll give it a miss. Promise.'

She stood on tiptoe, kissed him on the forehead and flitted out of the room, waving goodbye.

Fifty

Sir James Proud was the last man he had expected to see that morning. Or so Skinner told himself at first. But when he thought about it later, he realised that he had not been in the least surprised when his door burst open to reveal the Chief Constable's ample frame. Proud Jimmy, as he was known throughout his force, looked as imposing as ever in full uniform.

'Chief! What the hell are you doing here?'

'You know bloody fine,' said Sir James Proud. 'I couldn't settle for a moment out there, knowing all this nonsense was going on back home. Eventually it all got too much for her ladyship. Yesterday morning she said to me, "Jimmy. That's it. I'm packing and we're going to the airport. Get your Gold Card ready." So here I am.'

Skinner smiled at him. He realised at that moment just how much he had missed the solid support and advice of Sir James Proud.

'Well, I'm sorry it had to happen that way, but by God I'm glad you're back.'

'So what's been happening?'

Quickly Skinner updated him on the crisis. He showed him the MI6 file on Jesus Giminez, and the FBI sheet on Mary Little Horse.

'I am impressed,' said the Chief. 'You seem to draw these

people, Bob, like a flame attracts moths. So now I'm back, what can I do? How can I help?'

'You can chair tomorrow morning's press conference for a start. I'll be busy, doing something else. I'll have a Member of Parliament to arrest!'

Fifty-one

Neil McIlhenney was impressed by Macdairmid's choice of meeting-place. Edinburgh born and bred, he had never heard of the Kelvingrove Art Gallery and Museum, far less visited it. So when he ambled up the red sandstone steps and into the cathedral-like central hall, with its massive pipe organ at the far end, he was taken by surprise by its elegance and its scale. Neil had always liked organ music, and the fact that he had arrived in the middle of the Friday afternoon recital made the job the highlight of his week in Glasgow.

The tap had picked up Grant Macdairmid on the pub telephone as he set up his assignation at Kelvingrove. His call had been brief and to the point. 'Cassie? Grant here. Look I need you to run another message for me. Meet me this afternoon. Four-thirty, Kelvingrove Art Gallery.'

Haggerty had instructed Barry Macgregor to tail the MP from his office to the meeting-place, while McIlhenney had been sent on ahead.

Wooden seats were set out in rows across the hall. Those near the front were well filled, but in the row second from the back a girl sat alone, round-shouldered but relaxed in a pale blue T-shirt. McIlhenney looked at the back of her head and wondered. Rather than take a seat he wandered across to one of the display cases in an area off the hall. It was filled with an assortment of Cromwellian armour, out-of-place somehow in a Glasgow setting.

He could observe the main door from the far side of the glass case, and so Macdairmid did not see him as he glanced all around the hall on his arrival. Satisfied, the MP moved swiftly down the hall and made his way calmly between the seats towards the girl. McIlhenney noticed that he was carrying a black briefcase.

Macgregor entered a few seconds later, and sat down in the back row, a comfortable distance away from the couple. He had untied his pony-tail, and his long hair, with its white-beaded plaits, fell around his shoulders. He wore a crew-necked, short-sleeved shirt over faded jeans, split at the knee. McIlhenney looked at him and smiled. 'Crime Squad throws up some sights, right enough,' he whispered to himself.

The meeting lasted only a few minutes. Neither detective dared edge close enough to hear the conversation, but from what they could see it was one sided, Macdairmid doing all the talking. Less than five minutes after he had entered, the MP stood up and made his way out of the Gallery – without the black briefcase. Neither detective made a move to follow him. They knew that Glasgow officers were waiting outside at each exit from the Gallery, ready to pick up Macdairmid's trail. Instead they stayed, as ordered, with the girl.

She had little taste either, it seemed, for the fine organ music, for three minutes later she too rose to go. The briefcase looked heavy in her right hand. Outside, she made quickly for the car park, where she unlocked the door of a battered green Metro. She heaved the case on to the passenger seat, before jumping in and driving off.

Braided hair flying behind him, Macgregor sprinted over to

McIlhenney's Astra and jumped in, as the older man revved the engine and set off after the girl.

'Registration D436 QQS,' barked McIlhenney. 'Call it in.'

Using the car telephone rather than radio, Macgregor waited on the line while the number was checked. Eventually he said, 'Got that,' and put the phone back in its magnetic cradle. 'It's his sister, Neil. The bugger's using his own sister on a pick-up. The Metro's registered to Cassandra Macdairmid, date of birth 29 June 1969, listed address 124 Dundonald Road, Partickhill.'

'In that case, she's going home,' said McIlhenney, turning the Astra into Dundonald Road.

Fifty-two

Adam Arrow, Mario McGuire and Maggie Rose were all in position in the Chapter One Coffee Shop on the first floor of James Thin, in George Street, well before Cassie Macdairmid climbed the staircase at 11:25 am.

They were seated several tables apart. Wearing a light cotton jacket, Arrow looked for all the world like a tourist, as he sat reading the Saturday *Telegraph*. His view extended from the top of the stairs and into the second room of the cafeteria. He could see McGuire and Rose at their table through the open doorway which connected the café's two rooms. They looked for all the world like a thirty-something Edinburgh couple – which in fact they were – out on a morning's shopping expedition. Maggie's Marks & Spencer carrier bag, containing a few purchases made earlier that day, added authenticity.

They recognised Cassie Macdairmid as soon as she entered, not only from the description given by McIlhenney and Macgregor, but from the heavy black briefcase which she carried in her right hand. It tugged her shoulder down slightly as she moved.

Arrow's eyes were fixed on her back as she passed through the doorway, past McGuire and Rose, who seemed to take no notice of her. She made her way to the service counter, where she bought a cappuccino and a slab of thick brown cake. With difficulty she carried them, and the briefcase, in the direction of a table, somewhere to the left of McGuire and Rose, but out of Arrow's line of sight.

If being inconspicuous was part of the other messenger's brief, then, thought Arrow, he was inept at it. He wore the loudest black-and-white check woollen jacket that Arrow had ever seen on a man, with bright yellow polyester trousers. His lank jet-black hair, which emphasised his sallow complexion, looked as if it had been cut by a blind man. Apart from the fact that he looked so out of place, it was his briefcase which marked him out immediately as their second target. It was identical to that which Cassie Macdairmid had brought with her from Glasgow.

Arrow studied his *Telegraph* intently as the man looked quickly round the room, and, clearly having seen nothing to alarm him, moved through towards the service counter. He purchased a Coke, and, holding the bottle, looked round once more. At last, his eyebrows rose briefly in recognition as – Arrow guessed – he caught sight of Cassie Macdairmid. The messenger moved towards her table.

'May I join you?' he heard him asking in a Hispanic accent, just as he disappeared from view. Arrow switched his gaze to McGuire and Rose, ready to take his cue from them.

Five minutes had passed before he saw Maggie Rose make a sudden slight movement in his direction with her left hand. The little soldier stood up and moved towards the wide doorway, just as the man appeared in it. Arrow noticed at once that this time he was holding his briefcase in his left hand, while the other was plunged deep in the voluminous pocket of his jacket. As the two men's eyes met the right hand started to move.

Arrow stepped in, close and fast. With his left hand he grabbed the man's right wrist and immobilised it, just as the gun came into sight. At the same time the hard edge of his right hand smashed across the messenger's windpipe. With a choking sound, the man dropped his briefcase and crumpled to the floor. Arrow ripped the gun from his grasp and let his wrist go. He stepped over the writhing, pop-eyed form and through the doorway.

Maggie Rose was holding Cassie Macdairmid down in her chair by the shoulders. The woman looked terrified. McGuire held the second briefcase. He was about to open it when Arrow called to him.

'No, Mario. Leave that for Major Legge. He should have arrived outside by now. Let's get the public out of here, and fetch him in.'

Fifty-three

'Gammy' Legge shook his head. 'No damned explosive I've ever seen looks like that.' He stood in the second, inner room of the James Thin coffee-shop, still wearing his heavy black blast armour. 'You can come up now,' he called loudly.

Footsteps sounded on the stairs, and, a few seconds later, Arrow, Rose and McGuire appeared together in the doorway.

The black briefcase which the man had brought with him lay open on the table. It was full to the brim with fist-sized packages wrapped in brown paper. Legge had slit one open, and held it in the palm of his hand.

'What is it?' asked Arrow.

'Buggered if I know, old son. But it isn't explosive.'

Maggie Rose took the parcel from him. She looked at the powder inside and sniffed.

'You're wrong there, Major,' she said quietly. 'This stuff's explosive all right. It's high-octane and very dirty-looking heroin!'

Fifty-four

'I am Assistant Chief Constable Robert Skinner, and I don't believe I'm saying this, but, Grant Forrest Macdairmid, I am arresting you on suspicion of being a party to the illegal importation into the United Kingdom of a controlled substance, namely heroin, and of being involved in its illegal sale. You have the right to silence, but I must caution you that if you do say anything, it will be taken down and may be used against you.'

Macdairmid looked from Skinner to Willie Haggerty, and back again, in blank-faced astonishment.

As soon as the call had come through from Maggie Rose, they had gone in, four of them. McIlhenney and Macgregor made up the quartet, and all but Skinner were carrying firearms. They had brought a search warrant and, even as Skinner cautioned Macdairmid, the two detective constables were beginning to take his flat apart.

'Seems you didnae reform after all, Grant.' The intensely angry edge to Haggerty's tone was one that Skinner had never heard from him before. There was a passion in it which was totally unexpected in the normally cynical, worldly Glaswegian.

'Ah remember you as a tearaway, wi' yir heavies, and yir dirty wee protection racket. Ah wis one of the team that lifted ye the last time, but ye won't remember that. There were we thinkin' that ye'd seen the light, but ye had us kidded on, all along. You never gave it up, did ye? You jist got dirtier. How did ye get tae be an MP? How did ye get away wi that?'

'Most people in Glasgow are just as thick as you, so it wasn't difficult.' There was contempt in Macdairmid's voice.

Haggerty's fury was ready to erupt. He took a pace towards the man, his heavy fists balled, but Skinner held him back.

'You're the thickhead in this room, pal,' Skinner said. 'With all that's going on just now, you should have known that we'd have been on you like bluebottles on a turd, yet you still got involved in this deal. You must be fucking mad.' As he said this, it occurred to him suddenly that he might well be right. For a man in his predicament, Macdairmid's arrogance seemed beyond belief.

'Don't count your chickens, Skinner. I want my lawyer here now. I bet that any evidence you have against me won't be admissible in court. Once I'm out, I'll crucify you. The next election isn't that far off, you know. I expect to be a Scottish Office Minister, once it's over. Then you'll see.'

With lazy strength, Skinner picked Macdairmid up and slammed him against the wall, hard. The back of his head cracked against the plaster.

'Listen, boy, to what you are,' he said, in a controlled steady voice. 'You are a fucking horse trader. You're a heroin dealer. You are less than dog-shit on my shoe. Make no mistake, you are going away for a long, long time. There is someone in this room who's an expert with a hammer and nails, and you're looking at him. But before your public crucifixion in the High Court, you're going to tell me how a Glasgow snot-rag like you comes to be mixed up in a drugs deal with Jesus Giminez, international terrorist numero uno. How do you think old Jesus is going to like having had his messenger, his two hundred grand and his drugs all nicked? Maybe I *will* let you go, and see just how long you survive. Personally, I wouldn't give you a month.'

As Macdairmid stared at him, fear and amazement replaced the bellicosity. 'What the hell do you mean? Who's this Jesus whatever-you-called-him? I've never heard of him. My only contact was some Colombian. Even then, we only spoke over the phone, and only ever on secure lines.' Macdairmid was convicting himself with every word, but he cared not a bit.

'Not as secure as you thought,' said Skinner. 'We heard you talking to Giminez. He was identified by the best. You wouldn't believe some of the heavyweight things he's done, so why's he messing himself with a wee shite like you? That's what you're going to tell me – and bloody fast, too.' He let go of Macdairmid's shirt front. 'You've got some serious talking to do before the day's out. But not here. I'll see you again through in Edinburgh. Neil, Barry, finish up here, and take Mr Macdairmid, MP, though to Fettes. His lawyer can see him there. He'd better be bloody good, though!'

Macdairmid was handcuffed, and the two detective constables hustled him away.

'Well, sir,' said Haggerty. 'We didnae expect all this, did we?'

'No we bloody did not.

'Fucking ironic, Willie, isn't it. You and I have just made what for most coppers would be the arrest of a lifetime, yet here we are – well, me at least – absolutely pissed off. We started off thinking that Macdairmid was our best lead to the Fighters for fucking Freedom. Now we find he's just another drug-dealer. Look at the time we spent on it. A great result, sure, and I'm glad that stuff isn't going to hit the street. But as far as our main business in concerned, we're right back to square one!'

Fifty-five

Skinner was passing Shawhead, on the drive back to Edinburgh, when Brian Mackie's call came through.

'Boss, this is incredible. I thought you'd want to know right away. The lab boys ran a quick test on a sample of Macdairmid's heroin. Their report's just arrived. That stuff is lethal. First of all it's so pure that your average addict would off himself with just one fix. And, as if that wasn't enough, there's something else in there too. They haven't isolated it yet, but it seems to act as a catalyst to turn the heroin into pure poison. That's what Macdairmid was going to spread all over Glasgow.'

'Holy Christ, Brian! Look, don't let anyone say anything about it to our man. I want to break that piece of news myself.

'What about his sister? She saying anything since her arrest?'

'She can't stop crying. She says she knows nothing about anything – but how many times have we heard that before? She swears she hadn't a clue about the heroin. She says she thought she was picking up hot cash from Libya to fund some left-wing newspaper, and that the briefcase she brought with her was just a dummy for a swop, weighted down to make it look authentic.'

'What about the messenger?'

'He definitely isn't saying anything. He tried to pull a gun on Captain Arrow. The wee man hit him so hard he smashed his voicebox. He'd have died if Sarah hadn't been with the emergency team outside. She did an emergency tracheotomy. She kept him alive, but she reckons he might never speak again. He's in intensive care.'

'OK, Brian, thanks. Be back soon.'

Next, from the car, he called Six, then Joe Doherty, who for once had been spending a weekend at home. When he broke the news, it was the first time that Skinner had ever heard Doherty rattled.

'Christ, Bob! You really mean that? Giminez is running poisoned smack? I gotta feed that back to the Bureau and the DEA. Suppose he's doing that in the States as well. You any idea how many people you could kill with a case full of poison?'

'As many as there are needles to go round, my friend. Good luck.'

Fifty-six

The *Sentinel* broke the Carlie story on Sunday morning.

Bob and Sarah were still asleep when the telephone rang. It was Ballantyne in a panic which verged on hysteria. First, Bob calmed him down, then he dressed and drove down to the newsagent at the nearby road junction to pick up a copy of the newspaper. The *Sentinel* was a new, independent Scottish Sunday tabloid, launched three months earlier, and already struggling for survival.

The candid back-door shot was there, all right. But, much more serious, there was a second photograph, taken with a long lens through an upper-floor window, which showed clearly the Secretary of State and his lady in a fond embrace. Fortunately, Skinner thought as he studied it, they were both fully clothed.

'MYSTERY BLONDE IN BALLANTYNE LOVE-NEST' screamed the headline, crediting the 'Fighters for an Independent Scotland' as the source of the photographs, and printing in full their denunciation of Ballantyne. However, in neither the statement nor the *Sentinel*'s subsequent story was Carlie identified.

As Sarah sat down to read the story and study the photographs, Skinner called Ballantyne back on the kitchen phone.

'Alan, I'm sorry for you, but this isn't one that I can help you with. They've broken no law here. Any paparazzi could have done that; and I'm surprised that no one has before now. Best thing you can do is call Mike Licorish and ask him if he'll stretch the rules and issue a personal statement for you.'

'But, Bob, my career.'

'Alan, with respect, you should have thought of that before. What you do now is up to you and your conscience. You're either a man or you're a weasel. I know what I think you are. It's up to you to prove me right or wrong.'

As he hung the phone up, he noticed that Sarah was looking at him in astonishment. But he shook his head and said no more.

An hour later, as they were clearing away the breakfast dishes, the telephone rang again. This time, it was Michael Licorish.

'Bob, I thought you'd like to hear this before it goes out. You listening?'

Skinner grunted.

'It's a statement by the Secretary of State. It reads: "Mrs Ballantyne and I deprecate the publication in this morning's press of photographs of our close friend Miss Charlotte Mays, and the libellous story which accompanied them. One of these photographs was particularly intrusive in that it shows Miss Mays comforting me immediately after I had received the sad and unexpected news of the death of another close family friend, Lord Broadgate. Mrs Ballantyne and I wish to make clear that if there is any further publication of these photographs or these allegations, we will pursue libel actions against the perpetrators with the full rigour of the law." What do you think of that?'

'Jesus, that's our man all right. Where's Carlie now?'

'On a plane heading for the States. S of S bought the ticket.'

'Isn't he just the ticket himself, eh? Cheers, Mike.' He hung up.

Sarah, reaching up to put two mugs away in a high cupboard, looked across at him. 'Well? Which is he then?'

'I was right enough. He's a fucking weasel.'

Fifty-seven

The full team – police and SAS back-up – gathered in the Fettes Hall at 11:00 am, long after the last journalists had left the regular morning briefing. For the newsmen, the highlight had been Skinner's brief and completely unexpected statement that Grant Macdairmid, MP and his sister Cassandra had been arrested, along with a third man, identity as yet unknown, and charged with possession of heroin with intent to supply.

Faced with a threat by Skinner of prosecution for attempted murder, Macdairmid, on the advice of his lawyer, had made a full formal statement at 2:00 am. He had said that his contacts in London had taken him to meet a man in a pub, a Libyan who had told him that he had a connection to some cheap, high-quality drugs. Macdairmid had also admitted that he had been dealing for some years.

The contact had given him a number in Colombia, and he had talked price with the man there. The supplier had explained that he routed the heroin in through France, and across the Channel, easy since the borders had been opened. Macdairmid had decided to take a trial shipment, and had done well out of it. He had agreed to take a second batch, bigger this time. He had been astonished at the man's low price.

The same thought had occurred to Skinner. Two hundred thousand for a case-load of heroin was bargain basement.

But now Skinner's full attention was turned to his briefing for the Fringe Sunday event. From the rows of theatre seating which had been set out for the press, twenty serious faces looked back at him. Among them was Sarah's. He had attempted to persuade her that she would not be needed, and that her presence would be a personal distraction to him, but she had been adamant. 'You included me in this team. That means all the way.'

Now, he fixed his troubled gaze upon her as he stood up, behind his desk, to address the team.

'Well, ladies and gentlemen. Let me begin by giving it to you straight. This is going to be the devil's own job to police. Even in a normal year, Fringe Sunday gives your average pickpocket an orgasm just thinking about it. This time, well . . .

'For our army friends, who may be new to the Festival, let me explain what happens. Fringe Sunday is the one major gathering of all the Fringe performers, giving the public a chance to see them close-up and to sample their shows. You'll all by now have seen what happens at the foot of the Mound every lunchtime, and you'll have an idea of the crowds that gather there. Well, this event attracts about forty to fifty times that number. It takes place in Holyrood Park, it's open to the public, and it's absolutely free. We've only been able to guess at the possible numbers, but the experienced boys in operations reckon that there could be as many as one hundred thousand there, given a fine day – and this will be as fine a day as you could ask for. I've checked the forecast, and there's no chance of the weather breaking for a few days yet.

'You might expect the crowd to be less today, with all that's happened. Let's hope that's right. But it's been nearly a week since the last major incident. The press are even beginning to suggest that the enemy has shot his bolt.'

Skinner paused to look around the hall.

'Don't you believe it! These people want something big. They've had access to state-of-the-art equipment, and to people who know how to use it.'

Mario McGuire cut in. 'They're claiming they want an independent Scotland. Are you saying it might be something else they're after?'

'That's what I'm beginning to wonder, yes. How come we don't have a clue as to who they are. We led ourselves well and truly up the garden path with Macdairmid. All our known agitators have checked out clean – even that daft hack, Frazer Pagett. There is something else, Mario. I feel it in my water! Maybe it's really us they're after.'

'Us?'

'Yes. The police. Authority. Maybe that's what it's all about.' He turned back to the group. 'But that's irrelevant for now. Today we've got to be fully on guard against another terrorist attack. That's our job. Fringe Sunday presents a big target, and so far that's the pattern they've followed. Big, attention-grabbing events.

'There are four official entrances to Holyrood Park. We'll have uniformed officers guarding them all, and there will be plenty others among the crowds. The sight of all those flat hats might have a deterrent effect! But just in case it doesn't, I want you there, too, all of you armed and ready to react in whatever way seems necessary. You will all wear sunglasses, and one of these' – he held up a small lapel pin in the shape of a golden lion – 'so that if there is trouble, the uniforms will be able to tell the difference between the terrorists and the good guys. If we have action, and you SAS people get involved, then please leave the scene as soon as it's over. We don't want any of you identified by anyone. I take that very seriously. The uniformed detachment, all ninety-five of them, are being given their briefing separately for that very reason.

'By the way, people, the uniformed detachment is led by the Chief. The deputy and the other two ACCs will be there, too. I want you to know that the Command Suite is leading from the front on this one.' He looked around the room once more. 'Any questions?'

No one answered.

'Good. Let's go.' The group began to break up. 'And, hey!'

Twenty faces turned back towards him. He was grinning.

'Be careful out there!'

Fifty-eight

As Skinner was heading for the exit, he was stopped by the Chief Constable's staff officer, a uniformed superintendent.

'Sorry, sir, but before you leave, could you please call Mr Doherty. He's in his office. He said you would know who he is.'

'Thanks, Malcolm.'

Skinner sprinted up the stairs to his office, and punched in Joe Doherty's number on the secure line.

'Joe? What can I do for you?'

'Just listen, that's all. I have a story to tell you, about Giminez and your friend Macdairmid, the patsy. I've found out who was behind it all.'

Skinner sensed that Doherty was spinning out the suspense. 'Joe, come on, for fuck's sake. I've got a crisis here.'

The FBI man laughed. 'So have some cousins of mine. OK, I'll get to the point. It's the CIA. They've been running Giminez.'

'What!'

'Yeah. To be exact it's one man. A crazy hawk at Langley called Goodman. It seems that at some point during the last administration, the President was being given an inter-departmental briefing on the drugs problem, and he made some sort of throwaway remark, along the lines of: "If someone would just go away and come up with a miracle cure for all this, what a goddamned hero he'd be." A bit like your Henry II wishing to be rid of that turbulent priest of his. So Goodman's at the meeting, and his crazy little mind starts to work. He figures, "We'll never kill all the Colombians and the Burmese, or torch all their crops. So what we have to do is discredit their product."

'The health agencies all over the world have been saying it for years: "If you touch smack or coke you will die, eventually." But to an addict that just ain't true. We've had a boom in the drugs market, and in all the other crime that runs alongside it. So Goodman figures that what he's got to do is make the users believe: "If you touch heroin or smack you *will* die . . . now! No second chance." Then he does some more thinking and comes up with Giminez. The CIA have been running him for years, doing all sorts of things that we won't go into. Goodman tells him what he wants, Giminez says: "OK, gimme da money, I do it. But it'll take time." Goodman siphons off dough from a big CIA slush fund. Giminez drops out of sight, and stays in deep cover for years. What he's been doing is *one*, he's been building up supplies of horse and coke; *two*, putting some of the world's finest illicit chemists to work in making them lethal; and *three*, and most recently, setting up relationships with dealers around the world, like your MP friend, all of them greedy and in the market for cheap supplies. Say, Bob. Being an MP, that's pretty good cover, eh?

'The final stage of the plan, and it's a beauty, I have to say, is that Giminez, through his network, feeds the marks a little good stuff to whet their appetites, and get the street excited, then drops the bomb with the big shipment. End result is, dead users all around the world, stories leaked to the press, mass panic, and everyone too scared to touch the stuff, like ever again.'

Time was ebbing away, but Skinner was fascinated. 'So how did you get on to Goodman?'

'I passed the name Giminez on to Langley. They found the slush money, traced the payment to Goodman, and used all means necessary to make him talk.'

'So how do they stop it?'

'God knows. Maybe they can't. Goodman doesn't know names, or even how many Macdairmids there are, and the CIA can't get to Giminez anyway. He's operating blind. Broke contact with Goodman long ago. All the CIA can do now is put the word out on the street, and tell the Colombians about Giminez in the hope that they can stop him. But maybe they won't do that either. Because, goddamn it, crazy Goodman's crazy idea could actually work. I did hear that the DEA can't figure out whether to give you a medal for uncovering this whole operation, or put a contract out on you!

'Meantime, Interpol has started to log reports from Hamburg of dozens of coke users – some of them top people – suddenly winding up dead all over the city. And somehow I doubt if that'll be the last we hear of Giminez and his special deliveries. Hope your crisis up in Scotland turns out to be a damn sight easier to solve!'

Fifty-nine

Skinner's mind whirled with the consequences of Doherty's story, as he headed off towards Holyrood Park in his BMW, on the heels of his squad.

The Park is, in a sense, the biggest back garden in Scotland. Within its grounds, behind a high grey wall, stands the Palace of Holyroodhouse, modest in size but rich in history. Four centuries ago, as the machinations of the court of the doomed Mary, Queen of Scots tore her country apart, it was a place of intrigue and murder. Today it stands largely unchanged, as the official residence in Scotland of her heirs and successors, and as a venue for great gatherings of heads of government. Though Holyrood is a Royal Park in status, in practice it is one of Edinburgh's favourite and largest public open spaces, covering well over a square mile of greenlands, with three small lochs which provide lodgings for dozens of swans, geese and ducks, with – literally thrown in – a constant supply of food from children and tourists.

Holyrood Park is dominated by Arthur's Seat, an extinct volcano from whose vantage point the legendary king is said to have overlooked the first dwellings of what was to become the beautiful city of Edinburgh. Dark Age overtones continue to cling to the ancient hill. As he looked up at it in the fine August morning sunshine, Skinner recalled with a tug at his heart another morning twenty years earlier, when he had walked with his first wife Myra, the baby Alexis cradled in her arms, to the summit, with dozens of other parents, to wash in the midsummer morning dew. He closed his eyes for a moment, and could see again the clear vision of Myra gently dabbing her baby's face, and saying softly, 'There. That'll guard her beauty for life.' She had been right in her prediction for Alex. But, sadly, life had not been long for Myra.

Skinner tore himself back to the present and surveyed the Royal Park. It was still well short of midday, but thousands of people were there already, congregating on the flatter grassland around the palace and beyond towards the park wall, and the grey tenements of Royal Park Terrace. At intervals, flat-backed lorries and other temporary staging had been set up to provide venues for impromptu performances by Fringe players. He noted with approval the numbers of police caps which could be seen in the crowd. Occasionally, he saw casually dressed figures, looking around observantly through their sunglasses, and caught the glint of gold on their chests.

The first performers arrived just after midday: a student revue from Oxford University. They set out their props on one of the lorry stages and soon gathered a crowd as they began to perform snatches of their show, involving the audience whenever they could. Gradually, more and more spectators and more and more players filled the Park, until by 2:00 pm it was thronged with happy folk, singing, playing and laughing in the sunshine. The only people there who could not relax were Skinner's plainclothes team, the SAS soldiers, and the ninety-five policemen and policewomen in uniform, who continued to mingle with the crowd.

He was standing with Sarah, some way off, when it happened.

A few minutes earlier, a wide circle had opened amid the

crowd, perhaps one hundred and fifty yards across. A motorcycle had roared into life, then another, then a third, and a fourth.

'It's Le Cirque Mobile,' Sarah cried. 'Let's have a look.'

But he had held her back, seeing no easy way through the thick crowd. So Sarah had stretched on tip-toe, catching only glimpses of the riders' lightweight helmets, and occasionally the clown make-up on their faces, as they bucked and twisted their bikes in wheelies, or left the ground in acrobatic leaps.

Skinner was looking away when he heard the first screams, and Sarah grasped his arm tightly. He looked round, to see the wide circle of spectators burst apart as one of the riders revved his bike and roared through them, steering with his left hand alone. The bike carved a swathe amid the diving people as it ploughed through the panicking crowd. It headed straight towards a wide platform stage, on which a group of dancers were performing, dressed in a colourful folk costume. One by one, they stopped and stared as the cyclist roared towards them. They could only look on, frozen with shock, as he threw the object which he held aloft in his free right hand.

The grenade exploded in mid-air, among the dancers. Bodies flew everywhere, and a fine red mist seemed to hang in the air for a second or two.

As the screaming erupted and escalated, Skinner, running now towards the scene, saw the motorcyclist veer away from the makeshift stage, pulling a squat, ugly gun from his jacket. There was something about his movement, about the way he handled his bike, which made Bob certain that this was the same man who had shot at him in Charlotte Square. But this time he was carrying an automatic machine-pistol. As he roared through the scattering crowd towards the Meadowbank gateway, he sprayed fire from right to left and back again. To his horror, Skinner saw young Barry Macgregor go tumbling backwards, gun in hand, blood spraying from his throat.

And then the man had broken through the last of the crowd. The bike accelerated towards the exit, the rider steering now with both hands. He had thrown the gun, spent, on the grass behind him.

It was a hell of a shot, they all agreed later. Brian Mackie fired only once. Technically, Skinner might have rebuked him for failing first to call out, identifying himself as an armed police officer, but in the circumstances he decided to let this pass.

The rider's back arched and his arms flew wide, as the bullet cut through his spine. He seemed to rise out of the saddle, and to hang, cruciform, in mid-air for a second, before falling, almost gracefully, on to his back. At the same time, the front wheel of the motorcycle reared up, and the whole machine spun in a grotesque somersault, crashing, handle-bars first, to the ground with its engine still roaring, a few feet away from its spread-eagled rider.

Skinner ignored the biker, and ran instead towards Barry Macgregor. As soon as he reached him, he realised that there was no hope. The young man was convulsing. Blood pumped from an awful wound in his throat, squirting through his fingers as he struggled in vain to stem its flow, and running down his neck and shoulders to stain his braided hair.

Sarah arrived only seconds later, but even in that time the last of the life had ebbed from the boy's body.

For a time, Skinner knelt beside him, blood on his hands and tears in his eyes, though his jaw was set firm. When eventually Sarah took him by the shoulders and drew him gently to his feet she found, on his face, an expression which she had never seen before; not his, not Bob's, but that of someone she did not know at all.

Suddenly, in the stillness and silence which surrounded their little tableau, she felt very frightened; fear for her husband, and – for a flash – fear of him and yet not him, of someone cold, vengeful and absolutely deadly who dwelt within him.

Sixty

'Bob, isn't that our clown? Remember, on Saturday. The one on the unicycle at the Mound, with the leaflets.'

'It could be love, could be. But I do know I saw him somewhere else that same day.'

Skinner had banished his grief and rage, and looked his normal self again, controlled, hardened against the horror, and deferring his time of mourning until the job was done. They were standing with Andy Martin and Brian Mackie in the area which had been cordoned off around the motorcycle assassin. A hundred yards away, Sir James Proud stood at the head of an honour guard over the body of young Barry Macgregor, as his officers cleared the park slowly of public and performers.

In contrast to the stillness of the two groups, the ambulance crews were working feverishly to tend the casualties. There were some who were as far beyond help as Barry Macgregor. Four of the six members of the Belorussian Folk Ensemble, the on-stage targets of the grenade attack, lay sprawled in death. The lucky survivors were already in an ambulance which was screaming its way out of the Park, towards the Royal Infirmary, its blue lights whirling. Three members of the crowd had been killed, including a baby still clutched in the arms of her stunned mother, and fourteen others wounded either by the explosion's deadly shrapnel or by gunfire.

The motorcylist, in his turn, was very dead.

One or two colleagues had bestowed on Brian Mackie the nickname 'Dirty Harry' because of his legendary prowess with various firearms on the rifle range at St Leonard's Police Station. But Brian never acknowledged the title, nor played up to it in any way. Not for him the Clint Eastwood stride, or throwaway lines about days made. Brian took his role as an expert marksman very seriously indeed. It was an important part of his job as a policeman, and not the subject for humour. On the one occasion in his career when he had been called on to fire at a human target, his disciplined approach ensured that his reaction had been instant, emotionless, and absolutely effective. Afterwards, his conscience had been untroubled. He had not, as he said once in answer to Andy Martin's question, lost a single night's sleep.

So it would be again now, he knew. As he looked down at the body of the motorcyclist, he banished from his mind any feeling of elation that he had felled the man who had killed Barry Macgregor. This was just another job done well, and on that basis alone he was pleased. As an expert, Mackie believed in arming himself to suit the occasion and the possible circumstances. His choice of weapon that morning had been a Colt .45 magnum revolver. The gun, he noted as he looked at the body, had lived up to its awesome reputation. There was a fist-sized exit wound right through the biker's breast-bone. Mackie saw chips and slivers of white bone mixed in there. He surmised that the bullet had spread when it struck the spine, shattering it and sending fragments of bone and lead tearing through the heart.

Sarah had removed the man's helmet, but through the clown make-up it was difficult to tell anything about the man's appearance, other than that he was blond.

McGuire, Rose and McIlhenney were standing a little way

off, with the three other riders from the troupe, and one other: a muscular, short-haired girl who wore a vest with 'Le Cirque Tour' emblazoned on its front. Skinner waved them over.

The three riders cringed when they saw their dead colleague, but the girl merely whistled and shook her head. 'You guys don't miss, eh,' she said in a chirpy East London accent.

'This is Alison, sir,' said Maggie Rose. 'The three lads are all French. All the English they speak between them couldn't buy you a bag of chips, but Alison's one of the troupe too. She's a mechanic, and she knew this fellow.'

'Hey, steady on. I know he called himself Ricky, but that's about it.'

Skinner looked at the pass which he had taken from the back pocket of the dead man's jeans. It was made out in the name of Richard Smith.

'How long had he been with you?' he asked the girl.

'He joined us in France a month ago. Said he was a Scottie and wanted to work his way home. Didn't want much in wages – only his fare paying. The manager said he had a reference from a man in Marseilles. He was a mechanic, too, and good with the bikes. Mind you, he wasn't a regular in the troupe. Shouldn't have been riding today, only . . .'

'Only what?' said Skinner impatiently, as the girl's story tailed off momentarily – as if she was working something out in her mind.

'Only Paul, the fourth of our regular bikers, got mugged in Leith last night. Three geezers jumped him, apparently. He's in hospital now. They banged him up and broke his arm. 'Ere, you don't think . . .?'

'Fine, Alison. Just you leave the thinking to us. Any ideas you have, you keep them to yourself. Is that understood?'

'Sure, boss. Anything you say.'

'OK, now will you please give a statement to DS Rose here, give her also your address, and then take your pals home. From the look of them there's no show tonight.'

Sixty-one

'Her story checked out, then?'

'The mugging? Aye. The boy Paul was French too, but he spoke English. Apparently he was making his way home last night after the show, when three guys in suits came up to him, took him up a close, and gave him a doing.'

Skinner and Proud sat facing each other, over two large whiskies in the Chief's room at Fettes Avenue. It was still only 6:45 pm, but each looked tired and drained. Removed from the scene of the crime, a second wave of sadness had washed over them both at the loss of their colleague.

'Men in suits?' said the Chief Constable. 'That doesn't sound much like Leith.'

'No, it doesn't. Strangest thing of all, the boy said there was a woman with them, and she seemed to be giving the orders.'

'It wasn't this Typhoid Mary woman, was it?'

'No. This one was dark haired, and she was under five-six.

'I'm already pulling in all of our likely candidates to undertake a contract thumping, but I don't hold out any great hopes that any of them will fit the bill. These will either have been members of the team or out-of-town heavies brought in for this job alone, and so virtually untraceable. They were very professional. Apparently one of them said to the boy, "Sorry, mate, but it's in a good cause." Then he broke his arm with a mason's hammer. According to Paul, when the guy spoke to him, the woman said "Silence". And again, according to him, she said it in French. But since he's French himself, and he was having his arm broken at the time, I'm discounting that one.'

'What about the late Mr Ricky Smith? Do we have anything on him?'

'Yes. He has a French connection, too. Their police have dug out their file for us. According to his prints, his name wasn't Richard Smith at all. It was Raymond Mahoney, age twenty-six, birthplace Glasgow. Time-served mechanic. Lived in France since he was twenty. Bad boy, Raymond, or so they think: believed to have been involved in the gang scene in Marseilles. They had him marked down as a driver mostly, but he was known to have been in the vicinity of two or three shootings. The closest they came to doing him for anything was when he was picked up as one of a team in a freelance armed robbery. But then one of the police witnesses was killed on duty, and the other had a fit of amnesia – financially induced, they reckoned, so nothing came of it. Technically he's got a clean sheet, but they won't miss him now he's gone.'

Proud freshened up their drinks from a bottle of Highland Park. 'What're you doing about the press?'

'Royston's got a statement ready to go out, as soon as I've been to visit Barry's dad. He's a widower, and he's been away golfing with a pal. They're due back at eight according to the pal's wife. I'll catch him them.'

'No, you won't,' said Proud. 'I'll see that's taken care of. You've done enough.'

'Come on, Jimmy, he was my man.'

'My man, too. I was planning to see Mr Macgregor myself, but Eddie McGuinness insisted. He feels that he has to take on at least some of the tough tasks personally. A solid man is our Eddie.'

'So I'm beginning to realise,' said Skinner thoughtfully.

The Chief Constable took a sip from his glass, savoured the smoky taste, and swallowed it. 'So what do these bastards do next, Bob?'

'I'm trying to think like them, Jimmy. Looking at the pattern so far, I'd say it's got to be the Fireworks Concert, a week on Thursday. They know we won't let them near any more celebs, and the Fireworks are the last big event in the Festival. It's even on telly this year. They might stick in a couple of wee surprises between now and then, but I'll bet that's the next thing they'll go for.'

'Let's cancel it then.'

'I've already suggested that to Ballantyne, but there's no way he'll agree. He's got brave again.'

'Well, we'll just have to police it so tightly they'll have to use aircraft to hit it. Tomorrow you and I will go and see Mr bloody Ballantyne. It's time you had some back-up when you're dealing with him!'

Sixty-two

The inevitable communiqué was delivered to the Queen Street office of the BBC at 9:00 am on the following day. For the first time it was addressed to the media, rather than to the Secretary of State.

The News Editor, Radio, never a man to turn down a scoop, took a snap decision. He sent copies at once to St Andrew's House and to Skinner's office, then ordered that the morning's music programme should be interrupted and the text of the letter broadcast.

Skinner therefore heard it on the radio before he received his copy. He was alerted at once by the excitement in the newsreader's voice.

'The following message has just been received by the BBC. Because of its use of a special code word, we believe it to be genuine. It reads as follows:

> "*From the Fighters for an Independent Scotland.*
> "*Communiqué.*
>
> "It is with regret that we report the death of a fine young Scottish patriot, Raymond Mahoney, on an active service mission in Edinburgh yesterday. We regret too that a further demonstration of our resolve has proved necessary. However, the intransigence of Scotland's

colonial governor, the Secretary of State, left us no choice.

'As before, our target was selected with a view to focusing international attention on our struggle for freedom. We note with some satisfaction that one member of the enemy's security forces also fell yesterday. If the occupying government continues to deny Scotland its right to freedom, he will not be the last.

'The first phase of our struggle is over. We have claimed the attention, and we believe the support, of the nations of the world. From now on we will seek to strike at the heart of the tyranny, wherever the opportunity arises. Our fight for an independent Scotland will not end with the Edinburgh Festival. It will go on until the occupying government yields, or until the last of its members is cut down. The Secretary of State and his puppet-masters in London are legitimate targets. They must realise that their police cannot protect them for ever."

'That is the end of this newsflash,' said the newsreader breathlessly. 'Now back to the studio, and to Eddie.'

Sixty-three

'For Christ's sake, Sir James, don't you people ever listen! I've told Skinner, ever since this thing started, that we will not give in to terrorism. Now even you have joined the chorus of appeasers. I will not cancel the Fireworks Concert.'

Proud Jimmy looked at his most formidable, as thunder-clouds of rage gathered on his brow. Skinner sat back in the Secretary of State's comfortable armchair and waited for the storm to break.

But Ballantyne had not finished. 'Whatever these people may threaten, far from cancelling the event, I will attend personally! And I won't be alone. I spoke with the Prime Minister himself this morning and he has insisted on being present also! My information directorate has just made that announcement.'

'Sweet Jesus,' said Skinner softly.

Ballantyne shot him a haughty glance, but continued to address the Chief Constable. 'Protection and detection is what I asked of Bob last week. As our opponents point out in their so-called communiqué, his anti-terrorist squad has protected very little so far, and detected even less. Let's see if things will improve now that you're back.'

'Secretary of State,' Proud's tone was even, but Skinner knew that he was controlling himself with difficulty, 'I note what you say. However, I have to tell you that I believe that you are being foolhardy, and that the Prime Minister should know better than to go along with you. If you insist, the Concert will proceed. However, since my force is responsible for your safety, I will apply the following conditions. First, the general public will be barred from the Gardens, and only people with auditorium tickets will be admitted. Princes Street will be closed to all traffic between the Mound and Lothian Road. Spectators will be confined to the North side of the street, well away from the railings. They'll hear the music and see the fireworks, but they won't see either you or the PM.

'Second, the arena will be kept in darkness throughout. The conductor's rostrum and the players will be lit, to the extent that is necessary, but the rest will be blacked out. Third, the PM's armoured Jaguar will be used to drive you and him right up to your seats. Fourth, soldiers in protective clothing will be positioned behind you both throughout the concert, acting as human shields. Fifth, as soon as the concert is over, you and the Prime Minister will be collected by the Jag and driven from the Gardens to overnight accommodation of our choice, which will be made properly secure. On those conditions alone, the Concert may proceed.'

Ballantyne stood up behind his desk. 'Quite unacceptable. That is quite unacceptable,' he shouted. 'We will not skulk in and out like that.'

Proud rose up, too, massive and formidable in his uniform. His voice was still quiet and steady.

'Secretary of State, sit down, while I tell you something. If you do not accept every one of those conditions, and put yourself and the Prime Minister completely in my charge, then I will resign as Chief Constable, and will make it known, loudly and publicly, that I have done so because the Secretary of State for Scotland has no thought or concern for public or police safety and is prepared to put lives unnecessarily at risk, lives like that of young Barry Macgregor, who died yesterday obeying your orders, or of that baby who was killed because you thought it was right to have a party in the face of terrorism.'

Still standing, Ballantyne seemed to fight, for a few seconds, for breath and words. Eventually he gasped, 'You can't threaten me. I'll . . . I'll . . .'

The storm broke. Proud Jimmy exploded in a fury that Skinner had never witnessed before. He roared at Ballantyne. 'Don't be a bloody fool, man! I am Scotland's senior Chief Constable. You're just another tinpot politician. You have no jurisdiction over me. Of course I can threaten you. I have just threatened you. I am still fucking threatening you! And I will carry out my threat at once, if you cross me!'

He glared at Ballantyne for a moment, then went on, his voice lower, grinding out the words. 'I'll go further than that. I missed the first few days of this affair, but I've kept in touch with Bob Skinner here, who, in spite of your scorn, is in my opinion the finest policeman in Britain. I am now observing for myself the final stages of your transformation under fire from a moderately acceptable minister to a dangerous buffoon who is quite unsuited for high office. For now, Mr Ballantyne, Bob Skinner needs my support. But I tell you today that, once this affair is over, I will renew the promise I have just made to you, and will carry it out exactly as I have described, unless you yourself resign to make way for someone with the judgement and ability to do the job!'

He glanced down at Skinner, who sat in his chair marvelling silently at his Chief. 'Come on, Bob. Let's go and get on with the job of keeping this pathetic man alive!'

He turned his back on Ballantyne, and slammed out of the room. Skinner, for once in his life, followed silently and obediently at Proud Jimmy's heels.

Sixty-four

At the Chief Constable's insistence, Bob took the rest of that Monday off.

'Take your lovely wife away to the seaside, man. Recharge those batteries for Thursday night.'

So, with Sarah signed off from her practice and her police duties for twenty-four hours, they headed down to Gullane. All three of the golf courses were jam-packed, and so they decided instead to walk along the beach path to North Berwick, and back via the highway – a good twelve-mile hike. Dressed in T-shirts, shorts and Reeboks, they walked mostly in silence at first, finding and following a narrow path which wound down through a forest of head-high thorn bushes, then ran for a stretch along the perimeter of Muirfield golf course, before opening out on to the broad East Sands, far from the Gullane Bents car park. No day trippers knew of this attractive beach, and so it was always deserted, even on the finest of days. Sheltered, in a natural alcove among the dunes, from the light breeze which signalled the turning of the tide, they lay down to sunbathe for a while, stripping off their T-shirts to use as beach-mats.

Bob marvelled anew at the firmness of his wife's body as she lay on her back, high breasted, nipples erect, eyes closed against the sun which glinted on her auburn hair.

'Perfection,' he whispered, and suddenly into his mind

came a premonition of brown-haired sons and of a second shot at fatherhood. He felt himself harden, and laughed softly.

'Skinner?' She voiced his name as a question. Then, without needing an answer, she rolled sideways and on top of him, full of desire and with the suppleness of her youth.

She made love to him quickly, lustily, hungrily, in the hot August sunshine which bathed the deserted beach, mounted on him as if he were her stallion, calling out to him in her pleasure. When their journey was over, she lay upon him for a while longer, their foreheads touching, covering his face with kisses.

And then, as if she had read his earlier thought, she said: 'You and I are ready to be parents, my love. You deserve another shot, and I couldn't get any broodier if I tried.'

He held her breasts in his hands as she lifted herself up from his chest. 'Well, honey,' he said, huskily. 'If that happens, we'll just have to call him Jimmy. After all, he did give me the afternoon off!'

Sixty-five

The Mallard's Eighty-shilling ale was pouring at its best. The village clock showed 6:15 pm as they arrived back in Gullane. Their hike, and the excitement of their sudden, spontaneous, sun-washed coupling on the deserted beach, had left them with a raging thirst, which they slaked with two pints each of Scottish Brewers' finest product.

They gave some thought to dining in the bar, but eventually they agreed that the evening was too good to be spent indoors. And so, instead, they went back to their cottage and barbecued two thick steaks in the garden, with potatoes baking in foil in the red-hot coals, and sliced onions sizzling on the grid. They ate as hungrily as they had made love in the sand, washing down the succulent meat with good red Valdepenas, and finishing off with a whole pineapple quartered and soaked in Cassis.

Then, all their appetites satisfied, they sat in the garden and watched the day go down in the west – and with it, their brief break from the dangers which had so recently overwhelmed their lives.

'Will they ever stop, Bob?' Sarah asked him suddenly.

'Yes, love. They'll stop, when they've got what they want. And that isn't Scottish independence, or any of that crap. I don't believe that any more. They've got us tear-arsing around all over Edinburgh, and that's what they've been out to achieve all along. It's all being done with a purpose in mind, though I've no idea at all of what that could be. When I do know, that's when they'll stop. Because I'll stop them.'

The hard determination in his voice made her suddenly afraid again, just as she had felt in the Park, over the body of young Macgregor.

'Darling, promise me one thing. Please. That when you do meet up with these people, you'll take care. Of yourself. Inside and out.'

He looked at her in silence.

'There's someone in you that I don't know. It's like there's a closet inside you with something awful and dangerous inside: a real bogeyman. I'm just terribly afraid that if he ever really gets out, he could take you over.'

She held his gaze until his eyes dropped.

'Aye, my love,' he said with a deep sigh. 'I know the man you mean. I've met him. And I've no wish to encounter him again either. But I have to say that if I'm ever in that kind of danger again, I hope he's still around. Because one thing about my alter ego: he doesn't half get the business done!'

Sixty-six

Skinner saw the ball drop as the gun went off.

'This is where I'll be, Andy. I can see the whole show from here.'

The three of them – Skinner, Martin and Adam Arrow – stood on the Castle battlements, just at the angle where the Mills Mount Battery joins with the Western Defences, a part of the image which most visitors conjure up when their thoughts return to Edinburgh.

It was a few seconds after one o'clock. Close by, the famous gun still smoked, having just boomed out its time signal. When it had fired, Skinner had been gazing out, across Princes Street, over the Scott Monument and the Balmoral Hotel, at the roof of the round grey stone building on the top of Calton Hill, and had seen the huge green globe as it slid down its flagpole, in a visual time-check for navigators in the wide River Forth, simultaneous with the sounding of the gun for those on land.

Now all three looked downwards, observing the main Glasgow railway line at the base of the rock, and beyond it the chasm of Princes Street Gardens, all in the shadow of the great Castle. The tented roof had been removed from the Ross Theatre. Only the stage was out of sight, under the canopy of the open-air bandstand, which for all its grand theatrical title, it was for most of the year.

The air was heavy, the heat stifling. Skinner glanced up. There was a hint of purple about the sky.

'It's going to break, Andy.'

'You can set your watch by it, boss. Whatever else the weather does in Edinburgh, you can be sure it'll piss down on the Fireworks concert!'

Skinner laughed. 'Aye, that and don't forget the Queen's Garden party in July!' But their moment of light relief was a short one. 'Have we covered everything, d'you think?' he asked, deadly serious once more.

'Yes, I think so,' said Martin. 'Princes Street gets blocked off to vehicles at nine o'clock, but the crowd barriers will be installed along the north pavement this afternoon, and we'll close the pavement looking into the Gardens at eight, as soon as the last of the shops close.'

'Right,' said Skinner. 'And as soon as you see to that, you're off to Number 6 to meet up with Ballantyne and the Prime Minister. Although we've doubled the guard on him, like all the Scottish ministers, I want you and Brian to be as close to him and the PM as their underarm deodorant, until tonight's well and truly over. The PM's protection men are happy for us to run this one, not that they were given a choice. You and Brian will be in the Jag with our two VIPs when they leave Number 6. You'll have armed officers in cars in front and back, and four motorcycle outriders, one on each corner. Mind you, you should be all right in that Jag anyway. There's a ton-and-a-half of armour plating in it, and all its glass is proof against any sort of bullet. So listen, if the shit does start to fly down there tonight, the first thing you do is get Ballantyne and the PM inside that bloody motor. It'll be the safest place in Edinburgh.'

He turned to Arrow. 'Adam, you and your men will be stationed inside the theatre area, agreed?'

'Mm. That's right. We'll guard the perimeter, and keep watch on the seats, in case some fooker's planted himself in the audience. One lookin' out, one lookin' in, alternately, all the way round, using night glasses. I'd be happier with another couple of men, though.'

'You've got them. I'll give you McGuire and McIlhenney. In fact, why don't we kit them out in bulletproof vests and helmets and ask them take up position behind Ballantyne and the PM. They're both big wide buggers. They'll make good blockers. They'd have to volunteer, but I know them – they will. That'll free up all of your guys for what they're best at.'

'Thanks, Bob.'

'What about Maggie Rose?' said Martin. 'We mustn't forget about her. She'd be pissed off if she was left out of the action.'

'That's OK. Maggie will be with me, up here, watching for whatever happens. For believe me, boys, there *will* be something to be seen, and it won't be just fireworks. I've never felt as certain of anything in my life.'

Sixty-seven

Everything that evening happened on cue – even the weather. The storm broke, finally, at 8:45 pm, just as Skinner and Maggie Rose were driving up the deserted Castle esplanade between the high-tiered temporary grandstands, which on another night would have been filling with spectators gathering for the Military Tattoo in the wide parade ground which they flanked. But fireworks and orchestra had taken precedence over marching bands and military gymnastics, and for that, Skinner guessed, as the first flash of lightning lit up the gloaming, six thousand potential ticket-holders should feel truly grateful.

Heavy raindrops pounded on the roof of the car as he swung it into the tunnel which takes vehicles into Edinburgh Castle, resuming their bombardment as he drove back into the open, and up to the parking area between Butts Battery and the Castle Hospital, which had once been, ironically, its powder magazine. He felt glad of the long Burberry waterproof coat and hat which he had thrown on to the back seat as he had left home.

Maggie Rose was clad for wet weather, too. In knee-length boots, jeans and a hooded Barbour jacket, she looked for all the world like a countrywoman on a week-end walk, not a detective engaged on life-or-death duty.

Skinner opened the boot of the car and produced from it

two pairs of odd-looking, heavy binoculars.

'Here, take these,' he said, handing one set to Maggie Rose. 'They're light-intensifying, infra-red or some such. However they work; they'll help you see in the dark. You're going to need them before much longer.

'Are you armed?' he asked casually as they walked up to their vantage point on the Mills Mount Battery.

'No, sir. I didn't see the need for it up here.'

'Me neither. This is an army garrison, after all. There's guns enough all around us.'

The adjutant of the Castle garrison regiment, the Royal Scots, was waiting for them on the Battery. He held a large blue umbrella over his head. Soldier's bravado, thought Skinner, as lightning cracked across the sky, searching for a route to earth.

'Taking a chance, Major Ancram, aren't you?' he said, pointing at the umbrella.

The big, middle-aged officer laughed. 'Rubber soles, old boy! Anyway, if the bloody Argies couldn't hit me, what hope is there for this lot!'

Skinner shook his head and smiled. Daft as a brush, he thought.

He introduced Major Ancram to Detective Sergeant Rose. Then, moving forward to the edge of the Battery, he raised the night-glasses and swept his gaze along Princes Street, from the Mound to Lothian Road. Without its street lighting, the famous street, with its shops on one side, Gardens and Castle on the other, was beginning to resemble an island of darkness in the midst of the dramatic illuminations which show off historic Edinburgh by night.

In the deepening gloom, the north pavement was already well filled with people, braving the rain for the sounds and spectacle of this unique evening. Above the pedestrians was a second tier of spectators, those privileged ones with access to upper-floor windows, or to the wide galleried fronting of some of the buildings – memorials to an architectural eccentricity decades earlier which had envisaged the eventual creation of a first-floor walkway running the length of Princes Street.

The lights of the New Club, of which Skinner was a member, caught his eye. Through its high windows he could see clearly that the Fireworks drinks party was gathering momentum. He was suddenly glad that he had persuaded the Chief to make the Club his vantage point, out of harm's way yet able to observe the crowd. Further along, others, with glasses in hand, peered out of the upper apartments of the Royal Overseas League. Business was good, he noted, in the two-storey Burger King, bright on its corner in contrast to the gap site on the opposite side of Castle Street, where the Palace Hotel had once stood, and where rebuilding work was still far from completion.

'Fast food's selling well,' he muttered to no one in particular, as he registered that McDonald's too was packed.

From Princes Street, Skinner swung the glasses down into the Gardens, to the Ross Theatre itself. He checked his watch. It was still only 9:15, too early for ticket-holders, especially on a night like this. But already Arrow and his black-suited men were deployed there in waiting, hooded and with bulky automatic weapons in their hands.

The stage was hidden from his view, but twenty feet away from it, behind two seats in the centre, he saw two bulky figures, grotesque in their helmets, with rain tunics over their flak-jackets, but standing there solidly as human shields. Skinner was suddenly very touched by the loyalty of his team, and very proud of them.

His moment of reverie was broken by Major Ancram. 'Everything OK, Mr Skinner?'

'Yes, Major, so far. So far.'

'What do we do now?'

'We wait and we watch. And, if you're into it, you might like to do a wee bit of praying for those boys down there, and for the two clowns they're looking after.'

Sixty-eight

If smiles could cut you, Andy Martin thought to himself, Ballantyne would be bleeding all over the place.

The tension between the Prime Minister and the Secretary of State for Scotland was obvious to the six other people in the room: Martin himself, Brian Mackie, the ministers' two private secretaries Fowler and Shields, and the PM's two protection officers. From chance remarks it was also obvious that the appearance by the country's leader at this concert had been Ballantyne's idea rather than his own.

The Prime Minister was a small man, almost slender alongside the stocky bulk of Ballantyne, but his firecracker temper was known to equal that of even his most formidable predecessor. He was clearly not best pleased to be here in Edinburgh, in the firing line, in the rain. The conversation between the two ministers remained polite, but it was stilted. They were clearly not the closest of political allies. And although the PM was working hard to maintain an affable front, every so often the truth of his feelings would flash in his eyes, behind the spectacles, betraying the insincerity of his professional smile.

It was a relief to everyone when Martin's radio crackled into life on an open channel. Only he could hear the voice through his earpiece. It was distorted, but it was unmistakably Skinner. 'It's all secure up here, Andy. The punters are in their seats, the orchestra's tuning up, and the blue touch paper's lit. It's five to ten, so let's get the show on the road.'

Martin snapped an acknowledgement into the handset, then turned to his charges. 'All's well, gentlemen, so if you're ready . . .'

'Yes,' said the Prime Minister, fixing Ballantyne with his frostiest and least sincere smile. 'I love a good fireworks display in the rain, sitting behind a bullet-proof shield! Let's go, Alan, and do your duty!'

Sixty-nine

The rain still poured down, the thunder crashed and the lightning flashed, like some great overture to the fireworks to come.

The motorcyclists and the escort cars peeled off as soon as the convoy entered the Gardens. Watching from above, Skinner and Maggie Rose could follow the Jaguar's headlights as they cut a path through the dark to the entrance to the Ross Theatre. Expertly, the PM's driver swung the car round, and reversed it up to stop a few feet in front of four empty seats, two of them with massive sentinels positioned behind them.

Martin and Mackie, in heavy anoraks and flat caps, jumped out and scanned the audience. Then Martin leaned back into the car and spoke softly. The Prime Minister stepped out first, and then the Secretary of State for Scotland, each in heavy rainwear. Their arrival in the darkness went unseen by the great majority of the audience, but they were greeted by a round of polite applause nonetheless, led by the Concert's guest conductor, Daniel Greenspan, standing well back on his spotlit rostrum, only just out of the pounding rain.

The Prime Minister was ramrod straight, and smiled widely around him as he walked the few steps to his seat. Behind him, Ballantyne, glum and nervous, hurried to sit down under the cover provided by Mario McGuire. Martin took the seat immediately beside the PM, while Mackie flanked the

Secretary of State. Each detective kept a hand inside his jacket, on the butt of his pistol.

Greenspan turned to face the orchestra and raised his baton.

Seventy

Skinner felt Maggie Rose jump slightly beside him, in involuntary alarm, as the first firework, launched from the wide area around the foot of the Castle rock, exploded in synchronicity with the first bars of Aaron Copland's 'Outdoor' overture.

'Get used to it, Maggie. Keep looking around, and keep your fingers crossed that's all you'll see or hear.'

For some while it seemed as if Skinner's hope against hope would be fulfilled.

As the Concert unfolded, the unamplified music boomed up towards them on their battlement. Different shapes, colours and patterns of light burst all around them, as the pyrotechnics lit the night sky, in uncanny harmony with the music.

Skinner concentrated his view to the left, and Rose kept hers to the right. From time to time, flashes from the fireworks were channelled through the night-glasses and blinded them, but as the hour's duration of the concert wore on, they were able, between them, to keep under observation the whole of the area surrounding the Gardens and the theatre. They could see nothing untoward, only the enthusiastic crowds down in the Street, as they jumped and clapped with each new wonder of light in the dark sky.

At last, the programme reached its climax, Handel's *Music for the Royal Fireworks*.

'They're nearly at the end now,' Skinner called out above the noise to his two companions. 'So far, so—'

He was cut short by the sound of an explosion, carrying clearly through a lull in the music, and a momentary break in the fireworks. It came from their left.

Skinner swept his glasses along Princes Street to the Caledonian Hotel, but saw nothing untoward. Carrying on, he scanned along Castle Terrace. Saltire Court and the Traverse Theatre seemed undisturbed, and from what he could see of the Usher Hall and the Sheraton, they too looked undamaged. But beyond them, beyond the Royal Lyceum, in Lothian Road, to the left of the high top of Capital House, he saw a billowing cloud of smoke and dust rising and shining in the floodlights which illuminated the front of the building which had been home to the Film Festival.

His radio was in his hand in a second. 'Major incident, Filmhouse,' he barked into the open line. 'All emergency services required now. Every second officer in Princes Street go to the scene, immediately.'

Just as he finished issuing the order, he heard the tail-end of a second blast, this time sounding from the right.

Again Skinner swung round, searching through the glasses, but something took him instinctively to the Balmoral. The hotel's foyer was out of his line of sight, but his eye was caught at once by the shattered windows in its side. Then he saw the smoke of the bomb as it spread outwards in a mushroom from the front of the huge, square stone building.

'Jesus Christ, there's been another.'

The radio mike was in his hand once more. 'Second explosion, Balmoral Hotel. Emergency services respond again. Headquarters, let's get every policeman in Edinburgh into this area!'

He was still issuing his orders when Maggie Rose grabbed his arm. 'Sir, what's that over there, on the Mound?'

He followed her finger pointing into the night, until his glasses found the stationary lorry. It was big and flat backed, and it seemed to have been pulled right up on to the pavement, just at the point where the curving section of the Mound straightened to run down towards Princes Street, past the National Gallery. The lorry's cab was empty, but its curtain side, facing the Gardens, had been pulled open, and four figures stood on its platform. Skinner could see them clearly – and could see clearly what they were doing.

Two of them clasped bulky, box-like objects to their shoulders, while the others were braced against them, to hold them steady.

'Andy!' he roared into the radio. 'Get them into the car, now, they've got missiles! In the car! In the car! In the car!'

And as he spoke he saw the launchers fire, simultaneously. He followed the path of the squat fly-by-wire projectiles as each homed in on its target.

'Down! Down! Everybody down.' He screamed into the radio, and into the darkness of the Garden Theatre.

Seventy-one

The Prime Minister experienced a sudden sensation of flight. One second, having forgotten, temporarily, his anger over Ballantyne's ridiculous bravado, he was enjoying Handel's finest work. The next he was in mid-air, seized bodily by Andy Martin, lifted clear of his seat, and borne at speed across the short distance to the Jaguar.

Then its rear door was wrenched open and he found himself thrown across the back seat. An instant later, Ballantyne landed heavily on top of him, hurled there by Brian Mackie. Then Mackie himself dived in to cover them both with his large body.

Martin, his pistol drawn, slammed the door shut behind them, slapped the side of the Jaguar, and dived to the ground as it roared off.

He looked up, back towards the audience, and could spot McGuire and McIlhenney. Obviously they, too, had been alerted by Skinner's voice in their ear-pieces, since, arms outspread, they were gathering in as many of the people around them as they could and forcing them down between the seats.

On stage, the orchestra played on in triumph, as oblivious to the two explosions as were all but a few members of the audience. Overhead the fireworks crashed and sparkled, at their luminescent climax.

Seventy-two

There is no mistaking a Sidewinder missile for a firework.

Skinner watched, struck dumb by the horror, as one of them smashed right into the middle rows of the audience and exploded. He saw that, at the moment of impact, several people, noticing the sudden commotion in the front row, had stood up trying, vainly, to catch a view in the dark. By a small mercy, the other Sidewinder flashed across the front of the stage, exactly where the Jaguar had stood bare seconds before, over a figure lying face-down in the tarmac, and then off to explode in the trees beyond the theatre's iron gate.

Maggie Rose screamed out loud, and kept on screaming, until Skinner gripped her by the shoulders and shook her hard.

Even without night-glasses, Major Ancram could see the flashes of the missile strikes, and needed no telling what had happened.

'Mr Skinner, I'm calling out the garrison. I'll have to get every man down there.'

'Yes, Major,' said Skinner, recovering his power of speech. 'Fast as you can, too. Let's get down there.'

And then, suddenly, he changed his mind. 'No!' he said loudly, and the Major, who had been heading away to gather his soldiers, stopped in his tracks and turned to stare in surprise.

'There's something else,' said Skinner, vehemently. 'I said

that they want to get us tear-arsing around. That's what they've got now, in spades. But what happens next?'

He stood for perhaps twenty seconds, thinking hard, while Rose and Major Ancram stared at him. Then, decisions made, he looked again at the soldier. 'Major, OK, you get your men down there on the double, but leave half-a-dozen up here with me. Maggie, you go on down with him, and do what you can.'

She nodded silently, determined to be as tough as anyone in Skinner's command, and ashamed of her earlier weakness.

'Major, how many men have you got?'

'Just now, three hundred.'

'Good. When you get down there, I want you to put armed men on guard around the National Gallery, and at the big bank branches at the Mound, St Andrew's Square, George Street and the West End. I'll tell you why later. For now, get going, and send that half-dozen men to me.'

A germ of a notion was festering in Skinner's mind, one so bizarre that he thought that it surely had to be fantasy, and yet it was there and he could not totally dismiss it as a possibility. An afterthought struck him and he called after the disappearing Ancram. 'Major, see if one of your men can find me a whistle!'

Seventy-three

Andy Martin picked himself up from the wet tarmac, without even a thought of dusting himself off. When he heard Skinner's first alert, he had jerked bolt upright in his seat, and a voice inside him had screamed silently. For a second he had almost sprinted from the Prime Minister's side, off through the Gardens and into the night, to Lothian Road, the Filmhouse and Julia.

But then the second alert had come, and Skinner's frantic command. He had acted instinctively, and had ensured that the Jaguar and its passengers had made it to safety. Now he looked around him, and listened carefully. On the stage a percussionist was banging away, either lost in the score or refusing to believe what had happened. Daniel Greenspan stood in his spotlight, his baton by his side, staring into the darkness.

Martin re-holstered his pistol and took out his radio. He switched channels to call the operations room at Fettes. 'Find whoever can arrange it, and get as much light as we can in here. For a start, have someone turn on the lights in Princes Street. And get me any news you can of Filmhouse.'

A second later, he found that his first instruction had been anticipated by the stage manager of the Ross Theatre. Above the stage a row of floodlights flickered into life, illuminating the audience. Martin moved forward fearfully, into a world of death and desolation, unable to block out the fear that it might be the same where his Julia was.

There was carnage indeed in the Ross Theatre, and yet he soon saw it might have been worse. He looked around first for McGuire and McIlhenney, and to his great relief spotted them both, still huge in their jackets and helmets, shepherding uninjured spectators away from the scene.

And then Adam Arrow was by his side. 'God, Andy, I've never seen anything like this. What do you hear on that radio of yours?' Once again the accent had vanished.

'Three attacks one after the other. First Filmhouse, then the Balmoral – both bombs, from the sound of it – then here. We were attacked by missiles fired from the Mound. One missed. The other hit over there by the looks of it.'

'Sidewinders, I imagine. In that case we were lucky.'

'Not all of us, though.'

They had reached the heart of the missile's devastation. Neither could be sure how many had died, but a circle of twelve metal seats lay tangled and bloody under the floodlights, with broken bodies twisted among them. Around this immediate circle, perhaps two dozen people sat stunned and disbelieving. Some were bleeding, and several held their ears as if deafened. The silence was that of a mourning parlour. It had a power of its own, one which seemed almost to hold at bay the growing clamour from Princes Street, and the howling of sirens as police, fire crews and ambulances raced to their different destinations.

The soldier and the detective began to direct the men at their disposal to the care of the casualties, to render first-aid to those who were bleeding, and to confirm, as far as they were able, that none of the walking wounded was seriously hurt.

When he was satisfied that everyone was in good hands,

Martin called across to McGuire. 'Mario, you're in charge here now. I've got to check out Filmhouse.'

As he sprinted into the night, he glanced up at the Half-Moon Battery. Standing at its edge, framed in light, he caught sight of a silhouette unmistakable even in its overcoat.

'Thank Christ for the boss tonight,' he muttered sincerely. 'But what's he doing up there still?'

Seventy-four

The corporal looked puzzled as he handed Skinner the whistle. Skinner took it from him with a curt nod.

'Right, you all know me?'

'Sir!' said the corporal, speaking for all six men.

'Major Ancram will have told you that you are now under my command. What I want you to do is this: throw a guard around the Crown Square – that's the Great Hall, the Queen Anne Barracks, the War Memorial, and the Royal Palace. All the areas below will be empty by now, but there's nothing there that anyone would be after. What you must guard against is anyone or anything that shouldn't be there. The chances are that nothing unusual will happen, but if it does . . .'

He paused to let his words sink in, then went on. 'If any of you sees anything, and you don't know for sure it's friendly, don't ask for its name, shoot it. If it turns out to be the regimental mascot, or the RSM's tart, well, that'll be too bad, but they can both be replaced. Right, Corporal, get your men spread out.' He held up the whistle. 'I know it's old fashioned, but if I need you, I'll blow this thing. If you hear it, regroup here, by the One O'clock Gun. If any of you need me, chances are I'll have heard you shoot!'

Seventy-five

But Skinner was wrong.

He was standing by the gun, training his night-glasses on the National Art Gallery, looking for any sign of intruders. For he suddenly felt acutely aware that the building was currently housing an international exhibition of the life's work of Rembrandt. It had been brought to the Edinburgh Festival under the sponsorship of a major insurance company, and it was worth, conservatively, over a hundred million pounds.

'Forget the banks. That's only money,' he said softly to the night, his thoughts gathering speed. 'Anybody with the resources to fund what we've just seen doesn't need money. But what if he wants something else, something unique, just for himself, and will go to any lengths, any cost? There's only one other collection in Edinburgh as valuable as that exhibition, and we're up here guarding that.'

Then he heard the strange sound in the dark, and knew at once, with his detective's instinct, that the National Gallery was not the target – and that his germ of an idea had been right all along.

The Royal Regalia of Scotland are not nearly as famous as their English counterparts in the Tower of London, and they have been admired by far fewer tourists over the years. Indeed, most Scots do not even know they are there. Since the Union of the Kingdoms almost five hundred years ago, only King

Charles II, then an exile and outlawed by Cromwell, has been crowned in Scotland. Thus the Honours of Scotland – as they are sometimes called – are, in main, older than the Crown Jewels of England. They are also, in their own way, beyond price. Therefore they are guarded in the most effective manner possible, by the army itself, in the heart of the garrisoned citadel of Edinburgh, which stands impregnable on its rock – unless, in some dire emergency, that garrison were to be flushed out.

Without waiting to discover exactly what that sound in the dark had been, but sensing its meaning anyway, Skinner grabbed his radio and spoke urgently into the open channel.

'Get some back-up here to the Castle. They're after the Crown Jewels!'

Seventy-six

He stumbled over the body in the dark. The soldier lay face-down, near the Portcullis Gate, at the foot of the Lang Stairs. Skinner turned him over. The heavy clouds reflected the amber light of the city back down to earth, and in that dim glow Skinner could see that the man had been stabbed in the throat. The gurgling sound heard earlier must have been his death rattle, or a last attempt to raise the alarm.

The man had dropped his rifle. Skinner spotted the short, fully automatic weapon lying on the ground. He picked it up without further thought, thankful for his practice sessions with this same firearm on the St Leonards rifle range.

Leaving the dead soldier, Skinner hurried back to his rendezvous point by the One O'clock Gun. He hesitated for a moment about blowing the whistle, with the risk of alerting the intruders, but quickly decided that alerting his own men had priority. So he gave a single sharp blast, and hoped that the raiders would confuse it with the many other varied sounds now floating up to the Castle from the chaos in the city below.

Only three of the other soldiers answered his summons, including the corporal. Skinner glanced at him and held up the whistle, a gesture asking whether he should blow it again.

But the NCO shook his head sadly. 'Naw. They're good lads. They'd have come if they could.'

With twenty-twenty hindsight, Skinner cursed himself for

not commandeering twice as many men, then he addressed the remaining three. 'Look, lads, we've got a raiding party in the Castle. They're after the Crown Jewels. I don't know how many there are, but they must be inside the Palace by now. I've already radioed for back-up, but we can't wait that long. If they get what they're after, then get loose out there in the dark, we'll never catch them.

'Corporal, you take one of these two and go round behind the War Memorial to the main entrance to Crown Square. The other will come with me up the Stairs, and in by the side way. And, again ask no questions. You see it, you shoot it!'

The corporal slapped one of his soldiers on the shoulder, and together the pair headed off up a slight incline to the right, hunched in the dark and their rifles held ready. Skinner led the remaining man back past the body of his dead colleague and up to the top of the stone staircase, until it opened on to the topmost level of the Castle. Together they raced across the ground behind the Fore Wall and the Half Moon Battery, and flattened themselves against the side of the Scottish National War Memorial.

Slowly, Skinner eased forward to peer round the corner into Crown Square. At the edge of his vision he saw the corporal and his partner sprint into the square, away from the dangerous frame of the narrow entrance, bracing themselves, crouched, against the buildings.

There were two men stationed at the door of the Palace. They were dressed in black, and carried short, ugly guns which Skinner recognised at Uzis. They spotted the two soldiers as soon as they appeared at the far end of the square, and swung their weapons up to firing positions. But too slowly.

The corporal and his companion cut them down with

bursts of sustained deadly accurate rifle fire. Skinner saw both men thrown back against the wall of the Jewel Chamber by the impact. Then as the firing stopped, they crumpled slowly, limp and dead, to the ground.

He shouted across the square. 'Corporal, is there any other way out of there?'

'No, sir,' the man called back. 'Whoever's in there must come through that door at the foot of the Flag Tower.'

'Right, we wait. Our back-up should be here any minute.'

As he spoke, he heard, from within the building, a sound like the smashing of heavy glass. An alarm bell began to ring, pointlessly.

Skinner left his soldier companion in the lee of the War Memorial, and ran across to the steps of its only entrance. He shielded himself behind its arch, and blessed his luck and foresight as a grenade exploded in the square. He heard shrapnel zing against stone walls, and ricochet off into the night. Then he swung himself out from behind the grey pillar and waited ready for what he knew would happen next.

There were two others, also dressed in black like their dead colleagues. Each carried a hold-all in his left hand, and a blazing Uzi in his right. As they burst through the door, they sprayed fire blindly at unseen targets, but this kept the soldiers at the far end of the square pinned down nonetheless.

They could not see where their greatest peril waited.

Skinner dropped the first intruder with two quick shots. The other swung round towards the side exit from Crown Square, and straight into the path of the waiting soldier, who roared a battlecry as he emptied his magazine in revenge for his fallen comrades.

In the silence that followed, amid the reek of the gunsmoke, Skinner found time to look inside himself. He was pleased that he had been able to fire without hesitation, pleased too that he had handled the job so unemotionally, without any thought of Barry Macgregor in his mind. Perhaps, he thought, the closet door was locked for good. Maybe he did not need that other guy after all.

He held the other men in position for three full minutes, lest there were other intruders still inside the Jewel Chamber. But the next man to enter the square was Captain Adam Arrow, leading his silent troops in full combat array.

Arrow appraised the scene in a second, and realised why Skinner and his trio of soldiers were waiting immobile. At his signal, two men sprinted across the open space and threw stun grenades through the open door of the Flag Tower, holding their ears against the percussion. Then they rushed inside the building and up the stairs, their guns held in front of them.

A few seconds later they emerged, and waved the all-clear to Arrow.

As Skinner and the soldiers gathered at the doorway, the corporal found a switch, and soon the square was ablaze with light. Weapons at the ready, they approached the four figures lying crumpled on the flagstones. Three of the raiders were as dead as they could be, but the fourth still showed signs of life. Skinner radioed for an ambulance.

The two hold-alls lay on the ground nearby. The larger of them was streaked with blood. Skinner knelt down and unzipped it – and from within he took a sword still sheathed in its bejewelled scabbard. Not just any old sword, this one, but that which had been ceremoniously borne in state before the kings of Scotland. He held it up by its scabbard for a moment, feeling its weight and its fine balance. Then he handed it over to Arrow and bent to open the other bag, knowing also what he would find there.

First, the golden sceptre, finely worked, heavier than it looked.

And then Scotland's ancient pride, the crown itself. It was almost indescribably beautiful. Even in the harsh artificial light, its jewels glinted in the delicate gold circlet. Pearls, set in gold, gleamed on the red velvet inner cap, and six more, with four sapphires, formed the cross at its apex.

Skinner held it up by its white ermine surround, for all to see.

'There you have it, lads. This is what our Freedom Fighters were really after. Priceless, they call it, but for someone who wanted it badly enough, not beyond price, it seems.'

Seventy-seven

Skinner could scarcely believe that so many journalists would turn up sober for a 2:30 am press briefing. Extra seats had been brought in, filling the briefing hall completely. Yet they were all soon occupied, and the side aisles were also packed with correspondents, many standing, others crouching to allow the photographers and television cameramen a clear view of the table at the head of the room, and of the big dark-suited, steel-haired, stubble-chinned man who sat at it – his Chief Constable, in full uniform and clean shaven, by his side.

Skinner waited as Alan Royston and his uniformed assistants distributed the printed statement which he and Proud Jimmy had dictated together within the last hour. They waited for some minutes more, to give every man and woman in the room an opportunity to read and understand it fully. When he judged the time was right, Skinner rapped the table with his knuckles to recapture the attention of his audience, and began, slightly hoarsely.

'I'd appreciate it if everyone here could take that statement as read. It'll save my voice. But I'll sum up now for television and radio.' He glanced down the room towards the camera platform.

'In relative terms we have been fortunate tonight. This is no comfort to the families of the nine victims killed by the ground-to-ground missile fired into the Ross Theatre. However, things could have been much worse. There were no other serious casualties, either in the Gardens or due to the other explosions at Filmhouse and at the Balmoral Hotel. The first of these, we know now, was caused by a satchel of explosives placed against a wall in the foyer. It brought down the front of the building, but the rest stood firm. Fortunately all the audience and staff were inside the cinemas at the time, so everyone was brought out safely.

'We believe that the Balmoral bomb, too, was left in a suitcase in the foyer. Again fortunately, the receptionist had gone into her office, and the doorman was outside watching the fireworks. So that area was completely empty when the device went off.

'We believe that the second missile at the Ross Theatre was aimed at the Prime Minister's car, but the vehicle moved out of the line of fire just in time, thanks to the speed with which DCI Andy Martin and DI Brian Mackie acted to get the two ministers clear of the scene.'

On impulse, Sir James Proud broke in, pointing towards a stocky, blond, green-eyed man leaning against the wall. 'I'd like to single out Andy Martin for special commendation, but also congratulate all the other members of the team: Brian Mackie, Mario McGuire and Neil McIlhenney, who placed themselves without hesitation in the line of fire, and not forgetting DS Maggie Rose, but for whose keen eyes we could well have had a dead Prime Minister by now, not to mention her fellow officers and friends.'

As Al Neidermeyer raised a hand, Skinner eyed him without animosity. The American looked back with caution and new respect.

'We're putting this out live on TNI. Could you just run over the whole picture of what happened tonight?'

'Certainly. It's now clear that the so-called independence campaign was in fact a professionally planned operation to cause chaos and confusion among the police and emergency services, and to steadily stretch us to the point we reached tonight, when we had to call out every last resource at our disposal, including the garrison from the Castle. We know now that the real objective was theft of the Honours of Scotland, our Royal Regalia. Call it fantastic, call it audacious, but it actually happened, and it almost succeeded.'

'Do you think you've got them all, Bob?' The questioner was the grizzled John Hunter, looking slightly unkempt in the middle of the night, an unaccustomed time for him.

Skinner smiled at the familiar face. 'No, John, we haven't. We don't know yet whether the types who planted those bombs and fired the missiles were the same ones who attacked the Castle. Forensic tests should tell us, though. Also we don't know for sure that there were only four in the raiding party up at the Castle. A long rope ladder was found fastened to the Half Moon Battery, dropping down to the lawn below. That was their get-away route, so possibly someone was guarding it, then legged it.

'There's Mary Little Horse, too. We still haven't traced her. And there's someone else we haven't got. That's the one who set this whole thing up. Somebody who wanted so badly to possess the Scottish Crown Jewels that he or she was ready to provide the necessary finance for an operation as brilliant and as ruthless as this one. There is absolutely no clue as to who that person might be, but we can assume that he or she is extremely rich, and must have some very special interest in Scotland.'

'So what else have you got?' said Al Neidermeyer.

'Well, we've got a wounded man in the Royal, under very

special guard. An hour and a half ago we faxed fingerprints from all four intruders to various agencies around the world, but we've had no firm response as yet. So we still haven't identified any of them. However, we think we may have the getaway vehicle. We found a Mercedes saloon with false plates parked in Johnstone Terrace under the Half Moon Battery. Not the driver, though, and none of the four killed in the raid had car keys on him.

'Within the last hour we've learned that an aircraft, a De Havilland Dash, has been sitting in a hangar at Cumbernauld Airport, ever since it was flown in two weeks ago. The hangar rent was paid up until tomorrow, cash down, by the pilot who flew it in. The copy receipt is made out in the name of Mr Black. Unfortunately, the airport manager is away on holiday, but we're trying to trace him to obtain a description, and we're also tracing the ownership of the plane. My guess is it'll turn out to have been chartered, for cash.'

'This Mr Black, could he have been one of the men taken tonight?' asked Neidermeyer.

Skinner shook his head. 'I don't think so.'

'So Mr Black is still out there?'

Skinner nodded. 'I reckon so. Mind you, I don't expect him to turn up in person to collect his aeroplane.'

Seventy-eight

The getaway plane stayed where it was. But something else was picked up instead, something much more precious.

'One thing that niggles me, Andy, is not knowing if any of the bastards are still hanging around here.'

It was just over twelve hours since the press briefing. Skinner and Martin were settled in the DCI's office in the Special Branch Suite, going through the mountain of paperwork involved in the winding up of the enquiry. Each had snatched a few hours at home, although Andy had spent much of his break consoling Julia after her frightening experience with the Filmhouse explosion. 'If any of them *are* still here,' said Martin, 'they're bloody crazy. That guy in the Royal's going to make it. He's bound to bargain a few years off his sentence in return for telling us everything he knows.'

'Don't count on it. Those were pros. They'll have been well paid for this job, and it probably included something extra for keeping shtum if they got caught. And don't assume that he knows—'

Skinner was interrupted by an internal call on Martin's extension. Being closer to it, he picked it up. 'Skinner.'

The caller was Ruth. 'Sorry to bother you, sir, but I felt I had to. It's a Mr Morris, and he says it's important. It's about Alex.'

'Put him through.'

Skinner had never met the man, but he recognised the name. Bert Morris was the director of Alex's theatre company.

'What can I do for you, Mr Morris?'

The man hesitated. 'Look, I'm sorry to bother you, but do you happen to know where your daughter might be.'

The first faint chill crept into Skinner's stomach. 'What d'you mean?' He didn't realise that he had snapped at the caller, a hard edge suddenly in his voice.

Morris began to splutter. 'Well, it's just that – well last night her friend Ingo didn't turn up. Alex didn't know where he'd got to. We went on with the show, but without the lighting effects it was a bloody disaster. Alex did her best, but I still felt I had to give the audience half their money back. I called their number this morning to find out where the hell he had been, but I got no reply. So I went round to see them. The landlady said she hadn't seen or heard either of them all day. She let me in with a pass-key, but the place was empty. Not a sign. All his clothes, all of his things were gone. Some of Alex's stuff seemed to be there, but I couldn't see her handbag – you know, that big one she carries everywhere. So can you help me? Are they with you? I've got to know if he's coming back.'

Skinner replaced the receiver without a word.

Martin watched him anxiously as he sat staring chalk faced at the wall. His first thought was that his boss had experienced some delayed reaction to the night's events.

'What's wrong, Bob?'

The voice which replied was strange, quiet, shaky – unlike anything Martin had heard from him before. 'It's Alex. She's been snatched.'

'Eh!'

'That was her director. That guy Ingo didn't show up last

night. Now Alex has disappeared too. Andy, I *knew* he was wrong! He's taken her!'

'Steady on, man. She could be anywhere. Maybe he's just done a moonlight on her, and she's down at your place now, crying her eyes out to Sarah.'

Skinner shook his head, feeling cold all over.

'No, Andy. Since last night I've been wondering whether our Mr Black would have a Plan B. Now I know that he has, and I can guess what it is.'

Seventy-nine

The letter was delivered only ten minutes later. It had been found on a table in the first-floor coffee lounge of the busy Mount Royal Hotel, but none of the staff could describe the person who had sat there last.

It was addressed:

Assistant Chief Constable Skinner,
Police Headquarters.
Private and Confidential
To be delivered.

The hotel manager had brought it personally to Fettes Avenue.

Skinner could not stop his hand from trembling as he slit the envelope. He had recognised at once its style and its size, and the typeface on the address label. He withdrew the familiar single sheet of white paper, and steeled himself to read what he knew would be there.

He read it aloud to Proud, Martin and Arrow, who had all gathered in his office.

'Mr Skinner,

'You may know my name already. Let us say that I am simply someone who has undertaken to obtain something special for a client who wants it very badly. Last night I almost succeeded, but your own good fortune prevented me.

'However, I do not give up as easily as you might have hoped. Through the good offices of Ingo Svart, I now hold in my care someone who is very precious to you. I now propose that we exchange her for that which is just as precious to my client: the items which you prevented us from taking last night.

'I require that you arrange the following. The Regalia will be left, in the same hold-alls which my associates carried into the Castle, in the middle of the car park at the Gyle Shopping Centre, at 11:00 pm tomorrow night. Once the delivery has been made, the car park should be completely cleared. An aeroplane, with a range of at least three thousand miles, will be waiting, fully fuelled, on the runway at Edinburgh Airport. No attempt should be made to follow us at any stage. No personnel, police or military, should come anywhere near. No attempt should be made to hide tracking devices in the hold-alls. We have the equipment to detect them. No attempt should be made to track our flight-path. We also carry equipment that can detect radar.

'If any one of these conditions is breached in any way, Miss Skinner will be shot immediately. However, if all are met to the letter, she will be released safely, as soon as we reach our first stopping-off point.

Mr Black'

Skinner placed the letter slowly on his desk. He looked up at Andy Martin with absolute desolation on his face.

'Give that paper to me, Bob,' said Proud Jimmy gently, but with determination in his voice. 'I'm off to see the Prime Minister.'

Eighty

'I don't care whose daughter she is!'

'Secretary of State,' said Sir James Proud, hissing the words in a tone he had rarely used before in his life. 'If Bob Skinner had heard you say that, I would not guarantee your safety.' He took a menacing step towards Ballantyne.

'Sir James, please.' The Prime Minister restrained him with a light touch on the sleeve of his uniform. He turned to face Ballantyne, questioningly, across the drawing room of Number 6 Charlotte Square.

'I only meant that we can't give in to blackmail, PM,' said the Secretary of State, now flushed and flustered.

The Prime Minister walked slowly down the long room towards him, his eyes cold behind his spectacles.

'Alan, if you showed such bravery and courage with your own person as you do in putting other people's lives at risk – mine included – then you would probably make a great Minister. As it is, you're undoubtedly the biggest mistake I have ever made. Last night I said I wanted you to demit office, on health grounds, after a decent interval. You don't deserve decency, man. Give me your resignation now, please.'

He turned back to Proud. 'Now, Sir James, how are we going to help Mr Skinner?'

'With respect, Prime Minister, that isn't really a matter for you,' a voice interrupted.

There was a fourth man in the long room. Sir Hamish Tebbit, Private Secretary to the Queen, had flown to Edinburgh that morning for a personal briefing on the situation from the Prime Minister. The tall grey-suited courtier stepped forward from the window. He had been doing his best to make himself inconspicuous while the politicians and the policeman had their confrontation.

'I would remind you that the Honours of Scotland are the property of the Crown. Therefore their disposal is a matter for the Crown alone. If you will permit me, I will withdraw to another room, one with a telephone, and seek guidance from that highest authority.'

Eighty-one

'Andy, son, they'll kill her, whatever. You know that. This Mr Black won't leave her alive to identify him. He'll realise that if he does, it'll be too easy for me to find him. And when I do find him, I'll find his paymaster – his bloody client. Oh, believe me, Andy, I'll find him anyway, but unless we do it by tomorrow night, we'll be too late to help Alex.'

Sarah had joined them in Skinner's office. She sat beside Bob, on one of the low, cushioned seats, shocked and red eyed, sipping coffee.

Martin looked back at Skinner. He had no answer, for he knew the inescapable truth of what Skinner had said.

Bob pushed himself up from the seat, pounding fist into palm in a gesture of pure frustration. 'We don't know where she is, boys, and we haven't a clue how to find her. Oh, my lass. My poor, poor lass. Where in God's name are you?' As he cried out, he linked his fingers together, and covered his eyes with his hands.

Martin and Arrow gazed, helpless and silent, at his back and rounded shoulders. But Sarah rose quietly from her chair and crossed to him, taking him in her arms, cradling his bowed head against hers. They stood like that for a time, motionless. Then, slowly, steadily, Skinner's shoulders straightened, and his hands left his face. He now stood erect again, and it was almost as if Martin and Arrow were looking at a stranger. The man they saw – Skinner but not Skinner – touched them both, tough as they were, with sudden alarm. Distress and despair had been put aside and replaced by hope, the light of which gleamed cold and savage in his eyes.

'There's someone who does know, boys, or who'd better know. And he's lying in the Simpson!' The voice was little more than a whisper.

He eased himself out of Sarah's arms and started for the door, but Adam Arrow stopped him, and, using all his strength, held him back.

'Bob. Bob. Listen to me, Bob.'

Skinner looked down at him, still with that awful cold look.

'Man,' said Arrow quietly, making an effort at a reassuring smile, 'if you went near that man just now, the first time he said "No" to you, you'd rip' is fookin' head off and piss down his fookin' neck. He's got to be handled gentle if he's to tell us anything that'll help Alex. So you stay here with Sarah. Leave him to me. I'll talk to him, reasonable like. You know what I mean. If he does know anything, I'll get it out of him better than you could.'

His smile would have calmed the wildest beast – which, for a moment, Skinner had seemed to be.

Eighty-two

Sir Hamish wasn't out of the room for long. But he was gone long enough for Alan Ballantyne to scrawl out the briefest of letters of resignation, 'for reasons of health, and in the interests of my family', on Scottish Office crested notepaper. He handed it to the Prime Minister and, without even the briefest glance at Sir James Proud, stalked out of the room.

Scarcely more than five minutes had elapsed, by the carriage clock on the Adam mantelpiece, before the Queen's Private Secretary returned from his telephone consultation. To his huge relief, the Chief Constable noticed that he was smiling in satisfaction.

'Prime Minister,' the tall grey man said formally. 'Her Majesty has given me some very strict instructions, which should make your course of action quite clear. The demands contained in the letter to Mr Skinner are to be complied with in every detail. Her Majesty has said that, when seen in this context, no treasure is of greater value than a human life.'

He looked at Sir James. 'She has said also, Chief Constable, that knowing Mr Skinner from her many visits to Edinburgh, he and his daughter have her heartfelt sympathy in their predicament. She will pray for Alex's safe return. Her Majesty said also that she expects Mr Skinner to ensure that, once he has been reunited with his daughter, her kidnappers will not remain for long in possession of the Honours, or indeed of their own liberty.'

Warmly and spontaneously, the Prime Minister shook Sir Hamish by the hand. He turned to Proud, who was standing just behind him.

'There you have it, Chief Constable. Now go and get the girl back – and bag these people while you're at it.'

Eighty-three

Babies made Adam Arrow feel uncomfortable. He would never actually admit that he disliked them. It was only that, having been involved all too often, through his chosen profession, with the other end of the life cycle, they pricked his conscience with the thought that every one of the villains he had been forced to deal with had been some mother's son – or occasionally, some mother's daughter. A conscience was something which Arrow could not afford, and so it was to maintain his own efficiency – what others might call his ruthlessness – that Adam tended to steer clear of any close contact with babies. Thus it was that to him, the everyday sounds in the private wing of the Simpson Memorial Pavilion, in the Royal Infirmary of Edinburgh, were a little disturbing.

Andy Martin had arranged with the general manager, with whom he had frequent professional contact, that the wounded prisoner from the Castle should be housed in a private room in the maternity wing. The reason given was that the Simpson was the last place where any prying journalist would be likely to look. However, Martin's overriding consideration had been that not even Mr Black or his associates – should they feel the need to tie off a loose end – would have the idea of searching there, either.

None of the hospital staff knew of the wounded man's

presence, other than members of the theatre team who had operated on him, or were now overseeing his recovery, and these people had been sworn to secrecy. The surgeon was an RAMC major, with a career dedicated to repairing gunshot wounds. He and his chief nurse had been flown up specially from England.

Near the door of the private room, two men sat on opposite sides of the corridor, casually dressed in jeans and bulky jackets. They were reading magazines, and did not look particularly interested in each other, or in what was going on around them, but when Arrow turned into the corridor he saw to his satisfaction that each man glanced quickly up before – at his brief nod – delving back into his magazine.

Arrow rapped the door three times, the agreed signal, and entered. Another two SAS soldiers, also in plain clothes, were on guard inside. One watched the window, the other the door.

'Hello, lads. All secure?'

'Yes, sir,' said the man facing the door, in a thick Cornish accent. 'Quiet as a church, it's been.'

'How's our pal?'

'He's doing all right, the doc said.'

They turned to look at the bed. Its frame had been arranged to support the prisoner at an angle, presumably to guard against congestion. He wore no gown, and heavy bandages were wrapped round his chest, and extended down from his shoulder, covering the wounds where Skinner's two shots had torn through his right lung. The man seemed to be dozing, and Arrow noted the rough edge to his breathing. A tube ran into his nose, and another led out from beneath the sheets, into an opaque, flexible container which was hung below the level of the mattress. A long needle was taped down in place on the man's left forearm. It was connected by a third tube to a jar of glucose solution hanging high on a stand beside the bed.

'Has he had much to say for himself yet?' asked Arrow.

'Nah,' said the Cornishman. 'We tried talking to him, but he told us to fuck off.'

Arrow smiled pleasantly towards the bed. 'Maybe he'll talk to me. Let's see, shall we? You lads take a tea break. You can take them two outside, as well. I'll lock myself in. This must be a fookin' boring detail. Take 'alf-an-hour, at least. I'll look after him.'

The two soldiers left the room without protest.

Arrow said nothing for a while. He stood quietly at the side of the bed, looking down at the nameless prisoner. Mid-thirties, he guessed. As he studied the torso more closely, where it showed above the sheets, he noted several marks and disfigurements, including a ragged scar on the left shoulder, crudely treated at some time, from the size of the stitch marks. He guessed that it might be the relic of another bout of gun-play. Both upper arms were garishly tattooed. There was a lavishly endowed naked lady on the right, with the word '*Mother*' scrolled below, and on the left a snake entwined around a dagger, with four Chinese characters alongside.

'Well-travelled feller, ain't you?' Arrow said suddenly. 'Mercenary, I'd guess. That could be a problem. I hate fookin' mercenaries. Showing up in other people's countries and killing 'em, for no reasons other than they like it and 'cos they get paid. Hate 'em, I do. Still I shouldn't hold that against you. You're a wounded man, after all. So come on, my friend. Tell me: who are you?'

The pattern of the man's breathing changed. The closed eyes opened lazily. The laboured voice croaked. 'Go fuck your mother.'

Arrow laughed, out loud. 'She's dead, pal. And anyway, I'd rather fook yours.'

He sat on the edge of the bed. Idly, he touched the tube which led to the needle in the man's forearm. He was still smiling.

'OK, that's the pleasantries over. Now let's have a nice little chat. I'll go first. All you have to do is to listen – for now at least.

'I belong – as my friends who've been looking after you belong – to what you might call a closed organisation. No one's allowed to see us, and when we leave a place, it's as if we'd never fookin' been there at all. Only it's different. That place, I mean. It's been changed in some way or another. Sometimes a building or two won't quite be where it was before. Other times, there's some fooker doesn't live there any more, or anywhere else for that matter. Sometimes both. For a closed organisation, we're quite famous really. You'll have heard of us, I'm sure.'

He stopped and looked at the bed. Slowly the man nodded.

'In that case you'll know this, too. When we go into action, we go all the fookin' way.'

He paused again.

'People never quite believe us. So let me tell you a little story that'll help. Few years back, there were some trouble in a jail up here in Jockland. Some lads held a warder hostage, and the prison governor, he gets fed up. Decides to teach 'em a lesson, and so he gets authority to send for us. So half a dozen of our lot goes up there in a truck, with plans of the jail – Peterhead, it were called – that they studies on the way.

'It's after dark when the truck arrives. The plan is for us to go into action straight away. So the truck gets backed right up to the hall where the trouble is, and the first of our lads jumps out, hood on, fookin' submachine-gun in his hands. And there's the governor, and he sees our lad, tooled up like. And he all but shits himself. "How far are you chaps going to go?" 'e asks. And you know what our lad says? That's right, he says, "All the fooking' way, mate!" And he were right. They would have. Just gone in and wasted all the bad lads. 'Cos no one had told 'em different. Course they didn't that time, in t' end. The governor made 'em leave their guns behind. Gave them pick-axe handles instead. They didn't half cream the shit out of those bad lads, though.'

Arrow stood up again.

'So that's my little story. And the moral is, pal, I'm not here to piss about. You're going to tell me everything you know that I want to hear, or I'm going to go all the fookin' way wi' you. You'd better be ready to die, 'cos if you don't talk to me, you'll be dead within an hour.'

He looked at the glucose bottle on the stand, just about at his eye level, then continued.

'You see, mate, after your stunt last night didn't work, the guy who paid you did a really stupid thing. He decides he's not going to give up, so he snatches the daughter of a friend of mine – and I really hate it when my friends get upset – and he says he'll kill her unless we give him the swag and a plane out of the country. And that's really dropped you in it, mate. 'Cos you're the only bugger we've got that's alive to tell us anything about this fooker – what's his name, Black? – and where he might be hiding our lass. So this is the deal, mate.'

As he spoke his hands began to fiddle with the connection of the tube to the bottle.

'There's a way of killin' someone that works every time. As effective as a firework up the arse, it is, but a lot less messy. Untraceable, in fact. All you do is take a tube, like this, of stuff that's goin' into someone's bloodstream, and you pinch it tight, like this, to stop the flow. Then you disconnect it – like this, see.'

The prisoner watched, bug eyed, as he spoke.

'Then you squeeze out some of the stuff at the top – like this, see. Then you lets a little air in instead. Are you watching?'

He needed no reply.

'Then you reconnect the fluid, like this. See? Then you turn on the drip, like this. Then you let the tube go. And the little magic bubble works its way down the tube and up the needle and into the bloodstream, and round, and round, until . . . Embolism, I think they call it. Whatever they call it, it's fookin' fatal! And that's all that's to it.'

The man stared at Arrow's hand as it held the tube. He had gone rigid on the bed.

Arrow smiled at him. 'No, no. It's all right. I'm not going to let go – yet. I won't let go until you make me believe that you really want to die, and that you're not going to tell me what I need to know to help me find my friend's lass. But the second I do believe that, I let this tube go, and not long after that, my friend, you will experience very painful and quite inevitable death. Now. Let's start wi' your name.'

Eighty-four

Skinner was touched by the Queen's good wishes. Most of all he was relieved by Proud's news of her insistence that all steps necessary should be taken to ensure Alex's safe return.

'I'll take personal charge of this operation,' said Proud Jimmy. 'I promise you that no risks will be taken, I'll put marksmen in hiding around the aeroplane. If I'm completely satisfied that it's safe for Alex, I'll open fire. Otherwise I'll let them take off. We'll send word to every country within the plane's operating range to watch out for its landing, and that way we'll get Alex back as soon as possible.'

Skinner smiled: a tired, drained sort of smile.

'Two things, Chief. First, you will need to tie me down to keep me away from this operation. Remember, I'm still head of the anti-terrorist unit Ballantyne set up, until his successor tells me otherwise. Next, if you have men waiting at the airport, they'll be there all bloody night. Mr Black knows there's no way I'll let him get on board that plane with Alex. As soon as they were clear of our air-space, she'd be dead. They're not going to show up at Edinburgh Airport. That plane's just another feint. That's the way our Mr Black works. He sells you a dummy, every time. He's got something else planned. Well, so have I.'

His jaw tightened, and some of the tiredness left his face.

'Anyway, it might not come to that. Let's wait to see what our guest in the Simpson has to tell Adam.'

'What makes you think he'll tell him anything?'

Skinner laughed, quietly. 'You don't know Adam!'

Eighty-five

'Carl Stewart!'

The name broke out of him in a strange, half-strangled squawk, as if the man had been holding his breath in disbelief while he watched the last of Arrow's preparation for his execution.

'That's good. Seen the light, have we?' Arrow's right thumb and index finger were clamped tight on the clear plastic tube, holding up the flow of the nutrient – and of the deadly bubble. 'Let's have the rest, then. Nationality: Canadian, I'd guess by the accent. Right?'

The man nodded.

'And you are a fookin' mercenary, aren't you? Where've you been?'

It came more slowly this time, weakly, as Stewart measured each painful breath.

'I wasn't always a mercenary. I was a regular in the Gulf. I came out after that. Since then I've been in Bosnia, in Africa, in Guatemala – and a few other places.'

'What d'you know of this Mr Black, the fella who paid for the plane you lot were going to catch?'

'He does things for people. Difficult things they need done – or want done.'

'You worked for him before?'

'Twice. Once in the States. Once in South Africa. First

time, we busted into a gallery in New York – and stole a painting for a collector.'

'Who?'

'Don't know. We never know who the customer is – or the client, as Mr Black calls them. And we know better than to ask. Mr Black wouldn't like that. And you don't cross him.'

'So what did you do in South Africa?'

'We started a bit of a Civil War. We killed a black guy, a leader. Made it look like one tribal group did it. Then we killed some other guys; leaders on the other side – and made it look like the first lot was taking revenge. Once they were all killing each other, we killed some white guys – and all the black guys were blamed at once. Christ, man, we had them all chasing their tails down there. Just like we've had you chasing yours up here. Once the cops were all used up, keeping the sides apart, we hit a diamond mine. We cleared one hundred million dollars in uncut stones. The nearest cops were sixty miles away, caught in the middle of a gun battle. Mr Black's a great planner. What makes him so great is he thinks big.'

'So what's he like?'

'I've never met him.'

Arrow's hand moved on the tube. The man flinched in quick terror.

'Come on, Stewart. You expect me to believe that? You tell me that this fooker walks on water, then you say you've never met him.'

'It's true. None of us have ever seen him. He sends his messages, his orders, through someone else. A woman. Her name's Ariel. She's European of some sort. We all figure she must be his lady.'

'If you've never seen this Mr Black, how d'you know this Ariel isn't the boss herself.'

'Ariel could never do what someone did to Klaus. That had to be Mr Black himself.'

'Who's Klaus?'

'He was our explosives guy on the New York contract. We were holed up in a cabin in the middle of nowhere, up in the Catskills, ready to go – when Klaus decided that the money wasn't good enough. He told Ariel that he was out unless the dough was doubled. He said he wanted to see Mr Black himself, not deal with his whore. Ariel got very steamed up – as she can – but she said OK, she would arrange for Klaus to meet him.'

'So what 'appened?'

'Next morning we all came down to breakfast. Ariel cooked for us all in that place, and she dished it up in this big mess hall. Klaus was there, waiting for us. He was nailed to the timber wall. I mean he was crucified, hands and feet, man. There was a big knife through the middle of his chest, pinning a notice. It said, "A deal is a deal. Anyone else want to meet me?" Wasn't no Ariel did that to Klaus. The guy was a house. Six feet six. Looked like Hulk Hogan.

'Mary Little Horse, she was brought in to replace him. A genius with explosives, and pretty good with a knife too. I read in the papers you've tied her into this thing. But I never saw Mary here. She did the jobs she was paid to do, but she didn't know the whole story, or get to see any of my team.

'Mr Black let only me and my guys in on the whole plan. Ariel said he had a very big commission, money no object, from some collector. Each of us was on 200,000 dollars, and if anybody had to do time, there would be an annuity waiting when we were released, so we'd never have to work again. No, Mary just did her thing with the bombs. Then she came up to town and did the singer. Ray helped her get in, but it was mostly her. She went underground after that. Ray, the guy you killed, he stole the special explosive in France.'

Arrow nodded. 'So who was in on last night? Who planted the other bombs?'

'Ariel and Ingo did that.'

'Ingo!' Arrow's grip on the tube almost slipped.

'Yeah. Ingemar Svart. He's our pilot, engineer. An all-round mechanical genius. You need it built, Ingo'll build it. You need it fixed, Ingo'll fix it. You need it to run, Ingo'll run it. You need it screwed, Ingo'll . . .' For a second, the man laughed, weakly, then coughed with the effort. 'Ingo flies us out of the action, so he tends to be kept out of the shooting. But he has pitched in sometimes. I saw him in Cape Town. He is very good with a gun.'

Stewart looked pleadingly at Arrow. 'So how'm I doing, man?'

Adam shook his bullet head. Somewhere along the corridor a baby was crying, but he put the sound to the back of his mind. 'Not well enough, mate. You still haven't given me any clue where Mr Black might be keeping our lass. Wi'out that . . . well it's "Turn out the lights, the party's over." So tell me the rest of it. Then we'll see.'

'A farmhouse. That was where the four of us were holed up, and Dave our driver. He didn't know the plan – only where and when to be waiting, and where we were going. Dave used to drive Indy cars. We rehearsed there, in the barn. Practised handling the Sidewinders. Looked at videos of the Castle that Ariel had shot. She just walked in there like any tourist with a camera, and cased the place. The videos showed us the tunnel entrance and the way up to the Jewel building.'

'So where's this farmhouse?'

'The nearest name on the map is some place called

Longformacus – if that's how you say it. East of the City, and south. Way up on the moors, in the middle of nowhere. A shit-track road, way too far for traffic or tourists. Only snakes and sheep up there.'

'Does it have a name?'

'Stocksmoor, it was called. Ariel said Mr Black had rented it for the whole of August and September. So no one else would go up there until weeks after we were clear. If you want to find your friend's girl, that's where to head first.'

He stared at Arrow again, a plea in his eye.

Adam smiled at him. Along the corridor, the baby's crying had stopped. He sat on the bed, still holding the tube pinched tight. Gently, almost, he took Stewart's right hand in his left.

'A-1, Carl. A-fookin'-one. That's just what I wanted to hear.'

And then the smile left his face, turning it as hard as stone.

'But you know summat. I still hate fookin' mercenaries. Especially them as kills soldiers, like you lot did in the Castle last night!'

He let go of the tube. Now grasping both of Stewart's hands, and holding them vicelike, he stared into his eyes, without mercy or pity, as the man struggled in vain to find the strength and the breath to scream, as the air bubble made its way downwards, and finally out of sight.

Eighty-six

'So how's our man Stewart doing now?'

'Didn't you hear? He had a relapse, the poor bugger. Must 'ave been just a couple of minutes after I left him. What a shame, eh. Now he won't collect his pension.'

Skinner eyed him pensively, but decided to ask no more questions.

Their helicopter was flying low over the Lammermuirs, away from the setting evening sun. Skinner and Arrow, Martin and Mackie were crammed around the pilot in the small craft. Another helicopter, larger than their Jet Ranger, followed behind, carrying McGuire, McIlhenney, Maggie Rose and six SAS men in full combat gear. All of the police officers, including Skinner, carried firearms.

'So there could be as many as five of them?'

'Yes, Bob. That's if Mr Black's there too. There's him, Ariel, Ingo and Dave the Indy car driver.'

'Right,' said Skinner. 'We'll assume that they're all there, and that they're all armed. Your men have seen photos of Alex, yes?'

'Yes, Bob. Don't worry, man. They'll know her.'

'God, they'd better!' Skinner's voice betrayed, for just a second, the unbearable tension which gripped him. 'Right, when we get there, we watch for five minutes. Then your guys go in hard, upper and lower floors, in sync. Her life could be in your hands, Adam. I trust you with it, my friend. With everyone else in there, your usual engagement rules apply. Do what you think best, and I'll back you.'

Just as he finished speaking, the helicopters banked in to land, some two miles away from the farmhouse called Stocksmoor.

The group waited until it was fully dark, and until their eyes had grown accustomed to the night conditions, before beginning to move across the moorland towards where their maps indicated the farm buildings lay. They took bearings with compasses as they went, confident of the accuracy of the Ordnance Survey.

The ground was completely open for the first mile or so, covered by a mass of tangled heather, still soaking from the storm of the night before, which caught at their feet as they moved through the night.

'Christ, Bob,' said Arrow. 'What do they farm here?'

'Sheep, mate. Sheep and adders. Watch your ankles.'

Eventually the ground began to drop. The clinging heather began to thin out and gave way to grassland and gorse bushes. They found themselves descending into a narrowing valley, with a dark shape at its heart.

Arrow raised his night-glasses. 'Down there.' His voice was hushed, although they were still more than half a mile from their destination. They moved on.

Three hundred yards from the farm, Arrow drew them all together, police and SAS. He handed Skinner the binoculars. 'Take a look, Bob. Tell us what you see.'

Skinner put the bulky glasses to his eyes, and adjusted the focus wheel.

'There are two buildings. One's a steading or barn of some sort. Looks half ruined. The house is more of a cottage, two-storey, but the upper rooms are in the attic. There's a chink of light through the curtains of one of the upstairs rooms. There's a car in the yard. Looks like a Vitara. I can't see the registration from here.'

'We'll call it in for checking when we get closer,' said Martin.

'No,' said Skinner. 'We're keeping radio silence, and your mobile won't work up here. It's a blind spot on the network.'

'Any sign of movement?' said Arrow.

'No, none.'

'Right,' said the little soldier. 'My lads approach first. You coppers stay twenty yards behind. Stay quiet and keep your fookin' heads down. OK, lads, you three.' He pointed to the men nearest him. 'On the roof. But not a fookin' sound, mind. The rest of us, on the ground. Five minutes from now, if nowt's changed I fire one shot and we go in like shit off a shovel, through the windows, stun grenades first, then us. Now, you all know what Alex looks like? Confirm that everyone, please.'

Six voices each whispered 'Yes' in the dark.

'Right. Everyone else goes down. No one walks out.' Arrow turned back to Skinner. 'Right, Bob. Once we're in, and the shootin' stops, bring your people in. Better you don't see what we're up to. But don't worry about your lass. She'll be all right wi' us.'

He gestured to his men, and they moved off towards the house. Skinner led his group after them at the distance Arrow had specified, keeping low and taking whatever cover they could. Eventually, behind the dilapidated steading, they hid in waiting. Skinner checked his watch and counted down softly. He felt his heart race.

'Christ, Andy,' he muttered softly to Martin.

'I know, Bob. I know. But it'll be all right.'

Seconds later they heard Arrow's single gunshot. Its echoes still rang round the valley as the sound of shattering glass reached their ears, and the stun grenades exploded.

They waited for more shooting, but there was none.

Skinner waited for a call from Arrow, but none came.

'Come on, people,' he said grimly. 'Sounds like there's no one there. Let's go in.' They rushed from their cover towards the house. Light was blazing now from all of its windows.

Three of the SAS men stood in the lower hallway of the shabby dwelling. It smelled of damp, but of recent occupancy too. The aroma of ground coffee came from the kitchen, blown through on the night breeze from the shattered window.

Skinner stepped into the room to the right, off the hall. It was deserted. A small television set in the corner was switched on, but the sound had been turned down, either by the departed occupants or by the soldiers.

Martin, still standing in the hall, was the first to realise that none of the SAS soldiers would look at Skinner. A small knot of apprehension grew in the pit of his stomach. He looked up the narrow flight of wooden-banistered stairs.

Adam Arrow stood at the top. His voice was sad, desperately sad, and once again devoid of accent as he called from the upper floor – looking down not at Martin, but beyond him at Skinner, who had stepped back into the hallway.

'Bob. Can you come up, please. We need you here.'

Eighty-seven

Skinner almost fainted when he saw the body lying on the crumpled bed. Involuntarily, he turned his head away, grasping either side of the doorframe to hold himself steady. But at last he forced himself to look back into the small room, with its damp-stained yellowing wallpaper, its wardrobe, its cracked mirror, and its twin divans.

And on one of them, he saw his Alex, dead.

For it had to be Alex.

The girl, stretched out on her back, was tall. Alex's height. She was tanned all over; Alex's tan from sunbathing topless in the secluded cottage garden at Gullane, or on the beach in her early summer trips to their holiday home in Spain. Her legs – Alex's legs – were long and lithe, unpitted, still those of a girl rather than of a woman. Her small pink, proud nipples, set on young firm breasts – Alex's breasts – pointed towards the ceiling.

She was wearing only a pair of cream panties, wet at the crotch; and, grotesquely, a white pillow-case. It was pulled over her head like a hangman's hood, and it was blood-stained at the front. It reached down to her shoulders, covering completely her hair, face and neck.

Still braced in the doorway, Skinner, feeling his heart thundering in his chest, looked desperately at her hands for jewellery, for a wristwatch, for anything strange or new to him, anything that would let him tell himself, 'No, this is not my daughter.'

But he saw no sign, nothing there to give him that comfort.

Maggie Rose moved past him, towards the body.

'Stop, Sergeant.'

She froze in her tracks at the sound of his voice.

'I have to do this, Maggie.'

Dreadfully slowly, or so it seemed to those who watched, he walked towards the body. Andy Martin was not in the room. He sat at the foot of the stairs, trembling, the knot of fear in his stomach now grown to a grasping, twisting fist.

At last, Bob Skinner reached the dead girl. He leaned over her, then gently, reverently, lifted her shoulders up from the bed and drew the pillow-case away from her head.

As he did so he closed his eyes. It was only with an effort of will that he opened them again – and looked into the face of Mary Little Horse.

The girl's eyes stared back at him, lifeless. Above them there was a dark, round hole in the centre of her blood-smeared forehead.

Later Skinner would feel guilt at his immediate reaction, but in the moment of recognition he knew only a sense of relief deeper than any he had ever experienced in his life. And he gave thanks to whoever was there to hear him, that it was this girl who was dead, and not another.

He gave way suddenly to a great weakness. He felt unmanned, and so, afraid that his frailty might be recognised, he laid Mary Little Horse – a murderess but another father's daughter nonetheless – back down on her death-bed, walked from the chamber, head bowed and without a word, and locked himself in the bathroom across the landing.

He sat for a while on the white enamelled edge of the old

cast-iron bath and, alone behind the solid oak door of the little room, he wept tears of relief. He was trembling and his heart was still pounding. He had been certain that it was his Alex lying there, and in that short time from his first sight of the body to his discovery that it was not her, he had been swept by a sense of bereavement so profound that, even although it had now been lifted, the shadow of its desolation would remain with him for ever.

He lost all track of time for a while, but eventually he calmed himself and recovered his strength. But with it he found a feeling of new foreboding. His daughter was alive, but now his best chance of recovering her safely had evaporated. Mr Black had outguessed him. Now they would have to risk the Jewels, staking them, and most of all, staking his daughter's life, on the plan he had devised.

Feeling a sudden pressure in his bladder, he raised the wooden toilet seat and the lid, together, and urinated heavily into the bowl. Finished, he pulled the flush lever, zipped himself, and turned to wash his hands in the white basin. As he turned on the taps, his eye was caught by a piece of white paper folded and jammed under a plastic shell-shaped soap-dish which sat on a wooden shelf above the basin. Curious, he lifted the pink dish and picked it up.

The three sheets of paper appeared to have been torn out of a diary. They were folded across the centre. As he opened them out, his earlier foreboding was swept away by his sudden joy at the sight of his daughter's message, written in pencil on the torn dirty pages, scrawled but still legible.

Hi, Pops,

They let me watch TV today. I saw you, and know what this is about. Ingo says I'm Mr Black's second chance, so I can guess what my ransom is. He and an American called Dave brought me here during the night. On the way they picked up a girl called Mary. She'd been living rough in a hut near Gifford.

It's 8:00 pm. A woman called Ariel just turned up, and we're leaving in a hurry. She said Mr Black (?) assumed you'd get someone called Carl to talk. They've allowed me a quick pee and a wash first, though.

Ingo just killed my room-mate, Mary. He came in as she was changing, pulled a pillow-case over her head, and shot her. He said she was too risky baggage to carry further. I don't know where we're going now, but if I see a chance, I'll leg it. When you catch up with Ingo, Pops, be careful. He's very dangerous. I'm sorry I got you into this.

Love you.

Alex.

He was smiling as he walked out of the bathroom and down into the hall where Martin, Mackie and Arrow waited, anxious, none of them certain what sort of a man would emerge. He waved the note at Martin.

'Look at this, Andy. It's from our lass. She's something else.'

Martin took the note and read it, and, as he did, Bob Skinner laughed to himself, and shook his head again in wonderment at his daughter.

He had never been prouder of her. She had just seen murder done, sudden and shocking but she had still had the presence of mind to leave a note, to try to give what assistance she could. Bright, tough, and brave, too. He hoped in the hours to come he could live up to her example.

Eighty-eight

'If you were there, you'd be putting Alex's life at risk! There's no way, love, I'll let you do that!'

'Bob, that's an awful thing to say. How could you!' Sarah wore, for a moment, an expression which was completely new to him: one of pure hurt. Then it melted into one of anger and frustration. 'Dammit man, I'm a member of your team. You made me one, remember.'

'Well, as of now, you're off the pitch. I didn't tell you about last night's operation until it was over because I knew that, if I had, we'd have had this argument then.'

'But you could need me there! As a doctor. If there is trouble, if there's shooting, people could get hurt. Alex could get hurt. You could get hurt.'

He put his big hands on her shoulders and kissed her on the forehead. She leaned back against the larder cupboard of their kitchen at Fairyhouse Avenue, tears gleaming in her eyes.

He did his best to soothe her. 'Sarah, my darling, I hope with all my heart that, when I catch up with them, these people will decide that they are not on a suicide mission, and will let Alex go. In fact, I'm forcing myself to believe that's what will happen. If I'm wrong, then yes, there will be shooting. If there is, then believe me, the people on my team are the best – me included. But to give our best, we have to be completely focused on the job. If you were anywhere near, you'd be a distraction for me, and probably for Andy too. If the shit did start flying we'd have you to worry about as well. All our thoughts have to be focused on protecting Alex, and rescuing her. If you were there to distract us, then, as I say, you would be adding to her danger. Look, wherever we end up, if we need a doctor, we'll get one quick. If I *do* decide to take one, it won't be you; it'll be an Army medic. But Adam Arrow's probably as good as anyone. He'd seen action, and dealt with wounded.'

Slightly guiltily, a grin gleamed through her tears. 'Yeah, from what I've seen of little Arrow, with a point-four-five round in the ear!'

The tension between them eased. Bob chuckled quietly. He lifted up her chin and made her look him in the eye.

'That's better. You're smiling again. That's how you can help me most, love.'

She hugged him close, and very tight.

'Oh, but, my darling, I'll be so worried about you. About you both. About you all.'

'I know, honey, but we'll be all right.'

He was struck by a sudden thought.

'Listen. Wee Julia'll be in the same boat as you, in her case worrying about Andy. I'll have him bring her up here, and the two of you can hold each other's hands like the astronauts' wives did in Alex's play, when their men were in orbit.'

She brightened up again. 'Yeah. We can watch videos. Woody Allen rather than Kevin Costner, though.'

'What, not even *The Bodyguard*?'

'Especially not that!'

'What about *Batman*? That'd be quite appropriate really for you and Julia?'

She looked at him, puzzled. 'Why?'

'Well, what with Andy's nickname among the old-timer uniform PCs . . .'

'What's that?'

'Robin the Boy Wonder . . .!'

Her eyes widened. 'So that means yours must be . . .'

'Exactly! That's why I gave up wearing the black leather coat. Folk thought I was trying to live up to my nickname!'

They laughed together again in the midst of their troubles, and Bob kissed her once more.

'Right I'll fix that up with Andy. Now I must be off to Fettes. It's eight o'clock. All my plans are made. It's time to brief the troops. Brian's picking me up and he'll be outside by now. Next time you see me, Alex will be with me. Believe me.'

As the door closed behind him, the smile on her face dissolved. She leaned back against the larder door once more, tears flowing freely.

'Yes, my love, I do believe you,' she whispered. 'But will you both still be alive?'

Eighty-nine

Brian Mackie hefted the sniper's rifle, with its telescopic sight, to his shoulder, and settled it against him like a new lover, adjusting himself to its shape, making himself comfortable with its feel, and with the lines of its long body.

Skinner looked at the two of them, man and mistress, silhouettes in the little light which invaded the dark of the office. He took in the slender shape of the hand-built gun, and was struck by the contrast with the ugliness of the long silencer which extended its barrel.

Mackie nuzzled his cheek against the walnut stock and waited.

It was 10:58 pm. Outside, the Gyle Centre car park, cleared completely of vehicles as instructed, was illuminated brightly by its floodlights on their pillars, in contrast with the bulky darkness of the two superstores and the other, smaller shops which bounded it on two sides.

'It's nearly time, Brian,' said Skinner. 'Any second now. Remember, *our* car is a white Mondeo. Theirs might be a Vauxhall Senator.'

He felt the rush of adrenaline pumping him up, readying him for action. Though he was still fearful for Alex, he was glad that the moment had almost come. The last thirty, sleepless hours had been the longest of his life.

The rest of the farmhouse had offered them few new leads.

They had found Mary Little Horse's things, in a rucksack in the wardrobe in the bedroom. The only other signs of the house's occupants had been their refuse – the tins and discarded food wrappers which someone had thrown into a green wheelie-bin outside the back door – and the coffee pot and stained mugs which had been left on the kitchen table.

Eventually Skinner had returned to look again, more professionally and dispassionately this time, at the body of Mary Little Horse.

'Alex wasn't kidding about Mr Ingo, Andy. The man must be good. Our Mary here was a pro herself.'

'Yes,' said Martin, 'and she was strong as well, according to poor old Frank Adams. Ingo must have taken her completely by surprise. Pillow-case over her head and bang, before she had time to react. Poetic justice, I suppose.'

'Or dog eat bitch!'

Beside the Vitara in the yard, they found, and photographed a second set of tyre tracks in the setting mud. A tyre-centre manager, called out in the early hours of the morning, had identified them as belonging to the type normally fitted to a 24-valve Vauxhall Senator, the flagship saloon of the range.

'Vauxhall,' Skinner had grunted. 'Not exactly a rare model. Still, put the word out to all of our traffic cars, and to all traffic wardens, to look out for Senators. Anybody who sees one carrying a group of two men and two women is to call it in right away. But no one is to approach it. I don't want them getting nervy while Alex is still in that car. I want these bastards out in the open.'

The memory of his own instructions snapped him back to the present, just as the white Mondeo swept into the deserted car park, heading towards the centre of the pool of light. He had time to spot Maggie Rose in the driver's seat, before she swung the car around so that its near-side faced the office where Skinner and Mackie were hidden.

As soon as it had drawn to a halt, Neil McIlhenney jumped from the front passenger seat, and raced round to the boot. He pushed the release button and, as the lid swung up, reached inside and withdrew the two hold-alls, one long, the other squarish, which Skinner had seen before in another place. He wondered whether anyone had bothered to clean off the blood streaks, then found himself hoping that they had not.

Without even glancing around, McIlhenney – obeying to the letter Skinner's orders at his briefing earlier that evening – put the hold-alls down close together on the ground, right in the centre of the car park. He took three long strides back to the passenger door and jumped in. The door had barely closed behind him before Maggie Rose slammed the car into gear and raced off into the night, heading out of the Centre and turning in the direction of the city.

Skinner peered at his watch, holding it up towards the little light that crept in through the open window. It showed almost exactly 11:00 pm. He looked at the second hand as it swept up towards the hour, and waited, hardly daring to breathe.

The Senator was forty-three seconds late.

They heard it just before they saw it roaring through the car park entrance and into view. The high floodlights reflected strongly from its brilliant white bodywork, and gave the heavily smoked glass of its windows a mirror-like sheen.

Skinner, in his hide, read the number-plate from afar through powerful field-glasses. He struggled to catch a glimpse of the occupants, but the glass was impenetrable under the floodlights, and he was unable even to make out their shadows.

Driven very fast and very smoothly, the car zigzagged for a second or two as it entered the park, before straightening up and making directly for the two hold-alls sitting in the centre. Just as it drew close, the driver slammed on the brakes hard, and swung it round and to a halt, tail-first. At it spun, Skinner thought that he could just make out four heads inside, but it was the most fleeting of glimpses, and he could not be certain.

'Ok, Brian. Stay ready.' In the dark, renewed tension, almost overwhelming, gripped Skinner.

'Sir.' Mackie's reply was whispered, but certain.

The Vauxhall was positioned now between their office stake-out and the hold-alls. A few seconds passed with no sign of movement. Skinner guessed that the Senator's occupants were looking around for any sign of an ambush. Involuntarily he pressed himself back into the shadows.

At first he was unable to catch a clear view of the person who climbed out of the car. The only indication of any movement was a very slight drop in the suspension. Then, from his distant viewpoint, through the glasses he saw, under the Vauxhall's body, a shadow moving on the ground beyond, as the passenger door was opened. Left, then right; two feet in trainers appeared. He swung the field-glasses upward and caught the back of a blond head and broad shoulders, rising well above the level of the car roof.

'It's Ingo, I think,' he said to Mackie.

The powerful figure moved over swiftly to the hold-alls. For a second or two there was more of him in view, across the bonnet of the Senator – then none at all, as he crouched down, disappearing from Skinner's sight completely. Even his feet were hidden by the front wheels.

Some time passed.

'He must be giving those bags a good going over,' muttered Skinner. 'Just as well we didn't chance putting a tracking device in there.'

Mackie, who was concentrating all his attention on his view through the telescopic sight, offered no reply.

Only the shadow on the ground told Skinner that the searcher was on the move. Then suddenly he was in his clear view again, as he came round to the rear of the vehicle, still crouching, with a hold-all in each hand – but in the right hand also, a small black object not much larger than a walkie-talkie radio hand-set. Without putting down his burden he pressed the boot release button with his left thumb. The lid swung up. He placed the bags and the black object carefully inside, and quickly slammed it shut.

As it closed, the man stood up straight, and Skinner caught his first clear sight of him. Even if the view was only in profile, and at a distance, the power of the field-glasses left him in no doubt.

'Ingo, right enough.'

His mind swept back to their last meeting, in his own home, with Ingo as his guest – as his daughter's guest; as her lover. He remembered the man's cool arrogance, and Skinner's own certain belief that he was being sized up by someone with much more to him that met the eye.

As Skinner watched, Ingo swung round, scanning the surrounding buildings one more time, and he was able to look straight into his face. It was cold, intent, ruthless; a face he had seen before, yet never seen in this way. Even without the evidence of Mary Little Horse's corpse, he would have known at once why Alex had stressed this man's menace.

For a moment the Swede seemed to halt in the sweep of his gaze. It was as if his and Skinner's eyes had met. Skinner thought for that second, his heart dropping, that Ingo had spotted him, even from that far away. Then, with relief, he remembered that he was looking through field-glasses.

The gaze of inspection continued on past their place of concealment, and round the rest of the adjoining buildings. Then he spun on his heel and ran back to the passenger door, disappearing from sight.

The car started to move. Skinner stared after it, numbed by hatred for the man who had abused his daughter and now was threatening her life.

Beside him, Brian Mackie pulled the trigger without waiting for any order to be given. The soft thud of the silenced rifle broke Skinner's trance. He trained his binoculars on the Senator as it started to gather pace, and picked out, on the offside rear wing, something that had been not been there before. It was barely distinguishable against the white bodywork, but there it was, a big whitish-grey stain, looking for all the world like a seagull dropping.

'Nailed it, Brian. Good shot, son.'

'No problem, sir.'

Mackie looked over at Skinner as he stood in the shadows, staring after the car as it disappeared into the night.

'So that was Ingo himself, boss.'

'That was Ingo all right. No one else. He didn't spot us there, but he's going to see me again before this night is over. Oh by Christ he is!'

Ninety

There is no way that helicopters can fly quietly.

They heard the first whirr of the rotors barely twenty seconds after the Vauxhall Senator had cleared the car park. The Bell Jet Ranger which had taken them to Stocksmoor twenty-four hours earlier came in low, from the south, where it had been hovering out of sight and sound, waiting for the pick-up at a distance. The pilot swept in low across the car park, touching down as close as he dared to the building from which Skinner and Mackie were emerging.

Skinner sprinted up to the craft, ducking by reflex under the rotors. The door swung open as he reached it, and he saw Andy Martin and Adam Arrow seated inside behind the pilot.

Skinner jumped into the empty front seat, then turned to Mackie.

'Brian, did you bring regular ammo for that gun?'

Mackie looked offended. 'Of course, boss.'

'Let's have it, then. You never know, it might come in handy.'

He took the gun and ammunition from his aide and closed the door. Instantly, the Jet Ranger lifted off. Skinner turned to look at the two men in the seats behind him.

'Right, boys,' he said grimly, grasping the rifle by its stock and unscrewing the ugly silencer. 'Let's hunt some bears!'

Ninety-one

McGuire was inside the Jetstream parked on the runway at Edinburgh Airport. Alongside him were three of Adam Arrow's SAS contingent, fully armed and ready for action. The remainder were disguised as airport ground crew, with sidearms tucked inside their work tunics. Mario McGuire carried an H & K carbine rather than a pistol, for its extra accuracy even at close quarters, and its instant stopping power. He had once stood up against an automatic weapon when armed only with a handgun, and had good reason to be aware of the difference.

The small turbo-prop aeroplane stood on the tarmac in front of the main terminal building, just beyond the Loganair stand. A hundred yards away, twin gates lay open to allow the getaway vehicle access to the aircraft.

Skinner had asked for radio silence on the operation in the assumption that Mr Black's group would be covering all open frequencies. However, McGuire was linked by a short-range two-way radio to Sir James Proud, who was perched high in the airport control tower. He checked his watch, and spoke into the handset. 'It's 11:04, sir. See anything from up there?'

Up in the tower, the Chief Constable surveyed the wide carriageway which led from the landscaped A8 airport slip-road up to the terminal building. The last shuttle had long since landed, and no tourist flights were allowed to depart from Edinburgh that late in the evening. The road was empty. Proud Jimmy clicked the transmit button on his radio.

'Nothing yet, McGuire. Looks like Mr Skinner's right. This whole thing was a feint. They're going somewhere else. Give it to 11:15, then – hold on!'

Even as the Chief spoke, he saw in the distance a car shoot off the roundabout at speed and enter the approach road. Its headlights were full on, and badly adjusted. Even at that distance, he was blinded for a second.

'There's a car now. Can't make out colour or anything else, but it's travelling. It could be the target. Ready for action on my command. Officer at the terminal approach: route that car straight on to the tarmac. It'll be with you in no more than thirty seconds. Acknowledge.'

The uniformed constable on the road at the British Midland terminal raised a hand above his head to indicate that he had heard.

Proud had underestimated the car's speed. Less than twenty seconds later, it took the corner into the terminal straight, headlights still ablaze. The constable stepped into the roadway and flagged the car vigorously towards the open gates, and on to the tarmac. The driver slammed on the brakes and swung the vehicle round and through the opening. The policeman had no time to identify the make of the vehicle. He saw only a white flash as it sped past him.

Above, Proud watched the car as it slowed down to crawl. Even from his high vantage point it was half obscured by the first buildings of the terminal complex. But, as he watched, it cruised slowly towards the Jetstream, which was parked in the open beyond a Loganair ATP.

'Ready, everyone. They may be confused about which

plane to take, but they're getting closer. They're stopping. OK, wait for it. Door's opening. Now go!'

Down on the tarmac, the driver's door of the white car swung open. A stocky, ginger-haired man got out – and reeled back in surprise as six handguns were trained on him by airport ground-crew.

'What the fuck!' he cried reaching so high above his head that for a second it looked as if he would take off.

'What the fuck!' said Sir James Proud, up in the control tower. 'McGuire, get out and see what this is.'

Mario McGuire jumped from the Dash and ran over to the silent group surrounding the white car. The passenger doors had been torn open. There were no other occupants.

'Police,' snapped McGuire, as he reached the scene. 'Who are you and what the hell are you doing here?'

The red-haired man continued to reach for the sky. 'Harry Page. Ah'm Harry Page. Look, ah know ah wis speedin'. Ah'm sorry! Ma wife works as a stewardess fur Loganair. Ah'm here tae pick her up. Christ, mister, what is this? Ah'm late enough already. Ah should have been here at ten-fifteen. She'll bloody murder me, as it is!'

Ninety-two

'Remember, pilot, let it get more than two miles away, and we've fookin' lost it.'

'But it is working?'

'Sure, Bob. It's working like a fookin' dream. There's enough irradiated iodine in that paint-splash to give us a good strong signal. Cracking shot by Brian, that were.'

Arrow held a small box on his knee. It was wired into the helicopter's electrical system. A green glow from its screen reflected on his face.

'We can follow them forever with this, as long as we stay within two miles, and as long as the paint doesn't get washed off.'

'Can we make visual contact?' Skinner asked the pilot.

'Yes. But do you want to take the chance, sir? A mile is as close as I'd come, to be sure they won't see us.'

'No,' Arrow answered for him. 'Trust our little box, Bob. I'll wager that's the only car on the road with a big patch of radioactive bird-shit on its tail!'

'Ok, Adam.' Skinner's voice could only just be heard above the noise of the helicopter's engine. 'Let's go with it. What does it tell us?'

'Well, you were right. They've by-passed Edinburgh Airport. That were a con all along. I reckon they've just gone past the Norton House.'

'Unless they turn off for Ratho, it's Newbridge roundabout next,' said Skinner. 'From there they can go anywhere. North over the Forth Bridge, although I don't think they'll fancy stopping to pay the tolls; Falkirk and Stirling up the M9; or due West to Glasgow on the M8, and then, as far south as the road goes.'

'How far can they get on a tank of fuel in that thing?' asked Arrow.

'Hard to say, but the bigger the engine, the bigger the tank. Even though that's a three-litre, he should get to Birmingham easy, maybe London at a pinch, without stopping. If he goes south and gets into heavy traffic we've got a problem.'

'As long as he's got that paint on his arse, he's the one with the problem.'

'Let's hope so,' said Skinner. 'Watch that tracker. He should be at Newbridge any second now.'

Arrow bent close to the little screen. The reflected glow turned his face green in the darkness of the cabin.

'Here we go. He's swinging. He's going left. Yes, he's off. It's the M8, Bob. He's off to Glasgow.'

Ninety-three

No one came to the door when Maggie Rose rang the bell. The porch of the Skinner bungalow in Fairyhouse Avenue was lit and welcoming, but no one answered.

'Surely they haven't gone out?' she said to Neil McIlhenney.

'Can't imagine so. But then the boss didn't tell them we were coming. It was an afterthought of his, this baby-sitting idea.'

'God, Neil, don't let Sarah hear that. Remember, the party line is that he decided he should expect anything from these characters, so with him and Andy out of town, he sent us down here as protection.'

'She'll never believe that.'

'Maybe not, but she won't take it out on us. She's a nice lady, the doctor.'

'Try the bell again.'

They rang again, listening hard to make certain the bell had sounded, and waited for two full minutes more, before deciding to check round the back. They crept softly along the gravel towards the back door, and saw as they went that the garage door was open. Skinner's car was there, but Sarah's was gone. The garden was lit from the unshaded kitchen window and from the back door, which lay slightly ajar.

They had their pistols drawn as they slipped nervously into

the house. Moving quickly through the deserted kitchen, they went from room to room on the ground floor, checking each one cautiously. Then they climbed the short flight of stairs to the attic, to satisfy themselves that the three upper rooms were empty also, before returning to the living room for a second look.

They saw that Sarah had prepared for Julia's arrival. A big oval plate of freshly cut ham and tomato sandwiches, American-sized, sat on the low glass coffee table between the two sofas. Alongside it were two plates, two china mugs, knives, spoons and paper napkins. Nothing there was out of place.

They went back into the kitchen. The coffee filter was primed and ready, waiting to be switched on. Two glasses, a bottle of Smirnoff Silver and a tin of diet Coca-Cola sat on the work surface beside the tall fridge-freezer. Without touching anything, McIlhenney crouched down and studied each item closely.

One glass was three-quarters full. A few bubbles clung to the side, and a slice of greenish lime floated on the surface. Lipstick traces showed on the rim. He leaned over the glass and sniffed. 'Bacardi and tonic,' he said. He looked at the other glass. A slice of lemon was wedged at its foot in a finger of a clear liquid. He sniffed that, too, but found no trace of alcohol. He looked again at the bottle. Vodka and Coke in the making, probably.

'So what happened to them?' he asked Maggie. 'Sarah's got a drink on the go when Julia arrives, and she comes into the kitchen to mix one for her guest. She gets the ice and lemon from the fridge, drops them in the glass. Takes the Smirnoff and the Coke from the fridge as well. And that's as far as she gets . . . Then they decide to go to the pictures? Hardly!'

Maggie's face broke into a sudden, relieved smile.

'Neil, she's a doctor, isn't she? Not just with the police, but in a general practice. She's had an emergency call-out. Rather than leave Julia here, she's taken her with her. That's your mystery.'

McIlhenney looked sceptical. 'Oh aye, and being an ACC's wife she just runs out the back door and leaves it wide open, with all the lights on.'

Maggie grimaced. 'I see what you mean.'

Then she made a decision.

'Look, let's wait here anyway, as ordered. But in the meantime let's try and check her practice. Then we can call in to Brian Mackie, when he gets back to the office.'

Ninety-four

Glasgow reflected yellow in the night sky ahead. Closer at hand they saw below them the lights of the Harthill Service Area, as the helicopter continued to track the Vauxhall westward along the M8. They matched its speed, keeping a mile behind it. Occasionally, Skinner fancied he glimpsed tail-lights in the distance. The car was travelling fast, at just over 80 mph, but not so fast as to attract the attention of the motorway patrols.

Skinner checked his watch. The time was 11:23 pm, yet it seemed like an age since the Senator had raced into the Gyle Centre. He hated to be bottled up; it made him feel claustrophobic. Eventually he could stand the tension inside him no longer. He dug his mobile telephone from the top right pocket of his black leather jacket.

'Pilot, if I use this thing, will it work?'

'Shouldn't have a problem this close to the ground. We're right on top of a cell here too. You might find it a bit patchy, but go ahead.'

Skinner peered at the keyboard in the dim cabin light, and keyed in the stored number of Brian Mackie's direct line. He was answered after a few seconds.

'Brian, it's me. You made good time getting back. You'll know by now that we were right about that plane at Edinburgh. We're heading for Glasgow. I want you to call Willie Haggerty, give him the number of the Senator.' He dictated the number which he had memorised. 'Tell Willie I want people at all docks, and I want as many men as he can get under cover at Glasgow Airport.'

The line went faint for a second, then strengthened again. 'You think they'll go for another plane?'

'Has to be. Could be they're just going to drive in and hijack one, using Alex as bargaining power. But the way this thing's been planned, I reckon they've got a back-up ready. Needn't be very big. An 800-mile range will get you to a hell of a lot of places from Glasgow. Especially overnight. Whatever it is, wherever it is, I can't let them take off with Alex on board. Now give Haggerty the message, and tell him to make sure that nobody moves in without me there to give the orders. I don't want any of those Glasgow lads playing cowboys with my daughter's life on the line.'

Ninety-five

Suddenly the trace vanished from the monitor. Skinner could not actually see the screen, but he sensed its disappearance from the sudden look of panic which flashed across Arrow's face.

'Where's it gone? What's happened?' he snapped.

''S'OK, Bob,' came the calm, steady voice of Andy Martin. Seated next to Arrow, he had detailed maps on his knees and a torch in his hand. 'They're in the Charing Cross underpass, beneath that ugly office block that goes over the road. We'll have them back in a second. Yes, there it is. Still on course for Glasgow Airport. Just going on to the Kingston Bridge now.'

Skinner turned to the pilot. 'How fast can this thing go?'

'Twice as fast as they can. And dead straight, remember.'

'Good. I must be at the airport before they get there. We'll follow them for a minute of two more, then once we're absolutely certain that's where they're headed, we'll put the foot down and beat them to it. Suppose they see a chopper there at an airport, they won't think anything of it.'

Martin broke it. 'Hold on, boss. They seem to be turning off the motorway.'

'Eh! Which way?'

'Hold on. They're in a sort of a curve. They're still on the slip-road. I'll know in a minute. Yes, they're still heading west.

I'd say they're taking the off-motorway route to the airport, out through Govan. That's got to be it. It's one last feint. Tricky sods these.'

'God, Andy, but I hope you're right. Look, we can't track them street by street through this. Let's give them two more minutes, then we commit to Glasgow Airport.'

They hugged the line of the motorway as it headed towards the airport, and, as they did so, the trace from the dye on the Vauxhall Senator stayed to the north on Arrow's screen, moving much more slowly now, as the car wound through the streets of Govan.

Skinner tapped the pilot on the shoulder to attract his attention. 'How long to the airport?'

'For us, three minutes. For him, by that route, fifteen minimum.'

Skinner was about to commit himself finally to Glasgow Airport, leaving the trace behind, when Martin broke in. 'What the hell's this? They're doubling back.'

'What?'

'The trace. It's turned back on itself.'

'Dear Christ!' said Skinner, with a sigh of fear and frustration.

'It's gone again,' said Martin. 'Pilot, hover. Hold your position.'

Arrow and Martin stared at the screen. Skinner leaned back over the seat for a clear sight, and Arrow turned the tracer set half towards him, to allow him to view. The little cathode screen stayed obstinately blank.

'Damn it! Damn it! Damn it!' Skinner roared in his rage. 'Where's the fucker gone?'

Arrow offered a suggestion in hope. 'He could have gone into a garage to fill up.'

'Bollocks! You think this lot's planning includes running out of petrol in the middle of the night in fucking Govan! They'll have another car somewhere. The bastards have stashed the Senator and switched. We've lost her, boys. We've lost her.'

His despair was even greater than that of the night before, for then there had been that other slim possibility. But now . . .

'No!' The certainty in Martin's voice banished the darkness gathering in Skinner's heart.

'The Tunnel. The Clyde Tunnel entrance is down there. Pilot, head north.'

The helicopter banked sharply round and headed away from the bright lights of the motorway, towards the network of orange lines which crisscross the west of Glasgow by night, bisected by the dark slash of the River Clyde.

North they went, but the screen was still dead, even when they had almost reached the river.

'Andy, you sure about this?'

'What other chance is there? They'll have gone out of range for a bit. We'll have to catch them up. Look. There they are already!'

'Yeah, you beauty!' Skinner cried with delight. 'You bastards won't do that again,' he growled at the trace, as if, through it, Alex's kidnappers could hear him. He looked again and saw that the Senator was headed due north.

'So, now where're they off to?' asked Adam Arrow, and the atmosphere at once grew more sober again.

'What does the map say?' asked Skinner.

'I don't need the map for that,' said Martin. 'They're headed up Crow Road, towards Anniesland Cross. From there they can go in four different directions. It's anyone's guess now which one they'll take.'

'Whatever it is,' said Skinner, 'we've got to guess their

destination, and get there before them. Otherwise . . .' His voice tailed away wearily.

'Let's see what they do,' said Martin. 'They could even cut back across the Erskine Bridge and come into the airport from the other side. Anniesland Cross'll tell us that. They must be there now. The trace has stopped. That'll be the traffic-lights. Of course they're so complicated there, it's always possible the bugger could get lost!'

He stared at the screen. 'There he goes again. West is it? No, he's going north still. That makes it Bearsden, and Milngavie beyond that. That's the wrong way for a boat, and it's away from all the airports. Christ knows where he's off to, Bob. To lie low for a few days, d'you think?'

Skinner shook his head. 'No, they've got what they came for. They won't let the sun come up on them. Somewhere there's an aircraft. Any ideas, pilot?'

'No, sir. Not in this direction. I have to warn you, though, if they've got a full tank, they'll outlast us, especially if we're flying stop-and-start like this.'

Skinner nodded. 'Aye, I figured. Look, my last option is that if we're going to run out of fuel, we land on the road in front of them and shoot their tyres out. But that's nightmare stuff. It's the slimmest of all chances for my daughter.

'How long have we got?'

'No more than half an hour, sir.'

'Jesus.'

'Here, Bob. Hold on a minute. I've got it.'

Skinner looked over his shoulder to the rear seat. A sly smile showed on Martin's face. The green eyes, made even greener by the reflection of the screen caught in his contact lens, seemed to glow brightly in the dark.

'He's off to Balnaddar.'

Ninety-six

'Sorry to brother you, sir, but we've got a mystery here.'

Maggie Rose had come through on Mackie's direct line, not long after he had finished passing Skinner's message on to Superintendent Haggerty. She explained to him that Sarah and Julia Shahor had vanished, and that there were clear signs that their disappearance had been sudden and unplanned.

'So what have you done about it?'

'We've checked the doctors' call-out service. No emergency calls have been put through to Sarah tonight. Then we've checked the hospitals. She hasn't been seen at any of them. We've checked with Telecom. No calls to or from this number all evening. We've checked with UCI and the other cinemas that take credit-card bookings. None made by either Sarah or Julia. Oh yes, and we've even searched the garden, just in case they saw us and decided to play the fool. All in all, sir, so far not a trace of them.'

Mackie took a few seconds to consider what he had been told.

'OK, Maggie. You've done everything right so far. I'll take things from here. You two stay there and wait for them getting back from the Chinese or whatever carry-out shop they've probably gone to. I'll have an East Lothian car check out Gullane.'

'You going to let the boss know?'

'No bloody way. He and Andy have enough on their minds, without nonsense like this!'

Ninety-seven

The airfield was just where Martin had said it would be. It lay a few miles north of Milngavie – 'T' UK's least pronounceable town', as Arrow had dubbed it – on the A81 to Blanefield, and ultimately to Aberfoyle, just where the flatter landscape gives way finally to seemingly endless hills.

Skinner had committed the helicopter as soon as the trace showed that the Senator had taken the fork to Milngavie. Swinging wide round the car, the pilot had outpaced it easily. Now, the dead screen showed that they were well in front of it, but Skinner was unworried. He knew that there were no other forks or turn-offs on the road for their quarry to take, but if he was wrong, and this was not to be the stopping place, he still had fuel in hand for the gambler's last throw which he had contemplated earlier.

'What was this place used for, then, Andy?' he asked as the helicopter hovered low over the strip.

Martin did not answer for a moment, as he watched the searchlight beam follow the entrance road from the A81, sweep along the short grey tarmac runway, and finally pick out the hangar, the only building in the field.

'The University Flying Club used it in my day,' he said eventually. 'They ran three planes out of here. A few private pilots flew from here as well. Then some of them played silly buggers and got too close to the Glasgow flight-path, so the

CAA had it closed down. After that somebody rented it for a while and ran it as a go-kart track, until mountain-bikes and video games came along and killed that business stone dead. Since then it hasn't been used at all. As far as I know, the University still owns it, but they can't think of anything to do with it. They can't get planning permission for houses, and so they can't sell it. The last I heard of it was when I saw in a graduates' association circular in the spring that it was going to be used for a charity Bungee-jump.'

'Who'd be likely to know about this place, other than the locals and students?' Skinner asked.

'Just about any pilot with access to the right charts. It'll still be marked on them – like for emergencies only.'

As he spoke, the helicopter touched down, facing the hangar. The pilot switched off the engine and, as the craft settled, raised the beam of the searchlight and played it on the rusting doors. They stood slightly ajar. The policemen, the soldier, and the pilot jumped from the Jet Ranger and walked towards the hangar, their shadows on its doors growing smaller as they neared it.

They saw immediately that it was impossible for the doors to be pulled fully shut because of thick grass which had sprouted in their runner. One by one the men squeezed through the gap, although for Arrow, who seemed squatter than ever, it proved a tight fit.

Martin's torch had a wide beam adjustment. In the broad light it cast, they saw, in the centre of the hangar, its propellors facing the doors, a small twin-engined aircraft. Martin shone the torch into the aeroplane. It had four seats, two in front, two to the rear, with storage space behind.

'What make is it?' Skinner asked the pilot.

'Could be some sort of Fokker.'

'Range?'

'Depends on the load, but if it's fully tanked up, quite a way: Southern Ireland no sweat, well into France, the Benelux countries, Scandinavia even. And this one *is* fully tanked up. Look at the way she's sitting on the suspension.'

'That says it all,' said Skinner. He reached inside his jacket and took a Browning automatic from its holster. 'Right. We haven't got all night. We must get that chopper airborne again, now. Adam, you and I are the reception committee. You in that corner over there, against the wall and beyond the door. I'll take the other side.' He turned to Martin and the pilot. 'You two, get the hell out of here, and do what you have to.' He paused, then a strange look came into his eyes: a look with fear, hope and determination all mixed in.

'Me, I have an appointment with my daughter – and with one or two people who are going to wish they had never met her.'

Ninety-eight

They heard the Vauxhall Senator's tyres sizzle on the rough tarmac road, and saw the beam of its headlights swing round as it slowed to a halt, facing diagonally into the hangar. Arrow was almost caught in the sweep of the light as it lanced into the big shed through the gap in the doors. Just in time he jumped back into his corner hiding-place.

They heard a car door open. Then a voice, familiar to Skinner, said, 'Thank you, Dave, this is for you.'

The sound of the gunshot followed less than a second later, then sudden, reflex female reactions. *Two* women screaming, Skinner thought. Ingo could not have warned Ariel about his plans for Dave.

He tensed himself in the dark, and flicked off the safety-catch of the Browning. He was ready for instant action, but not for what came next.

'All right, Pops. You and your boys better come out now. Don't want pretty daughter to get hurt.' Ingo called directly into the hangar.

For once in his life, Skinner was taken completely by surprise.

'Come on, Bob,' Ingo called again. 'If you're in there, you step out within three seconds. If you're not there, well, I don't need her any more, so I just shoot her now. Just like poor Dave. I didn't tell him it was only a little plane. Come on out now. Your last chance.'

'OK,' Skinner roared from the shadows of the hangar. He left his place of concealment, the Browning still in his hand, but pointing to the ground, and stepped through the opening, out into the halogen light, out to face the kidnappers and his daughter.

Both the front and back offside doors of the Senator were wide open. Ingo stood beside the car, pressing Alex tight against him. His left hand held one end of a thick leather belt which was looped, through its buckle, around her neck. His right hand pressed a pistol to her temple.

Cold hard rage swept over Skinner like an Arctic wave. His right fist tightened on the gun. He wanted very badly to kill this man *now*, and knew that there was nothing left in him, no last shred of restraint to stay his hand. He looked Ingo dead in the eyes with such fearsome anger that for a second it penetrated the other man's coolness and made him flinch, even with his gun held close to Alex's head.

'You will let my daughter go now,' said Skinner in a hollow voice, 'and then I will deal with you.'

But Ingo held on to his nerve, and Skinner saw that Alex's note had not exaggerated the menace of the man.

'No, no, Bob. Let her go now? You must think I am crazy. Now you – you look a little nuts. If you are still trying to trick me, it will be bad for Alex.' He pushed the muzzle of his gun harder against the girl's temple. 'Now where are the rest? Tell them to show themselves.'

Skinner opened his mouth to call out, but then heard a movement behind him. He looked over his shoulder to see Adam Arrow step into the light.

'That's good. But where's the other one?'

'Who?'

'This Martin, the one that Alex told me all about. You

wouldn't leave your right-hand man out of something like this.'

'Where do you think he is? I sent him off in the chopper to call up the heavy squad.'

Ingo laughed. 'Then he'll be too late. We're fuelled up and ready to go, and no one will ever track me in this thing. I can go too low, too slow for the radar. It will just think I'm a fat bird. So, come on, let's get on with it. Your guns on the ground, please.'

Ingo glanced towards Arrow as he threw his pistol on the ground – and in that instant Skinner snapped his Browning up to a firing position, left hand on right wrist. It was pointed directly between the man's eyes. As he held his aim, Skinner felt an icy coolness sweep over him, felt the presence of the other man, the man in the closet, as Sarah had described him.

'No, son,' he said calmly and steadily. 'You don't understand. It ends here. You just said you weren't crazy. So work this out. I know for certain that if you take Alex away from here, you'll kill her just like you killed the girl in the farmhouse, and your driver there. So I will not let you take her away. If she is to die, she will die with me, her father, beside her. But if you do kill her, even if you harm just a single hair on her head, then I will shoot you at that very moment. Believe me, that is my solemn promise. If you're not crazy, you don't want to die. So let her go. Now!' The last word was as soft as a whisper, but it carried the force of a shout.

Death stood surely before him, and yet Ingo Svart laughed in its face. And in that second Skinner looked at his daughter, and saw only her concern for him, not fear for herself.

'Pops,' she mouthed silently.

'No, poor old Bob,' said Ingo, 'it is you who don't understand your situation. Time for our last surprise, I think.' He called over his shoulder. 'Ariel!'

The near-side passenger door of the Senator opened, and a

woman stepped out slowly. But it was not Ariel – not yet.

It was Sarah.

She looked helplessly at Bob, then shook her head.

And then another woman stepped out. Julia. But not Julia – Ariel.

The doe-eyes which Skinner had come to know so well were now hard as flints as they stared across at him. Her smile, previously warm and wide, was cold, tight and controlled. She held a gun to Sarah's side, and stood pressed close to her.

'So now, I think, you will take your pistol off my brother, and we will see if we can reach some agreement.' Her voice was as dark as her eyes.

Her accent seemed to have changed too. It was clipped, more European in origin. Her hair, usually flowing, was pulled back into a long heavy pony-tail. She was dressed functionally in jeans and a white short-sleeved top, far removed from either the flowery or the formal styles of the Julia Shahor that he had thought he knew.

'So how did you . . .?' he began. But he could guess.

'Don't blame Andy, Bob. He told me nothing we didn't know already – until he picked me up tonight. I was just about to leave his place to meet up with Ingemar when he called to tell me of your excellent idea that Sarah and I should look after each other. Then he said that he had to go catch a helicopter. Not a plane, a helicopter. That's when I knew for sure that you hadn't bought our escape story, and that you wouldn't just set an ambush at the airport but would try to trace us to wherever we were heading. We expected you'd probably find some way to track us in the end. I know you're a very dangerous man, especially where your beloved Alex is concerned. So when Andy said that, I decided we had to take Sarah too, just to make sure.'

A self-satisfied smile crept across her face. 'Did our little surprise give you a scare last night? Sorry about that, but you have really annoyed us. We have been planning this operation for two years. We committed finally when I was offered the Film Festival contract. Imagine, to be running an operation, and to be in on the police security briefings. We planned every detail, down to the last little item, even to "Auntie" staying with me, to give me an excuse to get away from Filmhouse at odd hours.'

She's enjoying this, thought Skinner. *Keep her talking, boy. Wait for the moment, then take it. By God, you take it.* The thought sent a thrill of anticipation running through him.

Ariel went on. 'We ran this type of operation once before in South Africa. It worked so well there, we really didn't think we'd need a back-up plan this time. But when we did, Alex working in the same show as Ingo was such a gift, and my getting involved with Andy was the icing on the cake. The break-in thing at my house was clever, wasn't it. Poor Ray staged that one for me, and Andy was hooked. That's Andy's one weakness, you know. He's vulnerable to love. Such a pity, because he turned out to be my one weakness too.'

For a moment Ariel paused, her boasting turned to wistfulness.

'If it had worked, I was going to stay here, not leave with Ingemar. I could have married Andy. How's that for funny. But when I had to let Alex see me last night, I lost that chance.'

'Ariel, enough. We have to go.' For the first time, anxiety showed in Ingo.

She nodded. 'Yes, we must. So here is the deal, Bob. We leave the ladies here. But we take you. Just you. Not your little friend – he's the soldier Andy mentioned, I imagine – we couldn't handle you both in that little plane. And we take our prizes here, of course – the Crown, the Sceptre and the Sword. We have a delivery to make to our client.

'You.' She turned to Arrow. 'Fetch the bags from the car and load them into the plane. Then we take off – and you make sure there is no attempt to stop us.

'Bob, you take your chance at the other end. Now throw down your gun. Let's get moving!'

Arrow looked across to Skinner, who nodded to him, and at the same time dropped his Browning on the ground. The little soldier moved past Sarah and Ariel, behind the car, and took the hold-alls from the boot. He carried them across to the hangar, shoving its doors further apart with his shoulders, and placed them on one of the two rear seats of the plane.

'That's good,' said Ariel. 'That's the most important part. Now, Bob, you get on board, please.'

Skinner shook his head. 'Not till the girls and Adam are free and clear.'

'Oh no, Adam is not going anywhere.' Barely looking to take aim, she snapped off a single shot. Arrow crumpled and went down.

'So that just leaves the five of us. Now, do you get on that plane or . . .?' She stopped and shrugged her shoulders, impatiently.

'But why bother? It's much easier if we just kill the lot of you. Ingemar. I'll shoot the women. You take Skinner – now!'

As she called to her brother, she pushed Sarah away from her and levelled her gun at her chest.

The shot was still cracking all around the airfield, even as she fell.

Ninety-nine

Andy Martin lay on the damp grass. He saw the car's approaching headlights, and saw it swing to a halt with its beams shining into the hangar.

He saw the muzzle-flash and even at that distance, heard the sharp sound as Ingo dispatched the driver.

He saw him pull Alex from the car.

He saw the eye-to-eye, gun-to-gun stalemate between Skinner and the Swede.

And then he saw Sarah's head and shoulders emerge from the far side of the car, and saw the profile of the woman who followed, pushing her forward but staying close, holding something to her side.

It was the profile he had come to know so well, in the moonlight not so long before, but different somehow. The truth came to him in a flash, and his heart sank. He had taken the devil into his bed and into his heart, in the guise and the garb of an angel.

He watched, helpless. Seeing her lips move, he strained to hear what she said, but of course he was too far away.

He saw Arrow take the bags from the car and carry them into the hangar.

He started in horror as she shot him down.

And then, still through the telescopic sight of the sniper's rifle which Skinner had taken earlier from Brian Mackie, he saw her push Sarah away from her, and knew instantly what she was about to do.

Tears flooded his contact lens, but only in the second after he pulled the trigger.

One Hundred

Ariel – who had been Andy's beloved Julia – twisted like a corkscrew as the heavy rifle bullet tore through her.

Ingo looked across in horror as his sister fell. His gun, which had been swinging towards Skinner, wavered aimlessly for a moment . . . And in that moment Skinner was upon him.

Not the affable if inquisitive Skinner whom he had met before as Alex's Pops. This was another Skinner: the cold, deadly Skinner he had glimpsed a few minutes earlier. The executioner Skinner, with no mercy in his eyes.

He felt his gun hand immobilised as an immensely strong forearm knocked it outwards and upwards. He felt his arm twisted and a hard hand clamping across his throat, setting his jaw at an angle. He felt no more after that, but he heard, crashing through his brain, a terrible thunder as the heel of Skinner's right hand slammed under his chin, driving it upwards, throwing his head backwards, and breaking his neck.

That thunderclap sound was the last living sensation of Ingemar Svart.

Skinner held the dead weight upright with one arm, as he hugged his daughter tight against him with the other. For a few moments, the three figures stood there in some terrible tableau, until Ingo's lifeless fingers loosened their grip on the belt around Alex's neck, and Skinner allowed his body to slip to the ground.

He felt Alex's long slender hands on his face, turning him towards her.

'Pops, Pops, are you all right?'

He blinked, and then smiled at her, as wide a smile of relief and happiness as she had ever seen. As they stood together, Sarah came to them and wrapped her trembling arms around them both.

As Bob embraced them, the women felt a violent trembling run through him, as sudden exhaustion, physical and emotional, overtook him. But quickly he brought it under control.

'It's all right now, girls. It's all right. It's all over.'

He led them across into the hangar and towards the plane. 'Now, you two sit in here, and look after the Queen's Sunday hat, while I get this lot sorted out.'

He held the door open as first Sarah and then Alex stepped up into the small craft. Then he turned to go to look for the fallen Arrow, and found, to his great delight, that the little soldier was sitting upright.

'Fookin' marvellous these new flak jackets are. Give us a hand up.'

Laughing with relief, Skinner pulled him to his feet.

'Don't know what's so fookin' funny, Bob. Takes your fookin' breath away does a bullet in the chest!'

A few yards away Ariel lay on the ground. Most of her white top had been stained blood-red, but she was still moving. Skinner knelt beside her. As he did, he glanced across the landing strip, in the direction from which the shot had come. The moon had risen, and in its glow he could see Andy Martin coming slowly towards him, a rifle in his hand. His shoulders sagged as he walked like a man with no desire to reach his destination.

Skinner looked down at the woman. Her lips were blood-frothed, and he saw that she was dying. 'Ingo?' she said faintly. 'No.'

He saw her eyes flood with tears.

'Ariel,' he asked, 'who is your buyer?' But he was not surprised when, with the last of her strength, she shook her head.

'Then who is Mr Black?'

'Not so clever after all, eh, Bob,' she whispered. 'Work it out for yourself.'

A final light of satisfaction shone in her hard eyes. Then it faded, and she was gone.

And in death she was Julia again, soft-eyed gentle Julia. Skinner unfastened the ribbon which tied her pony-tail, and let her hair fall loose. Then he stood up, as Andy Martin came to his side and stood, looking down with reddened eyes at his lover's body.

'I'm sorry, Bob,' he said very quietly. 'She took me in, hook, line and sinker. I even brought her to your house, and put Sarah in danger.'

'Andy, Andy. She took me in, too. She was Crystal Tipps, remember. I believed her every bit as much. Christ, it was me who told you to take her to Sarah. Andy, man, never blame yourself again. What you did was the hardest thing you'll ever have to do in your life, and because of that, it was the bravest, too. When I let my gun go, I knew I was putting all our lives in your hands, and I never doubted for one second that you'd come through.'

Then he and Adam Arrow took Andy Martin, now limp and exhausted, and led him away from the bodies of Ariel, who had also been his Julia, and of her brother with whom she had schemed, stolen, killed and finally died.

'Ah, but, lads,' said Andy as they walked away, in a voice full of almost unspeakable regret. 'When she *was* Julia, when she was good . . . I'll never find anyone again like the woman she pretended to be.'

Adam Arrow dug him gently in the side with an elbow.

'Sure you will, Andy. Sure you will. She were only an illusion, remember. She weren't real. There's plenty of women who are, though. Why for a start there's two in that plane over there. Mind you, one's spoken for, and the other – well 'er father's a bad fella' to cross!'

One Hundred and One

'So our Mr Black didn't exist after all.'

It was mid-afternoon, only one day and a half after the deaths of Ingemar and Ariel, and the end of all their plots, their projects and their schemes. Bob Skinner and Sir James Proud stood in the back garden of the bungalow at Fairyhouse Avenue. The blazing heat which had marked the first Festival days had gone, but there was still enough warmth in the sun for them to be in shirt-sleeves. Each held a drink in his hand: Proud Jimmy's a gin-and-tonic, Bob's the usual beer straight from the bottle.

'Well, Jimmy, you could say that in fact he did. He was – well, what would you call him? A trading identity, I suppose. Ariel and Ingo's joint trade name. And it really was their name, too. *Shahor* in Hebrew, which she wasn't, and *Svart* in Swedish, which he wasn't either. Both mean "Black". Interpol have finally tracked them down. Brother and sister they were indeed, but German by birth. And guess what? Their family name was Schwartz.

'Julia's story to Andy about her parents' marriage breaking up, and her being sent to Israel, that was a load of balls. Apparently the truth is that the teenage Schwartz kids joined a right-wing action group, one that went in for violent protests of various sorts. The police never caught on to them, but their father found out about it and threw them out. After that happened, they seem to have decided that terrorism had a limited future, not to mention very poor profit margins, but that the sort of things they had learned could be put to good commercial use, given the right sort of customer – one prepared to put up whatever funding they would need to get what he was after.

'They must have known they were both very young to be credible as the leaders of the sort of operations they were offering to put together. So they seem to have invented "Mr Black" as a sort of authority figure, a mystery man in the background, to keep their clients happy that they were dealing with someone really heavy-duty, and to keep even the hardest acts among the hired help well in line. When their bluff was called, they were tough enough – as anyone who crossed them found out.

'Interpol has been trying to get a handle on them for a while. They reckon they've been in business for six or seven years. That would have made them early to mid-twenties when they started: in no small way, apparently. They stole a twenty-million-dollar stallion in the States. It's never been seen since, but some very quick two and three year olds have started showing up in the Gulf States, and in Hong Kong! The Schwartzes disappeared around five years ago, and then Ingemar Svart and Julia Shahor showed up. Each had brand-new degrees – phoney of course, although they were both exceptionally talented. They followed different careers, well apart, but each, according to their passports, was able to do a lot of travelling. The stamps show that they were both in the vicinity of those jobs that Stewart told Adam Arrow about. They were a roaring success, until, eventually, they showed up here.'

Proud sipped his drink, the ice almost melted. 'Quite a pair. Quite a story. I'm just glad you were able to stop them. So how are Sarah and Alex? Are they getting over it? How are you, for that matter?'

'The girls are OK. A bit shaky still. So are we all, but we're leaning on each other. We're a family. We'll be fine.'

'And Andy? What about him, d'you think?'

'That's something else again. What a thing he had to do! I told him to take a month off. But all he said was that if I did, then he would, too. I'll keep an eye on him for a few weeks. Make him take counselling at least. Then, once he's justified himself to himself, and shown everyone he can carry on regardless, I'll sort out a sabbatical for him. Maybe we could send him off to do some research on security policing in another country, with another force. Somewhere far away.'

'That's a good idea,' said Proud Jimmy. 'I'll look into some possibilities. Oh, by the way, there'll be no FAI on Ingo or Ariel. I've fixed that with the Crown Office. They did a postmortem on him last night. The old pathologist told me he couldn't believe his eyes. He said the last injury he'd seen like that was thirty-seven years ago, and that bloke had been hanged. How bloody strong are you, Bob?'

'Strong enough to look after my nearest and dearest. That's all the strength I'll ever need.'

'Well, my friend, I hope you never have to call on it again!'

Skinner smiled. 'Go on, Jimmy. Get the girls, and Andy and Adam. Those steaks'll be barbied by now!'

Proud Jimmy turned to walk into the house, then stopped. 'Interpol haven't a clue about the client, have they?'

'No, not a sniff. You know, I'm beginning to think they might have done it on spec., and that they might not even have had a client. If they were risking their own money, that could explain why they pursued it to the very end. They'd have had cash enough from their earlier jobs to fund the whole operation, and there are enough wealthy weirdos around the world for them to have set up an auction for the Regalia, and pulled an incredible price. That could have been what it was all about. But, chances are, we'll never know!'

Epilogue

Everard Balliol sat in his den. He was a ten per-cent shareholder in TNI, and as such received daily transcripts of the station's output, as a matter of course. His jaw was working fiercely as he read the account of the foiling of the Edinburgh Castle raid, and of the failure of the follow-up attempt on the Crown Jewels of Scotland.

'Just as well for those two, they didn't make it,' he growled. 'Wouldn't have been no mountain high enough for them.'

Everard Balliol was a vengeful man. It ran in his family. He was also one of the richest in the world, and so had the resources to indulge his whims, in whatever form they developed.

It was that crazy book he had picked up on a hotel stop-over a few years back, when there was nothing else to read. *The Lion in the North* it was called, by some guy named John Prebble, and that had started him on his crusade. Until then, he'd no idea that he was the descendant of kings. The names had jumped out at him, early in the book, and he had read all night. John Balliol, and then Edward Balliol, Kings of Scotland and allies of the mighty Plantagenets of England, their throne usurped by the brigand Bruce, and so robbed of their birthright. His family's birthright. *His* birthright. For the finest genealogists his money could buy had confirmed his instant assumption. He *did* spring in direct line from the seed of those ancient kings. Royal Scottish blood *did* flow through his veins.

Everard Balliol's crusade to restore what he saw as his family's good name had been his driving force from that time on. He had paid frequent trips to Scotland. He had studied its later history, its laws, its institutions. He could have bought up much of it, but had decided early on that he wanted no part of contemporary Scotland. It had been corrupted, softened, Anglified, and its people had been spread around the globe. So instead, he had considered how to have his personal entitlement of Scotland, and eventually he had decided. If he could not have his kingdom, he would have its crown.

From a hugely wealthy and very unorthodox art collector friend, he had heard already about 'Mr Black', and the anonymous box number in Geneva. Very special assignments: you want it, you give him enough money, he'll get it for you. 'His team is good,' the friend had said. 'I know. Look at that painting they got for me. Even if I had been able to buy it at auction, it would have cost fifteen million dollars. Through Mr Black, I got it for eight.'

And so Balliol had contacted the Geneva box number, and Black had sent his messengers: that little woman and her blond brother. He had given them enough money, given it to them two years back, and he had waited. And now it was gone, and nothing to show for it. He slammed his fist on the desk, in his den, in his bungalow, in his fortified compound, in the deeps of Texas. As he read the report again, he fixed on one name – a memorable name.

Assistant Chief Constable Bob Skinner.

'Some day, my friend. Some day,' Everard Balliol said aloud.